NFL TOP 40

THE GREATEST PRO FOOTBALL GAMES EVER PLAYED

VIKING

Harold (Red) Grange

Bronko Nagurski

NFL football, circa 1930

Days of leather helmets and faces without masks, days of Bronko and Red and Slingin' Sammy. Stadiums seldom were full then, and, in the very early days, purists felt there were more respectable ways to make a living than playing pro football.

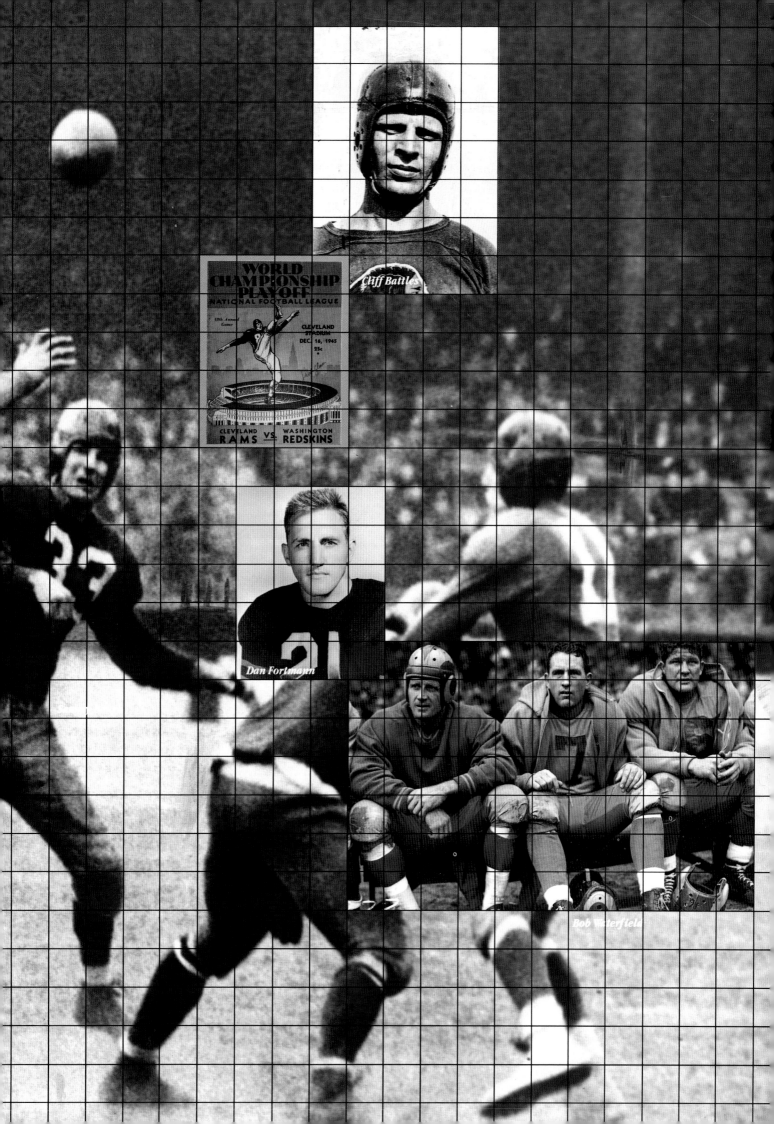

WORLD
CHAMPIONSHIP
PLAYOFF
NATIONAL FOOTBALL LEAGUE

18th Annual Game

CLEVELAND
STADIUM
DEC. 16, 1945
25¢

CLEVELAND
RAMS VS. WASHINGTON
REDSKINS

Cliff Battles

Dan Fortmann

Bob Waterfield

FIRST SUDDEN DEATH GAME
COLTS 23-17 GIANTS

Hugh McElhenny and Joe Perry

Bobby Layne

Norm Van Brocklin

Johnny Unitas

Fueled by a galaxy of stars, the game had new fire in the 1950s, still the golden age to some fans. Interest went off the charts —and pretty much stayed there—with the Colts-Giants 1958 Championship Game. The NFL rode on the wings of television, and, in the 1960s, Lombardi was its pilot.

Sayers

77

Don Meredith

Joe Namath

1966 Green Bay-Dallas title game

Bart Starr

George Blanda

Don Shula

Dan Fouts

Ask Americans (and even some Europeans and Japanese) to name their favorite sport, and chances are the response will be pro football. In the living-color world of the past two decades, the sport is king. A lot of teams have worn the crown, but none more than the Steelers.

Terry Bradshaw

John Elway

Landry

Joe Montana

VIKING
Published by the Penguin Group
Viking Penguin Inc., 40 West 23rd Street,
New York, New York 10010, U.S.A.
Penguin Books Ltd, 27 Wrights Lane,
London W8 5TZ, England
Penguin Books Australia Ltd, Ringwood,
Victoria, Australia
Penguin Books Canada Ltd, 2801 John Street,
Markham, Ontario, Canada L3R 1B4
Penguin Books (N.Z.) Ltd, 182-190 Wairau Road,
Auckland 10, New Zealand

Penguin Books Ltd, Registered Offices:
Harmondsworth, Middlesex, England

First published in 1988 by Viking Penguin Inc.
Published simultaneously in Canada

10 9 8 7 6 5 4 3 2 1

ISBN 0-670-82490-9

Library of Congress Catalog Card Number 88-40101
(CIP data available)

Printed in Japan by Dai Nippon

Edited by John Wiebusch
Designed by Cliff Wynne

Cover

Design–Cliff Wynne; Hand Lettering–James Whitaker; Photography–Clockwise from upper left: Wide World Photos, John Biever, Baron Wolman, Dick Raphael, James Flores, Lou Witt, United Press, Walter Iooss, Jr., Tony Tomsic, Al Messerschmidt, Alvin Chung, Malcolm Emmons, Fred Kaplan.

Back Cover

Top: Walter Iooss, Jr.; middle: Robert Riger; bottom: Pete J. Groh.

Photography

Legend: L-left; R-right; M-middle; B-bottom; T-top; TL-top left; ML-middle left; BL-bottom left; TR-top right; MR-middle right; BR-bottom right; TCL-top center left; TCR-top center right; ML-bottom middle left.

All Sport/Caryn Levy 6BL.
Arthur Anderson 7BL.
Associated Press 73BR, 120MR, 124TL.
John Biever 6BR, 57BL-TR, 58T-BL-MR, 59M, 140MR, 141BR, 142TL, 147MR, 160TL-ML.
Vernon Biever 5BR, 57BL-TR, 58TL-BL-MR, 59MR, 65TL, 68, 69TL-TR, 70BL-TR, 71TL-BR, 72, 75, 76T, 85TR, 87MR, 88BR, 100BR, 103TL, 140BL, 143TL, 145ML, 146ML-BR, 188BR, 189MR.
Chicago Bears 3BL.
David Boss 77TL, 78TL, 81TL, 82BR, 83TR-BR, 99BR, 100ML, 105BR, 129TCL, 142BR.
Chance Brockway 85BL, 87T-BL, 89TL-MR.
Cleveland Browns 43TL.
Dallas Cowboys 134.
Dave Cross 161MR, 169TL, 170TL, 171, 172TL-BR.
Dennis Desprois 178BL-MR.
Malcolm Emmons 5MR, 7BL, 84, 86, 88TL, 96BL, 99TL, 102, 104, 106TL, 107BR, 121ML, 127TL, 141TL, 153BR, 158.
Nate Fine 3BR, 165TL-BR, 166, 167TL-BR, 182BL.
James Flores 6MR, 79TL, 81BR, 82TL, 83ML, 122, 123BL-MR, 124TR-MR, 125TL-MR, 128TL.
George Gellatly 4BR-TR, 42, 43BR, 44TL-B, 45TL-MR.
George Gojkovich 184.
Pete J. Groh 187R, 188T.
Rod Hanna 105TL, 114R, 115TL-BR, 116MR.
Ken Hardin 74TL.
Jocelyn Hinsen 149, 150TL, 152TL.
John Iacono for Sports Illustrated 143ML.
Walter Iooss, Jr. 175.
Fred Kaplan 110, 111TR, 126, 127BR, 129BL.
Laughead Photographers 60, 61BL-TR.
Long Photography 128BR, 129TL.
Richard Mackson 174TR, 176BR.
Tak Makita 93TR, 144, 145BR, 147BR, 151TL.
Al Messerschmidt 154, 156, 157TL, 160BR, 162TL, 163, 168, 169BR, 170MR-BL, 173ML-BR, 181, 182TL-ML-TR, 185L-R, 186TL-MR, 187L.
NBC 90.
Anthony Neste 183TL-BL-MR.
New York Jets 103BR.
NFL Library 2ML, 3ML.
NFL Photos 28BL-BR, 29BL-BR, 56, 130, 133BR.
NFLP Library 4TL.
Darryl Norenberg 5BR, 6BR, 76BL.
Philadelphia Eagles 59TL-BR.
PRM 7ML-MR, 133TL, 176TL, 177TL, 178TL, 179TL-BL.
Pro Football Hall of Fame 2TR-MR, 3TR, 16, 17, 18, 19TL-ML-BR, 20TL-BL-R, 21TL-MR-BR, 22, 24, 30TL-B, 31B, 32, 33BL-TR, 34TL-MR, 35BR, 36, 37TL, 38, 39BL-TR, 40, 41, 64-65B, 66BL-MR, 67BR, 89B.
Dick Raphael 95TL, 97TL-BR, 107ML, 112, 113, 114TL-ML-MR, 116TL-BL, 117TL-BR, 118L-R, 119L-R-B, 120TL, 129TR, 137TL-BL, 139, 145TL, 146B, 147TL.
Russ Reed 47BR, 48, 91TL-BR, 92, 93BL, 94, 95BR, 96TL-MR, 109, 111ML-BR, 131R.
Robert Riger 4-5, 54
Frank Rippon 4TR, 46, 47TL, 49TL-B, 123TL, 124BL, 125BL, 174BL.
Fred Roe 4MR, 55L, 78ML, 79MR, 138L-R.
Ron Ross 152BR, 153L.
Manny Rubio 6-7, 106BL, 159BL, 162BR.
Fred Russell 5BL.
Russ Russell 73TL-ML, 136L, 137MR, 164, 165MR.
Sports Illustrated 50, 51BL-TR, 52R, 53L-R, 55R.
Vic Stein 77BR.
Damian Strohmeyer 1.
Tony Tomsic 5BML, 7ML, 74BL-TR, 78B, 101ML, 103ML, 107TR, 108, 129TCR, 135TL-BR, 136R, 140TL, 143MR, 148, 150BL-BR, 151MR, 153TR, 159TR, 189TL.
Corky Trewin 179MR.
United Press 21TL, 27TL, 28M, 31TR.
United Press International 52L, 80T-BL, 121BR.
UPI-Bettman 66TL, 67TL.
Washington Redskins 26-27B.
Herb Weitman 5TL, 161TL-ML-BL.
Wide World Photos 2-3, 29TR, 35ML, 37BR.
Lou Witt 62TL-BL-MR, 63TL-BL, 98, 100TL, 101MR, 155TL-BR, 157BR.
Michael Zagaris 131L, 132, 177BL-MR.

Acknowledgements

The author wishes to acknowledge a multitude of people at the Creative Services division of NFL Properties whose work behind the scenes made this book possible.

That long list of people includes David Boss, creative director; Chuck Garrity, Sr., managing editor; Phil Barber, Chuck Garrity, Jr., Jack Hand, Joe Horrigan (Pro Football Hall of Fame), Jane Morrissey, Jim Perry, and Beau Riffenburgh, editors, proofreaders, fact-checkers. . .and more; Bill Barron, Tina Dahl, Dick Falk, and Glen Iwasaki, quality control, printing, and manufacturing; Barbara Hager, design assistant and production manager; Marilyn Cauley, Brian Davids, and Rick Wadholm, typesetting and page assembly; Morrissey Gage, James Whitaker, and Paulina Yoo, pasteup and production; Miguel Elliott, Sharon Kuthe, Tom McGee, Mark Sherengo, and Paul Spinelli, photo services.

CONTENTS

PREFACE

Our Hit Parade

The Top 40. Hey, here's a musty, dusty, blast from the past and we'll be right back with a wax to watch and we'll dip the tune spoon into the platter batter, pull out the geeter with a heater, the boss of the hot sauce and here we go, bop till you drop, party animals. Here's one dedicated to Pudge from The Mad Stork. . . Now, would somebody please slap a quarter in the jukebox and make that sap-sucker sing. Get Casey Kasem on the phone. Hello, American Bandstand, is Dick Clark there? Good beat? Easy to dance to? How would you rate this one?

But hey, now, listen up. If everyone lights a match, and stomps his feet and chants loud enough, they'll come back out for an encore. Because, after all, they are the hardest-working men in show business.

The sweet, sweet music of professional football, the eternal stadium concert that lingers and bounces around the halls of memory like some song you can hear in your sleep, that transcends whatever fads might be jamming up the airwaves. Pro football is like the way someone once described Wagner's music— better than it sounds.

And selecting pro football's top 40 games is about as easy as picking up soap bubbles with chopsticks. I'm glad the Pro Football Hall of Fame Selection Committee did that. I'm even more glad I got the fun part: writing about them. It's like hanging onto the tail of a kite. You just wouldn't believe the view.

First, a confession. I don't know the words to any songs. And I love music. I also love football. But until I started this project, I didn't know how much.

I didn't know how great the game has been all along. Pudge Heffelfinger, the first pro player, set a standard of excitement for the resulting generations to follow back in 1892, picking up a fumble and bolting for a touchdown on pro football's first big play, first turning point.

But then Willie Nelson can sing "Stardust," can't he? And Chuck Berry made Beethoven roll over. Same music, different musicians and audience, that's all. Not a whole lot has changed in football except maybe the way to celebrate such heroics, like spiking the ball, high-fives, and that phenomenon known as the Wave. The games still are won the same way. Oh, the dropkick has given way to soccer-style kicks, and nobody runs the Single Wing anymore, although the Shotgun still employs a lot of the basic philosophies. It's still a game of blocking and tackling, as Lombardi once made quite clear. And, as this book will point out, it's also a game of opportunity.

Little windows fly open. Big doors slam shut. Opportunity. It's Preston Ridlehuber scoring the last touchdown in the incredible Heidi game. Or Reggie Harrison, or Tony Guillory, who crashed into the public eye as suddenly as a blocked punt. Little windows that flew open and slammed shut. A big door, half open, half closed. Who's coming on the blitz? Who's playing zone? Who's who? Their imprint remains indelible. For they were a part of something great if only for a moment. If only for a lifetime.

Conspicuous, as you will discover (just as I did), is the uncommon occurrence of last-second, implausible, improbable, impossible victory. Authors in this little book of miracles include notables such as Roger Staubach, Joe Montana, Terry Bradshaw, George Blanda, and, of course, the whole scenario has been guaranteed by Broadway Joe Namath.

Do you suppose Abner Haynes, who brought new drama to the coin flip, knew what he was doing all along?

Or that maybe Papa Bear George Halas had an inkling his Bears were going to hang up 73

Pro football is like the way someone once described Wagner's music—better than it sounds.

points on the scoreboard one day in 1940?

The Drive has been with us in pro football forever. There always has been some team, some quarterback, that pounds across enemy real estate like Sherman through Georgia, like Caesar through Gaul. How long, how quick, how dramatic? Unitas and the Colts for 86 yards at Yankee Stadium? Montana and the 49ers for 89 at Candlestick? Elway and the Broncos for 98 at Cleveland? How far? Far enough. Whatever it took.

And the defensive plays—the sack, the recovery, the interception. The tackle by Gino Marchetti on Frank Gifford on third-and-short. The tackle by Chuck Bednarik on Jim Taylor on the last play. Eric Wright's firm grip on Drew Pearson's jersey just as he was about to create yet another Cowboys fable.

And how ironic the way the ball bounces toward and away from its warriors. How thrilling the feeling for Warren Lahr to intercept a pass and save victory for the Browns in 1950. How cruel when the same Lahr was victimized in the closing minutes three years later by Bobby Layne and Jim Doran and the Lions.

A tableau of memories. . . .

The agony of Jackie Smith, rigid with frustration in the end zone, the touchdown pass dropped. The stunned look of Jan Stenerud, whose field goal hooked just outside. Of Uwe von Schamann, whose field goal was just blocked. The quiet agony of Bob Waterfield in defeat, the quiet joy of Bob Waterfield in victory. The total surprise of the Giants after Bronko Nagurski passed for two touchdowns against them.

Great coaches such as Don Shula, Tom Landry, and John Madden gasping disbelief over unbearable losses, pitchforks thrown into their dream balloons. The jack-o'-lantern smile of Vince Lombardi. Dan Reeves, the play-

er. Dan Reeves, the coach. Black Saturday in the Bay Area, when both the 49ers and Raiders were yanked out of the Super Bowl with heartbreaking swiftness. Frenchy Fuqua and The Assassin. Who touched the ball? Tatum in a tantrum, covered in funk. Fuqua in a frolic, covered in funky cape and shoes with fish in the heels.

Hail Mary and The Immaculate Reception. Last chance. First down. Kick or receive? Both feet in bounds. Lynn Swann dancing in the sky. Gale Sayers skating on mud. Ed Podolak chugging all over the place, 350 yards of total offense but still losing.

I tried to find a common thread with which all these games were woven. It seems to be the totality of football. Every aspect of the game must be there, executed. From the 99-yard pass play to Cliff Branch to the 90-yard run with a blocked field goal by Bobby Bryant to the one-yard sneak of Otto Graham to the simple heroics of Rocky Bleier recovering an onside kick to preserve a magnificent victory. Total football. Sixty minutes. Play till you hear the whistle, the final gun. Defense, offense, special teams, great punting, great coaching. Opportunity.

Tiny windows, big doors. . . .

Tom (the Bomb) Tracy coming out of mothballs for Detroit. George Blanda creaking off the bench to play quarterback for Oakland. Zeke Bratkowski and Max McGee rescuing Green Bay. Tom Matte and his crib-sheet wrist band.

Did Dwight Clark really jump over the moon to beat the Cowboys? Didn't Drew Pearson really push off on Nate Wright? How did Benny Barnes get the yellow flag when he fell before Lynn Swann did? Come on now, how did the Philadelphia Eagles win the championship in 1960 with that bunch?

Gadget plays? Ghost to the Post, Stabler to Casper on Christmas Eve. How about 31 Wedge,

Each one of them could stand alone... maybe even fill a book. Lumped together, they stagger the imagination.

and Bart Starr hitching his sled to Jerry Kramer's block in the Arctic wasteland between the 1-yard line and the NFL championship. How about Lenny Moore's block on the cornerback while Alan Ameche bulled straight ahead? Does Don Strock to Duriel Harris to Tony Nathan right before the half ring a bell? If you go way back, you might remember Harry Newman to Ken Strong to Newman to Strong in one amazing sequence in 1933. Honk if you love Garo Yepremian's passing form. Has anyone ever blocked kicks better than the Minnesota Vikings? Other than Ted Hendricks, that is.

Who is Ron Sellers and how many San Francisco hearts did he stomp flat in 1972?

The Purple People Eaters. The Steel Curtain. The Fearsome Foursome. The Doomsday Defense. The Flex. The Dawgs. You want colorful?

You want Jim (The Hammer) David, who was the real thing, and Fred (The Hammer) Williamson, who wasn't? You want Ben Davidson and Buck Buchanan and Lenny Ford and Gene (Big Daddy) Lipscomb and Verlon Biggs and Bob Lilly and Mean Joe Greene? You want the linebacking firm of Buoniconti, Nitschke, and Lambert? You want the Tyler Rose breaking loose for 81 yards near the end of the greatest Monday Night game of all time? You want a couple of Joes (Theismann and Washington) going crazy against the wild bunch (the Raiders) in a wild and crazy game? Or the Lions going crazy against the 49ers in 1957 because they heard a victory celebration at halftime over a game that was only half-won? You want games that blew hot, like Miami when it sizzled and smothered and stifled with humidity that San Diego has never felt? Or Cleveland when it's December and if you've never felt it, you've never been to Cleveland in December?

The thoughts get scattered and real justice

isn't allowed for these games. Each one of them could stand alone... maybe even fill a book. Lumped together, they stagger the imagination. Together, they seem so unlikely. How could there be so much greatness?

And then you realize there are 100 other games that have been played that arguably could have made the list and gotten into this book.

This book does not have to be read in order. Each chapter, each game is an island unto itself. Start with your favorite team, your favorite memory. Get unstuck in time, flip back and forth from 1932, when football went indoors, a hint of things to come, to 1987, when John Elway came away with Best of Show at the Dawg Pound in Cleveland. Find a game you knew nothing about and marvel at the big plays, the turnovers, the turning points. And don't feel bad about your ignorance. I did the same thing.

Look at the games that started with kickoff returns for touchdowns and note that each time, the other team came back to win. It's not how a game starts, it's how it ends. And remember, it's not played by robots or machines, even though they do appear to be men of steel. It's people. It's Jack Pardee fighting back tears. It's Ray Flaherty, Buck Shaw, Rick Volk, Bill Nelsen. It's George Atkinson chasing Don Maynard, Johnny Sample chasing Fred Biletnikoff. It's Nate Allen, Jim Plunkett, Elroy (Crazylegs) Hirsch, George Allen, Hank Stram. A thousand faces, half of them smiling. All of them proud, noble examples of the game.

Today the Roman numeral that was resurrected by the Super Bowl no longer is used simply to distinguish one world war from the other. Rocky movies and Wrestlemanias now are on the bandwagon.

Yet the important thing to remember is in

The games stay fresh. Like some song that reminds you of your first love. Hear the song and you can see the face.

the year 2066, barring man's tendency for self-destruction, Super Bowl C will be played. And maybe a sequel book. *NFL Top 40 II?*

It still will be a game of blocking—although you can't do much better than George Wilson's in 1940—and tackling—and they still talk about Bednarik's takedown of Taylor in 1960. It still will be a game of opportunity —how could Morrall not have seen Jimmy Orr?—those tiny windows and big doors opening and shutting as unpredictably as that ball, which, as we all know, has a mind of its own.

Like I said, I had the easy job. A small army of people worked a whole bunch harder to make this thing come out. From Heffelfinger to Elway, it was a helluva trip.

Personally, I cherish my tiny window for the privilege it gave me. The games came to me,

reborn by the magic of Xerox, long-distance dialing, and several wonderful lunches with gladiators you will meet pressed between the pages of *NFL Top 40*.

Even when they were on the wrong end of the final score, they all seemed to enjoy reviving the moment. And that's the name of that tune. The moment was special. Time and space, down and distance lost importance. The games stay fresh. Like some song that reminds you of your first love. Hear the song and you can see the face. You're still the same age you were then.

And so bittersweet when you play it again, Sammy Baugh. Or Dutch Van Brocklin. Or . . .whoever it is that makes you flinch lovingly and stare dreamily whenever people start rhapsodizing about football.

—Shelby Strother

THE FIRST PRO

Allegheny Athletic Association 4,
Pittsburgh Athletic Club 0
November 12, 1892

George Barbour couldn't believe what he kept hearing. It was the day of the big game with the Allegheny Athletic Association. And people were telling him they'd seen "the ringers" at the train station.

Barbour, an officer with the Pittsburgh Athletic Club, had told everyone his attempts to beef up the team with those big studs from Chicago had been turned down. One player, the great Pudge Heffelfinger, had said no even though the offer, besides the usual "cakes," the slang word of the times for travel expenses that sometimes were double and even triple the actual costs, also included a flat-cash bonus of $250.

What were Heffelfinger, Ben Donnelly, and Ed Malley, two other prime athletes, doing in Pittsburgh? Had they changed their minds?

Or, you don't suppose, could they, would they, were they going to play for Allegheny?

When the Civil War ended, and industrialization took giant capitalistic steps in all directions, leisure time for many nouveau-riche tycoons became almost a matter of one-upsmanship. Social clubs and athletic associations became fitting scenes for the Gay 90s to run their decadent course. Football, the Americanized version of rugby, became an amusement for the high-brows and well-heeled.

In Pittsburgh, a football rivalry developed between the AAA, which was formed in the city of Allegheny, an area that today is part of north Pittsburgh, and the older, more established PAC, which formerly had been the East End Gymnasium Club. After two years of playing games against outside competition, the two finally met on Columbus Day, 1892. It was a terrific battle that ended in a 6-6 tie. Gate receipts were good, but there still was the matter of which team was better. A rematch was a natural.

But charges were flying. Society always favors the best, the winners. Going back to Darwin, the survival of the fittest notion quickly transcended onto the playing arena. And the all-too-human

William W. (Pudge) Heffelfinger was the best football player in the nation when he competed for the Allegheny Athletic Association in 1892.

emotion of greed took the handoff from there.

PAC had played with a ringer named A.C. Read, who was listed on the roster as "Stayer." Read, claimed the AAA, had captained the Penn State team, and was brought in for the game with Allegheny to make sure of victory. Further, cried Allegheny, Pittsburgh's best player, William Kirschner, taught gym classes for PAC, but made twice as much money during football season and taught half as many classes.

An unofficial open season was declared. Amateur sports were policed at the time by the Amateur Athletic Union, which fought a constant battle with the blossoming concept of professionalism. Defining an out-and-out professional was simple. Play strictly for money and you were barely better than the scum that grows on theater floors. The (wink-wink) expenses deal made you a "semi-pro," which was considered only semi-bad. The AAU was proud of how it had banned that sneaky procedure of playing for "trophies," which often turned out to be gold pocket watches, easily redeemed at the nearest pawnshop for cash. The simple love of the game had yielded to the gluttonous love of winning and wagering on outcomes.

And it was all coming to a head November 12, 1892, at Exposition Park.

Oliver Thompson went to watch the Chicago Athletic Association play a game while he was in

New York "on business." Thompson, a lawyer and officer in the Allegheny club, coincidentally ran into one of the Chicago players, a former Yale graduate just as Thompson was.

The man's name was Heffelfinger.

William W. Heffelfinger was the best football player in the nation. Three times an All-America at Yale, a devastating lineman with the speed of a halfback, once described by Bernard Baruch as "The One-Man Army," Heffelfinger was a 6-foot 3-inch, 190-pound monolith of sinewy muscle. This business of helping a football team was nothing new to him. In high school, he'd done a little moonlighting, playing for the University of Minnesota varsity. It was the days when eligibility rules were, to say the least, lax.

After leaving Yale, he went to work for the railroad in Omaha. But, somehow, the Chicago Athletic Club had "convinced" him to quit his job and play football "for the sheer love of the game."

Meanwhile, Barbour was equally busy. An All-America back named Knowlton Ames, whose swivel-hipped running style earned him the nickname "Snake," was being courted to replace Kirschner, whose ankle was injured in the first game. And if that failed, there was Simon Martin, another great player from the nearby Steelton A.C.

Allegations were tossed back and forth like hand grenades. Word leaked that Ames also was being wooed by the Three A's, as Allegheny was called.

Consequently, fanfare was similar to a Super Bowl, which was still three-quarters of a century away from being invented. Betting was incredible. In midweek, Allegheny started offering 5-1 odds, the first indication something big was brewing. Local newspapers were caught up with all the rumors, and daily stories elevated interest in the big game even higher. A crowd of more than 5,000 was expected because everyone wanted to know just which team Snake Ames was going to join.

Nobody, as it turned out. Ames decided he wanted "to protect his amateur ranking," although insiders suggested the price simply wasn't right. And because of snow and rain and cold, the crowd was little more than 3,000.

And when Heffelfinger, Malley, and Donnelly all were spotted dressed in the blue and white of Allegheny, the PAC team was herded quickly back onto its horse-drawn bus. All bets were off as well.

Thompson smugly contended his club had done nothing that the other hadn't tried to do. "We simply were successful," he said.

Barbour was furious. He had waited in Chicago to talk to Heffelfinger and company upon their return from New York, only to be told they had inexplicably quit the team "in a huff."

It took more than an hour to argue and convince both teams to play the game, although all bets still were called off. In the crowd was a former divinity student who'd played with Heffelfinger at Yale but who now was coaching at the University of Chicago. His name was Amos Alonzo Stagg.

Negotiations finally were hammered out. There would be two 30-minute halves, but it would be an exhibition, not a game.

The three new players never had practiced with the Three A's. They made several mistakes and execution was poor, although it was apparent they were the best players on the field—especially Heffelfinger, whose odd semi-erect stance made him easily recognizable. Fifteen minutes into the game, Heffelfinger jarred loose a fumble, picked up the ball, and ran 35 yards to score. In 1892, a touchdown was worth four points. A conversion kick was worth two. But Malley, a champion shot-putter from Detroit, flubbed the kick and Allegheny led 4-0.

The game took on a vicious nature. Tempers flared, pent-up anger erupted. Several players limped off the field. A few, such as the PAC's Aull brothers, Charley and Burt, had to be helped off.

Eighteen minutes into the second half, it was too dark to see across the field. The referees called the game. Both teams promptly vowed never to play each other again.

Pittsburgh got its guaranteed gate receipts of $428. Allegheny, the host team, wound up with $621. And many years later, a slip from an account ledger was discovered.

"Game performance bonus to W. Heffelfinger for playing (cash) $500.00."

The paper was signed, "O.D. Thompson Esq."

The receipt, which identifies Heffelfinger as football's first professional, is on display at the Pro Football Hall of Fame in Canton, Ohio.

Heffelfinger was the first pro football player on record. This list of Allegheny expenses for the Pittsburgh game includes $500 paid to him as a "performance bonus."

RED!

Chicago Bears 19,
New York Giants 7
December 6, 1925

Harold (Red) Grange, who popularized pro football in the 1920s as a member of the Chicago Bears, could also be a fashionable dresser.

It's not so easy, stepping from your modest room at the Zeta Psi frat house out into a spot on top of the world. Vertigo, you know. Granted, Harold (Red) Grange was the big man on the Illinois campus. And he still beamed proud because that nice man down at the local theater had given him free passes to the movies just because he happened to be a football player. Then there was that free education and the simple privilege of playing a game he already loved. Really now, how much better could life get?

Dashing off to catch a national barnstorming train? Not so easy at all. Star of stars, savior of the pro football league? Pocketing a lot of that "terrible" pro money, playing football almost every day, only always someplace else. Doesn't up ever have a limit?

Grange said later it was hard to catch his breath, the way the world came at him so quickly. Nobody led him into temptation, he sprinted toward it in those galloping, ghost-like strides.

Sure, there was jealousy and resentment, but Grange always remembered the one basic truth that nobody wants to tackle anybody but the guy running with the ball. So some of the stuff he could take in stride. The rest he tried to sidestep. But mainly, he took the ball and he ran. To the bank. To history.

They say Red Grange saved pro football, him and C.C. Pyle, his fancy-pants manager with the spats and diamond stickpins on those two tours of America where, if the people in the outlying patches didn't feel like heading for the nearest pro football game, by golly, Red Grange and the Chicago Bears would bring it to them.

The Golden Age of Sports was striding along nicely in 1925, its heroes–Ruth, Dempsey, Tilden–larger than life. Grange fit the mold, too.

Everyone knew who Grange was. The University

The day after playing in his final college game at Illinois, Grange sat on the Bears' bench for a game with Green Bay in his new raccoon coat.

Grange and his teammates went on a 17-game tour to wind up the 1925 season.

of Illinois never had a more famous student, although most people knew about him because he ran with a football.

And now that he had just one more game left–against Ohio State in Columbus on November 21–the theater man wanted to talk to him. An usher yanked Grange away just as the featured attraction was starting. C.C. Pyle had a plan.

Pro football was listing severely, harpooned

tional tours, from Miami Beach to Seattle, exhibitions in which one team would play the other, but the real hook was the chance to see the great Red Grange in person. Grange's popularity, his instant recognition, would make him rich. Percentages of the gate and guarantees were rapidly tossed out toward the blinking Grange; the numbers alone made him dizzy. And that's not to mention all the endorsements. The market could be flooded with Red Grange products—candy bars and shoes and dolls and fountain pens. And, hey—don't forget about the movies. Hollywood would stand in line to get Red Grange.

So the senior from Wheaton, Illinois, the son of the police chief, was wide-eyed as he gave Pyle a hearty handshake and a definite "maybe."

His college coach was against it. Bob Zuppke, who had coached George Halas and Dutch Sternaman, the current owners of the Bears, told Grange, "Football isn't meant to be played for money."

And if he didn't believe that, Zuppke told him to ask his father. Lyle Grange told his son he'd rather he chose some line of work other than football. But he also told him that part of being an adult was making tough decisions. Because Harold was over 21, Lyle said, "The decision is yours."

Grange (with ball) faced the Chicago Cardinals on Thanksgiving Day, 1925, in his first pro game. He helped attract a standing-room-only crowd of 36,000.

by public apathy. Nobody was making any money and the image of the National Football League was vague. Pyle felt this all would change with a symbol, someone who could attract people to a game that was being hidden under a bad rap.

Someone like Red Grange.

Pyle also mentioned money to Grange. Lots of it, he promised, more than anyone could imagine. There would be na-

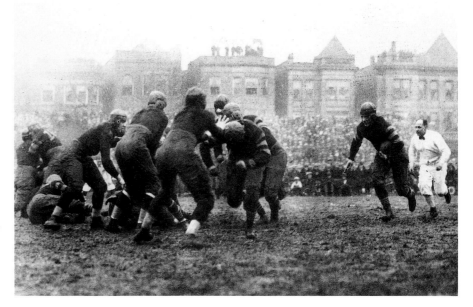

Owner Tim Mara admitted that Grange's appearance saved the Giants' franchise.

The world seemed to speed up after that. On Saturday, Grange rode with the Fighting Illini to Columbus, Ohio, where he ran for 192 yards, threw a touchdown pass, and intercepted a potential game-winning pass by the Buckeyes in the end zone to save a 14-9 victory. The next day, he was registered under a phony name in a Chicago hotel close to the one where Pyle was staying. Grange actually showed up at the Bears' game against the Green Bay Packers and sat on Chicago's bench. The new raccoon coat he wore suggested he was the recipient of a recent windfall.

The following Thursday was Thanksgiving, and the crosstown rivals, the Cardinals, were coming to Cubs Park. The news that Grange had joined the Bears caused a run on tickets. By the opening kick-off, a standing-room crowd of 36,000 was waiting. It was the largest crowd in NFL history.

Grange was unimpressive in his debut—40 yards on 13 carries, six passes thrown, none completed. More than that, he didn't get much of a chance to show his open-field running, because Cardinals star Paddy Driscoll carefully punted away from him all day. The game ended in a 0-0 tie. But the security guards on the sidelines could tell you about the excitement. Throughout the game, people left the stands and tried to get to Grange.

Pyle knew very little about football. His "tour" was more than ambitious; it was absurd. At one point, the Bears played eight games in eight different cities in 12 days. The pace would have been hard for musicians. Imagine what it was like for football players. Consider also that the Bears started the tour with only 18 players. Injuries took such a toll that Halas was forced to suit up his trainer when the number of able bodies dropped to 10.

But in the early going, it was a glorious dream for Grange and his adoring fans. On December 2, in St. Louis, playing a local mortician's team of all-stars, Grange scored four touchdowns. Three days later, in Philadelphia, where a driving rainstorm had turned the field into a flooded marsh, Grange had both touchdowns in a 14-7 victory over the Frankford Yellow Jackets.

Tim Mara, the New York Giants owner, was watching the wire-service reports the way someone else might watch the ticker tape at Wall Street. The Bears were coming to New York next.

Leaving Philadelphia at night, changing on the train, heading for the Polo Grounds and a game the next day with the Giants, Grange told teammates he was tired. It seemed a little awkward to think about playing football in a drenched, mud-stained jersey, but that's the way the tour schedule worked out.

When they reached their hotel, Mara was in the lobby waiting. It was no secret his first-year franchise was crumbling. To stay afloat, the Giants needed Grange and a big crowd.

They got it. There were 125 reporters on hand. And about 73,000 others. The Polo Grounds was under siege, as kids climbed ladders to sneak into the game. The seating capacity of 65,000 was surpassed with ease. People stood on Coogans Bluff to sneak a peek at the great Grange.

"There is no doubt he saved the Giants," Mara said later. "I never saw anything like it."

The game itself was almost nondescript in comparison. The Bears won 19-7, and the next day headlines suggested Grange had spearheaded

An NFL-record crowd of 73,000 turned out in the Polo Grounds to see Grange and the Bears play the Giants. Chicago won 19-7.

Although he was surrounded by tacklers on this play, Grange scored a touchdown against the Giants on a 35-yard interception return.

the victory. In fact, Joey Sternaman, who played all 60 minutes, had been the star, scoring two touchdowns and dropkicking an extra point. But Grange gave everyone what they came to see, intercepting a pass and running 35 yards for a touchdown.

The next morning, Pyle told Grange someone wanted to meet him.

"Hi ya kid," boomed the round man with the big smile. It was Babe Ruth.

A few days later, when the Bears checked into their hotel in Washington, D.C., Grange had a message to call Illinois senator William McKinley. Let's go out to the White House, the senator suggested. Meet President Coolidge.

Faster and faster, a blur. Grange was tired and beat up, but Pyle would quickly figure how much money had been made thus far, and Grange would try to get some sleep before the next day's game.

The tour headed south—Coral Gables, Miami Beach, a stop in Jacksonville where the local all-stars had brought in a ringer, a 37-year-old halfback named Jim Thorpe. In New Orleans a few days later, Grange was invited out to the Fairgrounds where the Red Grange Handicap was run. Out west, he met Charlie Chaplin and Mary Pickford, toured the San Simeon estate of William Randolph Hearst, and signed autographs up and down the California coast. In Los Angeles, 75,000 people showed up at the Coliseum. It seemed like Monopoly money by that point.

Pyle had gotten a private Pullman car for the team, complete with personal porters. But the

simple attrition of playing football games every couple of days was too much. Grange had made about $300,000 at this point. He had his own newspaper comic strip, and movie plans were taking shape. The pace had dulled everything into a simple case of survival. And if you think Grange was struggling, think of his teammates, most of whom were drawing pay of $100-200 a game.

There were 17 games on the tour. Grange played in 16. The one game he missed, in Detroit, prompted more than 20,000 customers to demand refunds.

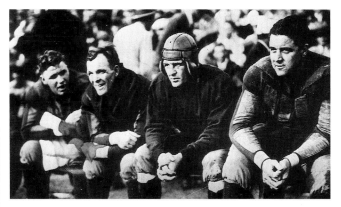

On January 31, 1926, the tour was over. It is a mistake to say Grange brought respectability to pro football. It never lacked credibility, just solvency. What Grange brought to the game was popularity. Once the game had to be advertised under billings such as "post-graduate football." Once the word "professional" carried a stain or brand.

Then came Red Grange.

Grange played in 16 of the 17 games on the coast-to-coast barnstorming tour with the Bears. Still wearing his helmet, he grabbed a short rest in this game, sitting between teammates Hunk Anderson (left) and George Trafton.

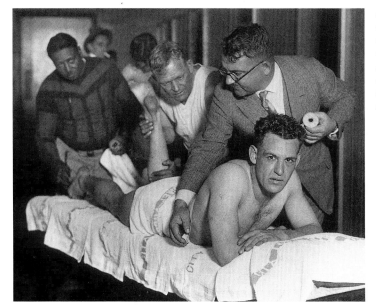

In Los Angeles, the final stop of the grueling tour, Grange had to undergo a thorough physical before being cleared to play.

ONE FOR THE RULE BOOK

Chicago Bears 9,
Portsmouth Spartans 0
December 18, 1932

Because waist-deep snow had made Wrigley Field unplayable, the first NFL Championship Game was held indoors at Chicago Stadium, home of the hockey Black Hawks.

Pro football owners made some sweeping changes in the rule book after the 1932 season because they wanted to make the game better. They also wanted to make sure there would never be another 1932.

It was a strange season highlighted by an even stranger championship game. Of course, the Great Depression was in full stride and very little could be considered normal anywhere.

"But I don't think anything could compare with the game between Portsmouth and the Bears in 1932," George Halas once said. "The only thing not ridiculous about the whole mess was we won the game."

Football still was tumbling in an incubator in 1932. Defenses ruled. Scoring not only was low, it was rare. Offenses were crude. And games tended to be dull. In 1932, one of every five games played ended in a tie. The Bears did not score a point in the season's first four games, yet lost only once. They finished with a 6-1-6 record, beating the three-time defending champion Green Bay Packers on the final day of the regular season to finish in a tie with the Portsmouth Spartans, who were 6-1-4.

Because a pro football season never had ended without an outright champion, the notion of a playoff game was born. But a blizzard had hit Chicago, and, as Portsmouth tailback Glenn Presnell recalled, "The snow was waist deep when we arrived. There was no way we could practice."

The game was supposed to be played at Wrigley Field. Halas, a man of common sense and business acumen proposed a change of venue.

Two years earlier, the Bears and Chicago Cardinals had played an indoor exhibition game at Chicago Stadium, home of the hockey Black Hawks. Now Halas moved the championship game to the same location. The site offered some unusual problems, however.

The playing field was only 80 yards long, and the end zones were not regulation size. And it was 15 feet narrower than a normal field.

"The place looked square the first time I saw it," said Portsmouth head coach Potsy Clark.

The sidelines were right up against the stands and the end zones were half-moon shaped, contoured to the shape of the wooden hockey boards.

The cement floor was only a mild nuisance because the Salvation Army had just held a circus at the stadium and there was a layer of dirt already down.

There also was a layer of organic residue deposited by elephants.

But it still beat going back outside for the 11,198 spectators. If such a thing as measuring wind chill had been invented in 1932, the sub-zero temperatures and the hawk wind would have teamed up for about a minus-30 chill factor outside. Of course, it wasn't real warm inside either.

The rules also got some special championship game revising. No field goals were allowed. All kickoffs were from the 10-yard line. Each time a team crossed midfield, it was penalized 20 yards, in effect making the field 100 yards long. The goal posts were moved from the end lines to the goal lines. And inbounds lines were created for the first time, so that each time the ball was carried out of bounds, instead of being placed where it went out (right next to a wall), it was returned to the inbounds line for the next play.

Like everyone else in the NFL, the Bears had a good defense, having posted seven shutouts during the season. Chicago was heavily favored because Earl (Dutch) Clark, Portsmouth's best player and the league scoring leader, already had bolted to his offseason job as basketball coach at his alma mater, Colorado College.

For three quarters, the game was scoreless. Red Grange had been knocked groggy in the first quarter, and Portsmouth keyed on the other legend in the Bears' backfield, Bronko Nagurski.

The first pass by halfback John Doehring wound up in the mezzanine level. Twice, punts bounced off the rafters—an automatic touchback. The setting was so intimate that spectators several rows back in the stands could hear what was being said in the huddle.

"Because of the confines of the field," Presnell said, "both teams could pull their defenses in. There were no long runs. Passing was almost impossible."

With 11 minutes to play, Chicago's Dick Nesbitt intercepted Ace Gutowsky's pass and returned it to the Portsmouth 13.

On first down, Nagurski rumbled to the 7. On the next play, he barged to the 2. But The Purple, as Portsmouth fans called their team, threw back Nagurski twice, and the Bears were still on the 2.

"We fooled them good on the next play," said Bears guard Joe Kopcha.

Nagurski got the ball once more, took a step forward, then started backpedaling. Finally, he threw a jump pass to teammate Red Grange, who was alone in the crescent area of the end zone.

Potsy Clark pointed his finger. In 1932, the rules stated all forward passes had to be thrown from a spot no less than five yards behind the line of scrimmage. Clark and the Spartans insisted Nagurski's pass was illegal. Referee Bobby Cahn, perhaps fearing the spectacle might wind up scoreless and necessitate an overtime, would have none of the argument. It was ruled a Bears' touchdown. Tiny Engebretsen's extra point made it 7-0.

The Bears poured it on after that, adding a safety. Actually, Portsmouth punter Mule Wilson mishandled a snap from center and the ball easily bounded through the end zone. At any rate, the Bears' 9-0 lead held up until the final gun, at which time everyone went home to shovel snow.

While the *Portsmouth Times*, hometown newspaper of the Spartans, ran a headline, "Sham Battle on Tom Thumb Gridiron" and sportswriter Lynn A. Wittenburg described the action as "a synthetic show," Halas and Spartans owner Harry Sydney took notice of the game's lingering appeal. The fans really did like it. The idea of having a final game was a good one.

And so the NFL Championship Game was born. In 1933, the NFL was split into two divisions, the champions of which then played for the title.

But the Spartans-Bears game had an even bigger influence. As a result of the successful use of that game's rules, the following spring the NFL, which long had followed the rules of college football, made a number of significant changes from the college game for the first time.

The owners passed a rule that the ball would be moved in 10 yards to an inbounds line (or hashmark) whenever it was in play within five yards of the sidelines. The goal posts were moved from the end lines to the goal lines. Passing from anywhere behind the line of scrimmage was permitted.

Unlike in the 1932 championship game, these rules in general made for more field goals, more points scored, and more wide-open, exciting play. They also made the game more entertaining, and, eventually, more profitable.

Kopcha, who was a four-time all-pro, remembers very little about the playoff game, which is probably just as well.

"I remember I hurt my shoulder in the last couple of minutes. And I remember the smell of the elephant dung. Everybody stunk of it," Kopcha said.

TRICKS UP THEIR SLEEVES

Chicago Bears 23, New York Giants 21
December 17, 1933

The 1933 NFL Championship Game was filled with wild, zany plays. For the Bears' winning touchdown, Bronko Nagurski threw a jump pass to bareheaded Bill Hewitt, who gained 14 yards, and then lateraled the ball (above) to Bill Karr, who ran the remaining 19 yards for the score.

Tommy Hughitt turned around. Several New York Giants wanted to talk to him. Because Hughitt was going to referee the NFL Championship Game with the Chicago Bears in an hour, they wanted him to be aware of this trick play they were going to try.

Hughitt listened, then gave them a certain look. One of those "you too?" smirks.

The Bears already had checked in with Hughitt. They also had a gadget play that would have been illegal the year before, but now that the rule had been changed, it was a fixture in the Chicago playbook. They wanted to make sure Hughitt and his officiating crew were aware of its legality.

Hughitt may have been confused as all the chicanery was explained to him. But, as the afternoon unfolded, as he saw what everyone was up to, Hughitt was the only person at Wrigley Field not wondering just what had happened to the once-stately game of professional football.

"That was kind of a screwy game all around," said Mel Hein, the Giants' Pro Football Hall of Fame center.

"There may have been unusual plays," said

George Halas, the Bears' owner, who had returned to coaching when Ralph Jones resigned before the season, "but in terms of drama, why, there were six lead changes. Both teams were magnificent. The winning touchdown came with less than three minutes to play. But the game still could have been won on the last play. I'd say it was a classic game, one of the greatest ever."

Particularly because his Bears won 23-21.

Pro football had broken off into divisions in 1933, guaranteeing a championship game. The owners also had adopted several rules changes designed to juice up the game.

In the battle of Bears and Giants, things didn't become surrealistic until the second half. The Giants clung to a 7-6 lead at intermission.

In the third quarter, rookie placekicker Jack Manders delivered his third field goal (he'd kicked only six in the regular season) to give the Bears the lead again. Then New York marched 61 yards for a touchdown to put the Giants on top.

"That's when things became very strange," said Steve Owen, one of four future Hall of Fame players on the Giants' offensive line. "Who would ever have thought of Bronko Nagurski as a passer?"

Nagurski was the greatest power runner in the game. The perfect fullback.

"Nagurski, what a man!" Halas said. "A couple of our players once asked him how he got so strong. And he told them he used to plow fields. The players then told him a lot of people had plowed a field at one time or another. And I'll never forget Nagurski smiling and saying, 'Without a horse?' Nobody could run inside like Nagurski."

Respect for Nagurski's bullish running set up the Bears' next touchdown. It also was the play they had mentioned to Hughitt. Nagurski took a hand-off, took a step forward, and lowered his head. Then he suddenly leaped and threw a jump pass. Bill Karr, another rookie, caught the ball and scored. The play went eight yards and the Bears led 16-14.

Enter Mel Hein and the hidden-ball trick. Hein was the center, Harry Newman the quarterback. But instead of lining up in the standard Single-Wing formation, Newman stepped up to the line, over center, like a T-formation quarterback.

"There was one man on my left, the end," Hein said. "All we did was have him take a step back, and the flanker on the right moved up into the line. Now I became an eligible receiver."

Hein snapped the ball to Newman, who handed it back to Hein. Newman faded back, as if to pass, then proceeded to "stumble" and collapse face first, with his back to the defense. While Newman waited to be smothered by Bears, Hein stuffed the ball under his jersey "and started strolling."

"The idea was to just walk down the field," Hein said. "I took four to five steps and I got excited and took off running. I made it about thirty yards."

That's when Bears safety Keith Molesworth discovered the deception and caught Hein from behind.

The Bears held and forced a punt, but had to kick back. What followed next belonged in a Charlie Chaplin movie.

Newman, who finished the game with 12 completions in 17 pass attempts for 201 yards, completed five consecutive passes, and the third quarter ended with the Giants on the Chicago 8-yard line.

On the next play, Ken Strong, the NFL's leading scorer, tried to run around end, taking Newman's handoff and heading left. But the Bears were waiting. Spontaneity took over. Strong braked, looked around, saw Newman near the line of scrimmage, and two-handed the ball back to him.

The surprised Newman caught the ball by reflex,

realized his predicament, and started retreating. At about the 15, he realized the Bears were about to bury him. So he threw a pass into the end zone.

That's where Ken Strong made the catch for the touchdown before tumbling into the baseball dug-out. He emerged with the ball and a broad smile. Red Grange, a defensive back for the Bears that day, said later, "If there has ever been a zanier play, it probably wasn't allowed by the officials."

As it was, Hughitt and his associates had their flags in their hands throughout the sequence. As it was, after a quick conference, they concluded nothing had been illegal. The Giants had the lead back.

Strong surrendered his hero status a few series later. As he tried to punt, he felt several Bears around him. He rushed his kick and it soared about 60 yards—unfortunately, 30 straight up and 30 back down—and only 8 yards downfield.

The Bears reacted quickly. Nagurski ran for a first down, setting up the Giants for another pass, which had a twist. Nagurski executed his fake run, then threw a jump pass. Bill Hewitt made the catch. Hewitt was easily recognizable because he was one of the few remaining players without a helmet.

The Giants closed in for the tackle and Hewitt suddenly wheeled and lateraled to Karr.

"Lateral?" Halas said later. "The ball must have traveled twenty yards. There were some passers in the league who couldn't throw the ball as far as that lateral went."

Karr turned and saw two Giants—Strong and Newman—directly ahead. What Karr didn't see was Bears halfback Gene Ronzani coming up from the rear. With clockwork precision, Ronzani raced between the impending collision and, he explained afterward, "I knocked them both right on their cans." Karr put the Bears ahead 23-21.

The Giants had one more chance. And one more trick. Newman's desperation pass was caught by Dale Burnett over the middle at the Bears' 40. Suddenly, a blur went racing down the sideline. Burnett "was going to lateral the ball as soon as he could," said Giants owner Tim Mara.

The blur was Mel Hein, this time determined not to be caught from behind. But the ball never arrived.

"Red Grange saved the game," Mara said. "He tackled the ball and pinned Burnett's arms so he was unable to lateral."

"I sure had a lot of room in front of me," Hein said. "Who knows what would have happened. To be honest, the things that did happen in that game were strange enough."

THE BIGGEST BLOWOUT

Chicago Bears 73,
Washington Redskins 0
December 8, 1940

Referee Red Friesel stepped into the huddle of the Chicago Bears. "What are you going to do?" he asked.

"Kick the extra point," someone said.

"Oh no, you're not," Friesel said. "We're almost out of footballs. They only give us a dozen for a game. I already talked to Halas. You're going to have to run or pass."

A few moments later, Solly Sherman passed to Joe Maniaci, and the Bears' lead over the Washington Redskins reached 67 points.

Unfortunately, about the same time, the public address system at Griffith Stadium offered an ill-timed promotional message advising Redskins fans it was never too early to order tickets for the 1941 season. The chorus of boos was the first emotion shown by the Washington fans since early in the third quarter.

The Bears eventually scored yet another touchdown, missed the extra point, and won the NFL championship by the most famous final score ever recorded.

The numbers stand alone. Ask any sports fan.

73-0? Sure, the Bears over the Redskins. No other game in any sport can stand alone simply by telling the final score.

"Everything we did, we did right. Everything they did was wrong," said George Halas, the Bears' owner-coach.

Bears quarterback Sid Luckman said, "The thing was none of us stood out that day. We were all good—every one of us."

Bears tackle George Musso said, "It was the perfect football game. You can't play better than we did that day."

Halas agreed, adding, "You can't blame the Redskins for what happened. They had nothing to do with the score. Or very little, anyway. It was us. The Bears played like no team before or after. There may never be a game again on the professional level so convincingly won."

"The funny thing was," said Washington tailback Frank Filchock, one of the few Redskins who felt like talking when it was over, "we really felt confident before the game. We'd beaten them just three weeks earlier on the same field."

Three weeks earlier, the Redskins had defeated the Bears 7-3 in Griffith Stadium. The same two numbers produced a vastly different result.

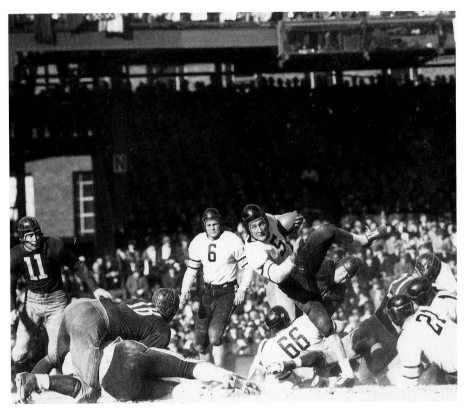

The Bears gained 519 yards in total offense, including 381 rushing. Ten Chicago players gained yards rushing, including George McAfee (5), who ran for seven yards on this play. Chicago led 21-0 by the end of the first quarter.

wouldn't be surprised to see his Bears win by a big margin. Why, that's ridiculous. I can't even understand why his team is favored [2½ points by kickoff]. Corinne, my lads will pass them silly."

Marshall and Halas were feuding. After the Redskins' victory in November, in which Halas and his players angrily vocalized about a controversial play in the final seconds, Marshall called the Bears "a bunch of crybabies."

"The Bears are front-runners, quitters," Marshall said. "They're not a second-half team."

Halas had been splashing reprints of Marshall's comments everywhere his players might see them for nearly three weeks. He was hoping to lure a strong sense of revenge from his Bears.

"I had no idea they would respond like they did," Halas said.

In the stands that day was Biff Jones with his square notebook. The Nebraska coach was preparing to take his team to the Rose Bowl to play Stanford. Jones figured he might see something helpful because Clark Shaughnessy's Stanford team, like the Bears, was one of only a handful of teams that

Filchock laughed weakly and added, "The final score then was 7-3. Today, same numbers but . . . ."

73-0. The day before the game, Redskins owner George Preston Marshall, who could swash and buckle with the best of them, read aloud from a newspaper to his wife, Corinne Griffith Marshall, over breakfast.

"Listen to what George Halas says: He says he

1940 Championship Playoff
Chicago Bears (73) vs. Washington Redskins (0)
at Washington, D.C., Dec. 8
Attendance 36,034

used the T-formation. In fact, Shaughnessy had helped contribute to the development of the Bears' T while he had been coach at the University of Chicago.

What Jones—or the Redskins—didn't know was that Shaughnessy had returned to Chicago to help the Bears prepare for this game. He took over the Bears' offense, tinkering with it here and there, installing new plays, and throwing out others. The result was to be devastating.

"I can only hope it was the Bears' players and not the T-formation itself that accounts for the game I saw," Jones said later that night.

As people entered the gates, they were issued song sheets. The Redskins' marching band was easily the most famous halftime show in the country. Marshall took almost as much pride in it as he did

in his football team. In the temporary bleachers that had been added, there also was a teepee that held a band that played old favorites as the milling fans headed for their seats for the big game.

Before the game, George Halas stood in the middle of the Chicago locker room and said in his usual gruffness, "I personally don't think you are quitters or crybabies. I think you're the greatest team in the National Football League."

And the heavy silence was almost too loud to stand for the next several seconds before Halas continued, "Now, go out and prove it."

In the broadcast booth, Red Barber whistled into his WOR microphone. The first pro football game ever to be broadcast over an entire network (120 stations received the game) was about to start. Barber skimmed the rosters of the two teams to make

On the game's second play, Chicago's Bill Osmanski (left) sprinted around left end and raced 68 yards for a touchdown. It looked as if he might be caught (lower left) at the Redskins' 30, but teammate George Wilson sliced behind him to take out two Washington defenders with one block.

sure there weren't names he didn't know how to pronounce.

And in a few minutes, from the "catbird's seat," Barber started sounding more like a tobacco auctioneer.

"The touchdowns came so quickly there for a while," Barber said years later, "I felt like I was the cashier at a grocery store. It is a very good thing I went over the roster of the Bears. I believe I wound up having to say every player's name on the list. In fact, I believe they all scored touchdowns. It seemed that way anyhow."

The steady diet that became gluttony began 55 seconds into the game. On the Bears' second play from scrimmage, fullback Bill Osmanski ran 68 yards for a touchdown, helped along the way by end George Wilson, who cleared two Redskins out of the way with one ferocious block.

The Bears scored two more touchdowns in the first quarter, and Marshall, at his usual position in his private box behind the Redskins' bench, heard the angry jeers of a disgruntled fan.

"Send these bums back to Boston," the heckler yelled, referring to the fact the Redskins once were located in Boston. Marshall was furious. He left his seat, walked back, and took note of the heckler's seat number, writing it down on a slip of paper. Marshall planned to find out who the fickle fan was and "make sure he'd never have to suffer through another Redskins game. I'd take his seat and sell it to someone else. Anyone else."

The Bears were held to one touchdown in the second quarter—it was 28-0 at halftime—which prompted the remaining faithful Redskins fans and most of the players to believe a second-half come-

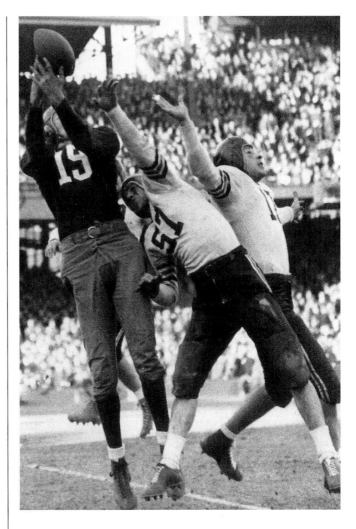

back not only was possible but forthcoming.

"I've seen bigger comebacks," Ray Flaherty, the Washington

Late in the first half, Redskins end Charley Malone made a fine 42-yard catch to reach the Bears' 5, but an interception killed the drive. Earlier, Malone dropped a sure touchdown pass from Sammy Baugh in the end zone.

In 1940, players went both ways. On this run, Washington's Jimmy Johnston was tackled by Bears quarterback Sid Luckman, with fullback Bill Osmanski (9) and halfback George McAfee (5) helping. The Redskins netted five yards rushing.

coach, said. "We should have scored on our first try, too. This game is far from over."

After Osmanski's long run in the game's first minute had startled the crowd into numbed silence, Redskins fullback Max Krause got them excited by returning the ensuing kickoff 54 yards. Two plays later, tailback Sammy Baugh threw a perfect pass to end Charley Malone, who was alone in the end

zone. But Malone dropped it. Then the Redskins missed the field goal.

"This game is far from over," Flaherty repeated as his players headed back for the second half.

This time, it took the Bears 54 seconds to score. Baugh's short pass was intercepted by end Hampton Pool and returned 15 yards for a touchdown.

"Live by the pass, die by it," Halas said later. "The Redskins hurt themselves all day by doing silly things like passing from their ten-yard line."

In all, the Bears intercepted eight passes, returning three of them for touchdowns. Flaherty tried switching tailbacks, Filchock for Baugh, but the Bears scarcely noticed the difference.

Three times in the game, the Redskins ventured inside the Bears' 20 and each time came away with nothing. The game with the famous final score also produced some misleading statistics. Like first downs, of which the Redskins had the same number as the Bears. It also produced some telling numbers. Like eight interceptions. Like the Redskins' rushing total, which was a net five yards. Like the Bears' total offense, which was 381 yards rushing and another 138 passing. Like the Redskins' 223 yards on kickoff returns, perhaps the most negative of statistics when you think about it.

Luckman didn't play in the second half. Most of the Bears' starters were pulled. It didn't make any difference. Ten different players scored touchdowns. Five different players kicked extra points. And then there was the game ball, saved from public consumption in the stands by the forced conversion pass from Sherman to Maniaci.

About the time the laughter and boos had settled following the announcement about tickets, Mar-

The faces on the benches told the story of the game. At left, head coach George Halas and quarterback Sid Luckman (center) of the Bears enjoyed the action...

shall left for good. When the final gun sounded, a wise guy in the press box cracked, "Marshall just shot himself."

To which another reporter quipped, "He should have shot his team first."

The aisles were littered with song sheets, trampled and smudged and about to be swept up and thrown into huge trash bins.

In the Bears' locker room, the entire team ran in a circle, arms raised, allowing the playful self-indulgence of cheering for themselves.

Marshall finally was spotted and asked for a comment. "Helpless, hopeless, hapless," he muttered.

And the Bears? Marshall scowled, then conceded, "Good. Very good. Too good for us today."

Marshall suggested his defense looked more like "a roomful of maidens going after a mouse" before launching into a tirade about his offense.

"Total embarrassment," he said.

He criticized everyone, but singled out Filchock for "passing the ball on almost every down and generally to the other team."

When asked for a rebuttal, Filchock snapped, "Listen, it was 35-0 by the time I got in the game. What else are you going to do but pass when you're so far behind?"

Marshall fumed a while longer, finally declaring, "My team quit, just plain quit. Too many of my guys are playing on reputation. Well, there will be plenty of changes."

As he walked out of the room, Marshall fidgeted with something in his pocket. He curiously pulled out his hand and opened it. It was the slip of paper with the seat number of the disenchanted fan. Marshall cursed softly, wadded the paper, and tossed it

After the game, Halas got a victory ride in the Bears' locker room. George Wilson (30), who made the key block on Bill Osmanski's opening touchdown, stood behind him. It was Chicago's third NFL championship, but first since 1933.

against the wall. His Redskins had just been treated like Indians in a Grade B western movie. His hated colleague Halas was gloating up a storm. Marshall had larger worries. Let the guy keep his opinion and his seat as well.

The next morning's front page of the *Washington Post* was filled with gloomy news. One story told of a Nazi ship being seized near Cuba by the British. The bombs of the Luftwaffe were hitting London. Hitler was marching in the streets of Paris. But the top story, the one with the boldest headline, the one with the most shocking news of all, streamed like a banner across the top of the newspaper:

"Bears Crush Redskins 73 to 0."

. . . while the Redskins' players looked on in shock. Sammy Baugh (second from left) sat between halfbacks Wilbur Moore (35) and Dick Todd (41).

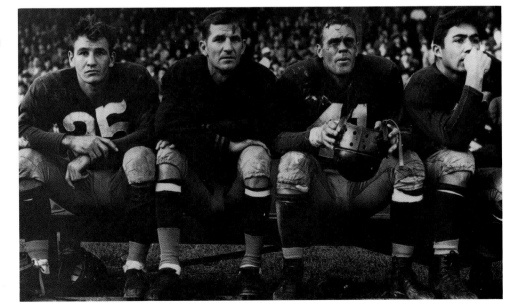

POSTWAR CLASSIC

Cleveland Rams 15,
Washington Redskins 14
December 16, 1945

Sitting with his back to his locker, halfback Jim Gillette swallowed and clasped his hands together.

"Are you nervous?" a teammate whispered.

Gillette looked up. He was beyond getting nervous. He had told some of his Cleveland Rams teammates about going down in the sea after enemy torpedoes had cracked the hull of his ship. He'd described the feeling of being in murky water, holding on to a lifeboat for several hours, of watching the fiery burial of his ship. Of not knowing who would show up next—Japanese gunboats or hungry sharks. Gillette had been a lieutenant in the U.S. Navy. He had come back from World War II and picked up his life as a professional football player.

He didn't want to go through it all again, so he just shook his head.

"Mainly, I'm just cold," Gillette said.

It was an hour before the NFL Championship Game with the Washington Redskins, and it was 3 degrees below zero. Gillette, a running back, blew into his hands and wiggled his toes. Football had been such a lark since getting back home. The Rams had won 9 of 10 games.

Then Gillette smiled. Here he was, not so long removed from hanging on for dear life in some distant, dark waters, flotsam in a war zone, playing football. He felt warmer.

Why not? It was 2 above zero when he walked onto Cleveland's Municipal Stadium field.

Sammy Baugh, the Redskins' great quarterback, was freezing. He noticed his passes had no zip. He couldn't grip the ball very well. And his ribs hurt. Two weeks earlier, he'd bruised several ribs but he hadn't told anybody except the Redskins' trainer. The night before the game against the Rams, he had told head coach Dudley DeGroot and assistant coach Turk Edwards.

There was talk of starting backup Frankie Filchock. But Baugh said he wanted to try, adding, "Maybe it'll warm up and I'll feel better."

At the opening kickoff, it was 6 degrees. Baugh's ribs ached.

Bob Waterfield, the Rams' first-year quarter-

The temperature was 6 degrees at the opening kickoff, so players on the sidelines huddled under blankets to keep warm. Hay was put on the field to keep it from freezing, but it was removed before the game started.

back, had the flutters. He had gotten up before
dawn and studied his playbook. He was worried
about turning the wrong way on a handoff. What if
he fumbled? Threw an interception?

"I never thought about the weather," Waterfield
said.

Before the game, Waterfield signed a three-year
contract with the Rams. In 1946, he would earn
$20,000 a season, which would make him the
highest-paid player in the NFL. It all was pretty
heavy stuff considering Waterfield was just completing his rookie season.

Baugh, the old pro, and Waterfield, the hotshot
rookie from UCLA, both noticed the bales of straw
piled up around the field. Each assumed it had
something to do with trying to keep the playing
area from freezing over. Both concluded someone
had done a lot of work for nothing.

Emil Bossard also was studying the field. As chief
groundskeeper, Bossard considered the bitter
weather as much an opponent as the Rams did the
Redskins. The idea to cover the field with straw for
insulation against the snow and freezing rain had
seemed like a good idea earlier in the week. It cost
Rams owner Dan Reeves a small fortune—winter
straw was not something farmers in Ohio are prone
to donate for the sake of pro football—and then
there was the matter of spreading it.

Vagrants and drifters were everywhere in Cleveland. Returning service-
men also responded to
the ads promising part-
time work and a free seat
for the championship
game. Bossard and his

army of 275 men set
about scattering the
9,000 bales to create a
four-foot-thick blanket of
insulation. Then, just before the teams came out

*As the players struggled on a field that
looked like it might be in Siberia, Bob
Waterfield's second-quarter conversion
teetered on the crossbar (far right), then
fell over good. It gave the Rams a 9-7 lead
at halftime.*

for warm-ups, the straw was swept to the sidelines.

Unfortunately, a few minutes into the game, the
field was frozen solid. Snow and ice started sticking
to the east side, where the wind coming off nearby
Lake Erie aided and abetted the abominable conditions.

In the crowded press box, reporters were counting their blessings. There was room for only 50 of
them. The rest of the large media corps had been issued seats outside in the stands.

Moments before the opening kickoff, umpire
Harry Robb ran into the dugout for a pair of gloves.
Twenty years earlier Robb had played for the Can-
ton Bulldogs. He'd seen weather like this often.

"But I'd forgotten how much your nose and ears
and hands hurt," Robb said. "It all came back to
me that day."

Soon the playing sur-
face had become so hard,
Baugh said later, "it was
like trying to play on a
paved surface. Like we
were out in the street."

A play nobody had
seen before came early.

The Redskins were set
back deep in their own
territory. They'd just
stopped the Rams at the
Washington 5-yard line.
In those days, it was common for a team with such
poor field position to
sometimes punt the ball
away on second or third

*With bales of hay stacked behind him,
Washington's Sammy Baugh took a center
snap deep in his own end zone in the first
quarter. His pass from there hit the crossbar and fell back for a safety, which gave
the Rams a 2-0 lead.*

Halfback Jim Gillette of the Rams (with ball) was the game's leading rusher, gaining 101 yards on 17 carries. He also caught the game-winning 44-yard touchdown pass from Bob Waterfield in the third quarter.

A few minutes later, Filchock connected with the fleet Bagarus for a touchdown. The Redskins, winner of their division six times in the last decade, had a 7-2 lead.

Waterfield responded quickly, guiding the Rams back upfield and throwing a 37-yard touchdown pass to end Jim Benton.

"He's [Waterfield] a great one," Baugh would say after the game. "I couldn't grip the ball too

down rather than risk a turnover. Baugh felt if he dropped back into a deep formation, it might look like he was going to punt and he could catch the Rams off guard with a pass.

"Steve Bagarus was going downfield a good lick," Baugh said later. "I had someone else on the other side also running deep. So I laid the ball up high."

Baugh took the snap and dropped into the end zone. He felt like a big play was there for the making. He'd completed more than 70 percent of his passes in the regular season. He found the switch from the Single-Wing to the T-formation the previous year easy. He was the most accurate passer pro football ever had seen. When he threw the pass, "I was thinking about a touchdown."

But the ball hit the crossbar.

In 1945, the goalposts were located on the goal lines. Baugh's pass, delivered from three yards inside the end zone, came bouncing back.

It was ruled a safety by the officials.

DeGroot couldn't believe the call. Baugh was just as confused. Even most of the Rams didn't know why they suddenly had a 2-0 lead. But the rule book was quite clear: "When a forward pass from behind the goal line strikes the goalpost or crossbar...it is a safety."

Early in the second period, DeGroot and Baugh talked on the sideline. Baugh's injuries had been aggravated; he had completed just one of six passes for just seven yards. It was time for Filchock, De-Groot decided. Baugh didn't argue.

good. But Frankie [Filchock] and Waterfield seemed to do fine in the same conditions. Waterfield's going to be a great one."

Waterfield had never seen weather like this at UCLA. He soon found out that as difficult as passing in cold weather is, kicking might be even harder.

"It's just so tough to get the ball up," Waterfield said. "The air is so heavy."

Redskins tackle John Koniszewski lined up in the middle as Waterfield, who also punted and placekicked for the Rams, lined up the extra-point try. Koniszewski got by the blocker and partially blocked Waterfield's low kick.

In the broadcast booth, Harry Wismer, the veteran sportscaster, was careful not to lean too far forward. If his tongue or lips touched the cold metal mike, "they would get shredded."

Wismer tried to describe what happened:

"There's the snap...the ball is up and...it hits the crossbar. No, it's...yes, it's good. It fell over. Let me tell you what happened."

Waterfield's partially blocked kick hit the crossbar, bounced and came back down on the bar once

Washington's Joe Aguirre (19) missed two fourth-quarter field goals, either of which could have won the game.

more, then tumbled over. The Rams led 9-7.

"It's certainly a strange day," Wismer said. "I can't remember ever seeing that one, either."

The half ended three minutes later with Cleveland still clinging to the two-point lead that had been provided by another ball hitting the crossbar.

In the locker room, Waterfield and Gillette talked about plays that might work in the second half. Gillette said the footing was better than it looked and "it only hurt when you hit the ground."

In the third quarter, the Rams moved to a 15-7 lead as Waterfield and Gillette completed an 81-yard march with a 44-yard touchdown pass.

But Waterfield missed the extra point.

"I just made a bad kick," he said. "Maybe my concentration wasn't good. I don't know."

Late in the third quarter, Filchock's eight-yard touchdown pass to Bob Seymour, and Joe Aguirre's extra point made it 15-14. In the south stands, a water main broke and for a few minutes, water cascaded down the concrete steps and froze.

Twice in the fourth quarter, the Redskins got close enough for Aguirre to try field goals. But

Rams halfback Don Greenwood (66) ran for 19 yards on nine carries. Note the early facemask he wore to protect his nose.

losing for so long."

To which one of the Rams shouted, "Who wants to celebrate? I just want to defrost."

Even in ultimate victory, the Rams were drowning in red ink. Reeves guessed he would lose $50,000 for the season.

Waterfield was trying to find a telephone. He wanted to call his wife, Jane Russell, the movie star. He wanted to tell her he'd be driving across the country as soon as he got a hot shower and a little rest. Gillette, who had rushed for 101 yards and caught what proved to be the winning touchdown pass, was sitting once more with his back to his locker, hands folded in front of him. A penny for your thoughts, someone said.

"Tomorrow's my birthday," Gillette said. "But I feel like I got my present today."

Washington's locker room was subdued and defensive. Answers to questions were curt. Then a photographer spotted Baugh, weeping, trying to hide his face. When the big flash of the camera went off, so did several Redskins.

"Have you no compassion?" Filchock said to the photographer. "It has been a very tough day for us all. Leave us alone."

A month later, following a vote by the league owners, Reeves announced his team was following Waterfield west and soon would be known as the Los Angeles Rams. The day prior, on January 11, 1946, the NFL rule book was revised. In the future, any pass hitting the goalpost, regardless of where it originates, would be an incomplete pass.

Some of the Rams' personnel joining in a locker-room celebration after their 15-14 victory included (from left) head coach Adam Walsh, halfback Greenwood, quarterback Waterfield, end Jim Benton, and backfield coach Bob Snyder.

Aguirre, whose nickname ironically was "Hot Toe," missed both times. The final gun sounded and the Rams celebrated by sprinting immediately to the warmth of the locker room. Most of the crowd of 32,178 likewise retreated to shelter. But a few crazies tore down the goalposts.

In the Cleveland locker room, Rams owner Daniel F. Reeves said he was almost afraid to celebrate, "I've been used to

SMASH DEBUT

Cleveland Browns 35,
Philadelphia Eagles 10
September 16, 1950

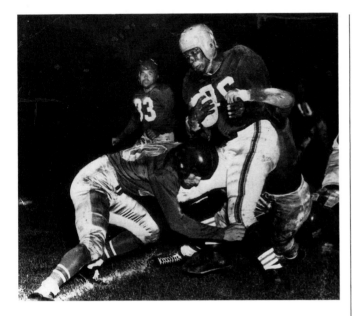

In their first regular-season game in the NFL, the Browns dominated the NFL-champion Eagles 35-10 on Otto Graham's passing and the running of Marion Motley, among others.

When the schedule for the upcoming NFL season was announced in 1950, the Cleveland Browns, one of the three new kids on the block, found out just what everyone thought of their ticket to the Big Top.

Game No. 1: September 16. Browns vs. Philadelphia Eagles at Municipal Stadium in Philadelphia.

The Eagles were the NFL's two-time defending champions.

Cleveland, Baltimore, and San Francisco all had been invited to join the old league that year. But the Browns were considered a special case. They had been the scourge of the All-America Football Conference, the most ambitious team in that post-war pro football league that had expired in 1949 beneath an avalanche of unpaid bills. What separated the Browns from the other two teams was their success: 52 victories in 59 games, four consecutive AAFC championships. Cleveland's dominance likely had helped the public's apathy toward the AAFC. They were *too* good.

NFL Commissioner Bert Bell felt a game between the established NFL and the young toughs from the AAFC would attract tremendous interest.

The Cleveland Browns were coached by Paul Brown, one of the most revolutionary minds in the sport's history. Brown had introduced formal playbooks, film analysis of games, advanced scouting, even a timing for running 40 yards.

And when he discovered the NFL was setting a trap for his team by having it play the NFL champions in its first official game, he reacted immediately. He had two scouts at the Eagles' 1949 NFL Championship Game against the Los Angeles Rams, charting plays and breaking down offense and defense with a meticulous intricacy. Brown obtained game films of several Eagles games—"not everyone hated the Browns," he said—and tendency charts resulted. By the time the Browns reported to their summer camp, a game plan on how to beat the Eagles already was drawn up.

The Browns were ready for the Eagles, who were confident but not ready. To begin with, the Eagles' scouting of the Browns didn't include several players—including Len Ford, Rex Bumgardner, Abe Gibron, and Hal Herring—that Brown had signed off AAFC teams that weren't coming into the NFL.

"We watched old films," said Eagles defensive tackle Bucko Kilroy. "But they weren't even the same team, really. We wound up playing an AAFC all-star team."

Philadelphia also was crippled. Steve Van Buren, the powerful halfback who had run for 196 yards against the Rams in the 1949 title game, had injured his foot. His running mate, Bosh Pritchard, also was down and out.

But the main disadvantage was the simple fact the Eagles never had seen anything like the Cleveland Browns' offense. Philadelphia head coach Earle (Greasy) Neale was proud of his 5-4 "Eagle" defense, which specialized in stopping enemy running attacks and throttling the T-formations that were the standard of the times.

But Brown figured if he put a halfback in motion, forcing a linebacker to cover him, one of his

The Eagles couldn't cover Cleveland's swift receivers, including Mac Speedie, who caught one of Graham's three touchdown passes.

receivers would get single coverage.

"There wasn't a defensive back alive who could stay with our receivers, Mac Speedie, Dub Jones, and Dante Lavelli," Brown said.

But the pervading thought still was that the Eagles were better; they'd win anyway. And Municipal Stadium (71,237) was jammed to capacity.

In the Cleveland locker room, Brown's voice had an even edge to it. He was certain his team was better than the Eagles at practically every position. But he wanted to instill a different emotion.

"We're new, and they don't like us," the coach said. "It may get rough out there. But remember just this—the worst thing you can do to an opponent is defeat him. Nothing hurts as bad as losing."

Cleveland kicked off, stuffed the Eagles on three straight plays, and forced a punt. The upset was in motion. It almost reached full speed when Don Phelps took the punt and bolted 64 yards into the end zone. However, a clipping penalty nullified the touchdown. And someone was lying on the ground . . .Lou Groza. His bruised shoulder finished him for the game.

Brown wheeled around.

"Where's Chubby?"

Not many teams in those days had backup kickers. Brown already had imagined the day Lou the Toe, who started in the offensive line, might get hurt. And he had Forrest (Chubby) Grigg in reserve.

Quarterback Otto Graham threw three incomplete passes in a row, but in the process, he found out all he and Brown needed to know. Each play, he sent Bumgardner in motion and the Eagles shifted by sending a linebacker. Dub Jones, the right halfback, ran a short square-out pattern each time. And Graham threw the pass to another receiver. But he noticed what was happening with Jones. The Eagles' defensive halfback, Russ Craft, crowded Jones more and more each time, closing forward.

"I'm sure he felt he'd intercept if I'd just throw the ball his way," Graham said.

Meanwhile, the Eagles, led by halfback Clyde (Smackover) Scott, the 1948 Olympics silver medalist in the high hurdles, had started a drive. They settled for a field goal.

When the Browns got the ball, Graham called another pass. This time he went to Dub Jones. But this time Jones didn't run that simple square-out. He broke back upfield and was 10 yards behind the stunned Craft, completing a 59-yard touchdown.

Chubby Grigg kicked the extra point and celebrated his achievement as though it were the final seconds. Instead there were more than three quarters still to play. But the reality was the Eagles were playing for second place. Their defense simply had too many vulnerable areas. When Brown noticed the Eagles didn't bother to cover fullback Marion Motley when he went in motion, Brown had halfback Bumgardner switch to fullback. Graham promptly completed three consecutive passes before the Eagles figured out they'd been tricked, and the Browns were on the way to another score.

Cleveland ran the ball only three times in the first period, five times in the second, and twice in the third. The Eagles were set in their 5-4 ways. Why change from the passing game?

In the third quarter, the Eagles marched and had a first down at the Cleveland 6-yard line. Then Motley, who had fumbled twice, checked into the game as a linebacker and made four consecutive atoning tackles.

In the fourth quarter, the Browns became haughty and decided to show off their versatility —to run against the defense that had been designed to stop the run. They pounded the ground with the mighty Motley, Bumgardner, Jones, and Graham, using only a few short passes. When they reached the 28, Graham called seven consecutive running plays. He kept on the last one for the touchdown.

Graham (next to Paul Brown) was honored as the game's outstanding player.

"I think Paul wanted to make a point," Graham said. "Neale had said Brown would make a better basketball coach because all we did was put the ball in the air. I also remember that the next time we played the Eagles after that, we beat them 13-7 and didn't throw a pass all game."

After the 35-10 victory, Brown said he'd never allowed such emotion to enter into his mindset.

"Four years of ridicule helped get us ready," he said. "Four years of being called a minor-league team. That game meant a great deal to us."

ONE FOR THE UPSTARTS

Cleveland Browns 30,
Los Angeles Rams 28
December 24, 1950

The Cleveland Browns still were waiting for somebody to show them why they couldn't be rookie champions of the National Football League. And now, on Christmas Eve, 1950, the NFL was down to its last chance to stop the sacrilege that a babe in swaddling clothes, dressed in the tattered defunct banner of the All-America Football Conference, might be football's king of kings.

In ice-cold Municipal Stadium, there were almost 50,000 empty seats as game time neared. Pro football, with few exceptions, was not yet enough of a magnet to lure people from last-minute shopping. Besides, it looked as if the upstart Browns finally were about to get their comeuppance anyway.

The Los Angeles Rams had more stars than the eastern sky.

"I don't know if there's ever been a team that had as many offensive stars as this Rams team," said Cleveland quarterback Otto Graham.

The Rams had averaged almost 40 points a game. And they seemed to have at least two of everything. Two future Hall of Fame quarterbacks, two future Hall of Fame ends, even two backfields.

The quarterbacks, Bob Waterfield and Norm Van Brocklin, had passed for more than two miles worth of yards. One of the wide receivers, Tom Fears, had led the league in receiving for the third straight season, catching an NFL record 84 passes. The other, Elroy (Crazylegs) Hirsch, had caught 42. Five Rams players had run 100 yards under 10 seconds. In one game against Baltimore, Los Angeles had scored 10 touchdowns.

Graham was the NFL's second-ranked passer (behind Van Brocklin), and he also had several good receivers, a quality running game, and an offensive genius on the sideline.

Cleveland head coach Paul Brown had spent most of the season exploiting the basic defenses used in the NFL. In only a dozen games, the Browns had rendered standard defenses almost obsolete. Using men in motion, screens, and little flare passes to loosen up the opponent, Brown had everyone trying to figure out how to stop him.

"We had better balance than most teams," said Browns tackle-placekicker Lou Groza. "Remember also that that year every team in the league was

Bunched together, the Rams and Browns watched Lou Groza's 16-yard, game-winning field goal sail over the crossbar with 28 seconds left.

trading information with each other, trying to find a way to beat us. They just didn't want some outsider winning the championship."

All week, the weather in Cleveland had been typically horrible. Three days before the game, someone figured that the field at Municipal Stadium was frozen to a depth of seven inches.

"We all wore tennis shoes because the field was frozen solid," Rams fullback Tank Younger recalled. "And, as I remember, it never warmed up any. We got a cold mist, but it sure never got warm."

The Rams had the ball first, setting up at their 18-yard line. Waterfield was the Rams' starter. It was a well-kept secret, but Van Brocklin had broken a rib the week before in a playoff against the Bears.

Waterfield had been a rookie quarterback in 1945 when the Rams had won their only NFL championship. Only then, the team had been located in Cleveland. The following year, owner Daniel F. Reeves had packed up the team and headed to Los Angeles. The Browns replaced the Rams in Cleveland.

On the first play from scrimmage, Waterfield flipped a short pass to Glenn Davis, who did most of the work in an 82-yard touchdown collaboration.

Brown fidgeted. He prided himself on preparation; his teams simply did not make mental mistakes. But on this first play from scrimmage, two of

Dick Hoerner's one-yard touchdown run, his second score of the day, gave the Rams a 21-20 lead in the third quarter. He led his team in rushing with 86 yards.

his linebackers had been suckered by movement and misdirection by the Rams' offensive line.

"When Paul was mad," Graham said, "he wasn't like Lombardi. He never screamed or yelled. But, oh, how he could burn a hole in you with his eyes. He just had a certain look."

While that certain look was aimed at the Cleveland defense, the offense went to work. Six plays later, the game was tied. Graham threw a 27-yard pass to halfback Dub Jones for the touchdown.

The Rams responded with a vengeance—a 44-yard bomb to Fears, an end-around by Verda (Vitamin T) Smith for 15 yards, and on the eighth play of the drive Dick Hoerner scored the game's third touchdown. The Rams led 14-7.

Browns receiver Mac Speedie shook his head. Speedie, like Van Brocklin, had a secret injury. His hamstring was torn. He could run once he got warmed up, but when he stood on the sideline he tightened up badly. He had told Brown he could play, "for a little while, anyway."

Speedie was aptly named, and even with a bad leg he was able to beat Rams defensive back Tom Keane on a fly pattern on the first play after the kickoff. Keane broke up the pass, but bumped Speedie and drew a pass-interference call.

"We decided to go right back at Keane," Graham said. "As long as Speedie could run those routes he would command attention."

A 17-yard pass to Speedie at the Los Angeles 37 had the Rams confused. Speedie ran the same pattern again and found himself triple-covered.

So Graham found end Dante Lavelli with a 37-yard touchdown pass.

Groza stepped back carefully, looking for bad spots in the ground, ready to kick the extra point. Assistant coach Weeb Ewbank once studied Groza's kicking style and found the kicker was so rutted in routine, "he could kick fifty balls and you'd only see one set of cleat marks."

Hal Herring's snap was high, and holder Tom-

Cleveland's Dante Lavelli caught 37- and 39-yard touchdown passes from Otto Graham and was the game's leading receiver with 11 catches.

Otto Graham, wearing a most un-quarterback-like number (60), dazzled the Rams by running for 99 yards and passing for 298 and four touchdowns. Note the blocker behind him who has his hand in a Rams player's face.

my James had to jump to stop it. Groza had no chance to kick. James scrambled to his right. All teams have emergency plays. The Browns' Tony Adamle recognized what was happening and drifted into the end zone. Adamle, a linebacker who played on the outside for extra-points, was alone and James threw a pass toward him.

Adamle dropped it. As he had drifted into the end zone, he had felt a familiar pain in his ankle. He started to stumble. It was just enough of a lapse in concentration to cause him to drop the pass.

Los Angeles led by a point, 14-13.

The Rams seemed undaunted and rumbled to the Cleveland 7. But an interception stopped them. A shanked punt near midfield gave them another opportunity. But, after rolling to a first down at the Cleveland 12, they were stopped again.

"When it looked like they were going to have to settle for three," Graham said, "we were kind of celebrating. We had no idea they'd come away with nothing."

Waterfield was an excellent short-distance field-goal kicker. He said later he couldn't ever remember missing one from 15 yards. But he did.

Len Ford could stand no more. The Browns' defensive end went to his coach and begged to play. Ford's jaw had been shattered near the end of the season. He had been forced to take food through a straw, and he was 15 pounds under his regular weight. He wore a special padding the Browns equipment manager had rigged up for his helmet. Brown nodded, and Ford headed onto the field, but

the half ended with the Rams leading 14-13.

In the third quarter, in one three-play sequence, Ford threw Smith for a 14-yard loss, sacked Waterfield for 11, and dropped Davis for a loss of 13.

"Lenny was a real inspiration out there," Groza said. "He got us going with those three plays."

The Browns marched 77 yards, and Lavelli caught a 39-yard touchdown pass from Graham for a 20-14 lead.

But not for long. In the middle of the third quarter, the Rams stormed back. A 38-yard pass to Smith set up the Dick Hoerner Show. He carried the ball seven consecutive times. On the last run, a fourth-down play at the Cleveland 1-yard line, he plowed into the end zone. The Rams led 21-20.

On the first play after the kickoff, Marion Motley took a pitchout. The Rams' defense had keyed on the big fullback all day—he would finish with six yards on nine carries—and once more, they gathered around him like ants on a piece of dropped cake. Motley tried to reverse his field, was stacked up by several Rams, and fumbled.

Rams defensive end Larry Brink picked up the football at the 6 and scored. In 25 seconds, the Rams had two touchdowns and a 28-20 lead.

With five minutes to play, the Rams tried to get the coffin-closer touchdown. But Cleveland cornerback Warren Lahr made a sliding interception.

Graham and the Browns then stopped the exodus of fans who were in the aisles, thinking the game was a lost cause. Graham ran for a first down on one fourth-down play, passed for a first down on another fourth-down situation, and then threw a 14-yard touchdown pass to halfback Rex Bumgardner. It was his fourth touchdown pass of the day, and the Browns trailed only 28-27.

Four plays later, the Browns' defense got the ball back. Graham steered Cleveland back downfield There was 3:16 to play, and the ball already was close to being in Groza's field-goal range, when Graham scrambled for a first down.

Linebacker Milan Lazetich, with Waterfield the only holdovers from the Rams' 1945 title team, hit Graham, who fumbled. The Rams recovered.

"I wanted to die," Graham said. "I walked off the field and I couldn't have felt worse. But coach Brown came over and said 'Don't worry, Otts, we're still going to get them.' I knew right then if we could get one more chance, we'd win it."

The Rams needed just one first down. But three runs gained only three yards. Waterfield dropped back to punt.

Into the wind, Waterfield kicked a 51-yard spiral, a clutch play that Rams coach Joe Stydahar felt might throw the Browns back far enough to save the championship for the Rams.

But Graham scrambled for 14 yards, completed passes of 15, 16, and 12 yards, and, with his head swiveling back and forth from the clock to the Rams' defense, signaled time out. There were 41 seconds left. The ball was at the 12-yard line.

In the coach's box, Browns offensive assistant Blanton Collier didn't like what he saw. The Browns were playing for a field goal by Groza. But the ball was being spotted on the far-left hashmark.

"Bad angle," Collier shouted. He got on the phone to Brown. "Run a quarterback sneak to the right," Collier said. "Get Groza a better angle."

Brown nodded and sent in the play: quarterback sneak to the right.

Collier later said, "In the next few seconds I aged a hundred years. I just called a running play from automatic field-goal range. What if there had been a fumble?"

Almost 40 years later, Graham laughed at the notion.

"Are you kidding?" he said. "After losing that one fumble, there was no way. You couldn't have gotten that ball away from me with a blowtorch."

Graham's sneak gained three yards and a better position for Groza.

From the 16-yard line, one yard back from where Waterfield had missed, Lou Groza kicked a field goal with 28 seconds left on the clock.

Outsiders 30, Aristocracy 28.

Stydahar walked over to Van Brocklin, who was warming up. "Can you throw deep?" he asked.

"I told him maybe one or two times," Van Brocklin later said.

Groza kicked off and because Yogi Berra's wisdom transcends all sports, this one wasn't over until it was over. Jerry Williams settled under the kick and found a lane.

At the Rams' 46, he was dragged down by Groza.

There still was time for perhaps two plays. One of them had to be a big one and then Waterfield might be able to try another field goal.

Van Brocklin faded back. Glenn Davis ran downfield, toward the goal line. Warren Lahr ran side by side. At Army, Davis was Mr. Outside, the Heisman Trophy-winning gamebreaker with great speed. Warren Lahr had played in college for Western Reserve, a small college in Cleveland. His speed never was a topic of conversation. His lack of speed was.

The pass came down at the Browns' 5. Four hands reached for it. Lahr had it. Davis had it. A two-second tug-of-war ensued, each pulling at the ball. On into the end zone they went as the final gun sounded.

"It was terrible," Graham said. "We didn't know for several seconds what the referee was going to call. We were sure Lahr had intercepted. But what if they gave Davis the ball and a touchdown? And what if they called it a safety or something? That would have been two points and a tie game."

Finally, the decision: Cleveland's ball. The game was over.

"Every team we played," Len Ford said, "we brought out the best in them. Nobody wanted us to win. Every team was a bunch of wildcats."

Groza kissed his shoe several times for the benefit of photographers, then dressed slowly.

"There really wasn't a formal celebration," Groza said. "Me, personally, I got in my car and drove to Martins Ferry, where my parents lived. The next day was Christmas. It was a long drive. Next day, in the afternoon, people found out I was home. And they drove me around in the fire engine."

The Rams' team plane landed in Los Angeles at 4 A.M. Waterfield was asked how he felt.

"Like I owe everybody on this team $750," he said.

Champions in their first year in the NFL, the Browns celebrated with great enthusiasm. That's Paul Brown in the center (with hat on), holding kicker Lou Groza's foot.

LIFE IN THE FAST LAYNE

Detroit Lions 17,
Cleveland Browns 16
December 27, 1953

As soon as Jim Doran stepped into the huddle, Bobby Layne asked gruffly, "Can you still beat that feller?"

For almost the entire 1953 NFL Championship Game between the Detroit Lions and Cleveland Browns—specifically, just about the time Jim Doran was forced into duty as a Lions wide receiver—Doran had been telling his quarterback he could get behind Browns cornerback Warren Lahr.

For just as long, Layne had nodded and said not just yet. But now, the Browns' 16-10 lead was not so much a concern as the clock. There was a little more than two minutes left to play and Layne was going to play his hole card at last.

"Just throw it," Doran said. "I'll beat him."

"Okay, men," Layne barked, looking around the huddle. "Let's run a Nine Up . . . and block them sons of bitches for me."

Doran trotted over to his position on the left end. Lahr crouched two yards ahead.

With about three minutes remaining in the 1953 NFL title game, Detroit's Jim Doran beat Tommy James and made an 18-yard catch of a Bobby Layne pass for a first down on Cleveland's 45-yard line. Three plays later, Layne passed 33 yards to Doran for the game-winner.

by called the play, I had to keep from smiling as I lined up. I was right in front of him and when the ball was snapped, I extended my forearm like I was going to block him."

Lahr was a veteran player, in his sixth season. In the 1950 NFL Championship Game, he had preserved the Browns' victory over the Los Angeles Rams with an interception on the game's final play. The night before, Lahr and quarterback Otto Graham, his roommate on the road, had talked about the big game. They went over assignments, talking about the Lions and which players might be the most dangerous.

"I was the one who had to deal with Jim Doran," Graham said. "He was a defensive player. At least that's what we thought."

Early in the game, when Leon Hart, Detroit's

"Lahr and I had been feuding a bit, you know, like you do in a tough game," Doran said. "He said he was gonna hit me in the mouth. When Bob-

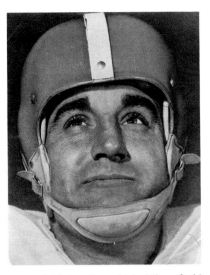

Dependable Lou Groza kicked three field goals to give the Browns a 16-10 lead.

regular right end, limped off the field, dragging his wrenched knee, Doran became an offensive player. He and Lahr tangled almost from the beginning. Just as quickly, Doran was telling Layne and head coach Buddy Parker, "I can beat this guy on an up pattern."

Doran had caught a total of six passes in the 1953 season in just such emergency situations. He was never the speediest runner, and his aggressive nature made him more valuable on defense.

"But he had good hands," Layne said. "And he just wasn't the type to go off saying things if he wasn't pretty damn sure."

A man's word usually doesn't mean much in today's modern game plans. Computer tendency charts rarely include gut feelings from converted defensive players. And who would go for such spontaneity in the closing minutes of the biggest game of the year?

"That's how the game's different today," said Jim David, a Lions cornerback in the 1950s. "What we had going for us back then was trust. We believed in each other. The team that year had a whole lot of adversity to overcome. Then, in the championship game, against the Browns, who were considered to have the best talent in the league, it was really a hell of a way to have it all end up.

"Bobby just had a way. He got you there. Say what you want about him and how he lived his life. But he got you there."

Layne looked over the Cleveland Browns' defense. The ball was on the Browns' 33-yard line. The Briggs Stadium crowd in Detroit was quiet. The Lions had started this drive moments ago, on their 20. It had begun with a 17-yard pass to

Doran, and, after the tackle, Doran and Lahr had traded their usual insults and threats. In the huddle, Doran had told Layne once more, "Really Bobby, I can beat him deep."

Layne nodded. But let's set him up. We'll get him. Soon.

The Lions had made it this far because, on a third-and-10 play, Doran had slid into a gap between two Browns defenders and made a lunging catch for 18 more yards and another first down.

"If he don't get that one," Layne said later, "we ain't going nowhere no how."

But now Layne looked over the Browns' defense and he noticed Lahr pointing an angry, threatening finger at Doran. Layne saw things the Detroit coaching staff couldn't. He saw human nature exposed. And he knew how to respond.

A few seconds earlier, during a time out, Lions assistant coach Aldo Forte had made a suggestion. Because of the hard rush defensive end Len Ford was getting on Layne, a screen pass might work.

Parker had relayed the play to Layne.

"Know what I think?" Layne told his coach, already thinking about Doran. "I think a cigarette sure would taste good about now."

Layne turned and walked back to the huddle and called the play that won the NFL championship.

Layne took the snap, and Doran took one giant step forward. Lahr made a similar move.

"Lahr came at me pretty hard," Doran said. "He really was going to knock my head off. But then I ran right by him."

Bobby Layne's pass

Layne, eluding Browns middle guard Bill Willis (60), led the Lions to back-to-back NFL championships in 1952-53. He completed 12 of 25 passes for 179 yards and ran for 46 in the 17-16 victory over Cleveland in 1953.

Doak Walker kicked a 23-yard field goal, after earlier scoring a touchdown, to give Detroit a 10-3 halftime lead.

wobbled rather than spiraled, which was nothing new. Doran was 10 yards behind Lahr when he caught the ball. He cruised into the end zone untouched. With 2:08 to play, the Lions had tied the game.

Doak Walker, who had played in the same backfield with Bobby Layne in high school, kicked the extra point and Detroit led 17-16.

Otto Graham pulled off his parka. If Bobby Layne was the embodiment of the Lions—a happy-go-lucky rogue, given to nocturnal escapades and bouts of excess and revelry, yet someone who knew how to rise up and lead and win—then Graham was the Browns' heroic counterpoint. Only the G-rated version—efficient, meticulous, straight arrow all the way. Otto Graham was the perfect extension for the great coaching dictator, Paul

Brown. Layne drew plays in the dirt. Graham had no such freedom.

But Graham was more than a machine. He had completed 64.7 percent of his passes in 1953, and the Browns were undefeated until the final week of the regular season. Now Graham had two minutes left to rescue the Browns.

In a private area of the press box, Edwin J. Anderson, one of the Lions' principal owners, could not contain himself. He stood up and shouted, "Oh, for a break now . . . just a fumble . . . or wouldn't it be wonderful if we could intercept? Anything, anything. Come on, give me a New Year's present."

Graham looked at his hands. He was having a terrible game—2 completions in 14 attempts. Blindsided on the game's second play from scrimmage, he had fumbled and the Lions had gone on to score a touchdown. He had thrown an interception that led to a Detroit field goal.

Now he had one more chance.

"My hands were chapped terribly," he said. "I had no feel on my passes. I don't know what it was —I tried spitting on them, everything I could think of to moisten them. But they were chapped, and, for some reason, I just could not pass well at all that day."

On the first play from

The Lions held the Browns to a net of 192 yards with defense like this on halfback Ray Renfro, who was two-timed by Joe Schmidt (on the ground), who had him by the leg, and Jim David. Renfro gained just 11 yards in four carries.

In the third quarter, Billy Reynolds of the Browns gained seven yards on a pass from Otto Graham, as the Browns drove 51 yards to the touchdown that tied the game 10-10.

scrimmage with 1:54 to go, Graham dropped back, ready to execute the play messenger guard Chuck Noll had just brought in from Brown, who called all the plays. Graham set and threw.

"It was a terrible pass," he said later.

Carl Karilivacz intercepted. The rookie defensive back, a twenty-third-round draft selection, simply slammed shut the door on the Cleveland Browns while Edwin Anderson stared up at the gray December sky in joyous wonder.

"You had to know those guys," defensive back Jim David said. "You had to know what all we went through. That team was special."

There were six rookies, eight second-year players, two returnees from Korea, and 13 players who came from other teams.

"But nobody was a stranger for long," David said. "That was Bobby's way. Once you were on the team, you were part of the gang. There would be a spirit party of sorts. There was rookie afternoon at some showbar in town. If you didn't show, we'd send a taxi for you. Bobby was the leader and we all followed. He knew the game and he knew people and he knew how to have a good time. There were some nights he'd be throwing $100 bills into a saxophone till all hours and there were other nights when some of us would kinda commandeer a trolley for a while. But when it came time to play, we were ready. They'd tell jokes that when we'd form the huddle, you could smell liquor and stuff like that. But that never happened.

"Not during regular season, anyway."

The Cleveland Browns were not allowed to smoke cigars in hotel lobbies. If they ever were seen drinking in public, said Graham, "they'd be fired."

On the night before the Lions played the Browns for the NFL Championship in 1953, as Graham and Lahr went to bed unaware both were about to play the poorest games of their NFL careers, nobody was totally sure Layne would even go to sleep.

Parker had a sudden good thought. "My team knows how to win," he told an assistant. "We know adversity and understand it and overcome it."

The next day, after it was over, the champions of pro football collected their thoughts and tried to say what it all meant.

"This team has it here," said assistant coach George Wilson, tapping his chest.

"Jimmy Doran don't tell lies," Layne drawled. "If he says he can get deep, you better get him the ball."

The celebration was on.

The Cleveland Browns showered and dressed quickly. There was a train to catch.

"Longest train ride I ever took," said Lou Groza, whose two fourth-quarter field goals had given the Browns the lead until the pass to Doran. "That one stuck in the gut longer."

On the train, Lahr showed little emotion. He talked matter-of-factly about the play. When they arrived, Lahr got in assistant coach Fritz Heisler's car and the two headed for the Cleveland suburb of Aurora. Warren Lahr cried all the way home.

"Now if we had lost that game," Layne said years later, "there wouldn't have been any tears. If I'd have overthrown Doran or if he'd dropped the ball or if I'd gotten my ass buried by Lenny Ford and a couple others, there wouldn't be nobody feeling sorry for themselves. We'd have gone out and had something cool to drink anyway.

"We didn't celebrate losses . . . we drowned them. See, winning and losing is nothing but an attitude. That game there was a good example. We just wasn't gonna lose, too damn stubborn to think any other way. Just the attitude we had back then."

When it was all over, head coach Buddy Parker was carried off the field after his team's second consecutive NFL championship.

COMEBACK AT KEZAR

Detroit Lions 31,
San Francisco 49ers 27
December 22, 1957

When you're playing on the road and getting your head handed to you and your championship hopes are evaporating like cheap perfume, the exasperation will come out.

"What the hell is happening to us?" yelled George Wilson, head coach of the Detroit Lions. He was running out of brimstone and fiery oratory. He'd given speeches at visitors' locker rooms everywhere and already had made several such impassioned pleas at friendly Briggs Stadium in Detroit.

Fans in Kezar Stadium in San Francisco were frolicking. The scoreboard at halftime read: 49ers 24, Lions 7.

"You guys are quitters," Wilson said. "We've totally given up out there."

Chins drooped. The coach's words had the sting of truth. They seemed to coincide with the ugly numbers on the scoreboard.

"How in the world did we get in this position?" moaned all-pro safety Jack Christiansen.

A dozen heads shook. Others just stared at the cement floor, numb with disbelief. The San Francisco 49ers were in the next room, gloating. At half-

R.C. Owens gave the 49ers a 7-0, first-quarter lead when he outjumped Jim David and scored on a 34-yard "Alley-Oop" pass from Y.A. Tittle. It was Owens's only catch of the game, however, and the 49ers, who led at halftime 24-7, lost to the Lions 31-27.

time of the playoff game to determine who would represent the Western Conference against the Cleveland Browns the following week, the Lions were getting embarrassed.

Quarterback Y.A. Tittle already had thrown three touchdown passes for San Francisco. He had completed 12 of 19 passes, humbling the famed Detroit secondary known as Chris's Crew, and had made it look as though his team could score whenever the mood struck. The Lions' offense also had been a no-show. And Detroit was unable to lick its halftime wounds in solitude because of the thin walls of the Kezar Stadium dressing rooms and the loud, obnoxious, already-celebrating 49ers.

"Oh, they were really jawing and talking about what kind of cars they were going to buy with their money," remembered Jim David, the Lions' corner-

San Francisco's explosive Hugh McElhenny (39) sent the 49ers ahead 14-0 when he took a pass from Tittle and raced 47 yards for a touchdown. McElhenny caught six passes for 96 yards and ran for 82 yards on 14 carries.

back whose sprained ankle had worsened despite several shots of Novocain. David couldn't help his team anymore this game. But as he changed into street clothes his anger remained.

"We sat there, all steamed and getting madder and madder with everything they were saying," he said.

Middle linebacker Joe Schmidt roared, "Listen to those SOBs! Listen to them!"

Listen they did. For a minute, the Lions' locker room was quiet. But the constant chatter in the other room brought more eruptions of temper.

Somebody threw a helmet against the wall. Christiansen lamented once more, "How did we get in this position?"

Wilson decided he didn't need to say anything.

The Detroit Lions had swum in dire straits before. All season—beginning before it ever began when head coach Buddy Parker had shocked everyone by abruptly resigning three days before the first preseason game—the Lions constantly seemed to be playing catch-up.

Halfway through the regular season, they had a 3-3 record. In one game, against Baltimore, the Lions trailed 27-10 with eight minutes left, then scored three touchdowns, the last one coming with 39 seconds remaining, to win 31-27. They fell behind Cleveland and its impressive rookie running back, Jim Brown, then, against Chicago, saw their leader, Bobby Layne, carried off the field with a broken ankle, but scrambled back to win both games.

On the final day of the regular season, with the Lions needing a victory to force a playoff with the 49ers, the Chicago Bears jumped on top quickly, led 10-0 at halftime, and were primed to be spoilers for their old rivals from Michigan. But, with Wilson, who was given the coaching job when Parker bolted, delivering a halftime tirade that assaulted

their sense of pride, the Lions rallied and pulled out the victory.

Christiansen wanted to know how they'd gotten in that position, trailing the 49ers 24-7 at the half, and yet the journey surely must have seemed familiar. The question was where was the escape route? And could the Lions find their way once more?

In a corner of the room, Layne leaned forward on his crutches and said, "It ain't over yet. We know what to do."

There was no rousing bedlam. The Lions quietly filed back out to the field, where the P.A. announcer was declaring that tickets to the championship game now were on sale at the box office.

On the first play from scrimmage, San Francisco's great halfback Hugh McElhenny swept right end, cut back to the left, and meandered through Detroit traffic on the way to the goal line and another touchdown. But the Lions were able to force McElhenny out of bounds at the Detroit 9.

"Hell of a way to start a comeback, huh?" David said later. "When you hold them to a seventy-one-yard gain on the first play, how are you supposed to feel good about things?"

Yet it was that play—the inability of McElhenny to get into the end zone—that started one of the great turnarounds in NFL history.

The 49ers could move only six yards in three plays against the Lions' defense, with Schmidt

Tittle's third touchdown pass, a 12-yard throw to Billy Wilson, stretched the 49ers' lead to 21-7. Wilson was the game's leading receiver with nine catches for 107 yards.

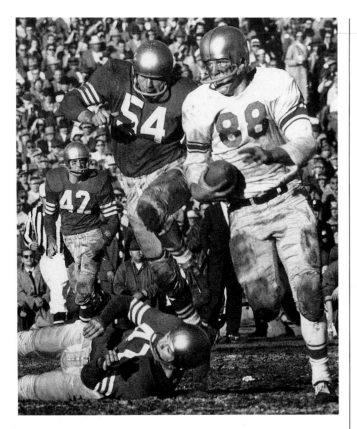

Detroit's Steve Junker caught eight passes for 92 yards, scored the Lions' first touchdown on a four-yard catch, and set up the game-winning touchdown with a 36-yard catch. The Lions scored 24 points in the second half.

screaming constant reminders of the halftime eavesdropping. San Francisco's Gordy Soltau kicked a 10-yard field goal.

"That was a minor victory in itself," Wilson said. "It was 27-7 and that didn't look good at all. But because we'd finally shown some spirit, I thought things were getting better. We just needed someone to make a big play."

The Lions took the ball and sputtered once more. Tittle and the 49ers' offense headed back onto the field, ready to resume the carnage. But the veteran quarterback was slammed from his blind side and fumbled. Detroit linebacker Bob Long recovered at the San Francisco 27.

"Normally, we'd give it to one of our running backs and just pound it down their throats," Wilson said. "But we really didn't have a healthy one . . . other than Tom Tracy, that is."

Tracy (nicknamed The Bomb) was a squat man who was neither a power runner nor a breakaway threat. He had not carried the ball for the Lions in any of the previous four games. Now, with Howard (Hopalong) Cassady and John Henry Johnson both banged up, Tracy became an obvious choice.

Nine plays later, behind the stubborn running of Tracy, and aided by a pass-interference penalty

against the 49ers, the Lions had a touchdown.

"That little one-yard run by Tracy really lit a fire," Layne said.

Layne's absence had thrown a big load on Tobin Rote, the backup who had been obtained from Green Bay in the previous offseason. A fellow Texan, Rote was bigger, stronger, and threw a tighter spiral than Layne. But nobody considered him the leader Layne was.

After Tracy's first touchdown, he got another one. The Lions' defense stopped the 49ers when three passes by Tittle fell incomplete. After the punt, Rote handed the ball to Tracy, who headed into the line, veered suddenly to the right, and broke open for a 58-yard touchdown run. Now it was 27-21.

"We got 'em, we got 'em," Rote yelled as he came to the sideline, where the Lions' frenzied defense was ready to go back.

"When one unit revs up, the other usually will, too," Wilson said. "For the rest of the third quarter, it was a question of which was more dominating— our offense or our defense."

Again, the Lions stopped the 49ers, forced a punt, and moved to a third touchdown within a span of 4 minutes and 29 seconds.

The 49ers now were keying on Tracy, and Rote noticed it. A fake to Tracy froze the San Francisco secondary, and Rote then dropped back and threw a 36-yard pass to end Steve Junker. Tracy got around the corner for 10 more yards. Five plays later, on the second play of the fourth quarter, halfback Gene Gedman scored from the 2. The game was tied, but after Jim Martin kicked the extra point, the Lions had a 28-27 lead.

But there still was a lot of time—more than 14 minutes—left to play.

"Don't forget what Tittle did to you in the first half," Wilson urged.

The swagger had switched sides of the field.

"Kick the hell out of them now," David yelled.

Schmidt slapped teammates' helmets, individually reminding them what was at stake. The seventh-round draft pick out of Pittsburgh had become perhaps the finest linebacker in the game. As the Lions lined up for the kickoff, Schmidt noticed how subdued the stadium had become.

The 49ers got the ball four more times in the game. Each time a different Lions defensive player claimed a turnover.

"You can't really say one was more important than the others," Wilson said. "We needed them all. But I would have to say Joe Schmidt's interception was fitting and appropriate."

Quarterback Tobin Rote, who directed Detroit's comeback, scrambled four times for five yards, but was more effective as a passer, hitting 16 of 30 for 214 yards. The following week, Rote led the Lions to the NFL championship.

Defensive end Gil Mains had recovered a fumble by Joe Perry. Carl Karilivacz had intercepted a pass by Tittle and so had defensive tackle Roger Zatkoff, his coming in the game's final minute.

But Schmidt's was the most special.

"Here's this guy who simply wouldn't let us lose," said Lions safety Yale Lary. "When he got his interception, I was hoping he'd take it all the way in. Because he deserved to have something special like that, the way he led us on defense that day."

As it was, the high-stepping Schmidt was run out of bounds at the 2.

"The thing a lot of people won't remember," David said, "is that we should have blown the game

wide open. We fumbled once on their three and couldn't get it in after Joe's interception with three tries from the two. It could have been a blowout."

Instead, the Lions got a field goal from Martin that made the 31-27 final score somehow deceiving.

"Goddamn amazing team," Wilson shrieked. "We did so much patching up because of injuries for this game. Then to come back from so far down . . . they just don't quit."

Rote and Tracy were surrounded by reporters afterward. Ken Russell, the rookie tackle, was able to dress almost unnoticed. Only his teammates would appreciate the job he did filling in for injured Charlie Ane.

Lions end Dave Middleton was headed for Tennessee. In a few days, the Detroit Lions would play for the championship of pro football. But before that, the medical school of the University of Tennessee had about 14 hours of exams for the third-year student.

Middleton made it back in time for the championship game with Cleveland. Tobin Rote threw four touchdown passes and scored another as the Lions routed the Browns 59-14. It was Detroit's third NFL championship in six years.

Afterward, Browns head coach Paul Brown blamed at least part of the loss on himself.

"I was personally scouting our opponent by watching that playoff game on TV. I had a clipboard and tried to pick out strengths and weaknesses that might help us.

"But I scouted the wrong team for a good part of the game."

Halfback Gene Gedman (26, on ground) put the Lions ahead for the first time, 28-27, with a two-yard touchdown run on the second play of the fourth quarter. The 49ers got the ball four more times, but turned it over each time.

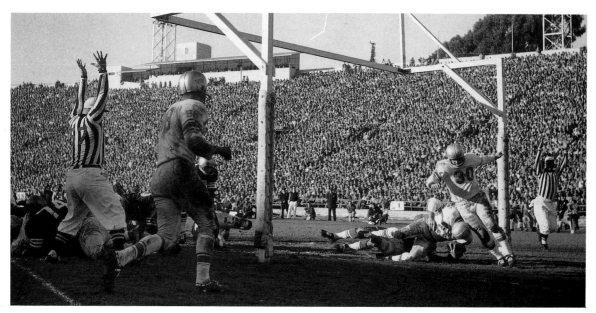

YANKEE STADIUM CLASSIC

Baltimore Colts 23,
New York Giants 17
December 28, 1958

Don Joyce remembered the feeling. It was something special, something big.

"It was dusk, the lights were on," he said. "Banners were flying. We were world champions and I was in such awe. I walked off the field and stopped three different times. I didn't want to leave."

Thirty minutes after the most important football game ever played had ended, Joyce, a defensive end for the Baltimore Colts, remained thunderstruck.

"World champions," Joyce said over and over.

A hundred yards away, Buzz Nutter, the Colts' center, chased down a Pinkerton security guard and retrieved the game ball. It was the same football Alan Ameche had delivered into the Yankee Stadium end zone in the first overtime game in National Football League championship history. The Colts had beaten the New York Giants 23-17 in sud-

With fans crowding the end zone, fullback Alan Ameche scored from the 1-yard line at 8:15 of overtime to give the Baltimore Colts a stirring 23-17 victory over the New York Giants for the 1958 NFL championship. The dramatic game sparked the pro football boom of the 1960s and 1970s.

den death on December 28, 1958.

The ball, Nutter decided, belonged to Gino Marchetti. His teammates agreed, and soon it was presented to the big defensive end. Marchetti apologized for not standing up. He broke his lower right leg making the tackle that allowed the Colts to win the game.

"But I'm not the only hero here," Marchetti said. "Hell, I oughta cut this thing up in fifty pieces. I never saw a game that had so much. So many players who made such big plays."

Alan Ameche smiled and excused himself from the postgame celebration. He had a chance to pick up an extra $500 just by showing up in the audience at "The Ed Sullivan Show" that night.

Johnny Unitas, 25, had the same invitation for $750, and said no. He was only a couple years removed from his days on the semi-pro sandlots for $6 a game, but a lot had happened to him since then. A lot had happened to pro football, too.

In one afternoon, the game that had been so provincial in interest, suddenly was thrust upon a national attention span.

It was 1958, and Ronald Reagan was making movies, and everyone seemed to like Ike.

Elsewhere, Fidel Castro was getting ready to come down out of the hills and attack Havana, Sputnik had everyone worried, and the best fighter in the world was Sugar Ray Robinson.

Also, Colts wide receiver Raymond Berry, who wore a corset for his bad back, contact lenses for his bad eyes, and special orthopedic shoes because one of his legs was shorter than the other, would stump the panel on "What's My Line?"

He certainly didn't look like someone who had caught a record 12 passes in a championship football game.

Nobody really wondered why Johnny U. didn't join Ameche as one of the toasts of the town after the game. Unitas already was driving around in the new Corvette he received for being named most valuable player in the championship game.

However, nobody had the nerve to tell him that when the first vote was taken, with five minutes left in regulation, the keys to the car belonged to Charlie Conerly, quarterback for the New York Giants.

Fantastic dreams such as artificial grass, indoor football, soccer-style kickers, white shoes, and even something called a Super Bowl were waiting

Raymond Berry gave the Colts a 14-3 halftime lead when he caught a 15-yard touchdown pass from Johnny Unitas in front of New York's Emlen Tunnell.

to come true on the encroaching horizon.

Sudden death at Yankee Stadium. Football at its intoxicating best. Who could know what was coming next?

Who could know that Don Shinnick someday would have a son who would fall in love with the cousin of Steve Myhra? Or that the Giants' offensive coach, a man named Vince Lombardi, and the Giants, defensive coach, a man named Tom Landry, would clone the greatness and later give it form in Green Bay and Dallas? Who could know that 15 men who were present that day at Yankee Stadium someday would be enshrined into the Pro Football Hall of Fame?

Somewhere, somebody probably still has one of the maps head coach Weeb Ewbank passed out to his Colts players before the game. Maps showing where all the soft spots were on the Yankee Stadium field. Somebody still might even have the Polaroid pictures of the Colts' defense Wellington Mara took from the press box. The pictures that showed how Baltimore overloaded its secondary to the right, the pictures that turned a 14-3 halftime deficit into a 17-14 lead and set the table for the feast of heroics.

The game has been called the greatest ever. Purists would disagree, pointing out the sloppiness that resulted when execution could not keep step with desire. There were six lost fumbles, numerous breakdowns on

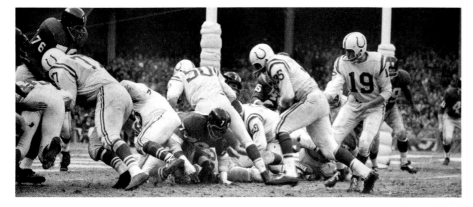

Trailing 3-0, the Colts scored the game's first touchdown in the second quarter when Ameche took this handoff from Johnny Unitas and rammed two yards off right tackle. Ameche led Baltimore in rushing with 59 yards on 14 carries.

each side of the line, interceptions, penalties, field goals missed and made, a controversy over forward progress and spotting of the ball, a failed four-play series that started inside the other team's 5-yard line, cries of conservatism that reverberated and butted heads with echoes of reckless play-calling, and all the deliciously smothering, snowballing suspense football is capable of manufacturing. Even a nationwide session of dead air, a total blackout that was allowed to extend almost three minutes because somebody tripped over a cable and

The Giants scored two second-half touchdowns to take a 17-14 lead. Fullback Mel Triplett squeezed through a crowd of Colts for a yard and the first touchdown, climaxing a 95-yard drive after a critical goal-line stand.

unplugged the big show, couldn't diminish the impact.

"It was a goddamn amazing day, to say the least," said Art Donovan, the Colts' defensive tackle aptly and affectionately known as Fatso.

The Giants were beat up before the game began. The week before, in a 10-0 victory over Cleveland to decide the Eastern Conference championship, they limited the great Jim Brown to eight yards rushing, but not without terrible cost. The defense that had been remarkable all season, allowing just 183 points in 13 games, was battered and limping.

And it had to face a Colts team that had scored 381 points in 12 games, the most by any NFL team in seven years.

Even though New York had beaten Baltimore earlier, the Colts were favored by 4½ points.

At noon, in room 626 of the Plaza Concourse Hotel, Baltimore trainer Ed Block was finishing off the last tape job. Normally, it would have been Len-

ny Moore, who could not stand the feel of adhesive tape on his bare skin so Block taped Moore's shoes, thereby creating the illusion of Spats, which of course was Moore's nickname. But this time Moore had come early.

This time, the last one in to get his ankles taped was Gino Marchetti.

"Gino said to do an extra-good job," Block said later. "He said he didn't want to break his ankle or anything."

Twenty minutes later, a chartered bus pulled away from the hotel and headed down East 161st Street toward Yankee Stadium.

Giants head coach Jim Lee Howell told Don Heinrich he was starting at quarterback. Then the coach went to Conerly and said, "Be ready. If Don can't make things happen, we're going to you."

At the same time, Ewbank was trying to figure out how to throw a believable Rockne routine at an audience of tough, grizzled veterans.

"Nobody wanted you. . . ."

Ewbank berated his own football team, pointed out that 14 of them had been cast off, released, or traded by other teams. It was a You and Me Against the World masterpiece.

"So you should win this game for yourselves," Ewbank said.

Curiously, the game wasn't a sellout—in fact, 6,000 more people watched the regular-season meeting. Chris Schenkel and Chuck Thompson were in the booth for NBC-TV. But because it was not a sellout, the game was not televised in New York City. In addition, there was a newspaper strike in New York.

The game began raggedly. Unitas fumbled on

End Bob Schnelker's 46-yard catch-and-run set up the Giants' second touchdown, which gave them a 17-14, fourth-quarter lead.

the Colts' first series. Heinrich promptly was intercepted. Then Unitas was intercepted.

Baltimore's Steve Myhra got a second chance at a field goal after the Giants were offside on his 24-yard try that flew wide. But, on his second try, linebacker Sam Huff blocked the kick.

Late in the first quarter, Conerly was calling signals. The Giants finally got something going. Pat Summerall kicked a 36-yard field goal to give the Giants a 3-0 lead.

On the first play of the second quarter, Frank Gifford fumbled, and Baltimore had the ball at the New York 20. Five plays later, Ameche took a handoff at the 2, lowered his head, and ran off right tackle into the end zone.

Remember that scenario—Ameche over right tackle.

But the Colts seemed to return the favor two minutes later as the Giants recovered a fumbled punt at the Baltimore 10.

Then Gifford fumbled again.

The Colts had the ball at their own 14-yard line.

Remember that place on the field. The 14.

Fifteen plays later, Unitas threw a 15-yard touchdown pass to Berry.

Giants guard Al Barry was limping badly from a smashed toe he'd sustained against the Browns the week before.

"Big Daddy [Lipscomb] heard about it, and before the game, he was real friendly and he seemed real concerned as he asked which foot was bothering me. Like an idiot, I told him. He must have mashed my bad toe five or six times during the game. The guy weighed 300 pounds. When he came down on your leg, it hurt."

Remember that medical explanation.

Late in the third quarter, the Colts almost turned the game into a rout.

First-and-goal at the 3. But three plays later, Baltimore still was a yard out.

"A touchdown would have killed them," Ewbank said. "If we'd scored there, they would have been buried."

But, on fourth down, Ameche was collared at the 5.

Five plays and 95 yards later, the Giants were back in the game. On third-and-two at their own

Baltimore's Steve Myhra kicked the 20-yard field goal that created the first sudden-death overtime in NFL Championship Game history.

13, the Giants took a gamble. Conerly passed to Rote, who had slipped behind the Colts' secondary. He ran to the Colts' 25 before Andy Nelson caught him and stripped the ball. But halfback Alex Webster was there and he took the fumble on the bounce and carried it to the Colts' 1-yard line.

Mel Triplett scored a touchdown two plays later.

On the first play of the fourth quarter, Conerly connected with end Bob Schnelker for 46 yards. Then Gifford scored on a 15-yard touchdown reception, carrying Colts cornerback Milt Davis on his

With the score tied 17-17, Baltimore's Johnny Unitas (19) met Kyle Rote (left) and Bill Svoboda for the overtime coin toss. The Giants won the toss, but were unable to make a first down, and the Colts went on to win.

back the last five yards.

Summerall's conversion made the score 17-14.

The drama began to compound itself. Bert Rechichar, the Colts' long-field-goal specialist, tried a 46-yard effort that fell short. A few minutes later, the Colts recovered another Giants fumble, and Unitas quickly moved them to the Giants' 27. But consecutive quarterback sacks for 11 and 9 yards ruined that threat.

The Giants took the ensuing punt and needed only a couple of first downs to kill off the clock and the Colts. They got one of them, but. . . .

"It was third down, right?" Donovan remembered. "They need four yards. And they give the ball to Gifford and it looks like he's gonna make the first down. If he does, we're in deep trouble."

At the New York 40, Conerly handed off to Gifford. Both guards pulled. Gifford cut back. Schnelker was supposed to block Marchetti.

He missed.

Marchetti got to Gifford first. Then Shinnick. Then Lipscomb.

There was a loud snap. And a groan.

"Big Daddy fell on Gino," Donovan said. "His leg snapped and it sounded like a gunshot."

Referee Ron Gibbs called for time. Head linesman Charlie Berry could see Marchetti was in terrible pain. He signaled for the stretcher crew.

"The ref forgot where he picked up the ball," Rote said. "He was too concerned about Marchetti. I saw him pick it up at his front foot and put it down where his back foot was."

Gifford could not believe what was happening. The chain crew was coming onto the field.

"The ball should have been spotted first," Gifford said. "Then they should have taken care of Marchetti. I made that first down. I know I did."

But, after the measurement, the head linesman held his hands up . . . five inches apart.

"A lot of the players wanted to go for it on fourth

Johnny Unitas started his journey to the Pro Football Hall of Fame when he led the Colts to victory in the 1958 title game. The 25-year-old quarterback completed 26 of 40 passes and directed 73- and 80-yard drives for the tying field goal and winning touchdown in overtime.

down," Howell said. "But we had a great punter in Don Chandler and the best defense in the league. And there wasn't but a few minutes left. I thought the only way we were in trouble was if they blocked the punt."

Carl Taseff made a fair catch of Chandler's 43-yard punt at the 14-yard line with 1:56 remaining.

"When we got in the huddle," Berry said, "I looked down the field and the goal posts looked like they were in Baltimore."

Lenny Moore felt the lump in his thigh pad. It was a miniature Bible. Berry bent over, checking his cleats. Unitas stepped in and said, "Okay, guys, here we go."

Lombardi was screaming for the Giants to beware of the sidelines: Don't let Unitas milk the clock with sideline passes! Two passes, both well-covered, fell incomplete.

"We need this one," Unitas said as the huddle re-formed.

And he hit Moore with an 11-yard pass. After another incompletion, Unitas saw that the only place that was going to be open was over the middle.

He hit Berry for 25 yards.

He hit Berry again for 15 yards.

He hit Berry for the third straight time, this one for 22 yards to the 13.

Steve Myrha ran onto the field. His 20-yard field goal tied the game with seven seconds remaining.

Schenkel, the Giants' regular announcer who had done the play-by-play for the second half, relinquished the duty to Thompson, the Colts' announcer who had handled the first half.

"Something historic that will be remembered forever is happening today, ladies and gentlemen," Thompson declared.

The Giants won the coin toss and chose to receive. The first overtime period in NFL championship play began.

Two plays later, the Giants faced another third-down dilemma: third-and-six at their 24.

Conerly rolled out to the right. Colts linebacker Bill Pellington pulled him down. The Giants were

Baltimore end Raymond Berry set a championship-game record with 12 catches, including two on the winning drive in overtime.

two feet short of the first down.

Once again, Howell ordered a punt. Nobody argued.

Chandler's 52-yard punt was taken by Taseff, who was tackled almost immediately at the 20.

"We felt we had the game then," Unitas later would say. "We had the game locked up in the third period and almost blew it. We were disgusted with ourselves and we struck back at the Giants with a sort of blind fury."

Two quick first downs moved the ball to the 41. Then Unitas was sacked by Dick Modzelewski.

On third-and-15, Unitas and Berry combined for 21 yards, reaching New York's 43.

"I called the same play again," Unitas said. "But as we lined up, I saw Huff dropping back a few steps to help his secondary. I called an audible."

Ameche up the middle on a draw. Huff was dropping back and one of our linemen got a good angle on Huff and the play went for twenty-three yards."

First down on the Giants' 20.

Three plays later, an NBC contact man frantically was waving to field judge Chuck Sweeney. Something had happened; a plug had been pulled or a wire had been tripped.

The game was off the air.

"You've got to stop play," the NBC man pleaded while trying to explain the situation.

"I knew the whole country was watching," Sweeney explained later, "I knew pro football was growing up right in front of everyone, thanks to TV. I gave the guy another minute beyond the usual ninety seconds for a commercial time-out. He was holding a walkie-talkie to his ear. Finally, I told him that was it. We had to resume play. But he was already smiling and I knew we were back on."

Just in time to see Unitas, from the 7, throw to tight end Jim Mutscheller, who was knocked out of bounds at the Giants' 1-yard line.

"There was no risk of interception," Unitas said, explaining his unusual, daring call. "If Mutscheller didn't get it, nobody would."

Then came Ameche, head down, barreling over right tackle into the end zone. Freeze frame picture. Everybody's seen it. It was 4:51 P.M.

"Champions," said Don Joyce. "World champions."

The total income for the game was $698,646, which someday would be enough to buy 30 seconds of commercial air time at the Super Bowl. The winners' share was $4,718.77 apiece, which was $1,607.44 more than the losers got.

Colts defensive end Gino Marchetti broke his right leg in the fourth quarter, making a game-saving tackle on Frank Gifford. It prevented a Giants' first down and gave Baltimore an opportunity to drive for the tying field goal.

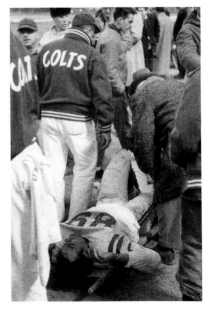

"That was damn good money in those days," Donovan said with a grin that soon became a laugh. "Even if we had to pull a shift of overtime to get it.

"What the hell, play a game like that, you might as well go ahead and win it, you know. It was just one helluva day. One helluva day."

LAST OF THE 60 MINUTE MEN

Philadelphia Eagles 17,
Green Bay Packers 13
December 26, 1960

It was the end of the game, the end of an era. Chuck Bednarik wouldn't get up. Beneath him, Jim Taylor, the Green Bay Packers' fullback, squirmed, wiggled, and cursed.

Bednarik rode Taylor like a rodeo rider, and he watched the clock reach zero.

"You can get up now," Bednarik grunted to Taylor. "You just lost."

The Philadelphia Eagles, whose Wheeze Kids had done it with mirrors and bandages during the 1960 season, were the champions of the National Football League. The Green Bay Packers' last swipe at victory was slammed to the ground at the Eagles' 9-yard line. With Bednarik sitting on top of it.

The 17-13 victory was the height of the 35-year-old Bednarik's career. Last of the 60-minute men, those tireless souls who never stood on the sideline,

but instead played every play on offense and defense, Bednarik had started his final season playing only center on offense. But regular linebackers Bob Pellegrini and John Nocera were injured in a game with Cleveland, and head coach Buck Shaw turned to the grizzled Bednarik.

"You're the only guy left," Shaw said. "Get in there. But don't try any hero stuff."

And Bednarik responded with such proud fire he would not surrender his double-duty the rest of the way. By the time the NFL Championship Game arrived, Bednarik wore his status like a medal.

Eagles quarterback Norm Van Brocklin also ended his career that Monday afternoon in Phila-

There were more than 67,000 fans at Franklin Field in Philadelphia when the Eagles won the 1960 NFL championship over the Green Bay Packers 17-13. It was the only playoff game Vince Lombardi ever lost as the Packers' head coach.

delphia. So did Shaw, the coach. The Eagles had a last-chance mentality about the season, and with good reason. The Eagles didn't overwhelm opponents. Five of their 10 victories in 1960 were by a touchdown or less.

"If it were college, we could credit our great senior leadership," said cornerback Tom Brookshier. "The Dutchman [Van Brocklin] and Mr. Eagle [Bednarik] are pretty good influences. They are steady, and they can be very inspirational."

Van Brocklin ran like a woman whose girdle was slipping. His once-great arm had lost some of its calibration. But he still had the bellicose instincts of being able to make men follow.

"No doubt Dutch was the leader," said Sonny Jurgensen, then the Eagles' backup quarterback. "What he lacked in diplomacy, he made up for with a certain kind of charisma. That charisma brought out the best in you."

Tommy McDonald, Philadelphia's 5-foot 9-inch flanker, said Van Brocklin's gift could be put into a single thought:

"He taught the Eagles to be winners."

And somehow they were. Philadelphia won 10 of 12 games with a defense that ranked ninth out of 13 teams and a running attack that was ranked twelfth. The offensive line was suspect and the linebacking corps was so hobbled it had to ask one of its walking museum pieces to step in.

While the heart and soul and brains of the Eagles were getting ready to lie down and take their places in the scrapbooks, the Green Bay Packers

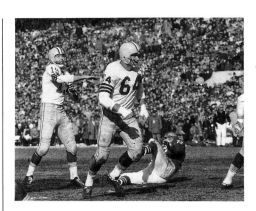

Green Bay's Bart Starr, working behind guard Jerry Kramer (64), passed for 178 yards and one touchdown in a losing effort.

were showing signs of becoming the next ruling class of pro football. In 1959, the offensive coordinator of the New York Giants had come to Green Bay and quickly set a once-lordly franchise right side up. Vince Lombardi had taken a benchwarmer named Bart Starr and made him his quarterback. He had fashioned the finest offensive line in the game. He had a converted quarterback named Paul Hornung at halfback and a bullish young fullback named Jim Taylor, and a defense with a perfect mix of experience and youth. Most of all, he and the Packers had momentum.

Years later, Van Brocklin would confess he could see how good the Packers were going to be. He said he told teammates that day in 1960, "If we're ever going to win the championship, it better be today."

Also years later, Lombardi would admit, "Losing that game hurt like hell. Losing is never acceptable. But that Eagles team was a great example. They taught us lessons that day that never needed to be discussed. There were many chances for us to win that game. But we were denied by them. In the years following, my teams were very good at turning the other team's mistakes into points and victories. That day, we were denied."

Imagine a Packers team that got to the opposition's 5-, 13-, 8-, and 7-yard lines, but only got a pair of field goals out of it.

"We had only one touchdown drive," Lombardi said. "One touchdown and two field goals. How did we lose? The Eagles were the reason."

On the second play from scrimmage, Van

Green Bay's Paul Hornung kicked two field goals and ran for 61 yards before being forced out of the game in the third quarter with a pinched nerve in his shoulder. Jim Taylor, his teammate, was the leading rusher with 105 yards.

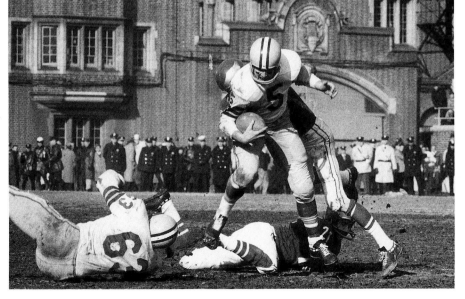

Max McGee caught a seven-yard touch-down pass for a 13-10 Packers lead.

Brocklin threw a swing pass that never made it past Packers defensive end Bill Quinlan. The interception gave the Packers the ball at the Eagles' 14-yard line. But moments later, it was fourth-and-2. Lombardi decided an early touchdown would be demoralizing for the Eagles. If the Packers had Hornung, who had led the NFL in scoring in 1960, kick a field goal, Philadelphia would draw some kind of strength from it. Taylor took the handoff and was tackled almost immediately by Bednarik. The two fell at the 5. The Eagles took over.

Philadelphia tried to push the ball out for better field position for Van Brocklin to start cranking. But rookie Ted Dean fumbled the ball away at the 22.

But the Eagles were equal to the challenge again. This time, on fourth down, Hornung was sent in to kick a field goal.

"Fourteen points were almost offered to us on a platter," Hornung said later. "We wound up with three. That's probably where the game was lost."

At any rate, a tone was set. Everything would come tough for both teams. The Eagles' only truly impressive advance consisted of a two-play drive— two completed passes from Van Brocklin, both to McDonald. The first was 22 yards; the second, 35

Following Mc-Gee's score, Ted Dean returned the kickoff 58 yards to Green Bay's 39 to set up the winning touchdown.

yards, produced a touchdown. Another time, Philadelphia went from its 23 to the Packers' 8, but most of the yardage came on a 41-yard pass from Van Brocklin to end Pete Retzlaff. All the Eagles got was a 15-yard field goal by Bobby Walston.

Inexplicably, Hornung missed a 13-yard field goal. An end-zone interception ruined an Eagles threat that had reached the Green Bay 5. The Packers tried for another fourth-down play at the Eagles' 23 with the same results: Bednarik stuffed Taylor.

"I should talk about our wasted opportunities," Lombardi said. "They had several as well. This is what made the game so dramatic. Frustration is a painful emotion."

In the game, the Packers would run 77 plays to the Eagles' 48.

The Eagles' inspired defense fell victim to a

Packers' trick that led to Starr's short pass to end Max McGee for a touchdown. Philadelphia had forced an apparent fourth-and-10 punting situation, but McGee, the punter, crossed up everyone by running around left end for 35 yards and a first down. In addition, Starr converted a third-and-15 dilemma into a first down with a 17-yard pass to Gary Knafelc.

"You look at the game," Bednarik said, "and you could see how either team could have won big or lost big. It was a hell of a battle, though."

After McGee's touchdown, the Packers had a 13-10 lead in the fourth quarter. But Eagles assistant coach Charlie Gauer had had an idea.

In studying films of the Packers' kickoff team, Gauer had noticed that one side was manned with considerably slower players than the other.

After Dean's kickoff return, quarterback Norm Van Brocklin pulled off a rare (for him) running play, when his receiver was thrown down. Green Bay was penalized for holding.

Dean scored the Eagles' winning touchdown with 9:39 left when he ran wide left behind guard Gerry Huth (65), cut back, and went in from the 5. Dean ran for 54 yards on 13 carries, caught one pass for 22 yards, and set up the winning score.

"Let's go for the slow side," he had suggested earlier in the week. Some blocking assignments also were changed. "In all, we worked on it about ten minutes," Gauer said.

Ted Dean circled under Hornung's kick and headed left, where he saw "a long tunnel just open up. There must have been four or five good blocks all in a row."

Dean ran the kick back 58 yards before he was tackled by Willie Wood at the Packers' 39.

Then Van Brocklin did the strangest thing. He *ran* with the ball. Intending to pass, he suddenly took off in a laborious canter befitting a war horse. The gain was almost nothing, but the Packers drew a penalty flag for holding.

"I was going to throw the damn ball and somebody just grabbed my receiver and threw him down," The Dutchman explained afterward.

The Eagles had another first down. And they took it the rest of the way without benefit of any more scrambles by their leader. Seven plays later, Dean ran wide to the left, cut back, and ran the final five yards into the end zone. Now the Eagles led 17-13, but there still were 10 minutes left.

The Packers quickly headed back upfield. But Starr's pass to McGee at midfield became a loose ball when Bednarik made a vicious tackle. And the ball was recovered by— of course—Bednarik.

The Packers' last hope began with 1:10 to play,

65 yards from the Eagles' goal. Starr passed for two first downs, but had to use the final two time outs along the way. At the Eagles' 22, he looked for one of his wide receivers running for the end zone.

"They were covered," Starr said. "Then my protection started to break down and I had to get rid of the ball. I saw Taylor over the middle."

Taylor broke three separate tackles. He spun and lunged and was one tackler away from scoring.

Chuck Bednarik.

Taylor had dirt in his mouth. He was out of

Jim Taylor ran for nine yards and a first down at the Eagles' 47 on this late fourth-quarter play. Three plays later, Taylor took a pass 13 yards to the Eagles' 9-yard line as the game ended.

breath. But he tried to get up, thinking that maybe there was time for another play.

"He couldn't see the clock," Bednarik said. "He couldn't see those big, beautiful zeroes."

Lombardi wondered what to tell his defeated Packers as he left the field. It would be the last time Lombardi lost a championship game; he would win five NFL titles in the next seven years and the first two Super Bowls. The Philadelphia Eagles would have to rebuild. It was the end of an era, the beginning of another one.

Eagles head coach Buck Shaw cradles the game ball between two of his stars, Norm Van Brocklin (11) and center-linebacker Chuck Bednarik, (60), who join in the celebration.

77 MINUTES, 54 SECONDS

Dallas Texas 20,
Houston Oilers 17
December 23, 1962

The chartered buses meandered through Houston, trying to find Jeppesen Stadium, a modified high school facility that was home for the two-time AFL champion Houston Oilers.

Hank Stram was worried. The blustery day and those tricky gusts of wind off the Gulf had the head coach of the Dallas Texans frowning all the way. Passing would be hard. Kicking would be harder.

"And we had the worst kicking statistics in the league," Stram said later.

Ten minutes later, security guards were waving the buses into the stadium lot. The Texans had arrived. Soon they would play the Oilers in a memorable AFL Championship Game.

"I hate this field," Stram said while examining the sloppiness before the game. "Look at it . . . mostly mud. But underneath it's concrete. Poorly laid concrete."

Stram raised his hand again, feeling the breeze.

Houston head coach Frank (Pop) Ivy wasn't

While an ABC-TV audience listened in through Jack Buck's microphone (right), halfback Abner Haynes of Dallas won the overtime coin toss, and then made a choice which forced his team to kick off against the wind. The Texans still managed to win in the sixth period.

much calmer. His team loved to pass and relied on quarterback George Blanda, the 35-year-old retread from the NFL who had found new life in Houston. The Texans were much more balanced. "If the wind bothers Blanda we'll be in a load of trouble," Ivy said.

But Ivy also felt Blanda would overcome the elements. He had before. A few minutes earlier, the quarterback had told his coach the wind wasn't as bad as it might seem.

In the locker room before the game, Stram took a quick inventory. Injuries had forced him to make some changes during the 1962 season. When end Chris Burford blew out a knee late in the season, Stram simply had his team throw more to running back Abner Haynes, who also had rushed for more than 1,000 yards. Haynes, the AFL's leading touchdown producer and number-two rusher, was joined in the backfield by fullback Jack Spikes, who had come on strong until he also injured a knee at midseason, when rookie Curtis McClinton stepped in.

Now a healthy Spikes joined a seasoned McClinton, who had just been named AFL rookie of the year. Even though Burford still was on crutches, the Texans were confident. They had good runners and pass receivers. But the real key was Texans quarterback Len Dawson.

Years later, Stram laughed as he recalled the circumstances that brought him and the former Purdue star together. Dawson had gone to the NFL and impressed nobody. The Steelers had cut him. The Browns were set to do the same. Stram called Cleveland head coach Paul Brown to find out if Dawson was available. Brown said yes, but he felt compelled to tell Stram something else. "Dawson's not the same player you remember," Brown said. "His skills have eroded. So has his attitude."

Stram said he wanted Dawson anyway. And, for a while, he thought he had a good combination with Dawson starting and Cotton Davidson, as backup quarterback and punter, in reserve. But Texans owner Lamar Hunt abruptly traded Davidson to the Oakland Raiders for a draft pick.

"I almost resigned over it," Stram said. "But the funny thing was that draft pick turned out to be Buck Buchanan, one of the greatest defensive linemen ever to play the game."

Dawson, the only Texan with NFL experience, became the AFL's top passer and most valuable player.

The stadium was packed, about 2,500 more than seating capacity, which was only 35,500.

It was the Texas State Championship, with the AFL flag thrown in. Houston had the top offense in the league, Dallas the second best. The Texans had

the leading defense, with Houston second. Both teams had 11-3 regular-season records. In the two games between them, each had won one.

"If we win the championship three years in a row," Ivy told his team, "we'll be considered one of the great teams in all of football, not just the AFL."

But Dallas dominated the first half, with Haynes scoring two touchdowns in the second quarter, one on a 28-yard pass

Haynes caught a 28-yard touchdown pass from Len Dawson and Dallas led 10-0.

and the other on a short plunge. The touchdown pass was Dawson's thirtieth of the season.

Houston's only real threat in the first half ended when linebacker E.J. Holub intercepted a pass by Blanda at the goal line and ran it back 43 yards, setting up the first score, a field goal by Tommy Brooker that contributed to a 17-0 halftime lead .

"Holub was an amazing player," Stram said. "One of the toughest men you'll ever see."

Holub eventually had 12 knee surgeries, all major operations because this was before the advent of arthroscopy. His knees looked like roadmaps.

"There's no doubt Holub's interception was one of the top two or three plays in the game," Stram said. "Instead of 14-7, it was 17-0. We were very confident at the half."

The Oilers' emotions ranged somewhere between embarrassment and outrage. Ivy was the Oilers' third coach in as many years. Ironically, both Lou Rymkus and Wally Lemm had resigned after posting league championships. Ivy already had promised Oilers owner Bud Adams he wouldn't be a one-year man. He would stick around.

The Oilers took the second-half kickoff and immediately went 68 yards in six plays, 51 of those yards coming on Blanda's completions to tight end Willard Dewveall. Dewveall's 15-yard touchdown catch signaled the start of a second half that was the opposite of the first half.

The Texans ran only one play in Houston territory in the third and fourth quarters. Only their defense kept the aroused Oilers from blowing open the game and turning the first-half mismatch into a second-half rout. Dallas safety Johnny Robinson intercepted another pass by Blanda in the end

Dallas linebacker E.J. Holub ended Houston's lone first-half threat with a 43-yard interception return. It also set up a field goal that gave the Texans a 3-0 lead.

Cornerback Dave Grayson returned an interception 20 yards to set up another touchdown by Haynes—this one a two-yard run—and the Texans led 17-0 at half-time. Dallas intercepted Houston's George Blanda five times.

zone to foil one threat. In all, the Texans intercepted Blanda five times.

But Dallas's kicking game kept it in constant trouble. Regular punter Eddie Wilson, who inherited both of Cotton Davidson's duties after the trade, averaged only 32 yards on six kicks, constantly giving the Oilers good field position. A frustrated Stram used backup halfback James Saxton for two kicks. Saxton squibbed 22- and 29-yarders.

Houston closed the deficit to 17-10 on a field goal by Blanda early in the fourth quarter. But Stram said later he was glad to get away with only a field goal. On the play before the kick, the Oilers' great runner and receiver, Billy Cannon, was just about to catch a touchdown pass. He had the ball —in fact, he already was holding the ball—when Texans defensive back Duane Wood somehow jarred it loose for an interception. "It probably was a game-saving play, as it turned out," Stram said.

After the field goal, Dallas still was unable to

Houston rallied with a 67-yard touchdown drive on the first series of the second half. Tight end Willard Dewveall made a falling 15-yard catch of a Blanda pass for the score.

move, and the punt again was a poor one. Starting at their 49, the Oilers moved swiftly to the tying touchdown. Fullback Charley Tolar, a fireplug who had been cut by the Pittsburgh Steelers of the NFL, made it around right end from the 1. With 5:58 to play, the score was tied 17-17.

Cannon remembered the mood on the Houston sideline. "We were very sure we'd win the game," he said. "They couldn't move the ball and we couldn't be stopped. It was just a matter of time."

Wilson's 23-yard punt rolled to the Dallas 41. Blanda already was thinking about a field goal. After a seven-yard completion, he was ready.

"It was muddy but I had no problem with the kick," Blanda said. "Other than it was blocked."

Sherrill Headrick almost never rushed a place-kick. He left that to his quicker teammates.

"But I took a step forward, saw a hole, and instincts took over, I guess," Headrick said.

The game went into overtime, and Stram was thinking. . .thinking about the wind, his slumbering offense, his pathetic kicking game. He put his arm around Haynes, his team captain. "If we win the toss," Stram said, "we don't want to receive. We want the wind. If they win the toss, we want to kick to the clock [meaning the direction of the stadium the wind was blowing]. We want the wind."

Stram figured the 15-miles-per-hour wind at his punter's back could only help.

Stram and Haynes still were discussing strategy when one of the officials, Bob Finley, interrupted.

"We're ready for the toss," Finley said.

Haynes said, "Okay, but coach wants to talk for a second."

"Abner, get your butt out here or it's fifteen yards," Finley said.

Haynes and Houston captain Al Jamison shook hands. Referee Harold Bourne held the coin in his right hand and flipped it into the air.

"Heads," shouted Haynes.

"Heads, it is," Bourne said.

Dallas safety Johnny Robinson's goal-line interception turned back the Oilers late in the third quarter.

Ignoring an attempted block by Dave Grayson (45), Blanda trimmed the Dallas lead to 17-10 on a 31-yard field goal early in the fourth quarter.

"We'll kick to the clock."

Jamison gasped. Bourne told Haynes he had the option to receive or defend.

"We'll kick," Haynes repeated.

Jamison said, "We'll take the wind."

While the Oilers celebrated their heads-we-win-tails-you-lose luck, Stram stomped in the muck.

"Abner just said it wrong," he explained. "Soon as he said the word 'kick,' the Oilers automatically had their choice of which side of the field they wanted. It was a mistake you don't like to make. But what can you do after it's made?"

You can play defense, which the Texans did. Robinson intercepted Blanda in the fifth period to help the Texans escape from one jam. But Houston's blitz still was bothering Dawson, who had no time to get set up.

"When we got the ball that last time," Ivy said, "I thought we were going to go all the way. Blanda looked like he had a hot streak going."

Four completed passes moved the Oilers from their 12 to midfield. Then Charley Hennigan, the Oilers' flanker who had been used as a decoy most

Late in the fourth quarter, Houston halfback Billy Cannon made a leaping, 21-yard catch at the Dallas 10 to set up the tying touchdown that sent the game into overtime.

of the day, gained 15 yards with another catch. Just about in field-goal range, Blanda thought.

A running play lost a yard, and Blanda decided to go with a short, safe pass to Hennigan. Bill Hull charged one step, then dropped back as Blanda backpedaled. The 6-foot 7-inch rookie defensive end raised his arms and leaped as the pass came toward him.

"It just stuck in my hand," said Hull, who returned the ball 23 yards to the Houston 49. Handoffs to McClinton closed out the overtime period.

Then came a record sixth period.

"We were a little tired, but I think we were more concerned with winning," Stram said. "After we had that big lead so early, we were very determined."

The next period began with the Texans facing a desperate third-and-8. But Dawson hit Spikes with a short pass, and Spikes ran for the first down to the Houston 38. Then, trying to use the swarming defense to his advantage, Dawson called for a simple cross-buck. Spikes took the handoff and bolted 19 yards.

"Their blitz had been coming from alternate sides all game," Dawson said. "This time they guessed wrong. They came from the right, and we ran to the left."

Dawson threw an incomplete pass, handed off to McClinton, and ran a quarterback sneak. It was time for the field-goal crew.

"We weren't much better at kicking field goals than we were at punting," Stram said. "Our kicker, Tommy Brooker, didn't have great range or much consistency. We always held our breath on field goals that year. Especially this one."

Teammates tried to relax Brooker, a rookie end from Alabama, in the huddle. Ivy called a time out. Ivy also ordered an 11-man rush for the kick.

Brooker stepped back in the huddle and said, "Boys, it's over. We've got it."

And it was: The 25-yard kick was good. Dallas won 20-17 in a game that took 77 minutes and 54 seconds.

Before the next season, however, the Dallas Texans would move. Competing with the Dallas Cowboys of the NFL was a losing battle. Hunt accepted an offer from Kansas City. Hank Stram and the Kansas City Chiefs went on to play in Super Bowls I and IV, the first and last championship games of the AFL and NFL. Ivy returned to coach the Oilers the next season, then was replaced by Sammy Baugh when the Oilers' record fell to 6-8, a slide that would continue for several years.

WUNDERKIND

Chicago Bears 61,
San Francisco 49ers 20
December 12, 1965

In the vernacular the Chicago Bears used for their scouting reports, a Category One player was "a player who will start in his first year in the NFL."

Gale Sayers was rated a Category One when he was a *freshman* at the University of Kansas. The measuring standards were speed, shiftiness, balance, strength, size, and instincts. Bears scouts felt Sayers was the perfect embodiment of those skills when he was 18 years old. If he could stay healthy, he could become a great one.

"A scout saw him and told us we wouldn't believe him when we saw him," said George Halas, the Bears' owner and coach. "The scout was right. He reverses direction like this," Halas snapped his fingers. "All at full speed. I've never seen anybody who could do that but him."

Halas was in the curious position of defending himself for his first-round selection of Sayers after the 1965 draft. The Bears took Sayers with their second choice, the fourth in the entire draft, right after the New York Giants had taken Auburn All-America back Tucker Fredrickson, the San Francisco 49ers had gone for North Carolina fullback Ken Willard, and the Bears had grabbed Dick Butkus, a linebacker from Illinois. The Bears felt they had pulled a fast one with the selections of Sayers and Butkus.

But then conflicting reports on the Kansas halfback filtered down from the camp of the Chicago College All-Stars. His stamina was suspect. He either couldn't or wouldn't block. His mental toughness was questioned.

"You'll see," Halas said. "I think I may have the best back in the game next to the fullback from Cleveland."

Gale Sayers scored the first of his six touchdowns against the 49ers on this first-quarter screen pass from Rudy Bukich (photo 1), which he took 80 yards. First, he got a good block from tackle Bob Wetoska on defensive back Elbert Kimbrough (2), then he cut sharply to the left (3). Guard Jim Cadile took out linebacker Mike Dowdle (4), and Sayers accelerated into the open (5). He appeared trapped by linebacker Matt Hazeltine (6), but he darted sideways (7). Now Sayers was in the clear (8 and 9).

Bears owner and coach George Halas predicted greatness for Sayers before he played a pro game.

To mention a rookie in the same breath with Jim Brown—who was playing his final NFL season—was a swipe of brashness that even the cantankerous Halas might have considered hot wind. Then again, Halas rarely ventured out on such limbs of hyperbole.

Gale Sayers, as projected, did step into the Bears' starting backfield. He never once showed any lack of tenacity or mental toughness. Stamina and endurance were among his strong suits.

"And he'll block any s.o.b. who's in front of him," Halas roared.

In December, the Bears still were in the playoff picture, however faintly. Several weeks earlier came the first real explosion of final proof that Sayers not only could play in the NFL but maybe even reshape it. Against the Minnesota Vikings, Sayers scored four touchdowns, two in the final three minutes, one on a 96-yard kickoff return. The Bears had rallied to win.

"Right then, I figured I had figured him wrong," said tight end Mike Ditka. "He was better than I thought. And I was one of his biggest fans all along. He was a special one."

While the San Francisco 49ers were warming up on the muddy bog known as Wrigley Field, a man on the West Coast fumbled with his television set in the Bay Area suburb of Tiburon. It was such a gray day in Chicago, it was hard to tell if the color fine tuning was on the blink or not. Ernie Nevers, who had been a charter member of the Pro Football Hall of Fame in 1963, twisted a couple of dials and concluded it was just another December day in the Midwest. He sat back to watch his favorite team, the 49ers.

"I had heard of the kid but I had never seen him play," Nevers said the next day.

Thirty-six years earlier, in 1929, Nevers had scored six touchdowns

In the second quarter, Sayers ran through an arm tackle by cornerback Kermit Alexander and stormed 21 yards to his second touchdown.

against the Bears for the Chicago Cardinals. In 1951, Cleveland's Dub Jones also scored six touchdowns against the Bears. On December 12, 1965, Gale Sayers tied their NFL record.

In the Bears' locker room, Ed Rozy, the equipment manager and trainer, was handing out shoes —shoes with longer nylon cleats. The treacherous footing might be overcome with the longer cleats, Halas said.

Gale Sayers fumbled with the laces of his shoes. The muddy surface, he decided, wasn't going to bother him any more than it would anyone else.

"When I run the ball, all I think about is scoring," he had said earlier in the season. "Where I'm running, what kind of shoes I'm wearing, who's chasing me—I don't think about those things."

The great ones don't think; they react. Sayers's

Sayers went seven yards in the third quarter for his third score of the game.

free-flowing, spontaneous style was not about to be bridled by a little bit of rain and mud.

Halas chided his team about the opponent. In the season opener that season, the 49ers had thumped the Bears 52-24.

"We owe them one," Halas said. "I don't believe in revenge, but I do want to win this game very badly."

Abe Gibron, the Bears' offensive line coach, nudged George Allen, the defensive coordinator. The Old Man was fired up. For someone who had walked the sidelines for so many games, for someone who had helped found the league, that a single game could ignite so much enthusiasm was an inspiration in itself.

Back on the field, Sayers realized the new cleats were definite improvements. He could cut. He could accelerate.

"The amazing thing about that day was that Sayers scored touchdowns in just about every way you can on offense," Halas said. "He caught passes, he ran inside, he ran outside. He returned punts. I

said it that day and I still feel it. It was the greatest performance I've ever seen on a football field by one man. Before that game, I felt George McAfee was our greatest game-breaker. But after that I had to include Gale Sayers as the equal of McAfee."

Sayers rang up 336 yards of offense against the 49ers, running for 113 yards on nine carries, gaining 89 on two pass receptions, and adding another 134 yards in punt returns. The Bears won 61-20.

"I just wonder," said Y.A. Tittle, then a San Francisco assistant coach, "what kind of numbers Sayers might have had if we hadn't geared our defense all game to stop him."

Ditka said if the field had been dry, "he'd have scored every time he had the ball. As it was, every tackle they made on him saved a touchdown. He was that close to breaking every time."

His uniform covered by mud, Sayers sprinted 50 yards through the right side of the line to score his fourth touchdown.

The Bears' lead jumped to 40-13 as Sayers went airborne to score from the 1, his third touchdown of the third quarter and fifth of the game.

"He looks no different than any other runner when he's coming at you," said rookie 49ers defensive back George Donnelly. "But when he gets there, he's not there. He's gone."

There was no morbid silence in the losers' locker room. No curtained looks on the 49ers faces. They were almost absolved of disappointment because Sayers's performance had been so startling.

Sayers tried to pass along some of the attention to his teammates, saying, "I got blocking, real good blocking, all day."

But Bears fullback Ronnie Bull shook his head as he heard the rookie's modesty.

"Gale," Bull said, leaning over, "it's a pleasure to block for you. You make us look good. We really seem to try harder because we know with you, every play could be a touchdown."

After Sayers's sixth touchdown—your basic, everyday 85-yard meander with a punt in which Sayers probably ran another 45 additional yards (no stamina, huh?) weaving through traffic —he was met on the sideline by assistant coach Sid Luckman.

"Sayers, you just tied a record," Luckman said.

Because Luckman had told him the same thing after he scored his fourth touchdown, Sayers was confused. The fourth

touchdown tied the *team* record, Luckman explained. The sixth tied the *league* record.

Sayers smiled.

The water-logged crowd cheered and chanted and demanded Sayers return to try for number seven. Halas refused.

"The 49ers were already whipped," the coach said. "I would never have forgiven myself if I'd put him back in and he'd gotten hurt."

Sayers also said he didn't mind not going back in.

"It wouldn't have done any good," he said. "They would have been laying for me. They would know why I was there, and, with me being a rookie, they might not have liked that and they might have tried to mess me up."

Years later, Sayers added, "See, I was a rookie. I figured there'd be plenty more chances for records. I was sure there'd be another day like that one."

Ernie Nevers heard the telephone the next day. Reporters wanted to know how he felt about his and Jones's record being tied by a rookie.

"Honored," Nevers said. "When it's someone special like him—such a great athlete—you don't mind one bit. I only hope he doesn't have so many great afternoons that people forget entirely about Ernie Nevers."

Gale Sayers had a spectacular but short career (seven seasons). Terrible knee injuries curtailed his greatness, but not enough to keep him from being elected to the Pro Football Hall of Fame in his first year of eligibility (1977).

Sayers flipped the ball in celebration as he tied an NFL record with his sixth touchdown, this one coming in the fourth quarter on an 85-yard punt return. He had 113 yards rushing, 89 pass receiving, and 134 on punt returns, for 336 overall.

A LOT IN RESERVE

Green Bay Packers 13,
Baltimore Colts 10
December 26, 1965

As he boarded the chartered plane that would take him and the Baltimore Colts to Green Bay that Christmas morning, Tom Matte felt for the lump in his coat pocket. Ulcer medicine isn't able to do what a credit card can. But you never leave home without it, either.

Especially when you are Instant Quarterback.

Matte, 26, looked down the aisle of the plane. The quarterback legend, Johnny Unitas, was in an aisle seat, his stiff leg and fractured kneecap extended. Gary Cuozzo, the backup quarterback, also was in an aisle seat. The right sleeve of his sports coat was slack; his separated shoulder was strapped and his arm was bound tightly to his chest.

The Colts were on their way to play the Packers for the NFL's Western Conference championship.

The Packers were the bullies of the NFL. They already had beaten the Colts twice in regular season. Worse yet, Baltimore had to come into frigid, unfriendly Lambeau Field, recently renamed in honor of Earl (Curly) Lambeau, one of the founders of the Packers' franchise who had died in June. They had to face the Packers with a halfback, who had a nervous stomach, disguised as a quarterback.

Matte tried to relax and rationalize things to keep the flutters inside from escalating into something more serious. A few minutes later, he got a blanket, then curled up and slept all the way to Wisconsin.

Baltimore head coach Don Shula had talked all week of rising to a great challenge. He had told his players that although the game plan had to be altered because of the injuries to Unitas and Cuozzo, the team would stick to its basic playbook. And, because he really believed it, Shula told his players: "We are still good enough to win this game."

Shula and his staff had pulled out the wrenches and screwdrivers and rubbed midnight oil all over the pregame strategy. They would remove as much risk from the offense as possible. Play selection would be kept simple. Intricate longer pass routes that required delicate timing between quarterback and receiver would be ignored. Matte would have enough problems calling cadences and with the basic mechanics of passing and handing off the ball.

Matte had worked hard throughout his short crash course. So hard, in fact, that his right arm ached from all the passes he had thrown. In college at Ohio State he had played quarterback on a run-oriented team.

Still, confidence grew among the Colts during

Halfback Tom Matte was pressed into action as an emergency quarterback (replacing the injured Johnny Unitas and Gary Cuozzo) in the Colts' Western Conference playoff against Green Bay. Matte, who completed 5 of 12 passes, wore a list of plays taped to his left wrist.

The Packers lost their starting quarter-back, Bart Starr, with bruised ribs.

the week. Maybe it was a Something From Nothing mentality, but there was a growing feeling things were not really hopeless. Shula had appealed to the commissioner for permission to allow either Ed Brown, who had been bought off the waiver wire for $100 the final week of the regular season, or taxi squad quarterback George Hafner to be activated for the game. The rules said that a player had to be on the active roster for the final two regularly scheduled games; an amendment would require unanimous approval by the rest of the league.

"I think we'll take our chances with Matte," said Packers head coach Vince Lombardi with a gap-toothed grin.

Lombardi had developed a machine in Green Bay. He had taken over a 1-10-1 team in 1959, turned them into Western Conference winners the next year, and NFL champions in 1961, and was in the midst of a decade of excellence the NFL had not seen before.

Knowing Matte would not throw long, Lombardi's plan was to pinch his secondary closer to the line of scrimmage. If he could deny dump-off and screen passes to Colts backs and have his defensive ends force everything inside, it would become a matter of tackling people coming straight ahead.

Lombardi also had appealed to his team's sense of pride. What if a team with a surrogate quarterback should beat the high and mighty Packers?

Lombardi also had a few surprises offensively for the Colts, whose defense in the two regular-season games had broken through and harassed Packers quarterback Bart Starr. To counteract the Baltimore rush, Lombardi planned a lot of rollouts.

A few minutes before the opening kickoff, Shula asked Matte how he felt. Matte smiled and said, "Nervous. . .real nervous."

The Packers won the toss and chose to receive. The first play from scrimmage began at the Green Bay 15-yard line. Starr dropped back to pass, hoping to surprise the Colts. Tight end Bill Anderson, who had been lured out of retirement before the season began, crossed over the middle from the

right and caught the 10-yard pass. He was immediately hammered from behind by Colts cornerback Lenny Lyles. The ball popped free, and Anderson slumped to the field, momentarily unconscious.

Veteran Zeke Bratkowski replaced Starr at quarterback in the first quarter and completed 22 of 39 passes for 248 yards. The Packers trailed 10-0 at halftime, but tied the score in the fourth quarter and won in overtime.

Linebacker Don Shinnick, who also battled an ulcer that flared up all week, scooped up the ball. At the Packers' 5, the only remaining obstacle was Starr. Shinnick, with Colts cornerback Jim Welch ahead of him, barged into Starr. Welch and Starr went sprawling in opposite directions, and Shinnick scored standing up.

Starr got up holding his side. The game was 21 seconds old. And now both teams had an Instant Quarterback.

Starr's bruised ribs kept him from playing any more, except to hold for extra points and field goals. Zeke Bratkowski, a 33-year-old veteran, hurriedly warmed up, trying to steel-wool a season of accumulated rust away in the length of a time out.

"There was a big difference, though," Shula said later. "Bratkowski had about ten years' experience. My guy had two weeks."

But the Colts had a 7-0 lead. And judging from the way they had hit on the first two plays, if they became any more inspired, Shula might have to send his trainers out for tranquilizer darts.

Lombardi fretted on the sideline. Not only had the Colts struck first, not only had he lost his star quarterback, not only were the Colts playing aroused football, but his team was making mistakes.

Later in the first period, when it appeared Green Bay had something going, Paul Hornung fumbled and the Colts recovered at midfield. Lombardi's notorious temper erupted.

Baltimore had momentum. If the Colts could score again, they could demoralize the Packers.

But Lenny Moore was popped hard by some awesome gang-tackling and fumbled the ball. Safety Tom Brown, who two years earlier was playing first base for the Washington Senators in the American League, cleanly fielded the grounder.

As the defensive unit came off the field, Lombardi stared straight ahead, arms folded. He would not let his team off the hook simply because of one good response to his anger.

The ferocious nature of the game sustained itself for the rest of the period. There were five consecutive possessions without a first down by either team.

In the second quarter, the Colts, helped by a late-hit penalty and a quarterback draw, nudged into scoring position. They moved to the Packers' 8, then were forced to a stop. But Lou Michaels's field goal was good, and, with five minutes left in the half, the Colts owned a 10-0 lead.

A 47-yard pass-interference penalty on the Colts push-started the Packers. At the Colts' 9, Bratkowski's pass to Anderson appeared to be a certain touchdown. But the Colts wrestled the squirming Anderson down inside the 1.

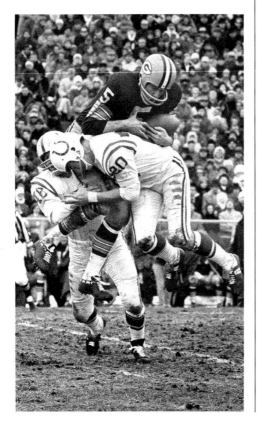

Sandwiched by defensive backs Jerry Logan (20) and Jim Welch, Green Bay's Paul Hornung still held onto the ball. He scored the Packers' only touchdown on a one-yard run.

The Colts shifted into a 5-1 deployment, something the Packers hadn't seen in their first two regular-season games. Packers fullback Jim Taylor was stonewalled on second down. Then Hornung, who had scored five touchdowns against the Colts in their last meeting, tried. Nothing.

On the sideline, Lombardi had a big decision to make. If he settled for the field goal this close to halftime and this close to the goal line, the Colts would get revved up even more.

Go for it, he decided. The handoff went to Taylor, who headed right, cut back, and was hit. Taylor spun and then was buried by linebacker Dennis Gaubatz. The ball trickled loose, but it was recovered by Taylor inches short of a touchdown.

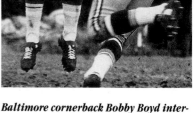

Baltimore cornerback Bobby Boyd intercepted this pass intended for Carroll Dale in the third quarter.

The second period ended a minute later.

On the first possession of the third quarter, Baltimore couldn't move, and punter Tom Gilburg came on. But the center snap was high. Gilburg, who also played tackle, bobbled it, then took off on an ill-advised scramble. He was tackled at the Colts' 35, where it was Green Bay's ball.

A handoff to Taylor gained a yard and got the partisan Packers crowd angry. They felt Bart Starr would have capitalized quickly; were Lombardi and Bratkowski being overly conservative?

But what the Packers really were doing was setting up the Colts' defense. On second down, Bratkowski faked to Taylor once more. It froze the Colts' secondary, and Bratkowski's pass to flanker Carroll Dale was caught for 33 yards to the Baltimore 1.

Shula called for the 5-1 defense again. But at the half, Lombardi had made changes in blocking assignments. Hornung scored.

The Packers had a drive foiled as Colts cornerback Bobby Boyd made a leaping interception. The Green Bay strategy of throwing on first down—seven times, of which five were complete and one drew an interference call—finally was shut down by the Colts. The adjustments Lombardi and Shula made were typically brilliant throughout.

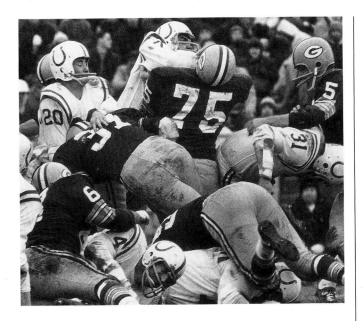

Green Bay fullback Jim Taylor (31) was held to no gain on this try from the 1-yard line in the third quarter, but Hornung scored on the next play for the Packers' first points of the game. The score cut the Colts' lead to 10-7.

Another interception, this one by safety Jerry Logan, ruined another Packers drive. The Colts were neutralizing the fact they were playing offense with a pop gun by playing overachieving defense.

The Packers ran for two first downs as the time remaining slipped under four minutes. Then Colts defensive tackle Billy Ray Smith rushed Bratkowski and delivered a right hook under the quarterback's facebar. The unnecessary-roughness penalty put Green Bay in Baltimore territory. The Packers drove toward the end zone. But the Colts, reaching once more into a reservoir most people didn't know they had, stopped the Packers at the 27-yard line.

In the gathering gloom of a heavily overcast day, kicker Don Chandler frowned as he ran onto the field. In the poor visibility of a fog-like shroud, the ball was spotted at a severe angle. Chandler would have to sight-adjust his kick. Starr eased down to receive Bill Curry's center snap, Chandler behind him, head down, arms swinging as the rhythm of a field goal wheeled into motion.

As soon as he kicked the ball, Chandler's head snapped back in apparent disgust. Colts defensive end Ordell Brasse clapped his hands as he watched the kick sail to the left. But field judge Jim Tunney had his arms raised, signaling the kick was good.

The Colts raised hell, claiming the high kick went outside the plane of the left upright. Referee Norm Schachter was surrounded by complaining Colts. But Tunney's decision stood. The game was tied with 1:58 to play.

The game went into overtime, the second in NFL playoff history. And, lest anyone forgot the 1958 championship thriller against the New York Giants, also the second in Baltimore history.

The Colts had the first chance to win. A punt return by Alvin Haymond gave them good field position at their 41-yard line. Matte scrambled for nine yards, ran a draw for five, then another for eight.

In the defensive huddle, Packers end and captain Willie Davis, boiling with anger, called a defensive switch. Davis was going to rush Matte. Middle linebacker Ray Nitschke would be responsible for the outside.

Three plays later, the Colts were stymied. Michaels came in to try a "winning" 47-yard field goal.

The snap from center Buzz Nutter was bad. Earlier, his snap to punter Gilburg had been high. This time it was low. Holder Bobby Boyd short-hopped the ball, and tried to get it in place. But the timing was shot. Michaels had to double-clutch and lost his momentum. His kick was short.

The Packers erupted. Bratkowski, who completed a playoff record 22 of 39 attempts for 248 yards, hit Anderson for 18 yards. Then Taylor and Elijah Pitts, subbing for Hornung who was injured on the previous series, combined for a first down and Dale caught a pass for another first down at the Colts' 26. Three running plays and eight yards later, Chandler and Starr set up for a field goal.

The ball was snapped and the Colts made a final, proud, desperate attempt, a tangle of arms straining in the air. Then, a forlorn look backward as the kick knifed through the uprights. After 13:39 of overtime, the Packers had won 13-10.

In the locker room, Matte took off the brown plastic wristband—"my crib sheet"—with the Colts' plays written on an index card.

"Coach Shula talked about rising to the occasion," said Matte, whose goal in the game was to be conspicuously inconspicuous. "I just wish I could have risen a little higher. But I guess everyone already knows I'm no Unitas."

The Colts' heroic effort ended when Green Bay's Don Chandler kicked a 25-yard field goal to win the game with 13:39 gone in overtime.

ONE FOR THE OLD GUARD

Green Bay Packers 34,
Dallas Cowboys 27
January 1, 1967

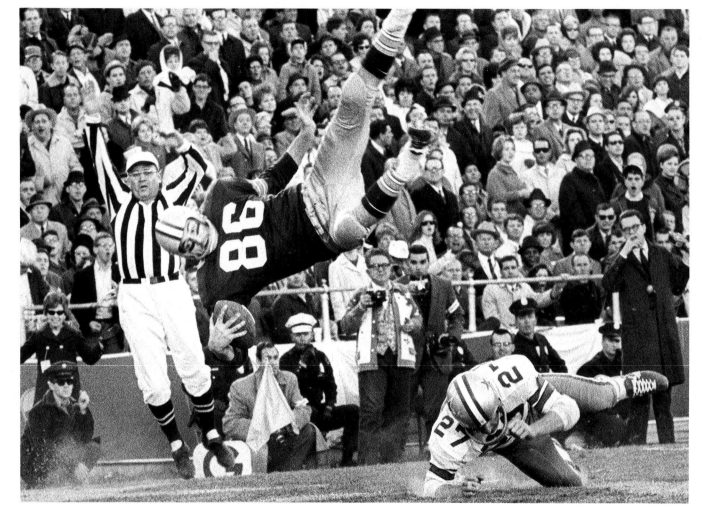

In the church that sometimes is the National Football League, the congregation can be just as condescending as in any other place of worship.

The Dallas Cowboys had a chance to win the 1966 NFL championship, having won the Eastern Conference with a 10-3-1 record. They also had a chance to be the first team to represent the NFL in that new-fangled, unify-the-titles bowl game with

Boyd Dowler gave Green Bay a 28-20 lead over Dallas with this 16-yard touchdown catch in the 1966 NFL Championship Game, but he paid a price. After the tackle by defensive back Mike Gaechter, Dowler landed on his head and neck and was knocked out of the game.

the American Football League.

But they were (shudder) Expansionist.

This bothered people.

If this NFL-AFL thing was going to come about, the old guard wanted their first representative to be one of their own.

It wasn't the Cowboys' fault they practically had been born yesterday. They had come into the NFL as an expansion team in 1960. Their head coach,

Elijah Pitts caught Bart Starr's first touchdown pass to give the Packers a 7-0 lead.

Tom Landry, had a background based in defense, but his teams were offensive innovators. The Cowboys averaged 32 points a game.

And that's why, on the dawn of the New Year, as the Cowboys prepared to host the Green Bay Packers at the Cotton Bowl, the game became unavoidably shrouded with spiritual significance. Because the Packers were the NFL's Rock of Ages— their franchise birth certificate was issued only a year after the league's—and because they still played football the old-fashioned way with between-the-tackles, stop-us-if-you-can power football, game day had turned into a matter of waiting for some kind of sign from this one-day holy war between Fundamental and Unorthodox.

Later Don Meredith, the Cowboys' quarterback, would say, "If God's got time to be a football fan, he musta really enjoyed this one."

Unlike so many great football games the two teams have played, there was no miracle performed

Trailing 14-0 late in the first quarter, Dallas opened a big hole, and Dan Reeves ran through it for a three-yard touchdown. Before the quarter was over, a 23-yard scoring run by Don Perkins had tied the score at 14-14.

in the closing seconds. Well, there was this one divine goal-line stand...

Four shots at six feet. A pass-interference flag at the Green Bay 2-yard line gave the Cowboys a chance to send an already-terrific football game into the stratosphere of overtime. There was 1:58 left in the fourth quarter, and the Packers led 34-27. But the Cowboys had first-and-goal at the 2.

"They hadn't stopped us all day," Landry said. "We felt we were headed for overtime, definitely."

That would have been almost appropriate.

The Packers had taken the initial lead with an alarming ease. Halfback Elijah Pitts, who was filling in for the injured Paul Hornung, had broken free for 32 yards on the game's first play. Right up the gut, straight handoff, crisp blocking. Football, according to the Book of Lombardi.

"We were flawless," said quarterback Bart Starr. "That drive was about as good as we can execute."

A 17-yard pass to Pitts for the touchdown quickly quieted the pro-Cowboys Cotton Bowl. Twelve seconds later, the place got even quieter.

Mel Renfro ran the kickoff back and was pounded at the 18. The ball fell loose, and Jim Grabowski, the rookie fullback from Illinois, picked up the ball and raced in for the Packers' second touchdown.

Landry's head dropped. The biggest game in franchise history seemed to be in ruins already. But Landry quickly looked back up.

"I don't show a whole lot of emotion on the sideline," Landry confessed. "I can't. I won't."

His eyes glinted. Down 14-0 and his team hadn't even run a play from scrimmage yet.

Landry says the business of cheerleading is somebody else's job in the Cowboys' corporation. Rooting, simply wishing and hoping your favorite team wins, is a luxury allowed only those who fork out the price of admission. A coach has to coach.

"If my players were to see me getting real emotional in a game," Landry said, "that would mean I was only watching instead of thinking."

Landry told his players, "There is no reason to go away from our original plan."

Dallas cornerback Cornell Green thought he had an interception, but the ball got by him, and the Packers' Carroll Dale caught it for 51 yards and a touchdown.

*Frank Clarke's 68-yard touchdown catch
gave Dallas new hope with 4:09 left.*

Carroll Dale, who had five catches for 128 yards, burned Cornell Green again with this 43 yard catch-and-run to the Cowboys' 31. It set up the scoring pass to Boyd Dowler that pushed the Packers ahead 28-20 in the third quarter.

Packers head coach Vince Lombardi once had taught Latin at a small Catholic school called St. Cecilia, in New Jersey. He particularly liked that Julius Caesar boast, "Veni, Vidi, Vici"—"I came, I saw, I conquered"—because it said something about power. Lombardi liked power. He liked football because it was power put into human form.

This game, with league pride on the line—his Packers against Landry's Cowboys—was about power. The Cowboys and all their gadgets and tricks were good, very good, perhaps more talented by position than his Packers. But power and teamwork and preparation, his building blocks, could overcome all that.

When the lead was 14-0, Lombardi put his hands into his overcoat. Landry had nothing on him when it came to hiding positive emotions.

But when things went bad, Lombardi's temper pushed aside any facades.

The Cowboys tied the game at 14-14 before the

first quarter ended, with halfback Dan Reeves and fullback Don Perkins both running for scores.

The Packers had surrendered only one touchdown in the first quarter in the 14-game regular season. Now the Cowboys had rammed two over on running plays, and Lombardi fumed.

In the second quarter, Cowboys cornerback Cornell Green looked up and saw the ball and had to make a decision.

"I could have intercepted it or knocked it down," Green said, talking about Bart Starr's pass that was addressed to Packers split end Carroll Dale, who was running a fly pattern from his own 49. But Green had the best position for the ball.

Linebacker Lee Roy Jordan already had turned around to lead interference for Green. Green said later the ball was slightly underthrown and maybe that's what caused him to miss.

It went through Green but not over Dale, whose trail to the end zone was just 10 yards.

"I still don't know how I missed that ball," Green added.

On the next drive, the Cowboys had it going again, advancing to the 4-yard line. On third down, Meredith stepped back and floated a pass to end Frank Clarke, who caught the ball several inches beyond the end line of the end zone.

"We had to take the dad-gum field goal [by Danny Villanueva]," Meredith said. "I was thinking that play was going to hurt us.

"Shows what I know, huh? The Packers came right back and marched it down on us and we were lucky Ralph Neely got his hand on a field-goal try."

In the third quarter, another field goal pulled Dallas to within a point, 21-20.

But on the first play after the kickoff, Starr and Dale burned Green once more, this time for 43 yards to the Dallas 31. Five plays later, Starr

This fumble recovery by cornerback Warren Livingston (at the bottom of the pile) set up one of the two Dallas field goals by Danny Villanueva.

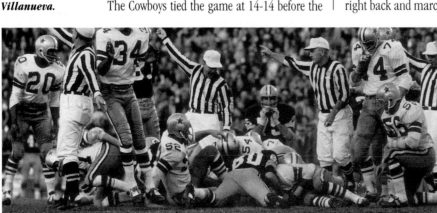

passed for the touchdown to Boyd Dowler, who was catapulted onto his head and literally knocked out of the game. Now the Packers led 28-20.

"We were making mistakes we hadn't made all season," Jordan said. "I'd like to count the mistakes but I'd probably get sick."

One Cowboys mistake particularly hurt. Bob Hayes, the world's fastest human, Olympic gold medalist, and one of the first track specialists who really could play football, made a terrible decision to field a punt at his 1-yard line. His momentum forced him back, into the end zone, and the Packers smothered him after he made it back to the 1.

After forcing the Cowboys to punt from their end zone, the Packers stormed to another touchdown by Max McGee for a 34-20 lead.

With little more than five minutes to play, those of little faith started heading for the exits.

But Bob Lilly blocked the extra point.

"I knew we still had a chance then," Lilly said.

Lombardi was roaring once more, but his defense calmed him briefly. The Cowboys were backed up, looking at third-and-20 with 4:22 left.

But Meredith found Frank Clarke all alone after Packers safety Tom Brown slipped. The 68-yard touchdown was so dramatic, so thrilling that Landry actually applauded on the sideline. His team had closed to within a touchdown, 34-27.

The Cowboys' defense shut down the Packers on three successive passes.

"Watch the punt block," Lombardi shouted. "Don't let them get the block."

The Cowboys roared toward punter Don Chandler, who had to hurry. Chandler's kick went only 16 yards. Meredith and Clarke took over. First came a 21-yard completion to the Packers' 26. Then, when the two tried to link up again, Green Bay linebacker Dave Robinson realized he was beaten and merely grabbed Clarke around the waist. The penalty put the ball at the 2-yard line.

Dan Reeves got the ball on first down, tried to squirm free but was stopped at the 1. Reeves blinked as he headed back to the huddle. His eyeball had been scratched. His vision was blurry.

On second down, Meredith threw a pass to tight end Pettis Norman, who was open but dropped the ball. There was a flag. Cowboys left tackle Jim Boeke had moved early. The five-yard penalty made it second down at the 6.

Reeves rolled into the flat, looked around for Meredith's pass—and dropped the ball.

"I was seeing double," Reeves said. "I should have told someone."

Packers safety Tom Brown hugged the ball after his interception turned back the last Dallas threat with 28 seconds remaining in the game.

Errors of commission. Errors of omission. On third down, Meredith tried to pass the ball to Norman, who was alone in the right flat. But the pass was low, and Norman had to dive to catch it going out of bounds at the 2.

Fourth down in the Cotton Bowl.

A quick fake by Meredith to Perkins was supposed to lure Robinson inside. Once Meredith got outside, it came down to an option play with Packers cornerback Herb Adderley on the spot.

But Robinson wouldn't bite. Instead he slanted outside and ran into Meredith.

"My job was to stop the bootleg," Robinson said. "But I was supposed to keep him from throwing. I got his left arm but I couldn't reach the right one."

Meredith had Robinson draped over him and was about to go down. With one last heave of determination, he wobbled a pass into the end zone.

"I thought I saw Hayes," Meredith said. "But I really was just throwing it up and hoping somebody would get it."

Somebody did. Brown intercepted in the end zone. The Packers were champions.

In the locker room, Lombardi smiled and hugged and saluted his warriors. Two days later, he called a meeting, his first step of preparation for the initial AFL-NFL World Championship Game against the Kansas City Chiefs. Lombardi's gruffness covered over his immense pride. It was time to go back to work. The heathen outsiders from Kansas City were even more of a threat to the moral fiber of football, the power game, the NFL game.

"Gentlemen," Lombardi said, "you are not only representing the Green Bay Packers, but the entire National Football League."

THE FIRST SUPER SUNDAY

Green Bay Packers 35,
Kansas City Chiefs 10
January 15, 1967

The chartered plane was several minutes late taking off. Teammates stood in the Green Bay airport lobby, trying to talk Bill Anderson into boarding.

Anderson, a reserve tight end for the Packers, was terrified of flying. In his white-knuckled view, he was struggling with the importance of flying

Vince Lombardi: first to win a Super Bowl.

all the way to California to play some team from another league. Why risk it? The Packers had already beaten the Dallas Cowboys to win the NFL championship. What was the big deal?

Reluctantly, Anderson eventually got strapped in his seat and the 727 took off. The Green Bay Packers headed for Santa Barbara, 90 miles from the Los Angeles Memorial Coliseum, site of the first—and maybe annual—clash of the National Football League and American Football League. In time, the thinking was, the game would become . . . super.

Cleared for landing, the plane circled, then dipped below the light clouds.

Max McGee slept.

Anderson bit on his lower lip and lowered his head. Teammates kidded him and he would not even recognize them with a smile or a curse.

"Then there was a big screech of the tires as we landed," quarterback Bart Starr said. "And we made this real sharp turn and everyone lurched forward and sideways."

"I knew it, I knew it," Anderson moaned. "We're going to die."

Suddenly, none of Anderson's teammates were laughing or kidding him anymore.

"It wasn't the smoothest landing in history," Starr said.

Anderson was first off the plane. A flight attendant had to wake up McGee.

The Packers had wanted to wait until just before game day to come west. The league office had convinced them to show up the week before—for public relations purposes.

As it was, they started out at a PR disadvantage. A Kansas City cornerback named Fred Williamson had been holding court with the media, not only bad-mouthing the Packers as old and tired and worn-down players but proclaiming himself as The Hammer, destroyer of enemy receivers.

"I have broken thirty helmets with my forearm alone," Williamson said. "I can't wait to add to my total against the Packers."

Flanker Carroll Dale usually was the quietest of Packers, a team that rarely spoke out anyway. But upon hearing The Hammer's boasts, Dale said flatly, "That kind of talk is good inspiration for working on downfield blocking."

In spite of Williamson's carnival-barking, the Packers were overwhelming 13-point favorites to win the game. "That's too much," said Chiefs fullback Curtis McClinton. "I'll give the Packers a point for being at the peak of their maturity. I give them another point for having played in a lot of big

Max McGee broke away from cornerback Willie Mitchell and went 37 yards with a pass from Bart Starr for the game's first touchdown.

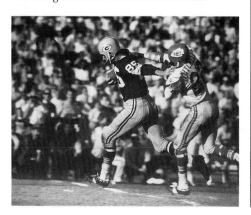

Fullback Curtis McClinton tied the score at 7-7 in the second quarter on a seven-yard pass from Len Dawson.

games. And I'll give them a point for their tradition. But that's all. Three points. All intangibles, too. Intangibles disappear when the whistle blows."

Head coach Vince Lombardi spent the first night in Santa Barbara worrying. He felt his team was superior to Kansas City in all facets of the game. But he could not allow it to be complacent. The California climate was so comfortable, too, mid-70s, blue skies. It made a man want to relax. Lombardi worried about relaxing.

The next day, at the first practice, Lombardi barked that all plays would be run in the opposite direction of the mountain range.

"We're not here to look at mountains," he said.

Coming from Green Bay, where the temperatures sometimes got above freezing in January, the Packers frolicked. Before practice, fullback Jim Taylor ran on the lush field, noticed the firm footing, and said, "Damn, I almost feel quick."

The practice was good, spirited but intense. Lombardi had relaxed a little himself. When he got back to the team hotel, two telegrams were waiting.

They were from George Halas of the Chicago Bears and Wellington Mara of the New York Giants, fellow senior partners of the NFL. *Good luck, best wishes. We are proud you and the Packers are representing us, the NFL, in this first game. . . .*

Lombardi felt the load crash down once more. The game was more than important.

There was a lot more to the Kansas City Chiefs than the mouth and forearm of one cornerback. Quarterback Len Dawson was a veteran with NFL experience. He had a game-breaking wide receiver in Otis Taylor. There were huge offensive and defensive linemen, a great linebacker named Bobby Bell, and, of course, head coach Hank Stram.

Stram was an innovator. He had devised the moving pocket and

claimed his team ran "the offense of the future." Defensively, the triple-stack was so effective against the run it practically dared opponents to pass.

"We think we can win," Stram said. "If the Packers represent the National Football League and all their wonderful tradition, the Kansas City Chiefs are the symbol of hope."

Being the first of its kind, the game contained a few quirks. For instance, it didn't sell out; the Los Angeles Memorial Coliseum—which seated nearly 100,000—was only two-thirds full for the opening kickoff. And the game was televised by two networks, NBC and CBS, each of which paid the unprecedented fee of $1 million for the rights.

Special uniforms had been designed for the officials, an all-star group from both leagues. There were even two different balls, the NFL and the AFL brands. The AFL ball was slightly thinner in the middle, which, according to some people, made it go farther when kicked and easier to catch.

"Is it easier to intercept as well?" Lombardi asked, with a toothy grin.

Two days before the game, at the daily media session Lombardi called The Five O'Clock Club, the Packers' coach said he never had seen an AFL game, live or on television.

"Come on, Vince, even Pete Rozelle has seen at least one AFL game," someone retorted.

"Maybe Pete has more time than I do," Lombardi said mischievously.

The night before the game, Starr and a couple of teammates were in the hotel lobby, reading newspapers. Williamson

Fullback Jim Taylor gave the Packers a 14-7 lead when he swept left end and barged 14 yards for a touchdown. The Packers led 14-10 at halftime, and Taylor went on to be the game's leading rusher with 53 yards on 16 carries.

Len Dawson had his arm hit by Packers defensive tackle Henry Jordan (74) as he threw a pass on the first series of the second half....

....and Willie Wood (24) intercepted and returned it 50 yards to the Chiefs' 5 to set up the touchdown that broke the game open.

had become a daily fascination for them, and they couldn't wait to get The Hammer's latest putdown.

Starr looked up and saw Max McGee headed out the door. "A late dinner," McGee said, with a smile.

"The next morning," Starr said, "I went downstairs to have breakfast and read the paper and I saw Max again. He was wearing the same clothes. He'd met a blonde from Chicago the night before. Now he was going to sleep before the game."

Starr might have been angry with a teammate who behaved like that before a big game. Except McGee, who was nicknamed Taxi, had been like that all his career. Besides, McGee wasn't expected to play. The veteran wide receiver had caught only four passes all season. Boyd Dowler was the Packers' starter; McGee was his backup.

When the big moment

arrived, with the respective captains at midfield, the genius of Vince Lombardi manifested itself. Nobody prepared for a game like Lombardi.

"Vince found out that the coin flip was going to be done with a silver dollar," Starr said. "He sincerely believed the engraved eagle made the tails side heavier."

Captain Willie Davis watched the coin fly into the air and yelled "Heads."

It was heads.

But the Packers did not move the ball well on their first series. The only incident of any consequence was that Dowler fell hard on his right shoulder. He slumped off the field, his arm limp.

"McGee," growled Lombardi.

McGee had noticed the Packers were on the home team side of the Coliseum. The shady side. He had scouted out the best place to resume his recovery from the night before. Lombardi's shout jolted him and he almost fell off the bench.

On the Packers' second possession, after they had established their running game and reached the Chiefs' 37-yard line, Starr sensed that a Kansas City blitz was coming.

"It's automatic then," McGee said. "I run a post pattern to the inside. The Chiefs didn't cover the inside like NFL teams did."

Max McGee gave the Packers a 28-10 lead late in the third quarter when he made a juggling catch of a 13-yard touchdown pass from Bart Starr. McGee, subbing for the injured Boyd Dowler, caught seven passes for 138 yards.

Our play fakes were useless. They knew we had to pass, and they just flew at the quarterback."

The Chiefs never got inside the Packers' 40 again. Green Bay put another touchdown up. . . then another. In all, the Packers converted an amazing 11 of 13 third-down situations.

All that remained to settle was The Hammer. In the fourth quarter, with Anderson carrying, the Packers ran a sweep to-

Elijah Pitts followed a block by Jim Taylor for a one-yard touchdown run and the game's final score. Pitts also scored from the 5, running for 45 yards in all. The Packers outscored the Chiefs 21-0 in the second half.

Starr's pass was not a classic. McGee's catch was. He reached back with one hand to collect it, then focused on the goal line. The first touchdown was a breathtaking bit of work by McGee.

Still, the Chiefs responded. Their pride asserted itself, and, at halftime, the Packers' 14-10 lead was far from overwhelming.

"They're old and they're getting tired," Williamson shouted.

In the Packers' locker room, the mood was not as jovial. Someone had written "Know Thyself" on a chalkboard. Lombardi was quiet for several minutes. Then he stood and said with typical emphasis, "Are you the world champion Green Bay Packers? Go out on the field and give me your answer."

Lombardi didn't like the blitz. He didn't like stunts. To him, they were signs of weakness, gimmicks that had to be used because a straight-up, man-to-man defense couldn't stop an offense. But he had decided it was time for a blitz.

The Chiefs were at their 45-yard line. It was third down, a passing down. Lombardi relayed the signal to middle linebacker Ray Nitschke. The Green Bay outside linebackers, Lee Roy Caffey and Dave Robinson, veered toward Dawson.

Dawson was trying to throw to tight end Fred Arbanas. Henry Jordan tipped the ball, and Willie Wood intercepted. Wood ran to the Chiefs' 5.

Running back Elijah Pitts scored on the next play, and Green Bay went ahead 21-10.

"It was over then," Chiefs offensive tackle Jim Tyrer said. "They wouldn't respect our run again.

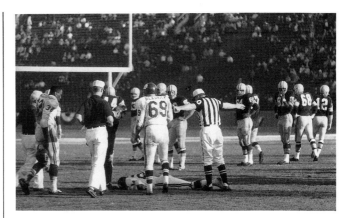

ward Williamson. There was the usual collision, the usual pileup. When everyone got up, Williamson didn't. As he was carried off the field with a broken arm, several Packers did a little gloating. Even Lombardi would remark later, "I didn't even know he was playing until I saw him being carried off the field."

Final score: Green Bay 35, Kansas City 10.

"Everything blew apart on that interception by Wood," Stram said. "We honestly felt we were going to win until then. But if you throw, throw, throw against Green Bay, you're going to lose."

Lombardi was asked to assess the Chiefs. He spoke honestly, but without diplomacy.

"The Chiefs are a good team," he said. "But they don't compare with the top teams of the NFL."

The next day, Lombardi scowled when he saw his words in print.

"I wish I could get my words back. It was the wrong thing to say and I came off as an ungracious winner." For several seconds he was silent, then with that jack-o'-lantern grin, he said, "I'd much rather just be a winner."

Chiefs cornerback Fred (The Hammer) Williamson suffered a broken arm when he collided with Green Bay's Donny Anderson on a sweep.

BLOCK PARTY

Los Angeles Rams 27,
Green Bay Packers 24
December 9, 1967

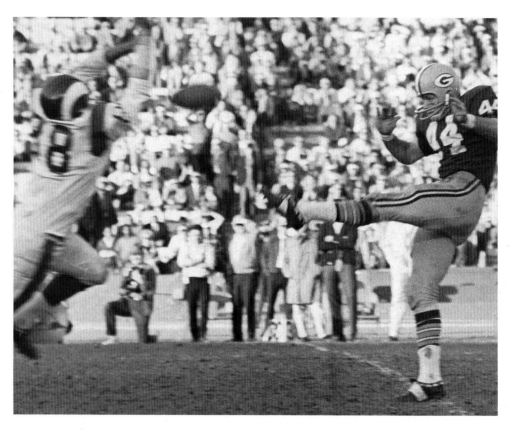

The Rams trailed the Packers 24-20 with 54 sec-
onds left, but, when Green Bay's Donny Anderson
(44, above) punted, linebacker Tony Guillory
burst in to block it. Claude Crabbe (49, below)
picked up the ball and returned it to the Packers'
5-yard line to set up the winning touchdown.

George Allen had this way of talking, of stating little prairie logics that transcended football, which if they had been transcribed, would have been presented best as needlepoint:

"The harder I work, the luckier I get."

"Hit and watch the good things happen."

"Only the winner is alive. The loser is dead, whether he knows it or not."

"You've got to give 110 percent."

The head coach of the Los Angeles Rams had come to Los Angeles in 1966, flipping corn and

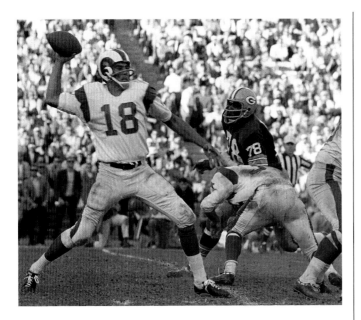

Rams quarterback Roman Gabriel had a big day, passing for 227 yards and three touchdowns, including the winning five-yard throw to Bernie Casey with time running out. He also fired two touchdown passes to Jack Snow.

pone left and right. As might be expected, Hollywood and the Rams were slow to accept him. But an 8-6 record in 1966 had become 9-1-2 in early December, 1967, as the Rams prepared for the final two games of the season.

Since July, when Rams training camp opened, Allen had insisted a portion of every practice be devoted to special teams—to kick coverage, to blocking for extra points, to rushing the other team's punter.

"A blocked kick has been the difference between winning and losing an awful lot of football games," Allen said. "Some teams use their youngsters on special teams because the regulars don't like the work. Not us. Our best players play on special teams and we practice over and over until we cover everything."

The Rams could make the playoffs by winning their final two games. But they had to face the Green Bay Packers, who already had clinched the Central Division title. If Los Angeles won, it would have to beat the Baltimore Colts the following week to win the Coastal Division and earn the right to play the Packers again for the Western Conference title.

The December 9 game with the Packers has been described as the day all of Allen's pie-in-the-sky platitudes turned into gospel.

Before the opening kickoff, Allen gathered his kickoff team around him. Keep the ball out of Travis Williams's hands, he ordered.

Williams was a rookie speedster teammates were calling "The Roadrunner." He'd already returned three kickoffs for touchdowns.

Squib kicks and the Rams' Fearsome Foursome defensive line kept the Packers at bay most of the first quarter. Then Green Bay showed that the Rams did not have an exclusive on special-teams play.

When a mild Rams' threat stalled and Bruce Gossett tried a 46-yard field goal, the Packers' Lee Roy Caffey slipped through and blocked it. Teammate Herb Adderley recovered at the Rams' 43.

"Desire is still very much a weapon in football," said Vince Lombardi. "The game will become sophisticated beyond my wildest dreams. But desire will always be the larger part of football. To block a kick requires the maximum effort and desire."

Four plays after the blocked kick, Packers quarterback Bart Starr threw a 30-yard touchdown pass to Carroll Dale.

"The game could have been over right there," Allen said. "Once upon a time, the Rams might have folded up right then and there. But when we came back, I knew the rebuilding years were over."

Quarterback Roman Gabriel quickly guided Los Angeles down the field, 72 yards in all, the touchdown coming on a pass to split end Jack Snow.

The Rams' new confidence showed. Their defense swarmed. Their offense became bold. Los Angeles tried to open up the game in the second

Les Josephson balanced Gabriel's passing with his hard running. He led the team with 800 yards in 1967 as the Rams went 11-1-2.

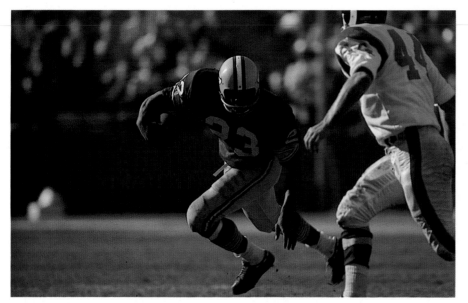

The Rams had just taken a 17-10 lead but made the mistake of kicking to Travis Williams, who eluded Chuck Lamson (44) and everyone else on a 104-yard kickoff return for a touchdown. It was his fourth of the season.

quarter when Gabriel tried to beat the Packers with long bombs. Adderley and safety Willie Wood made interceptions. Wood's gave Green Bay the ball at midfield with time running out in the first half. A pass from Starr to Boyd Dowler moved the Packers close enough for Don Chandler's field goal, which gave them a 10-7 lead at intermission.

In the locker room, Allen looked over the statistics. The game was practically even.

"Close games are won by attitude. . . .*winning* attitude," Allen said. "If we convince ourselves we'll accept only winning today, we'll win."

But Allen also had his toolbox open. Junk the long passes, he told Gabriel. Go to safer stuff.

"We can play with the Packers," Allen shouted. "If we cut out the mistakes, we can beat them."

Willie Ellison returned Chandler's kickoff 43 yards, and Allen was clapping his hands at the blocking by his special-team players.

The Rams steadily punched out yardage, regaining confidence with every first down.

At the Green Bay 11, Gabriel sneaked a glance at Snow, who was being covered by Wood, who was considered the best man-to-man defender in the NFL. Gabriel went to Snow anyway. The touchdown pass put the Rams ahead for the first time, 14-10.

When Green Bay had to punt the ball back, the Rams moved swiftly into Packers territory. Gossett kicked a field goal and the Rams' lead was 17-10.

Once more, giddy confidence got the best of Los Angeles. This time even Allen was caught up in it.

He told Gossett to kick away. Put the ball in the

end zone. If they try to run it back, nail 'em.

Gossett's kick went four yards into the Green Bay end zone. For a moment, Travis Williams hesitated, wondering if he should just down the ball and let his team take over at the 20. Then he took off.

The charging Rams raced downfield. Reserve tackle Bob Nichols was the first to greet the Green Bay runner.

Also the last. Nichols collided with Williams, who was knocked sideways by the impact. Williams somehow kept his balance and began running again. Nobody else even came close to him. The 104-yard kickoff return was Williams's fourth of the season, an NFL record. The score was tied.

"There are times when a big play like that can devastate an opponent," Lombardi said. "Instead, the Rams pulled together and it was us that made the mistakes."

Rams cornerback Clancy Williams intercepted a deflected pass and took it to the Green Bay 25. But the Packers' defense rose up and forced the Rams to settle for another field goal by Gossett.

When the Los Angeles defense shut down the Packers once more, people started looking at the clock. "We had the ball and we had some field position, about the forty-five," Gabriel said. "There were only about eight minutes left. I really thought we had taken control of the game."

But a fumble by Dick Bass that was recovered by the Packers changed everything once more.

"Here's the time to stop them," Allen yelled. "Now, do it now. Attitude!"

The Packers seemed to take control of the game with 2:19 left when Chuck Mercein (30) got good blocking and scored on a four-yard run. It gave Green Bay a 24-20 lead.

But the Packers coolly maneuvered back into the lead when Chuck Mercein punched over the left side for a four-yard touchdown, finishing a nine-play march. The Packers led 24-20.

When the Rams were thrown back on a fourth-down play at the Green Bay 44, the fans at the Coliseum started heading for the exits.

Or so they thought.

The Packers had to kill 80 seconds. But three running plays and time outs brought up a fourth down. There were 54 seconds left to play.

Tony Guillory lined up directly in front of Green Bay center Ken Bowman. Guillory, a reserve linebacker who was called Beowulf because of his unusual strength, never had rushed a punt before. He usually stayed put and tried to keep a blocker busy so someone else could get through.

"This time, I went," Guillory said. "I decided to go right because their kicker was left-footed."

Donny Anderson stood ready to receive the snap.

"I'd never had a punt blocked in my life," he said later.

Tommy Joe Crutcher was one of the up backs for the Packers. His job was to block whoever broke through.

Claude Crabbe lined up on the outside. The reserve defensive back got a good break on the ball, a

Tony Guillory, who set up the winning touchdown with a blocked punt, wasn't afraid to admit football is a game you can get your teeth into.

good reaction to the center snap. Crutcher quickly went over to block him.

Guillory burst up the middle. . .untouched.

"I tried to rush my kick but it was too late," Anderson said.

"I didn't see the kick get blocked," Crutcher said. "But I heard it."

"The ball hit my left wrist," Guillory said.

"I heard the thump and started looking around," Crabbe said later in the tumultuous Rams' dressing room.

Crabbe found the ball and picked it up, and suddenly there were seven Rams running for the end zone. Somehow Anderson looped around the tangle of bodies and made the tackle at the Green Bay 5-yard line. There were 44 seconds left.

The celebrating Rams quickly realized they still had to score a touchdown. And they were out of time outs. On his first snap, Gabriel quickly threw the ball out of bounds, stopping the clock. On the second snap, Gabriel dropped back and threw a soft pass that Bernie Casey plucked out of the air, his feet landing in the Packers' end zone.

On the sidelines, Rams defensive end Deacon Jones lost control. He ran onto the field, zeroing in on Gabriel as if he were the enemy.

"For just a second," Gabriel said, "my happiness turned to horror. When Deacon's coming at you with fire in his eyes. . .well, that's a sight you don't forget."

And a game you don't forget soon   over as linebacker Maxie Baughan intercepted Starr's last desperate pass.

George Allen danced onto the field, looking for players to hug. The tears in his eyes were pure. . . 110 percent pure.

Bernie Casey, who caught the winning five-yard touchdown pass, got a victory hug from fellow receiver Jack Snow.

Tight end Billy Truax congratulated head coach George Allen after Casey's game-winning touchdown catch.

THE ICE BOWL

Green Bay Packers 21,
Dallas Cowboys 17
December 31, 1967

Wrapped in warm clothing like an Eskimo, Vince Lombardi directed the Green Bay Packers to their fifth NFL title in seven years, defeating Dallas 21-17 in bitter cold.

"If you can't run the ball in there in a moment of crisis, you don't deserve to win. These decisions don't come from the mind, they come from the gut."

—VINCE LOMBARDI

No shadows on the ground. Just little patches of crystal sprinkled atop the cold rock of frozen ground of Lambeau Field. Just a bunch of football players from Green Bay and Dallas battling for the NFL championship. They'd both been here the previous year, and the Packers had prevailed in the final moments in Dallas. In the stands at Green Bay, people with ski masks and flasks of brandy might have sensed the Packers' era was nearing its end. Soon the Cowboys would be America's Team. But on this day, the last day of 1967, supremacy in the NFL was up for grabs.

Dallas defensive tackle Bob Lilly thought maybe if he could go get a screwdriver, some kind of tool, to punch some holes in the turf for traction,

Boyd Dowler's eight-yard touchdown catch of Bart Starr's pass put Green Bay ahead 7-0 in the first quarter. He later caught a 46-yard touchdown pass for a 14-0 lead, but the Cowboys rallied for a 17-14 edge in the fourth quarter.

Dowler caught four passes for 77 yards and two touchdowns to lead all receivers in the game.

"Maybe we could survive this thing."

Survive. Green Bay guard Gale Gillingham looked at his hands. They'd stopped hurting, and that scared him. Hands are supposed to hurt in football games, in times of crisis. Gillingham beat his hands on his hip pads. He felt nothing.

On the sideline, Lombardi and quarterback Bart Starr talked during the time out, the last one left. No shadows on Lambeau Field, 16 seconds on the clock. The Cowboys had a three-point lead and 24 inches of frozen ground left to protect. The wonderful irony would be talked about later. It was 364 days earlier, the first day of 1967, when the Cowboys had been the ones scratching along the goal line. The Packers were the ones trying to dig out a foothold on survival. Only that was in Dallas. This was Green Bay, the coldest New Year's Eve in Green Bay's recorded history. A year earlier, in the Cotton Bowl, the Packers had denied the Cowboys with a last-second interception in the end zone.

to get back into the game. Lombardi also knew that after a scoreless third quarter, some typical Dallas razzle-dazzle, or what Cowboys head coach Tom Landry thought of as imaginative play-calling, had put the Cowboys ahead. Now that 50-yard touchdown pass from halfback Dan Reeves to flanker Lance Rentzel separated Lombardi's Packers from a fifth NFL title. No frostbite ever hurt as much.

What Lombardi didn't know was which play do you call when the field has turned to glass. When it is so cold, do you wonder who else cannot feel his hands? Would your own field-goal kicker, the one who could nullify the three-point lead, maybe not feel his feet? Wouldn't that be a hell of a thing? If, two feet away from the other team's goal line, a field goal fluttered no good. What if the kick was blocked? What about overtime? What if it got colder?

Cowboys quarterback Don Meredith, who went on to become a television broadcaster on Monday Night Football, completed just 10 of 25 passes for 59 yards in the Ice Bowl.

Now, paybacks were one failed play away.

"Third down, coach," said referee Norm Schachter, limping over to remind the Green Bay Packers they had one more chance to win the NFL championship. Schachter's left heel was frost-bitten. He ran like a man who'd been shot in the thigh.

"This is your final time out."

Lombardi nodded but didn't look at the referee. He also didn't look at the scoreboard, which said the Cowboys were winning 17-14. He knew. He always knew. He knew his team had jumped ahead 14-0 on two touchdown passes from Starr to split end Boyd Dowler. Then a turnover—when defensive end George Andrie picked up Starr's fumble and lumbered into the end zone—and a short field goal by Danny Villanueva had allowed the Cowboys

"I can sneak the ball in," Starr said to his coach, easy and low because his throat hurt from calling signals in nasty wind and a 13-below temperature.

Lombardi looked down, then out at the field. Twice, his best running back had tried to score from inside the 1 and, slipping and sliding, barely avoided fumbling.

Lombardi looked at his quarterback, then out at the field once more. His team, the Packers, had one play left. Before he left the field, Starr asked his offensive linemen if any of them felt they could hold their footing for a wedge play.

"Hell, yes," said guard Jerry Kramer.

The wedge is a basic handoff to the fullback. But Starr's plan was to not tell anyone else that he would keep the ball. And just look for the end zone.

Green Bay was leading 14-0 when quarterback Bart Starr was hit by end Willie Townes (71) and fumbled at his own 7-yard line. End George Andrie (behind Townes) scooped up the ball and scored the Cowboys' first touchdown.

"When they come up high, they're easier to get a block on," Kramer explained. Maybe this time, because Pugh was tired and cold, he would mess up.

Center Ken Bowman also was supposed to hit Pugh. The Packers' center, however, was feeling a little gun-shy. On each of the previous two plays, when halfback Donny Anderson had tried to get in for the touchdown, Bowman had done little more than slip down. This time, he thought he *had* to keep his balance.

Packers tackle Forrest Gregg and Cowboys defensive end Larry Cole had battled all through the grim afternoon. Who'd been better? Who'd won the skirmishes? There were never thoughts of individual superiority that day. Nothing mattered but the teams and where they were and when it was. If the Packers scored this touchdown, if the Cowboys held them out once more, then somebody could

It would work, Starr told his coach.

With words straight from his gut, Lombardi said, "Then do it and let's get the hell out of here."

Kramer had noticed in looking at game films of the Dallas Cowboys that defensive tackle Jethro Pugh would raise up occasionally on the snap of the ball.

Packers punt returner Willie Wood dropped the ball late in the first half, and Dallas's Frank Clarke (not in the picture) recovered at the Green Bay 17. Danny Villanueva's field goal cut the lead to 14-10.

Dallas flanker Lance Rentzel caught a 50-yard touchdown pass from running back Dan Reeves on the first play of the fourth quarter, and the Cowboys went ahead 17-14.

talk of winning and losing. But not Gregg and Cole. Not now.

Lilly looked around, trying to imagine what Starr and Lombardi were talking about. They were going for it. He knew that. A team like the Packers always has that stop-me-if-you-can attitude. They're going for it, Lilly guessed.

"Hope they come right at me," he thought.

Lilly had been suckered a minute earlier. Gillingham had pulled out, as if he were leading a

With the field frozen, running backs were slipping and sliding all day. Donny Anderson led the Packers in rushing with only 35 yards on 18 carries.

when he saw Starr running back onto the field. But the little wooden ball inside the whistle was frozen just as it had been from the start. None of the whistles worked. The game had been played without whistles.

Lombardi pulled down the fur hat he wore. He often joked to his players that he got down on his knees and prayed for cold weather. Defensive tackle Henry Jordan would say after the game, "Vince stayed down a little bit too long for this one."

Lombardi had listened to the weather report until midnight the night before. It was zero then. But the National Weather Service predicted a new cold front sweeping down from Canada.

Lombardi had had an underground heating system installed at Lambeau Field. There would be 750,000 volts of heat about six inches under the field, not to keep football players toasty and comfortable but to keep the field playable.

But the heating system had been rendered use-

sweep. Lilly had followed him, and the Packers had sent fullback Chuck Mercein into the vacant hole for a big gain. But this time, third down, last play inside the 1, he was sure there wouldn't be any deception.

Schachter looked at his fellow officials. All of them were shaking from the cold. They'd been lucky that morning to find the owner of a sporting goods store who opened up early so the officiating crew could get ear muffs, thermal underwear, extra socks.

"Nothing kept you from being cold that day," Schachter said. "You just stayed barely alive."

Instinctively, Schachter reached for his whistle

The Packers' winning touchdown drive went 68 yards in the last 4:50. This eight-yard run by Chuck Mercein on the drive's second play earned a first down.

There were 52 seconds left to play when Anderson fought for two yards and picked up a Packers' first down at the Cowboys' 1.

less once the tarpaulin was removed. The ground immediately froze. And now, with 16 seconds left, even the weather was a questionable ally.

The crowd of 50,861 was standing and exhorting and freezing.

Pugh lined up inside Kramer's left shoulder. Kramer dug into his stance and felt something wonderful. His right foot had found a soft spot, a toehold. Both lines leaned forward, blasts of steamy breath shooting from their nostrils. Starr walked up and stood over Bowman, who was reaching for the football.

Mercein looked for a place that didn't look slick. The reserve fullback from Yale had made several big plays in this last drive. Rejected by the Giants, bought from the waiver wire for $100, Mercein was all business as he looked for somewhere he might find leverage.

He thought he was going to get the ball.

Starr had called for the wedge. That's all. Wedge 30. On a quick count. Starr said later he didn't want the Cowboys being able to dig in and time his cadence count.

Kramer said he's not sure if he jumped the count. He said he was so primed, so ready that he's just not sure.

"But I did get a good piece of Pugh," he said.

So did Bowman.

Pugh was knocked back. Starr ducked his head, leaped forward, and landed in the end zone.

In the broadcast booth, CBS broadcaster Ray Scott said, "You have just witnessed a mind-over-matter masterpiece."

The Packers had won their third straight NFL

championship. They were going to Super Bowl II.

Lombardi was asked about going for the touchdown as opposed to the tying field goal. "Why not?" he said. "Hadn't those brave fans suffered enough in this weather? I wanted the touchdown so everyone could go home and get warm. I am a man of compassion, you know."

Two weeks later in balmy Miami, Green Bay overwhelmed the AFL's Oakland Raiders in Super Bowl II. Two weeks after that, on February 1, 1968, Lombardi resigned as the Packers' head coach.

When the game ended, Green Bay fans ran onto the field as the Packers began congratulating each other and the Cowboys stood in disbelief.

With 16 seconds left, Green Bay quarterback Bart Starr (15) sneaked a yard for the game-winning touchdown, following a block by guard Jerry Kramer (64) on defensive tackle Jethro Pugh (75).

THE HEIDI GAME

Oakland Raiders 43,
New York Jets 32
November 17, 1968

Once upon a time, in a wonderful land known as Prime Time Television, an NBC gnome flipped this magical switch, and, lo—a storybook ending gave way so another storybook tale could begin.

Yes, Virginia, and the rest of the United States as well, it came to be known as the Heidi Game. Although, to many football fans, there usually is an extra salty adjective or two attached when recalling the Sunday afternoon in November, 1968, when the New York Jets crossed the continent to play the Oakland Raiders.

The game topped the weekend marquee of the American Football League. It was considered such a ratings draw that when the first game of the afternoon doubleheader, Buffalo-San Diego, ran long, the decision to preempt was swift. The obvious reason: so the Jets-Raiders game could be seen in its entirety.

Entirety took on different meaning, however, when the little hand hit 7 and the big hand was on 12 in the eastern time zone. Entirety stopped in a twinkling right about then. And this time, this story had a major network turning into a pumpkin.

In the late 1960s, New York and Oakland were the infant league's major drawing cards, each stocked with both good football players and colorful personalities. There also was the matter that neither

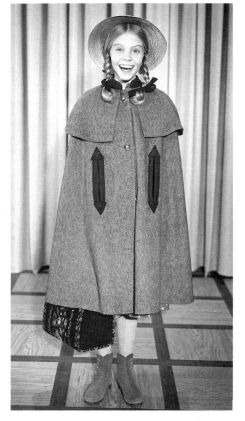

Heidi (played by Jennifer Edwards) was smiling, but football fans around the nation were irate when NBC left the Jets-Raiders game with 65 seconds to play and New York ahead 32-29. The fury got worse when Oakland rallied to win.

team liked the other, a fact borne out by brawl-filled games in recent meetings. If the game was anywhere near as good as expected, NBC executives reasoned, a good share of the national audience would be riveted in its seat for the duration. The game then would make a perfect lead-in for the network's special presentation of "Heidi," the Johanna Spyrl children's classic, which was scheduled to air after the game at 7 P.M. (EST).

In New York, Julian Goodman, president of NBC, settled in front of his TV set, not knowing the next several hours would set some kind of video broadcast history.

The game at Oakland turned out to be even better than expected as an emotional swirl of temper and big plays by both teams turned the afternoon into compelling jock opera. But just as the game entered its final spell-binding minute, the viewing world blinked as Jennifer Edwards, in the title role of the little Swiss orphan girl, suddenly was yodeling to a herd of goats.

When the last commercial of the game began, the Jets had taken a 32-29 lead on a field goal by Jim Turner with 65 seconds to play. The commercial ended and suddenly everyone was in the Swiss Alps, which is about as far away from Oakland-Ala-

The Raiders' Billy Cannon caught three passes for 89 yards and a touchdown.

meda County Coliseum as one can get.

The switchboard at NBC headquarters in New York City lit up almost immediately. Viewers were angry. Very angry. Livid. *"What happened to the football game?"*

The anger was compounded even further as the Raiders made a miraculous comeback, the kind you only read about in fairy tales, or see in far west time zones, scoring two touchdowns after that last commercial break. The Raiders beat the Jets 43-32. Most of the nation missed the thrilling conclusion to the game. And then hundreds of viewers tried, all at once, to call NBC to critique the decision.

Two decades later, the memory of the game still is caught in the shadow of NBC's ill-advised stick-to-the-script dedication. That might be the larger crime. The game deserved its own legend.

Before the game, at the Raiders' headquarters in Oakland, a huge blowup of a photograph summed up the Jets-Raiders rivalry. It was a black-and-white photo of Oakland defensive end Ben Davidson delivering a blow to New York quarterback Joe Namath's sideburns. Many believed it was this play that had fractured Namath's cheekbone in a game the year before. Nobody would say where the photo came from, or who had put it on the wall. This is the way of the Raiders and their owner Al Davis. Mystery and suspicion. Intimidation through photography.

By the time the Jets got to Oakland, the photo had been taken down. But not before word had reached them, not before the veins in their necks stuck out like cords in anticipation of another day of war with the bully boys in silver and black.

Namath, who also could swash and buckle with the best of them, grinned through his new Fu Manchu moustache when someone asked him if he thought the Raiders were gunning for him.

"If they want to win," Namath said, licking off a syrupy smile, "they'd better be."

NBC's Merle Harmon was in the broadcast booth, practicing some of the names, going over final preparations, dealing with his own pregame jitters.

"As many games as I've worked in my career,

that one really seemed special even before it began," Harmon said. "I could sense it was going to be a very entertaining afternoon."

In the Raiders' locker room, the mood was surly. Head coach John Rauch knew his team was playing well—they would go on to nine straight victories —but he wanted to guard against complacency. The Jets, he warned over and over in practice, didn't respect them. Nobody did.

In their last several minutes of solitude before heading onto the field, something was missing. The sound of wide receiver Fred Biletnikoff throwing up in the bathroom put everyone at ease. Biletnikoff threw up before every game; once he did, he felt fine. So did the Raiders.

The Jets were edgy. Head coach Weeb Ewbank sensed it. He was worried about the recent ineffectiveness of Namath, who had not thrown a touchdown pass in six games. But he was more concerned about his players' attitudes. They were too keyed up. There was an unusual tenseness. He warned his players to hold their tempers. "Be intense, not tense," he said. "Play football. Don't fight."

But, on the opening kickoff, the Jets were penalized for a personal foul.

The game began and Namath quickly guided

Oakland defensive end Ben Davidson towered over Jets tackle Winston Hill (75) and quarterback Joe Namath. Namath was sacked six times, but passed for 381 yards and a touchdown and ran for another score.

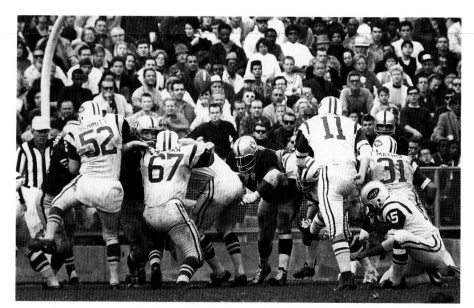

New York's Jim Turner kicked four field goals, including this one of 12 yards. His 26-yard kick gave the Jets a 32-29 lead with 65 seconds left.

the Jets downfield, where Turner kicked a field goal. He kicked another later in the period. After Raiders quarterback Daryle Lamonica threw a touchdown pass to Warren Wells, Oakland led 7-6.

Each play seemed to bring a snarl of anger from someone on the field. Yellow flags filled the air, and there was pushing and shoving and name-calling.

The Raiders got another touchdown pass from Lamonica, who, in typical Raiders intrigue before the game, reportedly was so heavily taped because of injuries that his status was unknown. But Lamonica looked healthy enough as he hooked up with tight end Billy Cannon for a 49-yard score.

The Jets battled back, overcoming several penalties, and Namath sneaked over from a yard out. On the extra-point try, the snap was bad, and backup quarterback Babe Parilli scrambled, looking for someone to pass to, but was tackled before he could throw.

The tempo was brutal. Namath would wind up getting sacked six times, Lamonica twice. Jets fullback Billy Joe would have his knee blown out on a tackle. Several other players on both teams would leave for medical attention.

In the halftime locker room, Ewbank was making some changes. Wide receiver Don Maynard was getting open a lot against Raiders rookie cornerback George Atkinson. Ewbank made a note to himself to call Maynard's number more often.

In the third quarter, New York took a 19-14 lead on a short touchdown run by Bill Mathis. But the Raiders fired right back.

Jets safety Jim Hudson, who was Namath's assigned roommate for road games, blew up on the next series, his temper finally frayed to the snap-

ping point. As the Raiders marched steadily toward the Jets' goal line, Hudson went out of control, yelling at the Raiders while they were in their huddle, yelling at the officials, yelling at his own teammates.

On the next play, Hudson was whistled for grabbing the facemask of Oakland fullback Hewritt Dixon. Hudson got even angrier, screaming at field judge Frank Kirkland, who shook his finger at Hudson and yelled back. A second yellow flag (unsportsmanlike conduct) was thrown, and Hudson was ejected from the game. As he walked off, Hudson made a gesture to the jeering Oakland crowd, which only succeeded in making things even noisier. The penalties moved the ball to the Jets' 3-yard line, where rookie Charlie Smith took a handoff and scored a touchdown.

On the play, Jets linebacker Larry Grantham fell hard on his neck and had to be helped off the field, suddenly leaving Ewbank another hole to fill.

The Raiders went for two points, which was one of the differences between the AFL and the older National Football League. The ball went to Lamonica, who scooted right and threw a pass that was caught by Dixon. The Raiders led 22-19.

A few minutes later the Raiders were driving for another touchdown, one that would have allowed them to open up and finally shake free from the Jets. But at the Jets' 3, Smith fumbled on a big hit by Paul Crane—Grantham's replacement—and New York's Gerry Philbin recovered.

Two bombs later—a 47-yard pass from Namath to Maynard followed by 50-yard collaboration between the same two men—the Jets had the lead again. Maynard would finish the day with 10 catches for 228 yards.

With 8:49 to play, Turner kicked a field goal to give New York a 29-22 advantage. But Lamonica brought the Raiders back once again. Lamonica threw a 22-yard touchdown pass to Biletnikoff, and George Blanda's extra point tied the score.

In New York, at his home, watching the terrific football game that was coming at the TV audience like a heavyweight championship brawl, Julian Goodman looked at his wristwatch. It was getting late. The three-hour time slot might spill over. Probably because of all the penalties—there would be a combined total of 19 for 238 yards. At any rate, the scheduled starting time of "Heidi" was approaching fast.

The Jets, with Namath coolly using the clock and the sidelines, maneuvered into Raiders territory, finally settling for Turner's 26-yard field goal with 1:05 remaining.

That's when all hell broke loose.

Back in New York, Lucy Ewbank, wife of the Jets' coach, saw that the children's movie had come on the air. So she went to dinner, thinking the Jets must have held on for the victory.

Meanwhile, back in reality, the Raiders decided they would test safety Mike D'Amato, who had come into the game when Hudson was ejected. They would try to isolate Smith, who had good speed, on either a linebacker or D'Amato.

Lamonica passed to Smith for 20 yards. On the play, D'Amato was penalized for grabbing Smith's facemask. On the next play, Lamonica threw a pass to Smith, who ran 43 yards for a touchdown with 42 seconds to play. Blanda's kick made it 36-32, which meant a Jets field goal was meaningless. They needed a touchdown.

The Raiders took the lead for good when Charlie Smith escaped on a 43-yard touchdown pass play with 42 seconds to go. Then, nine seconds later, they scored with a fumbled kickoff for the final 43-32 margin.

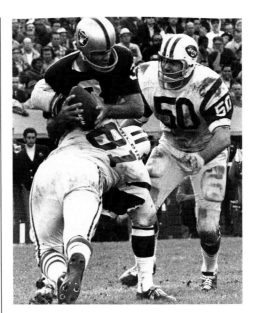

End Gerry Philbin of the Jets had six tackles, including this sack of Oakland's Daryle Lamonica. But Lamonica threw four touchdown passes in the Raiders' victory.

As the Raiders lined up for the kickoff, halfback Earl Christy was thinking how much a long runback would mean. There wasn't much time. But there was enough.

Mike Eischeid's kick was a squibber that bounced three times and finally was fielded by Christy at the 15. It rolled through his legs, he retrieved it at the 10, then tried to spin and twist his way through the Raiders' mob. As Christy was slung around, the ball squirted free. Reserve fullback Preston Ridlehuber picked up the ball at the 2 and stepped into the end zone for the second Raiders touchdown in a nine-second span.

At the end of the game, Jets assistant coach Joe Walton chased after the officials, complaining about their judgment. Ewbank ripped the officiating as well in his postgame press conference. Even Dr. James Nicholas, the team doctor, banged on the door of the officials' dressing room, complaining bitterly. Ultimately, Commissioner Pete Rozelle would fine the Jets $2,000. In addition, several individual fines were handed down, including one for Hudson's unfortunate gesture.

But it all was mild compared to what was happening at NBC. The following day, Goodman made a public apology, describing the decision to switch from the game to the children's show as, "a forgivable error committed by humans who were concerned about the children."

Complaints numbered in the tens of thousands. But eventually NBC found one sympathizer. Ewbank said later he thought NBC had the right idea. Then with a wide smile, he added, "I also think the game should have ended right after Turner's field goal put us ahead."

PAINFUL VICTORY

New York Jets 27,
Oakland Raiders 23
December 29, 1968

Pain is easily forgotten. Women with many children prove that. It's why rich and famous men dare to play quarterback.

Jeff Snedeker, trainer of the New York Jets, shook his head in despair as he saw Joe Namath trudging to the sideline, his left hand dangling limp in front of him. It was the second quarter of the 1968 AFL Championship Game, and the Jets' pass protection had just collapsed. So had Namath.

The ring finger on the left hand of the Jets' quarterback was threatening to become an isosceles triangle. It curled up and out, badly dislocated, due to the sandwich job a couple of Oakland Raiders just applied.

"Oh, Joe," shrieked teammate Winston Hill, who walked over to see what was the matter. "Joe, look at it, man. That's hideous."

Hill turned away as Namath held out his left hand to his trainer. Snedeker warned Namath it was going to hurt.

"It already hurts," Namath said.

Snedeker yanked on the dislocated finger with a knowledgeable tug, and Joe Namath closed his eyes for a moment. The finger went back into place. Dr. James Nicholas, the Jets' team physician, asked Namath if he wanted a shot of painkiller.

The 1968 AFL Championship Game was played on a cold, blustery day, but before it started, Jets coach Weeb Ewbank learned that the Raiders insisted on the removal of his team's protective bench shelter.

"No, not my hands," Namath said, looking out on the field where the Raiders were getting their punting team into position. "I have to have feel in my hands."

A quarterback needs feel. He needs touch. Even if the feel is pain. Even if it hurts to touch. Namath's right thumb, the one on his passing hand, had been badly jammed for several weeks, and a couple of hits by the Raiders had caused it to swell and throb. His tailbone was bruised, too, a holdover from the last time he ran into the unfriendly folks from Oakland.

But if you want to talk about pain with Joe Namath, you start with his famous knees. Orthopedic repair had turned them back into reasonable facsimiles of the originals. At halftime on this particular chilly afternoon in New York, Namath got the usual shots of painkiller in those terribly delicate and damaged hinges.

Across the field, the Raiders' linebacker coach was eyeing Namath as he received his medical attention. In a matter of weeks, after Oakland head coach John Rauch would resign unexpectedly, 32-year-old John Madden would be elevated from linebackers coach to the top job. But for the moment—that being the game that would determine who would represent the AFL in Super Bowl III—Madden was more concerned with how to throw a bucket of sand on the Jets' offense. Namath had guided New York to a quick 10-0 lead in the first quarter. It was 10-7 now, and Madden was his usual animated self. He saw Namath being worked on, and he knew that if the Jets lost him, they would be in trouble.

Then he saw Namath trotting out to the Jets' huddle. And his now-celebrity body English almost made words unnecessary.

"Joe Namath is one of the toughest football players I ever saw," Madden said later. "You could never intimidate him."

Later in the second quarter, as Jim Turner and George Blanda traded field goals, making it 13-10,

Shrugging off a dislocated finger, jammed thumb, and sore knees, New York's Joe Namath passed for 266 yards and three touchdowns. His six-yard, fourth-quarter scoring pass to Don Maynard clinched the victory.

"I'm willing to practice anywhere, in any vacant lot," Rauch said, "as long as it's got a fence."

In their last regular-season meeting, which would become forever known as the Heidi Game, the Jets had lost their poise, not to mention the game. Tempers always raged whenever the two teams played, but the Jets' composure totally eroded and the Raiders scored two touchdowns in the last 65 seconds to win. The rematch did not figure to be any less emotional.

"We have to keep our poise," Jets head coach Weeb Ewbank said earlier in the week. "Losing control is what the Raiders try to get you to do. We've got to do a better job this time."

In the first half, the same battle lines that had existed in the game at Oakland were drawn again. Rauch didn't think Jets cornerback Johnny Sample could stay with Raiders flanker Fred Biletnikoff, who had caught seven passes for 120 yards in the Heidi Game. Ewbank also figured his receiver, Don Maynard, an antenna with sideburns and incredible speed for someone on the flip side of 30, would have another highlight-film day against George Atkinson, the Raiders' rookie cornerback. Maynard had burned Atkinson for 10 catches and 228 yards in Oakland.

Atkinson had borrowed a team film projector and watched that game over and over at home. He said it was embarrassing, adding, "I almost have the whole thing memorized."

Ewbank gave Sample explicit instructions before the game: "Don't let him run a post pattern. The first one he runs, you're coming out and we're going with [rookie Cornell] Gordon."

Sample nodded. But 48 seconds into the second quarter, Fred Biletnikoff swiveled and juked and ran a post pattern. He took Lamonica's pass in full stride, broke a feeble tackle by Sample, and scored a touchdown.

The score helped narrow the lead the Jets had taken 3:39 into the game on Namath's 14-yard pass

Jets' favor, the playing conditions deteriorated. Wind constantly whipped in from nearby Flushing Bay, sending the dirt from the baseball infield swirling, making the expected aerial showdown between Namath and Daryle Lamonica unlikely to reach maximum liftoff. The blustery climate also enhanced the nasty disposition of the two teams.

The Raiders had come to New York with their usual cloak of mystery and paranoia pulled around them.

After trampling Kansas City in a divisional play-off game the week before, Rauch was asked where the Raiders would practice in New York before the championship game.

Wide receiver Fred Biletnikoff scored the Raiders' first touchdown on a 29-yard pass from Daryle Lamonica. He led all receivers in the game with seven catches for 190 yards.

Elusive Don Maynard caught six passes for 118 yards and two touchdowns to help send the Jets to the Super Bowl.

Oakland's Daryle Lamonica, often referred to as the "Mad Bomber," bombed the Jets for 401 yards passing, but couldn't pull out the victory.

to Maynard, a yard past the stumbling Atkinson.

Gordon replaced Sample, as promised.

As the half was shivering to an end, Namath dropped back in hope of a big, momentum-setting play to take into the locker room. Dave Herman, the all-AFL guard who had been switched to tackle specifically to block Ike Lassiter, the Raiders' pass-rushing specialist, was beaten for the only time all game. He shouted, "Look out, Joe," as he saw Lassiter bearing down on Namath.

Namath got the pass off and it was incomplete. Then he was belted by Lassiter, accompanied by Ben Davidson. The three men fell to the frozen turf in a tangle. Namath's eyes rolled. He blinked and staggered to his feet, looking more like a newborn horse with quivering legs and a dazed look.

Inside the Jets' locker room at halftime, Namath was acting strange. Dr. Nicholas took him to a side room for examination. Then Snedeker stood watch while the doctor went to Ewbank and said, "You'd better get Parilli ready."

Babe Parilli was the Jets' backup quarterback. Courage was one thing, obvious danger was something else. Knees and fingers and thumbs and sore tailbones can be ignored. Concussions are different.

"But he started to come around a little bit," Ewbank said later. "When the third quarter began, we were all watching him real closely."

On the first play, Namath took the handoff and stumbled backward for a four-yard loss.

"Uh-oh, he's not right yet," Parilli said to a teammate as he instinctively snapped his chinstrap, then watched as the Raiders forced a punt.

Two plays later, Cornell Gordon thought he would be the next star on Broadway. He saw La-

monica's pass coming to him. He was going to intercept and run it all the way back.

But Biletnikoff stole the dream before it ever took form, for a 37-yard gain. When Warren Wells grabbed another bomb from Lamonica for 40 yards, down to the New York 6, Ewbank was looking around for Sample.

Jets safety Jim Hudson was ranting in the defensive huddle: "Poise! Let's keep our poise. Let's stop them right here."

Hudson was in on three straight tackles that forced Blanda to kick a field goal for a 13-13 tie.

By then Namath was back to seeing only one of everything. And the Jets got their act together for the first time since early in the second quarter.

With less than a minute left in the third quarter, tight end Pete Lammons grabbed Namath's 20-yard

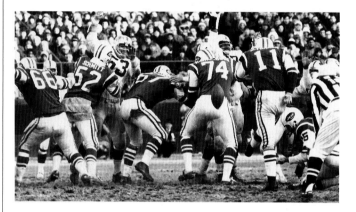

strike for a touchdown.

A repentent Sample sprinted onto the field, ready to show Biletnikoff what he had learned while serving his sentence on the Jets' bench.

New York's Jim Turner (11) kicked two field goals, including this one of 33 yards in the first quarter which extended his team's lead to 10-0. Turner also made a 36-yard field goal for a 13-10 halftime lead.

Lamonica arched a 57-yard parole revoke into Biletnikoff's stickum-covered hands as he beat Sample again. But once again the Jets forced the Raiders to kick a field goal, and the Jets led 20-16.

On the first play after the kickoff, Namath looked for the old reliable Maynard, and single coverage by the bedraggled Atkinson. But when Maynard ran eight steps and cut abruptly to the sideline, Atkinson was right there with him. "I'd seen that move before," Atkinson said later. He intercepted at the Jets' 35. At the 5-yard line, he was pushed out of bounds by Namath.

Rookie halfback Pete Banaszak scored on the next play. For the first time, Oakland led, 23-20. There was 8:18 to play.

The Jets got a lift when Earl Christy, whose fum-

George Blanda (16), the Raiders' old warborse, teamed up with holder (and quarterback) Daryle Lamonica for three field goals. Blanda still is the NFL's all-time scoring leader in postseason play with 115 points in 19 games.

ble in the closing seconds in Oakland had been so costly, returned the kick-off 35 yards.

After gaining a first down, Namath decided to test Atkinson once again, passing to Maynard.

Atkinson said later, "We both could see the ball fine. Then all of a sudden, it moved cross-wind. He made a great adjustment and a hell of a catch. It's tough to do stuff like that when you're running so fast." Maynard made an over-the-shoulder grab at the Raiders' 6.

Namath then wanted to throw a flare pass to halfback Bill Mathis. He was covered. So he looked for George Sauer, but Raiders all-league corner-back Willie Brown was all over him. Namath wondered about Lammons, spotted him, and saw he too was smothered. Finally, he sidearmed a low liner diagonally across the field. Maynard made a sliding catch for the touchdown and a 27-23 lead.

"How many quarterbacks can go through four different options in, what—five seconds?" Sauer asked later.

Madden was batting himself in the head with his fist. Rauch was staring at the clock. The Jets had been behind all of 31 seconds.

But almost eight minutes remained. The Raiders and Lamonica, who would finish with 401 yards passing for the day, quickly moved to the Jets' 26. A sack not only spoiled the threat but took the Raiders out of Blanda's field-goal range.

With 3:30 left, Oakland got its last chance. Completed passes to Bilet-nikoff and Wells for 37 and 24 yards, respective-ly, and a personal foul against the Jets had the crowd on its feet. There was more than two min-utes remaining, and Oakland had a first down at the New York 24.

Jets linebacker Ralph Baker saw something painfully familiar in the way the Raiders lined up. Pain does not always have to be physical.

"Out there [in Oakland], they scored the win-ning touchdown on a pass to one of their half-backs," Baker said. "But the thing was, they sent both halfbacks out on the same side. One would go deep. One stayed in the flat."

Baker's sense of *deja vu* was true. Lamonica backpedaled, looking downfield. But Verlon Biggs, the Jets' defensive end, had slipped his blocker. La-monica looked to the flat for his safety-valve.

Charlie Smith was a rookie from Utah, a big kid with speed who had come into his own in the late stages of the season, running for more than 500 yards and scoring seven touchdowns, including a 43-yard run with a safety-valve pass against the Jets in November. In the next moment, Smith would break one of football's cardinal rules: You play un-til you hear the whistle.

Lamonica's pass was behind Smith, who reached with one hand for the ball but only could tick it with his fingertips. Smith was behind La-monica.

"It wasn't a pass. . .it was like a lateral," Baker said. It was a backward pass—a lateral— and a free ball. Smith froze, staring at the ball. Baker meanwhile scooped it up.

The Jets were in the Super Bowl.

"I don't know if I even could have gotten to the ball," Smith said. "Baker was on the ball so quick-ly. But I did not know it was a live ball. It all hap-pened so fast. You either react or you don't. I didn't."

Later that night at a party, Namath looked and acted the picture of hedo-nistic health. Meanwhile, the Oakland Raiders could tell you all you wanted to know about pain. Real pain.

The Raiders' last chance evaporated at New York's 24-yard line when rookie running back Charlie Smith couldn't catch a swing pass that was ruled a lateral. Linebacker Ralph Baker (51) was only too happy to recover it.

HE GUARANTEED IT

New York Jets 16,
Baltimore Colts 7
January 12, 1969

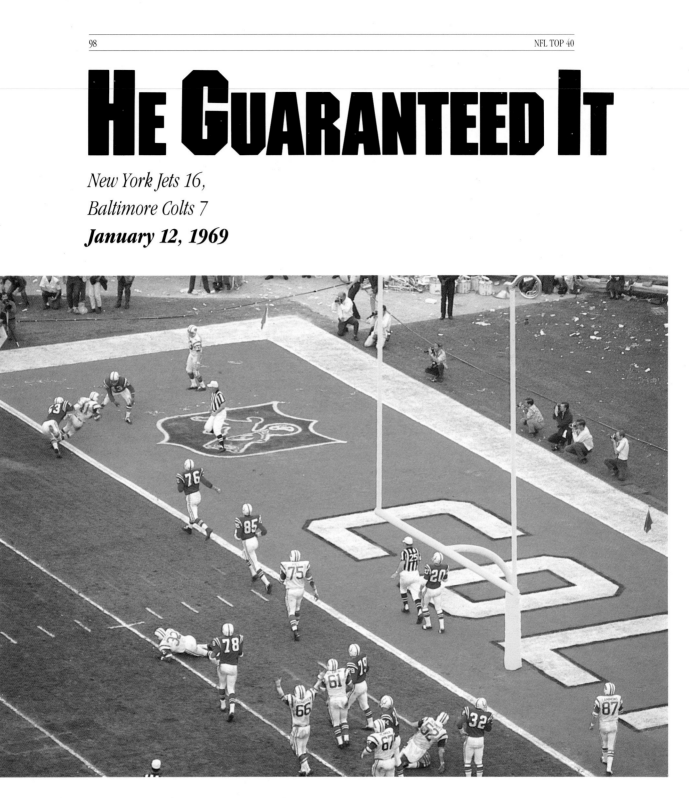

The Jets' Matt Snell (far left) dragged Baltimore linebacker Dennis Gaubatz into the end zone to score the game's only touchdown on a four-yard, second-quarter run. New York's 16-7 victory in Super Bowl III is considered one of the greatest upsets in NFL history.

Before the dawn's early light, workers were busy at the handsome beach-front home of Carroll Rosenbloom, the icono-clastic owner of the Balti-more Colts. They were getting ready for the big party. The victory party.

As soon as the Colts took care of those other-league nuisances from New York, Rosenbloom and hundreds of friends were going to celebrate under a big tent, with magnums of French champagne, dancing to a 10-piece band dressed in tuxedos. What better way to toast the football team some people were calling one of the greatest of all time?

"I'll never forget Carroll telling me before the game about his party," Jets head coach Weeb Ew-bank said years later. "I told him I appreciated the invitation, but I was hoping I'd have my own victo-

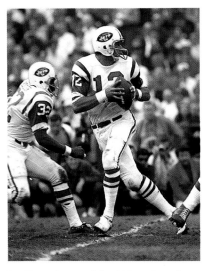

Joe Namath passed for 206 yards and was named the game's most valuable player.

ry party to attend that evening."

In the early morning hours of January 12, 1969, CBS Television also was busy. At the locker room that would be used by the Colts, camera positions were being marked. They put pieces of tape on the floor. One piece went where Don Shula would be interviewed. And, at the one over there, Rosenbloom would get the championship trophy from NFL Commissioner Pete Rozelle.

Super Bowl III was more a foregone conclusion than a contest. The Colts were 18-point favorites over the New York Jets.

The Jets promised they would show up at the Orange Bowl anyway.

In fact, their quarterback, the guy with the searing green eyes, the mink coat, the white shoes, and the delivery that was quick as a crossbow, even went so far earlier in the week as to "guarantee" victory for his team.

Broadway Joe Namath had been dropping outrageous bombs of arrogance ever since the Jets beat the Oakland Raiders to fill the American Football League's spot in the Super Bowl. Namath said there were at least four quarterbacks in the AFL who were better than Baltimore's Earl Morrall, who had been named most valuable player in the NFL.

"Including me," Namath added.

A lot of cynics nudged each other knowingly. When you have a mismatch on your hands, you must beat the public relations drums long and hard. Many perceived Namath's outbursts as plain and simple loudmouthing.

"But Joe believed it," said Jets tackle Dave Herman. "He really thought we were going to beat them. Then eventually, we all did."

On the evening of Super Sunday, Carroll Rosenbloom held his party, but much of the gaiety was missing because the Jets had won Super Bowl III.

The team with a snowball's chance in Havana of winning, had rubbed the Baltimore Colts' noses in it, 16-7.

And the slouch-shouldered quarterback with the number 12 on his jersey jogged triumphantly toward the locker room, his arm raised, his finger

waving number one in the cool Miami night air.

The biggest upset in Super Bowl history—then and now—also sent out quivers of change in pro football. The result put the official stamp on the 1970 merger of the AFL and NFL, and the message was: if you *can* beat 'em, join 'em.

In a delirious Jets locker room, Johnny Sample, a former Colts defensive back who felt he had been blackballed out of the NFL a couple of years earlier, wadded up a faded newspaper clipping he had carried in his wallet for more than a year.

"Lombardi Says AFL Inferior," read the headline.

Sample laughed and asked the mob of reporters around him, "What's the headline tomorrow?"

The so-called Mickey Mouse League was yesterday's news. Joe Namath's word was good. So were his passes. So were his teammates. It was nothing artistic, just decisive and convincing. The scenario of Super Bowl III was as compelling as the game.

Five hours before the opening kickoff there was an unexpected knock on the door at Namath's hotel room in Fort Lauderdale. It came only minutes after his wakeup call. The bellboy handed Namath a dozen red roses. There was a card: To Joseph, From Lou Michaels and the Baltimore Colts.

Namath laughed. Gamesmanship had bloomed fuller than those roses all week. Besides, they were roses. If they'd been lilies or if it had been a funeral

The Colts ruined their chances with several big errors. After Tom Matte's Super Bowl-record 58-yard run to the Jets' 16, for example, Earl Morrall threw an interception to Johnny Sample. Morrall, the NFL's MVP, threw three of Baltimore's four interceptions.

Baltimore tight end Tom Mitchell bobbled this tipped Earl Morrall pass late in the first quarter. Cornerback Randy Beverly (barely visible at bottom left of photo) made a diving interception, and then (right) displayed his trophy.

wreath, Namath might have read some hidden meaning into it all.

"Just another gift from an admirer," Namath would say later.

The game was supposed to be a mismatch, but it had juicy little twists stuck all over it.

Like the head coaches.

The Jets' Weeb Ewbank was 61, a grandfather, and, once upon a time, coach of the Colts. In fact, Ewbank called the shots for the Colts' 1958 and 1959 NFL champions.

Before Ewbank came to Baltimore, he was an assistant with the Cleveland Browns. In 1951, Ewbank, who helped with scouting and player personnel, traveled to John Carroll University to check out a prospect named Shula. Later that year, based on Ewbank's recommendations, the Cleveland Browns selected Don Shula in the ninth round of the college draft. Two years later, Shula was traded to Baltimore. The following year, Ewbank was named the Colts' head coach. Three years later, Ewbank put defensive back Shula on waivers. Seven years after that, Ewbank was fired and replaced by

33-year-old Don Shula, who became the NFL's youngest head coach.

And five years after that, the two were getting their teams ready to play in Super Bowl III.

Meanwhile, sociological lines were being drawn around the football world. Whose side are you on? Are you square or hippie? As always, sport remained society's mirror. The Jets were young, brash, anti-establishment—like their quarterback. The Colts were experienced, solid, conservative.

Namath did the talking, but, behind closed doors, the rest of the Jets were just as confident. They had seen the Colts on film and were not awed.

For one thing, they could see the Colts had no breakaway running threat.

"That meant we could play their receivers tighter," said Sample.

Ewbank also spotted a glaring weakness in the Colts' secondary. Veteran cornerback Bobby Boyd was painfully slow. So slow, in fact, the Colts tried to protect him by rolling their coverage toward him. The Colts, Ewbank figured, would double-cover Jets flanker Don Maynard.

The Colts threatened on their first series, but Willie Richardson dropped a touchdown pass in the end zone, and Lou Michaels (below) then missed a 27-yard field-goal attempt. Baltimore failed on four first-half scoring opportunities.

"That meant George Sauer, our other receiver, might have a big day," the Jets' coach said afterward. Sauer caught eight passes for 133 yards.

Ewbank and his staff added some new wrinkles, too. One of them moved a linebacker into the defensive line, making a five-man front. Another was a revamped offensive line in which Ewbank moved Dave Herman to right tackle and inserted Randy Rasmussen at right guard. The Jets would remain a left-handed team, running primarily behind left tackle Winston Hill and left guard Bob Talamini.

"But throwing something new at them might make them have to do some extra thinking," Ewbank told his team.

Matt Snell gained 121 yards on 30 carries.

The Colts, who were 15-1 through the regular season and playoffs, were perhaps more talented than the Jets, Ewbank figured. But they weren't Supermen. And they definitely were beatable.

Baltimore split end Jimmy Orr was open for a touchdown pass late in the first half, but Morrall never saw him and threw this interception to safety Jim Hudson.

An hour before the game, Namath lay on a training table while Jets trainer Jeff Snedeker taped his crystal-fragile knees. Ewbank had one last piece of advice.

"I don't think we should try any sweeps," the coach said. "Their linebackers are so good at pursuit." Namath's eyes were closed. He heard. But he was trying to relax.

On the game's second play, Namath stood over center, called an audible... and sent Matt Snell around left end on a sweep.

Snell ran for a first down. On the play, Colts safety Rick Volk was knocked out. Two lessons were learned.

The Jets could go outside.

The Colts were not indestructible.

Namath was audacious and irreverent, which wasn't really a lesson because everyone knew it.

New York was forced to punt, and Baltimore went to work. A screen to all-pro tight end John Mackey gained 19 yards. Halfback Tom Matte took a pitchout for 10 more.

"They looked vulnerable on defense on film," Shula explained later. "They were not overly impressive from what we could see. We really felt we could run and pass freely."

And from what everyone at the Orange Bowl had seen so far, they had to agree. A pass to reserve tight end Tom Mitchell picked up 15 more yards. The Colts were at the Jets' 19-yard line.

Then the Colts started a self-destruct pattern that would last the entire game. Wide receiver Willie Richardson had a sure touchdown when he cut and broke into the end zone. Jets defender Jim Hudson had fallen down.

But Richardson dropped the ball.

Then Morrall overthrew Mitchell, who also was open. On third down, the Jets finally got some pressure on the Colts' quarterback, forcing him out of the pocket, where he was tackled for no gain.

Lou Michaels came in to try for a 27-yard field goal.

Boyd was the holder, and he noticed the swirling wind. The Colts were kicking into the open end of the Orange Bowl. Even the short field goals, Boyd was thinking, would be tests.

Boyd took the snap and turned the ball around, laces to the front, and heard the thump of foot on ball. Michaels's kick was wide to the right.

A celebrated encounter between Michaels and Namath earlier in the week had put a charge of ex-

Joe Namath's passing was instrumental in two second-half field-goal drives for the Jets, and New York got another field goal after recovering a Tom Matte fumble. Namath completed 17 of his 28 passes, with no interceptions.

citement into the festivities. They had called each other names, playing a macho game of verbal territorial imperative, but they had parted with smiles, no hard feelings, and plenty of publicity.

Now Michaels had faltered.

And it was Namath's turn.

On the second play, Maynard ran a deep go pattern. He easily beat Boyd, and even got a couple of

Johnny Unitas, still recovering from an elbow injury, replaced struggling Earl Morrall and produced three long drives, but Baltimore scored on just one of them. Unitas completed 11 of 24 passes for 110 yards.

steps behind Volk.

The pass was too long, out of the end zone beyond Maynard's reach.

"But it was an important play," Namath explained later.

You were not supposed to be able to throw deep against Baltimore. The Colts' zone allegedly was bomb-proof. In one incomplete pass, another concept of invulnerability was shattered.

"The rest of the game, Maynard had them scared," Snell said.

Later in the period, Sauer took a pass, was hit, and fumbled, the Colts recovering. In each of the first two Super Bowls, a similar miscue had opened the gates for the Green Bay Packers to seize command of the game. Mistakes such as this had forced the AFL representatives (Kansas City and Oakland) to lose their poise.

But the Colts could not capitalize as the Packers had. Morrall's pass to Mitchell was tipped by Jets linebacker Al Atkinson then intercepted by cornerback Randy Beverly on a dive roll in the end zone.

The day before, Beverly, a free agent who had been playing semi-pro ball two years earlier, confessed to teammates he was scared, adding, "I don't want to look like a clown."

The interception also stoked life into the Jets' of-

fense. With 9:03 left in the first half, Snell rumbled over the goal line for the last four yards of a 12-play, 80-yard drive.

That was followed by an exchange of missed field goals...and another Baltimore mistake. Two plays after Matte had broken loose for a Super Bowl record 58-yard scamper to the Jets' 16, Sample intercepted a pass by Morrall. As was his incandescent nature, Sample got up and tapped Richardson, the intended receiver, on the helmet with the ball, gloating and yapping as he walked to the sideline.

Stymied again and again, the Colts got one last chance before the half ended. With 25 seconds left in the second quarter, Morrall handed off to Matte. Jets safety Bill Baird committed and charged forward. Matte flipped the ball back to Morrall.

Beverly was assigned to cover Colts flanker Jimmy Orr short. Baird would take him if he went long.

Orr was 10 yards behind everyone, waving his hands frantically. The Colts had a certain touchdown if Orr caught the pass.

And if Morrall threw it to him.

Morrall didn't. He said later he never saw Orr. Instead, Morrall threw to fullback Jerry Hill. Hudson intercepted.

The Colts had tried the play against Atlanta in the regular season. It was completed—for a touchdown—to Jimmy Orr.

The Jets' last defensive play in the last practice before Super Bowl III was the same play. Ewbank knew the Colts had it, and would use it in just such a situation. So he had backup quarterback Babe Parilli try it in practice. It was completed then, too, for a touchdown.

"We were simply lucky," Ewbank said.

At halftime, Shula struggled with his options. Morrall obviously was having an off-game. Shula had the great Johnny Unitas available as an alternative. Unitas had lost his starting job because of an elbow injury. It still bothered him, but he told Shula he could play. Shula had to make a decision. Were things desperate?

On the first play from scrimmage in the third quarter, Matte fumbled, and the Jets recovered. Things became more desperate.

The Colts could have gotten the ball right back but safety Jerry Logan bobbled a sure interception. Two plays later, the square-toed shoe of Jets kicker Jim Turner produced a 32-yard field goal and a 10-0 lead.

"That's a hell of a lot more comfortable than just a 7-0 lead," Ewbank said.

The crowd of 75,377 stirred, almost as if they all

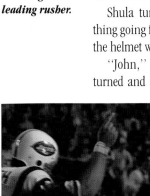

Matt Snell complemented Joe Namath's passing by running for 121 yards on 30 carries. He was the game's leading rusher.

saw the same thing at the same time. As Morrall attempted to drive the Colts, Unitas was warming up.

At the same time, Namath was coming out. After Morrall's last-chance series ended uneventfully, the Jets were on the move again. But Namath suddenly jogged to the sideline, shaking his right hand. His thumb had been sprained for several weeks.

"But this time all it was was a cramp or something," Namath explained.

While he was out, Parilli underthrew a pass, and Turner kicked another field goal from 30 yards.

Shula turned to Unitas and said, "Get something going for us." Unitas nodded and strapped on the helmet with the blue horseshoes.

"John," said the voice behind him. Unitas turned and saw Morrall, who said simply, "Good luck."

Namath left the Orange Bowl signaling the amazing AFL Jets' number-one status.

Ewbank said later, "All of a sudden, I was scared to death. All of us were. We'd seen him [Unitas] make so many big plays for so long."

But Unitas began as if he had nothing up his sleeve but a sore arm: three plays and a punt. And now Namath was back. Passes of 11 and 39 yards to Sauer and strong runs by Snell and Emerson Boozer moved the ball to the Colts' 10.

"Make sure we get points," Ewbank yelled.

Namath nodded. Even rebels understand caution. Ninety-four seconds into the fourth quarter, Turner kicked his third field goal—nine yards— and it was 16-0.

Unitas suddenly got hot. In what seemed like moments, the Colts were at the Jets' 25. Orr broke into the end zone, and Unitas tried to reach him. He pushed the ball, cringing from a shiver of pain. The pass was short. Beverly intercepted.

Later, there was one last consolation prize for the Colts. Using a fourth-down completion, three

Jets penalties, and three tries from inside the New York 1-yard line, the Colts finally scored. Hill's touchdown stopped the shutout after 56 minutes and 41 seconds.

After recovering the onside kick, the Colts still clung to hope. They made it to the Jets' 19 before stalling. On fourth down, Shula decided to forgo the field goal, to try for the touchdown and keep the flickering chance at victory alive. But Unitas's pass to Orr was tipped and the ball flew incomplete.

In the stands, the suddenly large legion of Jets fans chanted, "AFL, AFL, AFL...."

A few minutes after that, as Commissioner Pete Rozelle walked into the locker room, Turner yelled, "Hey Pete, welcome to the AFL."

Later, back at the team hotel, the Jets celebrated their impossible dream with their own party.

Jets assistant coach Walt Michaels was introducing his 73-year-old mother to everyone. He and brother Lou had pooled their winner's and loser's share and each had given half to Mom.

The party lasted long into the next morning. The newsstand ran out of aspirin before it did newspapers. And then because a souvenir doesn't necessarily have to be something you can touch and feel and hold, when the team charter left for New York, somebody, everybody, left behind the 21-inch sterling silver Tiffany trophy and the game ball that had been stored in the hotel vault.

An ecstatic Namath celebrated in the locker room with head coach Weeb Ewbank (left) and Namath's father John. Ewbank also coached the Colts to two NFL championships.

STUNNING VINDICATION

*Kansas City Chiefs 23,
Minnesota Vikings 7*
January 11, 1970

left before their 23-7 victory over the Minnesota Vikings was finished. But Dawson, the Chiefs' quarterback, had to get away.

In the trainer's room, in the luxurious solitude that would not last very long, Dawson tried to let loose, sitting on a table, his bright red Chiefs helmet in his hands. What emotions do you have when the most traumatic week of the most traumatic season has just ended in sublime victory? The Chiefs had scored a huge upset over the Vikings, who had come into the game favored by two touchdowns, and Dawson didn't know whether to laugh or cry.

So he prayed.

A few moments later, he rejoined the world that had thrown so much pain and chaos and confusion at him. And got his fair share of joy, for a change.

Dawson began, "No one can appreciate how much torment...."

A smile interrupted his words, a big ear-to-ear grin that had been stuck inside for a long time.

"I'm vindicated. There's just such a tremendous burden, an emotional burden that's been lifted."

Dawson's smile stopped as an involuntary reaction overcame him. The events started replaying

Kansas City quarterback Len Dawson was named the MVP of Super Bowl IV.

A few minutes earlier, when he came out of the game and the cheers that were for him went unacknowledged because he didn't know how to let loose what he was feeling, Len Dawson walked stoically off the field. The Kansas City Chiefs had a minute

NFL Commissioner Pete Rozelle (left) greeted Chiefs owner Lamar Hunt.

themselves in his mind. The more he relaxed, the more the bizarre lead-in to Super Bowl IV came back to life. For several seconds, he stared at something only he could see. Then blinking back to the moment, he repeated, "Nobody could ever know what this all has been like."

He wanted to think about football, about the three controlled drives he guided that wound up with Jan Stenerud kicking a field goal each time. He wished he could think about the way the Chiefs had cashed in the Vikings' fumbled kickoff, taken over on Minnesota's 19-yard line and suckered Minnesota's defense for the touchdown that gave them a 16-0 lead at halftime. He should have taken time to relish the simple turn-in that resulted in a 46-yard touchdown pass to Otis Taylor that caved in any thought of a Minnesota comeback.

The 23-7 victory was a majestic example of ball-control football with a quarterback dictating the way the game would unfold. Dawson had been that quarterback in charge, and, at the end, the game's most valuable player. But he couldn't enjoy it. Not for a long time.

"It was almost too much to take for a while," Dawson said.

The 1969 season had begun full of promise. In October, though, Dawson's knee had ruptured. He'd rejected surgery, knowing it would put him out for the year. In November, after missing five games because of the injury, Dawson was back, playing on one stiff leg. A week later, two nights before an important game against the Jets, Dawson's father died. The week after that, on Thanksgiving, Dawson reinjured his knee.

Dawson dragged his leg even more, and the Chiefs had to scramble into the revamped AFL playoffs, in which, as the second-place team in the West, they had to play the Eastern champion Jets.

The Chiefs won 13-6 on Dawson's touchdown pass to Gloster Richardson at blustery, cold Shea Stadium. In the AFL Championship Game, with Dawson completing just seven passes, the Chiefs upset the Raiders in Oakland to earn the trip to New Orleans and Super Bowl IV.

Six days before the game, the Chiefs arrived about the same time as a freezing rain. Vikings weather, joked some of the Chiefs. One asked if Minnesota didn't already have everything in its favor.

It sure seemed so. The Vikings had lost their first game of the regular season and their last. In between, they had won 12 straight. The Purple People Eaters defense had allowed an NFL modern-record low 133 points. The Minnesota offense, led by maverick quarterback Joe Kapp, had been dominating, three times scoring more than 50 points in a game. Oddsmakers immediately declared the Vikings would win easily. The game seemed to border on a mismatch.

George Blanda, the ageless Oakland quarterback, scoffed at the swift rush to judgment.

"They're doing it again," Blanda said. "They haven't learned a thing since last year. They're underestimating the AFL all over again."

But a lack of respect soon would become the least of their problems. Dawson and road roommate Johnny Robinson, a safety who had gone to college at LSU, promptly found a restaurant specializing in Cajun cuisine. It was the last happy meal Dawson would have all week.

The next morning, Kansas City head coach

The first time they touched the ball, the Chiefs drove to a 48-yard field goal by Jan Stenerud. He kicked two more in the second quarter as Kansas City took a 9-0 lead, which rose to a surprising 16-0 at halftime.

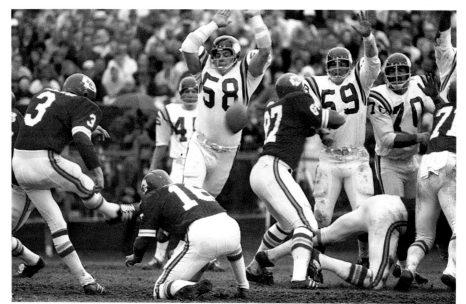

Mike Garrett gave Kansas City a 16-0 lead when he took a handoff from Len Dawson (16) and ran five yards for a touchdown. Garrett's run came on third down.

Hank Stram received some disturbing news from an NFL security man. NBC was going to air a story during the Huntley-Brinkley evening news of a "special Justice Department task force conducting what is described as the biggest gambling investigation of its kind ever...."

The report would say there were seven professional football players and one college coach who were going to be subpoenaed to testify about their respective relationships with a known gambler in Detroit. A man named Donald (Dice) Dawson had been arrested on New Year's Day with several hundred thousand dollars in checks and alleged gambling records in his possession.

In those records were the names of the players and the coach. One of the football players allegedly was Len Dawson.

Stram and Dawson spent most of the day in meetings. NFL security people wanted to know how much, if any, of the report was true. The gambler's name was Donald Dawson. Was he any relation to Len Dawson?

"None...he's just a man I met several years

Minnesota rallied in the third quarter with a 69-yard touchdown drive that cut the Chiefs' lead to 16-7. Dave Osborn (center) got the score with a four-yard run, after Joe Kapp completed four successive passes on the drive.

earlier, when I played for Pittsburgh," Dawson said, his words trembling as they came out. "Bobby Layne introduced him to me."

Donald Dawson had called the Chiefs' quarterback twice during the regular season. The first time was after the knee injury. The second time was after the death of Len Dawson's father. There had been no business dealings, no exchange of information involving football. In summary, no gambling.

The names of four professional quarterbacks, including Joe Namath, were supposedly mentioned among Donald Dawson's records. But only one of those quarterbacks was getting ready to play in the Super Bowl—Len Dawson.

Jackie Dawson, Len's wife, was bombarded with telephone calls the next day. Their children were afraid to go to school.

The year before, similar rumblings had been heard by the NFL, and Dawson had been asked to take a polygraph (lie detector) test. Dawson passed.

After talking to Dawson and reconfirming his player's innocence, Stram became furious.

"This is not fair," Stram snarled. "This is very unfair, not only to the player, but to the human being. Very unfair and very cruel."

The NFL office issued a formal statement echoing Stram's feelings, claiming the report was "totally irresponsible." Commissioner Pete Rozelle said, "We have no evidence to even consider disciplinary action against any of those publicly named."

It was this unsettling atmosphere that welcomed Len Dawson and the Kansas City Chiefs to Louisiana's Crescent City.

Robinson said later that Dawson barely slept all week. Mail arrived daily, more and more as Sunday neared. Dawson said he hadn't received a single piece of negative mail. But Robinson worried for his teammate.

"He never had a tougher week in his life," Robinson said. "It ate him up. From the day it all started, up to game time, he looked like he aged five years. One night I forced him to go out and have some oysters...before the walls closed in on him. And the night before the game, I doubt if he slept three hours. He was so bothered by everything that he got sick to his stomach."

That same night, Ed Sabol of NFL Films, asked Stram for a favor.

"Let me put a live mike on you," Sabol said.

"Don't you think this has been a tough enough week?" Stram responded. "Why me?"

"Because [Vikings coach] Bud Grant isn't animated," Sabol said. "Besides, I think the Chiefs have a great chance to win. Also, Hank, you don't use profanities."

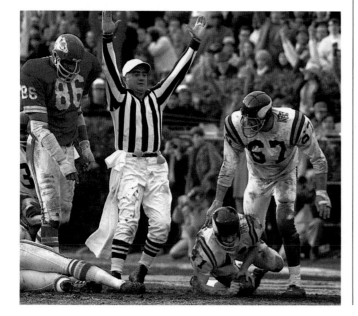

"You're damn right I don't," Stram said.

On game day Stram went for a walk before dawn with a friend who was a priest. It was still cold. Stram noticed that a fountain in front of the hotel still was frozen, and he wondered if his building optimism was a fool's folly. But within an hour a warming trend had begun.

The game films Stram had labored over all week were so obvious: The Vikings couldn't run on the Chiefs' defense.

Vikings center Mick Tingelhoff would not be able to scoot off the line and make blocks on middle linebacker Willie Lanier. That's because Chiefs tackle Buck Buchanan would line up inches away from the center. Using an odd alignment along the scrimmage line, the Chiefs would shield Lanier, who then could make tackles at will.

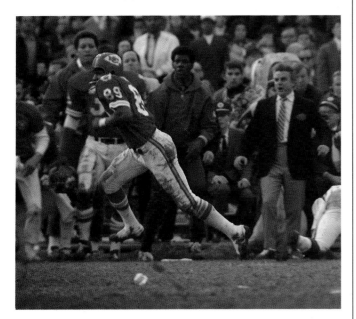

Kansas City's Otis Taylor broke two tackles on a 46-yard touchdown catch-and-run that built the Chiefs' lead to 23-7 in the third quarter. The elusive Taylor caught six passes from Dawson for 81 yards in the game.

Defensive end Jerry Mays said the triple-stack plan would work only if the Vikings ran to the strongside, their normal offense. If Minnesota ran to the weakside, the Chiefs were vulnerable.

"But they never varied from their game plan all game," Mays said later. "They kept running into our strength. It never changed. Strongside, strongside—all game long."

It wasn't until the third quarter that the Vikings were able to rush for a first down. By then, the game was in the Chiefs' clutches. In the third quarter, after the Vikings had made their first offensive thrust and scored on a Dave Osborn run, the Chiefs had countered with the look-in pass to Taylor.

"That thing was just a little pass," Dawson said. "It's really not designed to go all the way. Otis is just a great athlete. He made the last forty yards on his own."

Interceptions by Robinson and Lanier put out mild Vikings fires, and, in the fourth quarter, Joe Kapp, the NFL's most valuable player during the regular season, staggered off the field after being sacked and injuring his shoulder.

The Chiefs intercepted three passes, including this one by Willie Lanier.

Dawson watched Kapp, trying to feel what he was feeling. He remembered Super Bowl I against Green Bay, and the empty feeling he had as the game slipped out of hope's reach.

In a few minutes, backup quarterback Mike Livingston was sent onto the field to replace Dawson. At the sideline, Stram tapped Dawson on the shoulder and said into his hidden microphone, "Great job, Lenny. . .great day."

And Dawson started walking to the locker room.

It was getting easier to celebrate now. His smile was freer. He was thinking about football again. Then somebody told him he had a phone call.

"It's President Nixon."

Dawson smiled and graciously accepted the congratulations of the President. Moments later, his 11-year-old son was hugging him.

"Dad, you did good," the boy said.

The quarterback smiled. And yawned. It wouldn't be hard to get some sleep tonight.

The Chiefs held the Vikings to 239 yards and 13 first downs with inspired defense such as this embrace of Bill Brown by 275-pound defensive tackle Buck Buchanan.

MIDDLE-AGED MAGIC

Oakland Raiders 23,
Cleveland Browns 20
November 8, 1970

George Blanda, 43, was a miracle-worker for the Raiders in 1970.

The word spread quickly around the Oakland Raiders' locker room. Stay away from George. He's edgy. George Blanda, quarterback, placekicker, and inspiration to middle-aged people everywhere, walked around the room in T-shirt and football pants, thinking about the Cleveland Browns.

"I never liked the Browns," he said later.

The more the 43-year-old Blanda thought about the Browns, the Raiders' opponents that day, the more angry he became.

Twenty-one years of pro football and never once

a win over the Browns. Blanda never had played on a team that beat Cleveland.

Blanda told a couple of teammates he never wanted to win a game as much.

"If I have to keep playing until I'm 100 I'm going to know what it feels like to beat that damn team," he said.

In 1970, Monday Night Football was new, and Blanda was flipping the pages of the calendar the wrong way. The Raiders had put him on waivers before the season, which might have been a jolt to someone else's pride. But because he had been released twice—in 1959 by the Chicago Bears at age 31, in 1967 by Houston at age 39— enough calluses had grown on his ego to withstand just about any-thing. Except another loss to the Browns.

Blanda remembered the time he was with the Bears, the quarterback for head coach George Halas, the next NFL superstar. But a separated shoulder cost Blanda his starting job and he never got it back. It was the only serious injury he ever had.

"I got it playing against the Browns," Blanda said.

The Raiders' game against Cleveland was going to start soon, and Blanda paced impatiently. In the last two weeks he had come off the bench to direct great escapes. Against Pittsburgh, Blanda had relieved Daryle Lamonica when Lamonica's bad back hampered his passing.

"The Old Man came out firing," said John Madden, the Raiders' head coach who was nine years younger than Blanda. The proud old warhorse was called on against the Steelers before halftime, and he threw two touchdown passes and kicked a field goal. The Raiders never looked back, winning 31-14. The following week, in Kansas City, where the annual Chiefs-Raiders free-for-all was winding down to its final seconds, Blanda had wheezed out to midfield, taken a step forward, and popped a 48-yard field goal that salvaged a 17-17 tie.

"We've made some big plays with Blanda," Madden said in the week before the Browns game. "He's played great. But Lamonica's back is better. He's going to start against the Browns."

Personal disappointment quickly was put aside. Blanda wanted to play. But he knew the younger Lamonica probably was the better quarterback at this stage. After all, Blanda was playing in his fourth decade, having come into pro football in 1949. There were lots of other quarterbacks breaking into pro football around that time. Johnny Lujack, Y.A. Tittle, Charlie Conerly, Bobby Layne, Harry Gilmer, Norm Van Brocklin. All of the rest of them were long gone from active rosters in 1970.

"As long as we win, that's all that really matters," Blanda said.

When Blanda kicked a 43-yard field goal in the first quarter to give the Raiders the early lead at Oakland-Alameda County Coliseum, the place erupted. The sheet banner that said "Welcome to the Old Folks Home" rippled in the Bay Area breeze.

Blanda was among the first to run onto the field to greet Lamonica after his touchdown pass had put the Raiders ahead 10-0. When Blanda added another field goal and the lead jumped to 13 points in the second quarter, he started to feel like today was going to be his lucky day against his hated rivals.

Madden also was feeling confident. The Browns were stymied by the Raiders' defense. Quarterback Bill Nelsen was having trouble throwing downfield. Cleveland's running back Leroy Kelly was slipping out and catching little dink passes.

But when one of those little flips finished off a Browns drive and Kelly scored a touchdown, Madden became alarmed. His offense seemed to have gone into deep slumber.

The Browns came back again, a field goal by Don Cockroft cutting the Raiders' lead to 13-10.

At halftime, Blanda was feeling some old twing-

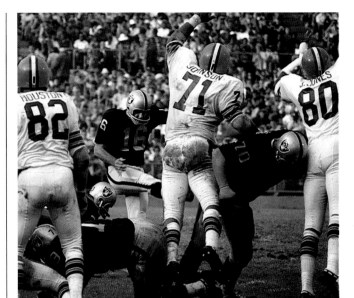

es. Madden was concerned with Lamonica, who suddenly was sputtering. Madden already was thinking about a possible change. But he decided to stick with Lamonica a while longer.

In the third quarter, the Raiders got as close as the Cleveland 19 before rolling to a stop. And when Blanda's 27-yard chip-shot field goal missed, Madden kicked the ground in front of him.

On the last play of the third quarter, Browns running back Bo Scott took a handoff, slipped out of a tackle at the line of scrimmage, and broke free. Only one Raider had a chance to catch Scott, and safety George Atkinson seemed to be closing fast.

"But I saw [Cleveland wide receiver] Fair Hooker running beside me," Scott said. "I faked a lateral to him and it made the guy chasing me hesitate."

It was just enough. On Scott's 63-yard run, the Browns went ahead 17-13.

An interception in the end zone ended another Cleveland threat.

With 10:20 to play, Lamonica dropped back, looking for a home-run throw. Tight end Raymond Chester was the deep man. But Browns defensive end Ron Snidow crashed through and blindsided Lamonica. Worse, Lamonica landed on his left shoulder and needed help to leave the field.

Madden sweated in any kind of weather. And he was sweating. He looked for the Old Man.

"George!"

Blanda nodded. Again the familiar waddle. The silvery sideburns. He may have been a physical wonder, with a body still finely tuned, but he still looked every bit of 43.

The Raiders couldn't move. They punted, and Cleveland got another field goal for a 20-13 lead.

In the first half, Blanda kicked 43- and 9-yard field goals as the Raiders took a 13-0 lead. But the Browns scored 20 successive points to go ahead 20-13 in the second half.

Then Blanda was intercepted by linebacker Bob Matheson. The reign of the miracle worker in Oakland seemed at an end. But because nobody could see the internal fires being stoked by white-hot anger, nobody could know that George Blanda had decided the Raiders were going to win.

"Somehow I had this angry feeling," he said. "It's not going to happen again. I wouldn't let it."

So while he was looking up and noticing there still was 4:11 to play, Blanda suddenly felt the humbling circumstances falling into place: This is it.

Passing almost exclusively, Blanda guided Oakland into field-goal range. But only a touchdown would do, so, on fourth-and-16 at the Browns' 31, this old fossil felt he had to make something special happen.

Lamonica twisted and turned on the bench, his body English matching the route his elderly replacement was taking in an effort to get away from the Browns' pass rush. Lamonica's ice pack slipped off his shoulder when Blanda, throwing off the wrong foot, off-balance and awkward, hit wide receiver Fred Biletnikoff with a 17-yard completion to the Cleveland 14.

Even though he got tired and had to inhale oxygen on the sideline, Blanda completed 7 of 12 passes for 102 yards and a touchdown after replacing Daryle Lamonica in the fourth quarter. He also kicked three field goals in the game.

Several Browns leveled Blanda on the play. At least one of them, Blanda thought, had been uncommonly aggressive.

Blanda fired off a few unkind words, and got some back in return.

He called a time out and talked strategy with Madden while squatted like an Indian. Between gulps of air, Blanda said he wanted to pass. Madden said he thought a run would be better. Blanda argued. And won.

He called a pass, and told wide receiver Warren Wells, "It's going to be low and it's going to be fast. No more interceptions."

Wells made the catch, rolling into the end zone. Blanda kicked the extra point, and the game was tied 20-20 with 79 seconds to go.

"What a comeback," gushed Bill King, the play-by-play man on the Raiders' radio network. King had no idea he was being premature.

Cleveland head coach Blanton Collier felt the Browns would be able to move back into a position for Don Cockroft to win the game with a field goal. "Make all the passes safe ones," Collier told Nelsen. "No high-risk passes."

Cleveland tight end Milt Morin flashed open in the secondary. The outside defender, cornerback Kent McCloughan, realized where Nelsen was throwing and closed toward Morin. It's a play that Nelsen said he'll always regret. McCloughan stepped in front of Morin, and there was a moment of struggle. But McCloughan had the interception, and the Raiders had the ball at their 46-yard line.

Blanda took a couple of blasts from the oxygen tank. He looked exhausted.

"Unbelievably tired," he said later. "The emotion had gotten to me. But the adrenalin kept it from coming out until later."

Blanda's first pass was incomplete, but an interference call moved the Raiders to the Browns' 39. Then Blanda was decked by defensive end Jack Gregory for a 10-yard loss. Gregory and Blanda had been trading insults for several minutes. Gregory was taking the heat for all 21 seasons of Blanda's frustration.

With no time outs left, and 16 seconds on the clock, Blanda threw an incompletion. On third down, running back Hewritt Dixon started in motion a half-count early. The Raiders picked up four yards on the short pass, but Oakland was called for illegal procedure.

If the Browns had refused the penalty, they would have forced Blanda to try a 56-yard field goal. That same day, Tom Dempsey of the New Orleans Saints kicked a 63-yard field goal, the longest in pro football history. The old record was 56 yards.

Collier gave Blanda the ultimate respect. He was

afraid a 43-year-old man, who'd just been flattened and obviously was tired, was capable of kicking a field goal of 56 yards.

"I couldn't believe it when they took the penalty," Madden said.

The repeated third down was a calculated risk, Collier said.

"If we make one play, we've stopped them and I'm sure they're out of Blanda's range," the Browns' coach said.

Blanda's pass was caught by Dixon, who dived out of bounds after a nine-yard gain. Gregory was just about to unload on Blanda when the ball was thrown. Instinctively, Blanda wheeled around and appeared to throw a punch at Gregory.

The ball was on the 45—seven seconds left.

Wide receiver Warren Wells caught a 14-yard touchdown pass from Blanda to tie the score 20-20 with 1:19 left. Then the Raiders got the ball back on an interception.

Blanda looked around. Who's holding for the kick? If Lamonica's out, who's holding?

Ken Stabler trotted by Blanda, who nodded. Some kickers worry about new holders.

"They're probably the same ones who can hear the crowd. . .or other players," Blanda said.

Not Blanda. He went into his solitary bubble, alone with his thoughts, which were nothing more than trying to think about basic fundamentals. But then a thought interfered: It was the end of the frustration. . .kick the Browns.

While everyone else's pulse was pounding like a frog's throat, Blanda was alone in the bubble.

"When my toe hit the ball," he said, "I knew it was good. Distance didn't matter. It was going through."

His distance was a couple yards more than the needed 52. In the booth, King was babbling bonkers, assaulting perspective. Blanda went to the sideline, where Madden smothered him with a hug.

One kickoff later, the game was over. Oakland celebrated so hard the Bay Bridge probably vibrated.

"The Lord's been with us the last few weeks," Blanda said. He acted nonchalant after the game. But it was more like he was busy purging a lot of out-of-date frustrations from his system. The 251st field goal and 228th touchdown pass of his everlasting career had made all the rage go away.

But there still were more miracles lurking inside. The next week he threw a touchdown pass with a minute left to beat Denver 24-19, then made it five miracles in a row by kicking a field goal as time ran out to defeat San Diego 20-17.

Blanda was named the NFL's player of the year, but he said, "To be honest, all forty-three of them have been pretty good. This one just seems to be the best. At least until next year."

In 1976, George Blanda, an American story of ongoing dignity, retired. America was 200 at the time. Blanda was 48.

Just seconds remained when Blanda boomed a 52-yard field goal to win the game. He saved three games in five weeks with last-second field goals.

There was no Presidential election in 1970, but if there had been, Blanda would have carried Oakland.

CHRISTMAS CHEERS

Miami Dolphins 27,
Kansas City Chiefs 24
December 25, 1971

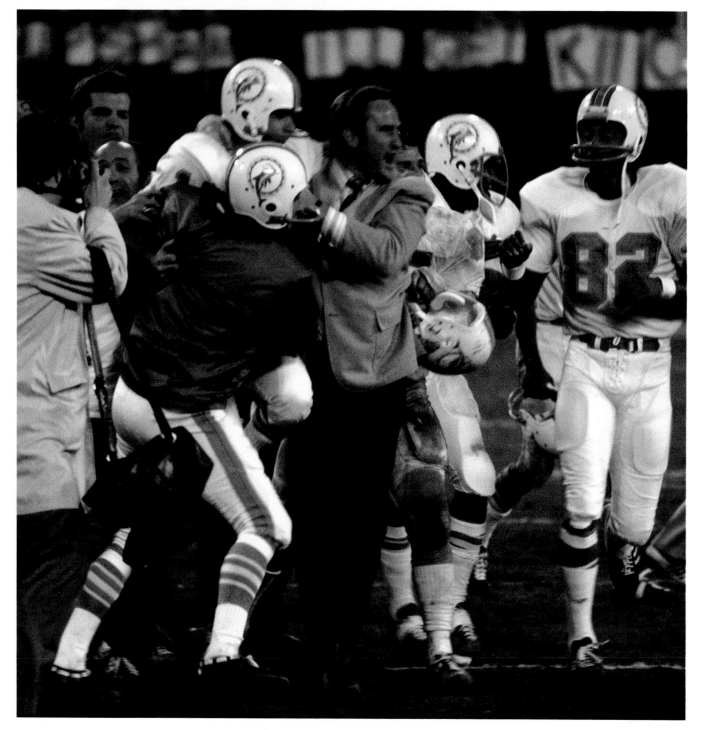

At Gate 77 of Miami International Airport, two policemen and an airline attendant watched the door of the charter plane open.

"Are you Garo Yepremian?" one of the policemen asked.

The short man with the bald head nodded.

"You'd better come with us."

At 11:50 P.M. there were only 10 minutes left of Christmas Day. But about 100 feet away, an expectant mob was so rabid with anticipation you'd have thought Santa Claus was making a return trip.

"It's for your protection, Garo," said the other policeman. "They're so happy to see you guys, they might kill somebody. Especially you."

Several other Miami Dolphins went first. The plan was that they would deflect some of the attention away from Yepremian, the least likely looking hero of the most unlikely football game ever played. Earlier Christmas Day, the Dolphins had beaten the Kansas City Chiefs 27-24. In the longest game ever played—82 minutes and 40 seconds—the Dolphins had claimed their first-ever playoff victory on a 37-yard field goal by Yepremian.

"There are probably seventeen, eighteen thousand people in there," the policeman said.

Five years earlier, the Dolphins and Chiefs had played a game at the Orange Bowl that had also gone down to the final seconds. The Chiefs had won that one. The announced crowd was 17,884.

"We've come a long way," beamed Joe Robbie, the Dolphins' owner. "I can remember that game, how disappointed I was that we couldn't attract anybody. Now look."

The Miami International concourse was jammed. The screams and cheers were deafening. Remember, it was 10 'til midnight on Christmas Day.

Yepremian was bordered by police. Someone spotted him, and people rushed toward him. His escorts started to flex their authority. Yepremian stopped them.

"It's okay," he said. "I love this. Today I am the happiest man. Can you believe this?"

Two time zones away, the Kansas City Chiefs already had gone to bed. Sleep came not as hard as someone might expect for Jan Stenerud. A few days later, after watching a replay of the game, Stenerud would struggle considerably more, confess his pain and guilt were unbearable, and say he never wanted to play football again. But tonight, he didn't have to wrestle with any memory of a fluttering football for long. He was comfortably numb and was able to pass out from exhaustion.

"I guess it was some kind of shock or something," said the Chiefs' placekicker. "I think, though, the last thing I thought about before sleeping was how I couldn't believe what had happened."

A tale of two feet. A left foot that won a game. A right foot that was wrong. Garo Yepremian, the disbelieving hero. Jan Stenerud, the man who would like to take his right foot and kick himself.

In Miami, the mob inched closer to Yepremian, pushing their way with smiles and cheers toward their hero. Then Yepremian held up both hands and made a serious plea.

"My feet, please don't step on my feet," he said.

Twelve hours earlier, Dolphins head coach Don Shula had flinched. He didn't like the familiar feeling as his team climbed aboard the buses that would take them to Kansas City Municipal Stadium. On the road, playing on Christmas Day. "I hoped this one would be a little merrier," Shula said.

The year before, the Oakland Raiders had bounced the Dolphins out of the playoffs two days after Christmas. The memory was double-edged.

Kansas City's Ed Podolak gained 350 all-purpose yards and scored twice, including this seven-yard reception of a pass from Len Dawson. Podolak ran for 85 yards, caught eight passes for 110 more, and had 155 yards on kick returns.

Miami head coach Don Shula helped carry Garo Yepremian off the field after he ended the longest game in NFL history (82 minutes, 40 seconds) with a 37-yard field goal. The Dolphins outlasted the Chiefs 27-24 in their 1971 playoff game.

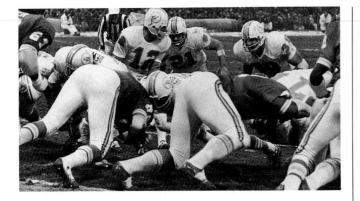

Trailing 10-0, Miami scored for the first time when reliable Larry Csonka (39) took a handoff from Bob Griese (12) and bulled a yard in the second quarter. Csonka led the Dolphins in rushing with 86 yards.

Shula wanted his players to remember the empty feeling. He also didn't want them to repeat the situations that led to that gnawing pain.

"And this time, we had the Kansas City Chiefs, who had probably the best overall personnel in the league," Shula said. "And we had never beaten the Chiefs."

In fact, that game in the Orange Bowl five years

The Chiefs took a 17-10 lead in the third quarter when Jim Otis (35) sailed one yard for a touchdown.

earlier was easily the closest to victory the Dolphins ever had come against the Chiefs. In six meetings, Kansas City had outscored Miami 183-47. The Dolphins had been shut out four times.

The Chiefs, who had won Super Bowl IV in 1970 with almost the same team, were favored to defeat the Dolphins again. On the morning of the game, Kansas City quarterback Len Dawson watched the fog quickly burning away and didn't like what was taking its place.

"It was really nice out," Dawson said. "Kansas City at Christmas time can be bitterly cold at times. We were hoping for that. But what we got was Miami weather."

By the opening kickoff, it was 63 degrees, and, according to Dawson, "like no other Christmas I ever saw in Kansas City."

Chiefs head coach Hank Stram had figured if his team could control the Dolphins' ability to run outside, they would win the game. Miami had Larry Csonka and Jim Kiick and a speedy bunch of linemen. Stram said the Dolphins reminded him of the old Lombardi Packers when they ran a sweep.

"But I've got some awful good linebackers," Stram said, "so it's going to be interesting all day."

Linebackers Jim Lynch, Willie Lanier, and Bobby Bell were masters of pursuit, and, by shading to the outside, they did control the Dolphins' offense for

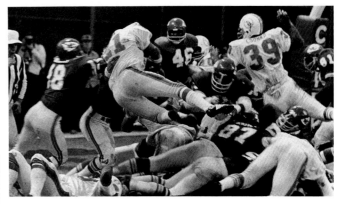

After the Chiefs drove 75 yards for a third-quarter touchdown, Miami retaliated with a 71-yard drive that ended when Jim Kiick went airborne for another one-yard touchdown. Kiick's touchdown tied the game at 17-17.

most of the game.

Shula felt the key to stopping the Chiefs was not letting Otis Taylor break any long pass plays.

"He's excellent after he catches the ball," Shula said. "We've got to find some way to make sure he doesn't hurt us."

A standard double-team did it. Second-year cornerback Curtis Johnson, with safety Dick Anderson assisting, controlled Taylor with three harmless catches for 12 yards.

"But a good team finds other ways," Shula said. "That day, both teams made great adjustments. For us, Bob Griese was on the money with his passing and play-calling. And, for them, Ed Podolak was just unstoppable. We still haven't stopped Podolak. That's what made it such a good game— both teams were doing the things defensively they needed to be doing. But both offenses still were finding ways to move the ball."

Of course, the resulting marathon meant a lot of Christmas dinners burned, got cold, or went uneaten. And Garo Yepremian and Jan Stenerud, respective natives of Cyprus and Norway, seized the responsibility of winning and losing with two feet.

Fact is, Yepremian's field goal never should have happened. An hour earlier, Stenerud should have

With 1:36 left in regulation, Griese eluded linebacker Bobby Bell (78) and fired a five-yard touchdown pass to Marv Fleming.

kicked a field goal that would have won the game.

"I still don't know what went wrong," Stenerud said. "I had missed earlier because we were trying a fake and, instead, our center hiked the ball for the kick. I had missed another one because it got blocked. But this one, everything went perfect. I thought. I should make those kind in my sleep."

The Dolphins had just tied the game. Yepremian had kicked off and everyone already was thinking about overtime because there was only about a minute to play in regulation. But Podolak took the kickoff and found a little hole and then a big one. At midfield, there was one player to beat and it was Yepremian, all 5 feet, 7 inches and 165 pounds of him. Podolak already had rushed for 85 yards, caught passes for 110 more, and now he had one little guy to beat to put the exclamation point on one of the greatest one-man offensive shows ever.

"I gave him a shove," Yepremian said. "He didn't go down."

But Podolak did have to shift gears, break stride, and rev back up. And that allowed Curtis Johnson to angle over and drag him down at the Miami 22.

"It saved the touchdown," Stram said, "but we were in Jan's chip-shot range. We figured it was all over. I think everyone in the stadium, maybe including the Miami Dolphins, figured it was over. Jan just doesn't miss from there."

Three safe handoffs later, with 35 seconds left in regulation, Stenerud jogged onto the field. In between the 31- and 32-yard lines of the Dolphins, quarterback Len Dawson knelt and patted the ground. This is where he would place the ball down. Stenerud nodded.

The game the Dolphins had just tied with a desperation drive in which Bob Griese had passed brilliantly, converting three third-down dilemmas into first downs, and tight end Marv Fleming had made a nifty catch for the tying touchdown with less than two minutes to play, was just about to be untied.

A perfect snap, a perfect catch, and a perfect

placement preceded what Stenerud thought was a perfect kick. So accustomed were Chiefs fans to Stenerud's dependability that they cheered immediately. Even when the ball curiously hung to the right, not hooking like the usual soccer-style kicker's ball does, the crowd cheered out of reflex response. Stram himself raised his arms.

Referee John McDonough did not.

By inches, the ball was wide right.

Stenerud hung his head, then looked back at the goal posts.

"All day, we let them have new life," Lanier said. "Early in the game, we were up by ten and we had them third-and-long. I figured if we held that one play, we'd be right back in the end zone. It would be over early and everyone could go home and enjoy Christmas. But Griese hit a big pass to Paul Warfield. They got new life there. They kept getting new lives all day."

The Dolphins had scored a touchdown in the second quarter to trim Kansas City's lead to 10-7, but the Chiefs responded with a quick charge back upfield. When the drive stalled at the Miami 22, Stenerud came on for the apparent field goal.

"But it was a fake," Stenerud said. "Bobby Bell [who snapped on field goals] was supposed to center the ball directly to me and I was supposed to run around end."

But Bell didn't think Stenerud had heard the audible call. And he wasn't sure what he had heard, either. He decided to snap the ball regularly for a kick. A surprised Dawson caught it, placed it down,

After Griese's pass to Fleming tied the score 24-24, Kansas City's Ed Podolak returned the next kickoff 78 yards to the Dolphins' 22. The long return set up Jan Stenerud for a potential game-winning field goal, but he missed.

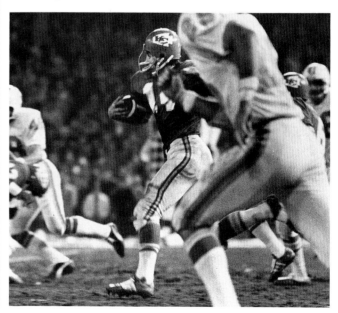

Kansas City's Jan Stenerud stared at the ground in frustration after missing a 31-yard field goal with 35 seconds left in regulation that would have won the game. He also missed a 24-yard kick and had a 42-yard attempt blocked.

In the third quarter, the Chiefs drove 75 yards for the go-ahead touchdown. They used up almost 10 minutes, scoring on fullback Jim Otis's short plunge up the middle.

"Except for those couple plays right before the half," said Miami fullback Larry Csonka, "we hadn't been on the field for a long time."

But the Dolphins came back. Kiick scored, and it was tied again. On the first play of the fourth quarter, Nick Buoniconti recovered a fumble at the Chiefs' 47-yard line. Griese had the Dolphins rolling again. Then Chiefs linebacker Jim Lynch intercepted at the Kansas City 9.

"That time, we got some new life handed to us," Lanier conceded.

A few plays later, the Chiefs looked totally resurrected. Dawson, unable to throw long most of the day, spotted Elmo Wright breaking free over the

Early in the first overtime, Stenerud's 42-yard field-goal try was blocked by Dolphins linebacker Nick Buoniconti (85).

and yelled, "Kick it, Jan! Kick it!"

Stenerud already had taken a step in motion. He stopped, tried to get in rhythm, and his kick was wide to the right.

The Dolphins capitalized on a fumble recovery to get a field goal by Yepremian with 16 seconds left in the half to tie the score at 10-10.

"We could have buried them two or three times already," Lanier said.

middle. Dolphins safety Jake Scott finally rode Wright down at the Miami 3. On the next play, Podolak took a pitch and scored standing up. Now the Chiefs led 24-17.

There would now be no surprises. Griese had to pass. The Chiefs knew it and almost disregarded the Miami running game. Shula felt a reverse might break a big play. Instead, Warfield fumbled and only the alertness of center Bob DeMarco, who recovered, prevented total disaster.

On third-and-13, Griese passed to Warfield for 17 yards. Two plays later, he hit Warfield with a 26-yard completion. A pass to Howard Twilley set up a five-yard touchdown pass to Fleming, tying the game 24-24.

And that set up Podolak's kickoff return and Stenerud's failure with 35 seconds left.

While Bob Griese discussed strategy with coaches in the press box, head coach Don Shula talked with backup quarterback George Mira.

The Chiefs won the coin flip in overtime and chose to receive. Yepremian's kick went out of the end zone, but the Dolphins were flagged for illegal procedure. They had to kick again.

"This one I didn't kick very good," Yepremian said.

The ball went to Buck Buchanan, normally a defensive tackle who blocked on kickoffs. Buchanan turned and lateraled the ball to Podolak, who once again almost broke free before he was pulled down at the Chiefs' 46. Podolak would be involved in 350 of the Chiefs' 606 total yards. Moving to the Miami 35, Stenerud came on to try to win the game once more. But Buoniconti smothered the kick.

Lanier slammed his helmet against a bench.

Later in the first overtime period, Yepremian tried to end it. But his 52-yarder was off to the left.

"I was very close to making that one," he said. "It gave me confidence. If I got another chance, I knew I'd make it," he said.

The chance came 7:40 into the second overtime, a point in time at which no pro football game ever had been.

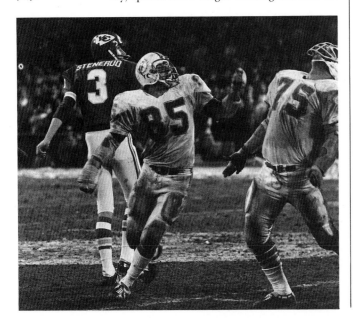

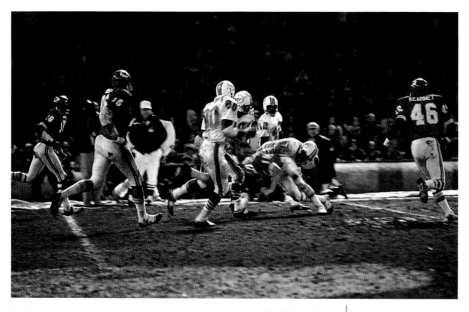

In the second overtime, Larry Csonka set up Miami's winning field goal with this 29-yard run to the Chiefs' 36. Garo Yepremian's winning kick went 37 yards to send the Dolphins to their first AFC Championship Game.

Miami had been frustrated all day by the Chiefs' defense and their ability to shut down their outside running game. Csonka and Griese combed their brains for a play that might work. Finally they decided: Roll Right, Trap Left . . . the Csonka special.

The flow of the play was to the right, Kiick moving that way and Griese as well. Only as he moved, Griese made an inside handoff to Csonka.

"Larry Little and Norm Evans were leading for me," Csonka said. "I hooked behind Larry and we looked like a convoy of eighteen-wheelers."

Buchanan had the only legitimate shot at tackling Csonka near the line of scrimmage. He missed. Csonka ran 29 yards before he was stopped at the Kansas City 36.

"Now they were in my territory," Yepremian said.

Yepremian had led the league in scoring, kicking more field goals than anyone else, but he had been beaten out for the AFC Pro Bowl spot . . . by Stenerud. The chance to show that everyone had been wrong was moments away.

At the 37-yard line, Karl Noonan reached for DeMarco's snap and placed it onto the ground. Yepremian took one short step, then chopped at the ball.

"It was good, I knew it was good," Yepremian said. "But then I thought, 'Garo, this is the most important field goal of your life. Turn and watch it.' I looked back just in time to see the signal."

Referee John McDonough's hands were up. The game—more like the game and a half—was over.

Yepremian forgot. He was headed to the sideline for a kicking tee. He was going to kick off.

"Then I realized it was over," he said. "We had won."

Delayed reactions were the order of the day. Buoniconti said, "My emotions are stuck inside. When it's eighty-two minutes and then it's over, you don't feel much of anything."

Norm Evans said there shouldn't be a loser in games such as this. But he didn't think about what he was saying.

After all, who wants a tie for Christmas?

A few years later, Stenerud was asked if he considered the game the best he'd ever been a part of. Even then, the disappointment still registered.

"I suppose that if you look at it from an unselfish point of view, it was a fantastic game," Stenerud said. "But, to my mind, it will only stick out as an unbelievable personal disaster, the worst feeling I ever could have in football."

Two years later, Yepremian, who played with the Dolphins in three Super Bowls, said of that Christmas in Kansas City, "I still consider it the best feeling I ever had in a game."

A tale of two feet. A left one and a wrong one.

Yepremian celebrated his winning field goal, which ended the Christmas Day classic in the sixth period.

THE IMMACULATE RECEPTION

Pittsburgh Steelers 13,
Oakland Raiders 7
December 23, 1972

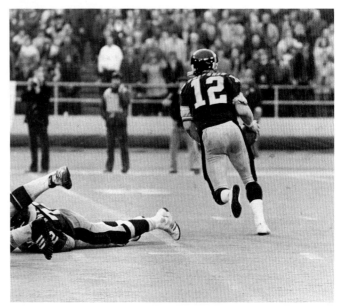

With 22 seconds left in their 1972 playoff game, the Steelers trailed the Raiders 7-6 as Terry Bradshaw faded to pass on fourth-and-10 at his own 40...

In the upper-level stands at Three Rivers Stadium in Pittsburgh, Mario Camaioni looked at his hand siren that just quit working on the last incomplete pass.

"All I can do now is pray," said Camaioni, a bus driver for the Pittsburgh metro transportation department.

On the third level, Art Rooney, owner of the Pittsburgh Steelers, smushed out his cigar, rose slowly, and headed for the private elevator. A security guard said something to him about next year. Rooney nodded. He wanted to get down to the locker room to tell his players not to forget what a great season it had been anyway. He wanted to talk to the players privately, without any media, without any fanfare. That's why he was taking the elevator before the fourth-down play.

On the field, in the Steelers' huddle, quarterback Terry Bradshaw licked his fingers and said, "66 Option."

Several yards away, in the huddle of the Oakland Raiders, hard-hitting safety Jack Tatum wore his usual scowl and said, just barely loud enough for his teammates to hear, "One more time."

It sounded more like a hiss. It was fourth down at the Pittsburgh 40-yard line. There were 22 seconds left in the AFC Divisional Playoff Game, which Oakland led 7-6. It had been a monstrous defensive struggle, and Pittsburgh had led most of the game because of two field goals by Roy Gerela. But with 1:13 remaining, backup quarterback Kenny Stabler, taking over for flu-ridden and ineffective Daryle Lamonica, had scrambled 30 yards to score.

Three consecutive passes by Bradshaw had been incomplete. There was one play left.

Somewhere between the mezzanine and ground levels, Art Rooney and six friends, including the late baseball announcer Bob Prince, rode in complete silence. There just wasn't anything to say.

Just before the ball was snapped, John Fuqua, the outrageous running back everyone called Frenchy, shot a somber glance downfield and whispered a final wish.

"I was thinking how I wished it didn't have to end like this," Fuqua would admit 15 years later. "But I never dreamed, not in any of my lifetimes, it

...He rolled to his right to escape defensive end Tony Cline (84), looking downfield for John (Frenchy) Fuqua...

could end like it did. You could never wish something like that."

Twenty-two seconds. The Steelers had been one of the nice stories of 1972 but now there appeared to be less than half a minute left to their season. After so many years of being everyone's whipping boy, decades and decades of never making the playoffs, Pittsburgh finally had a legitimate contender. An 11-3 record and an AFC Central Division championship had charmed a tough blue-collar town. The season-long love affair had spawned so many

field. Ten yards behind Fuqua, Tatum already had his foot planted. Tatum had it timed so if the ball did come to Fuqua, he'd be there to stop it.

The ball and Jack Tatum arrived at Fuqua at the same time. The collision was violent.

"It always was with Tatum," Fuqua said. "When I made my hook, I was wide open but Terry was getting pressure. Then all I can hear is Tatum coming up. I can hear him breathing. I can hear his steps. With Tatum, you knew he was going to knock your crown off. I didn't consider him a dirty

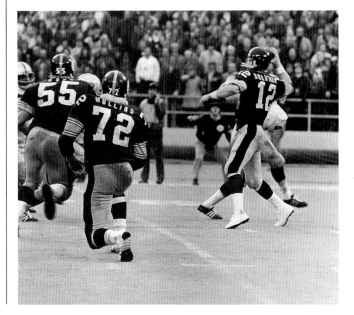

...As Bradshaw planted his feet, end Horace Jones closed in on him while Pittsburgh tackle Gerry Mullins (72) watched...

fan clubs—from Franco's Italian Army to Fuqua's Foreign Legion to Gerela's Gorillas—that it seemed a shame to Rooney things should have to come to such a sad and disappointing end.

"It's easy to say we didn't deserve to lose after we played so well," Rooney would say later. "It's easy to feel selfish or sorry for yourself. But those players and those fans— they deserved to win that game. They really did."

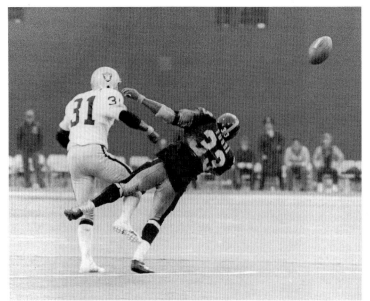

...Finally, Bradshaw wound up and threw for Fuqua (33, below), who was hit by Oakland's Jack Tatum as the ball arrived. It rebounded off one or both of them 15 yards backward...

Bradshaw took the snap and took the standard seven-step drop. But Oakland's Otis Sistrunk and Tony Cline broke through, and Bradshaw was flushed from the pocket. He was scrambling to his right when he saw Fuqua flash open 20 yards down-

player or a cheap-shot artist. He wouldn't grab your finger in a pileup and dislocate it. He didn't kick. He just hit the hell out of you. Every play."

But when Fuqua sensed Tatum was closing upon him and the approaching pass, he adjusted

. . . Running back Franco Harris plucked the ball out of the air off his shoe tops—the Immaculate Reception—and kept running 60 yards for the winning touchdown . . .

his body. "I was trying to make sure I was between him and the ball," Fuqua said. "I was always taught that. And see what I was figuring? If I could catch the ball, maybe we'd be able to try a field goal. Hell—I might even break the tackle and go all the way, win the game, and be on Johnny Carson as the first black king of Pennsylvania. But first I had to make sure Tatum couldn't get to the ball."

What happened next has been analyzed thousands of times and from every angle. Video replays of it do little but prolong arguments. Bradshaw's pass ricocheted backward at least 15 yards where, at shoe level, it was plucked out of the air by Steelers rookie running back Franco Harris, who galloped into the end zone.

Art Rooney heard the roar even before the elevator door opened. Fuqua watched it all upside down. It didn't look any less strange from that viewpoint. Bradshaw flung down his helmet in despair and couldn't figure out what all the excitement was about. He never saw Harris catch the ball; he thought it was just another incomplete pass.

Raiders head coach John Madden sprinted toward the closest official, criss-crossing his arms and screaming, "No good, no good, no good."

Harris wasn't supposed to be where he was when the miracle—the Immaculate Reception, as it came to be called—dropped out of the steel gray winter sky. Harris was supposed to help block for Bradshaw, but when he saw his quarterback scramble to the right, he decided to drift downfield and "either be another target or help block for whoever caught the pass."

In 1972, the NFL rule book stated that any thrown pass touched, tipped, or bounced off one of-

fensive player directly to another was an incomplete pass and a dead ball. Madden and the Raiders pointed accusing fingers at Fuqua, then at Harris. The play was illegal, screamed Madden. It touched two Steelers.

Fuqua, who was knocked backward several yards by Tatum's crashing tackle, said, "I'll never forget the look on Tatum's face while everything was happening. It was like slow-motion; he was smiling and celebrating and then it slowly melted and turned into anger."

There still had been no official signal for a touchdown. Referee Fred Swearingen disappeared into the baseball dugout and reached for the field-level phone. He called league supervisor of officials Art McNally in the press box. Swearingen admitted he didn't know what had happened or exactly who had touched the ball. Umpire Pat Harder and field judge Adrian Burk had told Swearingen they thought both Fuqua and Tatum had touched the pass. McNally agreed.

Swearingen emerged from the dugout, ran onto the field, and raised his arms. Touchdown, Steelers.

Tatum grabbed Fuqua, who still was sitting on the field, and shouted, "Tell them you touched it. Tell them you touched it."

Fuqua then erupted with cackling laughter.

Later, Fuqua, who thrived on stirring up controversy of any kind, refused to tell what had happened. Even teammates, who asked him to explain, couldn't get a straight answer. Fuqua told them it was a planned play all along—"me and Franco met in private and dreamed it up"—and said they wanted to keep it a secret because "the Raiders

. . . Harris completed the bizarre play by running down the left sideline and scoring with five seconds left. It was the first playoff victory in Steelers history.

might have had Terry Bradshaw bugged."

Fuqua still gets asked frequently about the play. He offers the same mysterious non-explanation.

"Only I know what happened," Fuqua said. "Physicists and mathematicians can only guess how the ball could have bounced that far back. What'd it hit? A shoulder pad? Maybe I sneaked my glass cane onto the field and batted it back to The Stallion [Harris]. I've never told. Someday I will. But for now, it's Frenchy's Little Secret."

After Swearingen's touchdown signal, celebrating fans jumped out of the stands and ran onto the field, only to be shooed off by officials, who pointed out the 15 remaining seconds on the clock.

By then, Rooney had been told by a delirious security guard the Steelers had won the game. He didn't believe him.

Because of the mob celebration, Fuqua said there never was any doubt the touchdown would be allowed.

"Are you kidding?" he said. "This was the Iron Hat City. We hadn't been in the playoffs since 1947. There would have been a riot if it didn't count."

Harris (left), a rookie in 1972, appeared stunned after his winning score, while Bradshaw only could smile.

Moments later, it really was over. The Steelers had won. In the Oakland locker room, Tatum insisted he never touched the ball, explaining, "I was zeroing in on the receiver, not the ball. I never touched it; it never touched me."

Madden lamented long and loud, saying, "There is no tomorrow. You're down to a fourth-down play. One play. You play twenty-one ball games for this moment—fourth down. Then the ball bounces off one man's chest into another man's arms and it's over. No tomorrow. I'm telling you this will hurt for a long, long time."

Stabler drawled, "I guess that's football but I can't accept it. It doesn't seem fair. What an awful way to lose a game."

In the Steelers' locker room, Harris retold over and over what had happened. Or at least what he

thought happened. Bradshaw was doing the same thing. An hour later, the question still bounced around: What really happened out there?

At Fuqua's locker, where the big Joker's Corner sign was a marker for guaranteed mischief and unrelenting jive, the middleman in the Miracle of Three Rivers dressed slowly. He said he was talked out, needed some spiritual rest, and added he didn't know there was so much fatigue involved in these modern miracles.

Fuqua claimed, with tongue in cheek, to be the ebony reincarnation of a French count, who played football only to earn enough money to travel back in time to reclaim his stolen castle and resume his life as a playboy soccer player. He rightfully had earned a reputation for being a flake. And a well-dressed one at that. A new outfit for each winning game, he had promised earlier in the year. He would arrive at the stadium early, his special wardrobe wrapped in a garment bag. Then, after his shower, he'd step into the trainer's room and reveal his secret Le Duds du Jour. At one time he had goldfish in his clear-plastic heels.

After the Steelers' 13-7 victory over the Raiders, Fuqua emerged in red knickers, a velour sports jacket peppered with tiny stars, star-flecked patent-leather shoes, and matching socks.

"One of these is our lucky star," said the Count. "Maybe all of them are."

With a grand flourish, Fuqua strutted to Harris's locker, where the rookie hero was pulling on a necktie.

"Stallion, my man, my main man, you look . . . Immaculate."

And his laugh was a cackle once more.

While the scoreboard flashed "Merry Christmas," Oakland head coach John Madden slumped off the field in disgust after learning Harris's touchdown would count.

MIRACLE WORKER

*Dallas Cowboys 30,
San Francisco 49ers 28*
December 23, 1972

All that remained to be done was for the coroner to come draw a chalk line around the corpse.

"They're dead," yelled Cedrick Hardman. "We got this one nailed flat. Dallas is dead."

The rowdy defensive end of the San Francisco 49ers had just come off the field at Candlestick Park. He'd watched Craig Morton's long pass bounce off the hands of Dallas receiver Bob Hayes.

Roger Staubach came off the bench with a minute left in the third quarter and rallied the Cowboys from a 28-13 deficit to a 30-28 victory. He completed 12 of 20 passes for 174 yards and two touchdowns, including the 21-yard, game-winning throw to Ron Sellers.

"Even when they do something good, it comes out bad," Hardman said, noticing that Hayes had gotten behind the 49ers' secondary.

Dick Nolan, San Francisco's head coach, looked up at the scoreboard. It was just the third quarter but his team's 28-13 lead in the playoff game sure did look convincing, especially considering how well his team had been playing and how self-de-

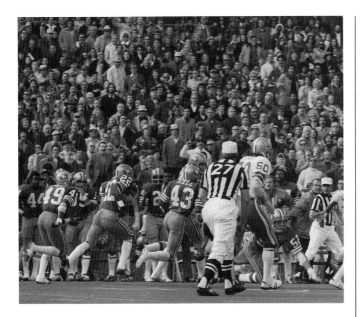

San Francisco's Vic Washington (22) took the opening kickoff and raced 97 yards down the left sideline for a touchdown. From then on, the 49ers never trailed until Dallas scored the winning touchdown in the last minute.

structive the Cowboys had been.

Nolan didn't see Roger Staubach start warming up on the other side of the field.

Tom Landry, the Cowboys' head coach, was going all out; he was switching quarterbacks.

"Bring him on," Hardman roared when he spotted Staubach. "He's not gonna make any difference today."

With a minute left in the third quarter, Staubach headed for the Cowboys' huddle. Staubach hardly had played all season. In a preseason game against the Rams, his shoulder had been separated, and, for a change, there was no quarterback controversy in Dallas. Craig Morton was Landry's man. But

Larry Schreiber (35, on ground) gave the 49ers a 14-3 lead in the second quarter with the first of his three one-yard touchdown runs.

now it was time to try something different.

"Roger has this way about him," Landry explained later. "He can turn things around."

When Staubach first came into the game, however, the only thing that got turned around was Staubach himself. His first pass was incomplete. He would wind up getting sacked four times in 10 minutes. One time, he was hit so hard he lost the ball. San Francisco recovered.

Moments later, Bruce Gossett, normally a regular maker of routine field goals, missed a 25-yard attempt, his second miss of the game.

Then a remarkable comeback began. At first, Staubach had little to do with it. He can take some credit for flawlessly getting the ball to fullback Calvin Hill on a draw play that wound up gaining 48 yards and setting up Toni Fritsch's third field goal

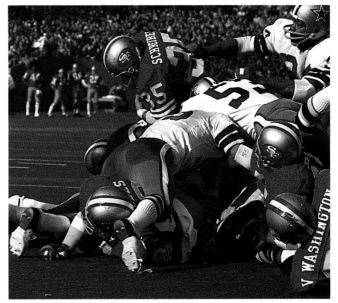

of the game. San Francisco still led by 12 points with less than nine minutes to play.

"The 49ers were being very conservative on offense," Staubach said. "They seemed content to sit on the ball."

Schreiber squeezed over the line for his second touchdown in the second quarter, pushing San Francisco in front 21-3. Schreiber ran for 52 yards in the game, and Vic Washington led all 49ers rushers with 56 yards.

But when a poor 49ers punt went just 17 yards and Dallas took over at its 45-yard line, a strange rumbling began on the Cowboys' sideline.

"I'm at a loss for words to explain it," Landry said, "but I got the feeling we were confident things were going to turn around. Even when it looked like the clock was winding down, we were acting like it'd only take one break to get back in contention."

The good field position quickly was turned into

Lance Alworth broke a tackle by cornerback Jimmy Johnson and went 28 yards to score with a pass from Craig Morton as Dallas cut the lead to 21-13 at halftime. Morton, however, was replaced by Roger Staubach in the third quarter.

Linebacker Skip Vanderbundt intercepted two of Morton's passes, with the first one leading to a touchdown, and the second stopping a short Dallas drive.

a touchdown. Four plays, 55 yards, and, suddenly, Staubach was untouchable, hitting every pass. There was 2:02 left to play on the fourth play of the drive when Staubach stepped into the huddle. There wasn't enough time for Landry to send in the plays. The messenger shuttle took too much time. In the two-minute offense, it was up to Staubach.

Billy Parks abruptly said, "I can run the post."

Staubach smiled and said, "Great . . . do it."

And that's how the Cowboys scored a touchdown —a 20-yard strike to Parks—on a post pattern. The 49ers' lead had been cut to 28-23.

"Once Billy caught the ball, this feeling came over me," Staubach said. "We were going to win. Everyone had the same feeling. There wasn't but a minute and a half left that the 49ers had to waste. We only had one time out left. But we were going to win that game."

Ever since the opening kickoff, when Vic Washington had taken Fritsch's kick and returned it all the way, 97 yards, the Cowboys had been behind. They'd turned the ball over five times, and Larry Schreiber had converted three of them into short touchdown runs for the 49ers. "We still needed the biggest break," Staubach said. "We needed the ball, and the only real hope we had was to recover the onside kick."

Nolan sprinkled wide receivers and running backs all along the front line as Fritsch put the ball on the kicking tee. Fritsch stepped back and tried to pull a surprise on somebody fully expecting it.

When Fritsch kicked, the ball scooted toward Preston Riley.

"Riley had great hands," Nolan said. "We used him in those situa-

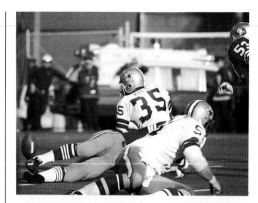

Turnovers set up three San Francisco touchdowns, including this fumble by Calvin Hill at the Cowboys' 5. Safety Windlan Hall recovered at the 1.

On the first play after Hill's fumble, Larry Schreiber scored his third touchdown. It gave the 49ers a 15-point lead.

tions all year."

But the ball was behaving strangely. "It spun weird, crazy-like," Riley said.

Riley reached for the ball just as linebacker Ralph Coleman unloaded on him. The ball popped loose, and Mel Renfro recovered for the Cowboys.

Staubach dropped back on first down, and "my instincts took over. I saw a little hole and took off. I never thought about passing."

The 21-yard scramble had everyone standing. When Staubach followed with a 19-yard sideline pass to Parks, the worst fears of San Francisco were coming true. Already that day, their neighbors on the other side of the bridge, Oakland, had been shocked by a last-second touchdown in Pittsburgh that would come to be known as the Immaculate Reception. Now the Cowboys were 10 yards away from pulling the same horrible trick on the 49ers.

On the pass to Parks the play before, Cowboys flanker Ron Sellers noticed he was all alone over the middle. So in the huddle, Sellers suggested, "I can get open on a curl over the middle."

Instead, Staubach called a play—62 Wing Sideline—that was designed to go back to Parks. But he told Sellers to be ready anyway.

"If they had a blitz coming, I'd have to throw fast," Staubach said. "There wouldn't be time for Parks to run his pattern. If the middle linebacker was one of the blitzers, Sellers would be clear."

After Mel Renfro recovered an onside kick, Staubach concluded the miracle comeback with this 10-yard scoring pass over the middle to Ron Sellers that won the game.

"That gave me a big boost."

But there were 52 seconds to play. The 49ers needed only to get back into field-goal position for Gossett. San Francisco quarterback John Brodie quickly completed three passes, and the last, with Preston Riley holding onto the ball for dear life at the Dallas 22, seemed to be enough to reverse the miracle. But back up-field there was a yellow flag. The 49ers' Cas Banaszek was slapping his head with both hands. The holding penalty brought everything back. On the next play, Brodie was intercepted.

When Staubach first came into the game, he was sacked four times in 10 minutes, including this double-team hit by Charlie Krueger (70) and Cedrick Hardman.

After the ball was snapped, Staubach threw as soon as he could. That's because 49ers middle line-backer Ed Beard was in on him immediately.

Sellers caught the ball in the end zone. Safety Windlan Hall was a second late.

"I threw the pass as hard as I could," Staubach said.

The first player to reach Staubach, hug and congratulate him, was Morton.

"He'd come up to me when I first went in and told me he was rooting for me," Staubach said.

Staubach's first touchdown pass went 20 yards to Billy Parks, who eluded Bruce Taylor and scored to cut the 49ers' lead to 28-23 with 1:30 remaining.

Nolan still was in shock when Landry walked across the field to speak with his former teammate and assistant coach.

"Tom, I never had anything happen like this before," Nolan said.

"You will," Landry said. "I have, I will. It's part of the game."

As the players from both teams filed off the field, Dallas guard Blaine Nye looked at the ground. He was afraid to show his happiness.

"I felt so sorry for those guys [the 49ers] that when it was over, I couldn't even look at them," Nye said. "That one had to really hurt."

Brodie also stared at the ground as he walked off. Later, he said, "You can never say a game is in the bag. But this one looked awfully good. Right now, though, the feeling is awfully bad."

THE PERFECT SEASON

Miami Dolphins 14,
Washington Redskins 7
January 14, 1973

The Dolphins, particularly defensive end Vern Den Herder, attacked Washington quarterback Billy Kilmer all day.

ring," said cornerback Lloyd Mumphord, "we all had a serious case of the goose bumps. Personally, I wanted to play right then and there. And we still had a week to wait."

Super Bowl VII offered the strangest of propositions: An undefeated, untied football team, the Miami Dolphins, was a three-point underdog. Dolphins head coach Don Shula welcomed the oddsmakers' prediction that the Washington Redskins were going to win.

"My team faces enough pressure, as it is," Shula said. "It's not easy being undefeated."

No team before had gone through an entire season, including playoffs, without losing or tying a game. The Dolphins had won all 14 of their regular-season games and had scored two playoff victories to earn the trip to Super Bowl VII. But they had been unimpressive at times and lucky at other times, and their quarterback, Bob Griese, was coming back from a broken ankle and had played only two serious quarters of football since early October.

The Redskins, who lost three games in the regular season, seemed to to be playing their best football. In playoff victories over Green Bay and Dallas, their defense had not allowed a touchdown. Suddenly, the Over-the-Hill Gang had asserted a seniority that made the unbeaten look beatable.

"It's nice to know some people have faith in my bunch of old men," said George Allen, the Redskins' head coach, as his team checked into their

Marv Fleming made a fist, which made the ring on his finger protrude even more.

"Super Bowl rings have special powers," Fleming said to the cluster of teammates standing around him. "This is one of the ones I got when I was with the Packers. Win one of these and you're the best. To win it all . . . man, you guys just have to know what it's like."

Several Miami Dolphins stared like children at a pet store seeing their first python. Fleming sensed their awe and tried to turn it into inspiration.

"Take a good look, fellas. You know, we have a chance to be the best ever. Undefeated Miami Dolphins. We can get rings like nobody else ever had."

The Dolphins usually were an even-keeled team, not given to demonstrations of emotion.

"But after hearing Marv talk and looking at his

Larry Brown, Washington's outstanding running back, was held to 72 yards.

hotel the week of the game. "I know I sure do."

Allen was all smiles—for about five minutes. When he walked into his hotel room and saw the blue bedspread and the blue towels, he erupted with anger.

"I think Rozelle was expecting the Cowboys," Allen said.

It became obvious Allen was feeling the building tension every bit as much as Shula. In the next few days, Allen would blame the media for his team's bad practice that day, claim the Dolphins' record was aided by a "soft" schedule, and then proclaim with syrupy sarcasm, "Miami is the best team I've ever seen in my career. We'll be lucky to stay on the same field with them."

In a more serious vein, Shula said the fact the Redskins and their veteran defense were strong at stopping the run wouldn't deter his Dolphins from trying anyway. After all, the Dolphins had set an NFL record with 2,960 yards rushing and boasted the first two players, Larry Csonka and Mercury Morris, ever to gain 1,000 yards for the same team in the same season.

"It's what we do best," Shula said.

Shula then smiled and added, "I'd also like to announce we're going to shift our practices to Tijuana. I say that now so George can start scouting the area for our practice field. At our practice today, a little old lady the size of [Redskins assistant] Charley Winner got past everyone and was watching our offense. I tried to shoo 'her' away."

When asked about spying on Miami, Allen slung counter-charges: "Their defensive back, Foley, what is it? Tim Foley? The one who's supposed to be injured? He was hiding in among you members of the media. Interviewing my players. He was even talking to me before I knew who he was. I could have told him something that would have helped the Dolphins."

Told that Foley, who definitely was not able to play, was writing special daily stories for a Miami newspaper and that his press credential was legitimate, Allen shook his head. The problem is, the Redskins' coach continued, "There's too much talking about football. The game is being ruined by all these distractions. It's taking too long to play."

By starting Griese, Shula was leaving himself open for criticism and second-guessing. Veteran Earl Morrall, who had been bought off the waiver wire the year before, had come on to lead Miami to nine consecutive victories after Griese had broken his leg in the season's fifth game. But Shula also knew his best combination was Griese starting and Morrall as backup. And, as everyone had been saying, Miami had struggled lately.

Miami quarterback Bob Griese threw only 11 passes, but completed 8, including a 28-yard, first-quarter touchdown strike to Howard Twilley. Griese was making his first start since suffering a broken ankle in October.

A good block by guard Bob Kuechenberg (67) helped clear the way for Jim Kiick on his one-yard touchdown run, which gave the Dolphins a 14-0 lead.

As the game started, the Dolphins dominated the early going. Their 53 Defense, the one that disguised a player as either an extra lineman or a spare linebacker, stymied the Washington running game. Larry Brown, Washington's all-pro runner, was not a factor. Redskins quarterback Billy Kilmer —playing in place of injured Sonny Jurgensen, who was on crutches—was under constant pressure from the Dolphins' strong pass rush, led by tackle Manny Fernandez. Kilmer struggled with his passing.

Miami scored in the first period on a six-play, 63-yard march. At the Washington 28, Griese correctly guessed that wide receiver Howard Twilley was going to be covered only by Redskins cornerback Pat Fischer.

"I got beat on a good inside move," Fischer said. "Twilley then broke out and Griese hit him in the numbers. Griese read us real good all day. Some can throw harder and longer but I doubt if anyone's more accurate."

Twilley's 28-yard touchdown looked as if it would be the only score of the first half. With Fernandez and end Bill Stanfill harassing Kilmer, the Redskins floundered. Griese threw a touchdown pass to Paul Warfield, but it was called back because reserve wide receiver Marlin Briscoe had made a false start.

Less than two minutes before halftime, Dolphins middle linebacker Nick Buoniconti, the most recognizable of Miami's No-Name Defense, intercepted a pass and returned it to the Redskins' 27-yard line.

Griese promptly stuck

a 19-yard pass into reserve tight end Jim Mandich's chest. Two plays later, Jim Kiick plunged over for a touchdown with 18 seconds left on the clock.

In the locker room trailing 14-0, Allen and Kilmer talked about things that might ignite the Washington offense. They both agreed they'd have to pass to open things up.

"Miami's ball control was good enough that fourteen points was a lot to make up," Kilmer said.

In the third quarter, Washington took the kickoff and drove to the Miami 15. But, on third down, Fernandez sacked Kilmer. And Curt Knight's 32-yard field goal was wide to the right.

"That was an obvious turning point," Allen said later. "We had other chances earlier. But none as big as that first possession of the third quarter."

Later in the period, Csonka broke free for a 49-yard rumble to the Redskins' 16, but an interception by Brig Owens kept Miami from scoring again.

"It seemed like we were clearly outplaying them," Buoniconti said. "But we kept looking up at the board and seeing it was only 14-0."

Washington later drove from its 11 to the Miami 10, but Jake Scott, who was named the game's most valuable player, made one of his two interceptions, this one in the end zone. He returned it to the 48.

On the sideline, Fleming sensed his teammates were getting tired. He felt the same way about the Redskins. The California heat was taking its toll.

So Fleming bellowed a favorite quote: "Fatigue makes cowards of us all."

It was one of Vince Lombardi's best proverbs. Fleming tried to wake up the Dolphins, shouting, "They're thieves, trying

Miami safety Jake Scott stopped two Redskins drives with interceptions and was voted the game's most valuable player. In the fourth quarter, he jumped for the ball in front of Charley Taylor (42) and returned it 55 yards.

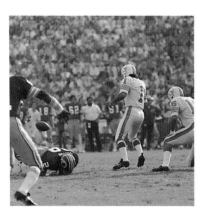

to steal our money, take away our ring. Remember the ring. Remember the ring."

As the game wound down, the Dolphins moved close enough to where they seemed assured of at least getting a field goal that would put the victory safely out of the Redskins' reach.

But defensive tackle Bill Brundige broke through the middle and blocked Garo Yepremian's kick.

"When something like that happens," Shula said, "Garo's just supposed to fall on the ball."

Yepremian let enterprise overrule common sense, however, and he tried to pick up the ball. Washington's Mike Bass said he knew Yepremian wasn't going to try to run with the ball.

"I was on the taxi squad with him in Detroit," Bass said. "I knew he couldn't run."

Bass closed on Yepremian, who suddenly tried to pass the ball. Only it slipped off the palm of his hand. Yepremian batted at the ball in mid-air, but it poofed weakly toward Bass.

"It was pretty much a straight line from there," Bass said.

The 49-yard touchdown run was a very real conclusion to what seemed like a comedy routine spliced onto the end of a game film. But it now was 14-7 instead of 17-0.

The Dolphins had no more gag gifts. The game ended, almost appropriately, with Kilmer getting sacked by Stanfill and Vern Den Herder. Shula accepted a ride on his players' shoulders.

Inside the locker

Left to right: Washington defensive tackle Bill Brundige blocked a field-goal attempt by Garo Yepremian (1), who tried to run with the ball, chased by Brundige (77). Then he tried to pass, but the ball squirted to cornerback Mike Bass (41), who carried it 49 yards for a touchdown.

Larry Csonka, Miami's powerful fullback, was the leading rusher in the game, rumbling for 112 yards in just 15 carries.

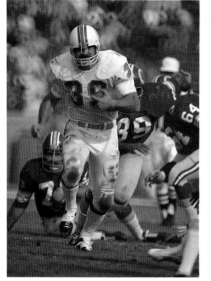

room, the head coach stood among his victorious players and said, "This team went into an area where no one had ever been before. Undefeated, seventeen-and-oh—it's the ultimate."

Den Herder slipped away from the celebration and into the washroom. Looking into the mirror, he surveyed his mustache. The rookie defensive end had grown it before the season.

"I thought I'd try one, to see what it looked like," he said. "Then, when we started winning, I was afraid to shave it off. I guess it'll be all right now to cut it off."

Griese had thrown 11 passes in the game, completing 8. His return to the lineup had not dictated any de-emphasis of the passing attack, Shula said. "It's just that Bob had such control out there. Our running game was going well at times, and when it wasn't, Griese was able to hit a pass or two."

Kilmer shook his head and said, "We're probably lucky Griese didn't throw more or it might have been worse. I wasn't sharp at all. Good as their defense is, I still should have thrown better. I think my best pass hit the goal post. And my two next best hit Jake Scott. The interception by Buoniconti was a big play. I was under the gun and just rushed the throw. We got beat by a pretty solid team. But I guess everyone figured that out by now, huh?"

Den Herder decided his shaving cream might be better suited being sprayed into teammates' hair. Foley was interviewing Mumphord. Shula, who had lost the first two Super Bowl games he'd coached, was asked if President Richard Nixon had suggested any plays like he had the year before, when the Dolphins had lost to the Cowboys in Super Bowl VI.

At first Shula scowled. What kind of question is that? But then the Dolphins' coach, relaxed at last, said with a huge smile, "Well, there was this fake-field-goal pass, but. . . . ."

END OF A DYNASTY

Oakland Raiders 28,
Miami Dolphins 26
December 21, 1974

Clarence Davis of the Raiders outfought Miami linebacker Mike Kolen for the winning touchdown pass with 26 seconds left in a 1974 AFC playoff game.

After the Miami Dolphins won their second consecutive Super Bowl, in January, 1974, head coach Don Shula took a quick inventory. His team was young, yet still had experience. It had both cohesiveness and chemistry. "I couldn't see a reason why we just couldn't go on and on and on," he said.

Shula was aware of the on-any-given-Sunday capability of the rest of the NFL; he knew any team could surprise his Dolphins. But that's just what it would be. His team had become so efficient, so routinely superior, that, yes, everybody expected the Dolphins to win every game. Given the cast he had assembled, with an offense that ran as smoothly as a sewing machine and a defense that quietly smothered opponents, Shula felt the only way his team could be stopped was by some unknown, outside factor.

Enter John Bassett.

At the same time Shula was counting his blessings, three of his best players—running backs Larry Csonka and Jim Kiick and wide receiver Paul Warfield—were nailing down the final terms of a multi-million-dollar package deal that would whisk them away to the infant World Football League. Bassett, a Toronto businessman, was ripping out the guts of the Miami offense and claiming them as his own. The three players would be gone as soon as the 1974 season was done.

Most people assumed that would be after the Dolphins won Super Bowl IX.

"We're disappointed, of course," Shula said. "But we'll go on. We're thankful we have them this year so we can start grooming replacements."

As expected, the Dolphins rolled to the AFC East championship. The "replacements"—Don Nottingham, Benny Malone, and rookie Nat Moore—were integrated slowly into the Dolphins' offense.

Miami's Nat Moore raced 89 yards for a touchdown with the opening kickoff.

None took a starting job away from the defectors. Instead, Shula felt his team was bolstered by the need to develop the younger players, and, in fact, the Dolphins were an even stronger team as the playoffs began.

In the divisional playoffs, they had to play the Oakland Raiders. The Raiders had pro football's best record in 1974, winning 12 of 14 games.

"It's almost a shame," Raiders head coach John Madden said. "This probably is the real Super Bowl."

The NFL had some new rules in 1974, mostly concentrating on safety, but with the residual effect of generating more offense. The main one was that, after hitting a pass receiver within three yards of the line of scrimmage, defensive players were allowed only one more bump on pass coverage. The bump-and-run pass defense, in which a receiver often would resemble a human pinball as he tried to run a route, no longer was allowed.

This helped and hurt the Raiders, a team that specialized in aggressive, physical pass defense but also one that had utilized the long pass as a weapon since coming into the league. The '74 Raiders were the top offensive team in the AFC.

The Raiders ranked only twenty-first against the run, which was the Dolphins' strength.

On the day of the game, Oakland-Alameda County Coliseum filled early. As the Dolphins prepared to receive the opening kickoff, Csonka walked over to Kiick and slapped his shoulder pads. No words, just the ritual message that it's time to play, time to win. Paul Warfield stood a few feet away on the sidelines staring at the Dolphins' deep man, Nat Moore, who would replace him in 1975.

Moore squinted as the kick went into the overcast sky. He took a couple of steps forward to the 11-yard line, and fielded the kick. He weaved and then burst free, racing 89 yards for a touchdown. Fifteen seconds had elapsed.

Madden turned away in disgust.

"Gotta get it back," he shouted as his offense readied to go onto the field. On the Raiders' fifth play from scrimmage, Miami safety Dick Anderson intercepted a pass by Kenny Stabler. The Dolphins

Although cornerback Tim Foley had his right arm pinned, Oakland's Fred Biletnikoff pulled in a 13-yard touchdown pass with his left, while keeping his feet in bounds, to give the Raiders a 14-10 third-quarter lead.

had the ball back at midfield.

The Raiders were in trouble. If Miami got another touchdown, even a field goal, Madden's team would have to stray from its game plan.

But another rule change worked in Oakland's favor. Before the season started, in an effort to stop glorified kicking contests and generate more touchdowns, the goal posts had been moved from the goal line to the back of the end zone. The Dolphins got one first down, but were unable to get into kicker Garo Yepremian's range and decided to punt.

Neither team mounted any additional threats until the second quarter, when Stabler finally got the Raiders moving. At the Miami 31, the Dolphins' defense anticipated a pass. Miami middle linebacker Nick Buoniconti knew that if running back Charlie Smith broke deep, he'd have to cover him. Most linebackers can't stay with a running back.

"I think I covered him perfectly," Buoniconti said. "I couldn't have been in better position."

But Stabler's looping pass to Smith was caught, and the game was tied. A 33-yard field goal by Yepremian gave Miami a 10-7 halftime lead. The electric beginning with Moore's kickoff return had turned into an unglamorous war of inches for field position. And the Miami offensive line, which featured four Pro Bowl selections, usually did its best work in the latter stages of games.

Shula liked the way the first half had gone.

Madden was more concerned. The Raiders were going to have to outscore the Dolphins. You can't beat a team like Miami by waiting for them to make mistakes. The only Miami touchdown had come on the runback. The Raiders' defense had done its job. "Now let's have some offense," he shouted.

The Raiders took the second-half kickoff and methodically drove downfield. (As a rule, the Dolphins could stop the long, sustained drives; if you scored on them, it usually was a big play.) At the Miami 13, Fred Biletnikoff spread toward the sideline. Defensive back Tim Foley followed. Foley had studied the Raiders' wide receiver on film all week. He had seen all the classic moves. Recognition of what Biletnikoff was running had to take place in a fraction of a second.

Foley guessed right. Biletnikoff curled left into the end zone, and Foley was right by his side. Biletnikoff had only a yard or so of the end zone in which to maneuver.

Stabler's pass arrived, a little high, in the corner of the end zone. Foley reached for Biletnikoff, pinned his right arm, sure there was no way the ball could be caught.

With his left hand, Biletnikoff hooked the ball, at the same time dragging his feet. Foley was draped over his right side but Biletnikoff was able to pull the ball in to his left for the touchdown.

Foley's eyes still were filled with shock as Buoniconti tried to console him. "Not a whole lot more we can do about those kind," the linebacker said to his dazed teammate.

"I just don't think I can cover someone any better than that," Foley said in his own defense.

Trailing for the first time, 14-10, Bob Griese opened up the Dolphins' attack. He sent Kiick deep, hoping to catch a Raiders linebacker covering him. He did, and Oakland's Phil Villapiano was beaten and forced to interfere with Kiick to save the touchdown. At the Raiders' 16, Griese hit Warfield with a touchdown pass to put the Dolphins back in front 16-14, but the conversion failed. Another field goal by Yepremian stretched the lead to 19-14.

The Dolphins' secondary was crippled. Starters Curtis Johnson and Jake Scott had been injured. Stabler picked on the reserves immediately. Cliff Branch took off on a straight fly pattern. Reserve cornerback Henry Stuckey had him covered pretty well. Stabler cranked up and threw the pass, but it was underthrown.

"Cliff was very underrated as a receiver," Madden said. "He had a great ability to adjust to the flight of the ball."

Seeing the ball would be short, Branch came back toward it and made a sliding catch.

He didn't touch me, Branch thought to himself, and he got up and sped into the end zone, finishing the 72-yard play. In the NFL, even if you're lying on the ground, you're not considered down unless a member of the defense touches you while you're down. The Dolphins argued, but to no avail. The Raiders were ahead 21-19.

Griese looked at the clock. About four minutes remained. He completed a 23-yard pass to Moore. Csonka bulled for seven yards, then 15. The Raiders were backed up to their 23. Malone took a pitch and headed around right end. Two Raiders had him hemmed in near the sideline, but Malone spun away, stayed in bounds, and sprinted into the end zone. The Dolphins had reclaimed the lead, 26-21.

Cliff Branch burned Miami on a 72-yard scoring play on a pass from Kenny Stabler. He made a sliding catch of the ball (left) and then, because he hadn't been touched by a defender, got to his feet (center) and raced into the end zone.

Miami's Benny Malone put the Dolphins ahead for the last time, 26-21, on a 23-yard scoring run with just 2:08 remaining.

There was 2:08 left to play. Shula's team had scored too quickly. The Raiders and Stabler still had a chance to come back.

The Dolphins forced Oakland to third down, then almost got to Stabler for the sack that might have finished off the Raiders. But Stabler somehow got a pass off, and Biletnikoff grabbed it for 18 yards. Stabler went to Biletnikoff again, for 20 yards. A short pass to Branch set up another quick throw, to reserve wide receiver Frank Pitts. Pitts had caught only three other passes all season. Pitts tried to make it out of bounds but Miami linebacker Bob Matheson pulled him down at the 14. It was third down, and a yard still was needed for the first down. The Raiders used a time out. They had one left.

"We needed the first down more than we needed our last time out," Madden said. "We decided to run for the first, then call the time out whether we made it or not."

Clarence Davis took the handoff and ran inside, gaining six yards for a first down at the 8. There were 35 seconds left to play as the Raiders used their final time out.

"Now we're able to throw four passes if we need it, knowing the clock's gonna stop after every incompletion," Madden said. "We didn't feel like we had to hurry anymore. We had a chance to get four good plays."

In the huddle, Stabler said, "Ninety-one Flare Seven."

Biletnikoff was the primary receiver. Tight end Bob Moore was supposed to delay, then drag to the right side and find an open area.

The Dolphins dropped seven defenders back.

"It was all clogged up back there," Stabler said. "I looked around for [fullback] Marv Hubbard. Even he was covered."

Clarence Davis also had run out for the pass. However, he had a reputation for having bad hands —"supposedly the worst on the team," Stabler said. But now the protection was caving in, and a

couple of Dolphins were closing in on Stabler as he drifted to his left, no longer picky about his receiver.

"I saw Kenny in trouble," Davis said. "I came back to help."

Miami's Vern Den Herder got to Stabler, who by then was thinking he might have to throw the ball away. Den Herder had Stabler around the waist and the Raiders' quarterback was falling forward.

"I just wristed the ball, no arm at all, a little floater," Stabler said.

Shula watched as the ball went toward a cluster of Dolphins. Linebacker Mike Kolen looked to be right in front of the pass. Davis arrived, and so did the ball.

"I had my hands on it for a second," Kolen said.

"I don't know how," Davis said, "but I got above everyone else. My arm was under the ball. The Miami guy had it from above. And I wound up with it."

Davis and the touchdown pass crashed to the grass. There were 26 seconds left in Miami's dynasty.

The kickoff went to Moore, who could not end the game the way he had begun it. A desperation pass by Griese was intercepted, and it was all over. Shula was visibly shaken as he walked off the field, still disbelieving, not noticing the victory ride Madden was taking on his team's shoulders.

"That was my toughest loss in coaching," Shula said. "When you lose like that. . .you know it just wasn't meant to be. Your dreams just go down the drain."

The following week, Pittsburgh defeated the Raiders, then went on to win Super Bowl IX.

The next ruling class moved to the front.

Completing 20 of his 30 attempts, Stabler passed for 293 yards and four touchdowns and rallied the Raiders to a thrilling come-from-behind victory.

THE HAIL MARY

Dallas Cowboys 17,
Minnesota Vikings 14
December 28, 1975

As cornerback Nate Wright fell down, Drew Pearson of Dallas caught Roger Staubach's 50-yard touchdown pass to stun Minnesota 17-14. Note the orange (by Pearson's left hand) which flew out of the crowd.

Before the game, after running through a pass drill, Drew Pearson stopped and looked up at the big scoreboard beyond the end zone in Metropolitan Stadium. Pearson stared at the big cutout cowboy on top of it, the Marlboro Man.

"If I score one today, you get the ball, big guy," Pearson thought to himself. And he laughed.

Back upfield, Roger Staubach was trying to get loose. His bruised ribs from the week before were bothering him. The infamous Minnesota weather —gloomy and an overcast 27 degrees for the open-ing kickoff—wasn't helping. The Cowboys' quarterback told teammates his injury only affected his playing "when I throw deep. That's when I can feel it. It's going to be hard to really uncork one today."

Dallas was a big underdog. They had been all year. Bob Lilly and Walt Garrison had retired before the season, and several other Cowboys were getting gray in the muzzle. Twelve rookies had made the team. But they'd earned a wild-card spot in the playoffs on the strength of their Doomsday Defense and Staubach's big-play magic.

Minnesota's Chuck Foreman accounted for 98 yards from scrimmage, rushing for 56 yards on 18 carries and catching four passes for 42 yards. His one-yard touchdown run gave the favored Vikings a 7-0 lead at halftime.

But now they had to play the Vikings, perhaps the premier NFC team. Minnesota had won 12 of 14 games and was eager to atone for two consecutive losses in Super Bowls VIII and IX.

In Savannah, Georgia, the Reverend Dallas Tarkenton and two of his sons were clustered around the television set. The 63-year-old minister wasn't a particularly rabid football fan but he usually found time to watch a game if his son Fran was playing. Fran Tarkenton was the Vikings' quarterback.

"I don't know if we can contain Tarkenton," said Dallas head coach Tom Landry. "You really have to be patient against him. Our defense is very young. But it will grow up today."

On the Dallas sideline, Staubach was encountering another problem. His center, John Fitzgerald, was erratic with his snaps when Staubach lined up in the Shotgun formation. The ball was coming back on short hops—off to the right, off to the left.

"My elbow's messed up still," Fitzgerald said. "Maybe it'll work itself out. But sometimes it's stiff and I can't make it work. Other times it's okay. I'll have to see."

Vikings head coach Bud Grant had said earlier in the week his team had to be ready for a Cowboys team "that's much more balanced on offense than other teams they've had. Their fullback [Robert Newhouse] has become very productive. They don't seem to have to rely on the big bomb so much anymore."

There was a nondescript nature about the game almost from beginning to end. Like the skies, it was varying shades of gray. The opening kickoff and everything that happened until the last half of the last quarter were one big bland cardboard box. And the prize was inside.

In the second quarter, the Vikings scored in a fashion that typified them. Bogged down on the Dallas 37, Minnesota punted, and Cliff Harris returned it to the 13. But center Mick Tingelhoff had been downfield too quickly, so the Cowboys, hoping for better field position, forced Minnesota to punt again. The punt bounced in front of Harris and apparently touched him before Fred McNeill recovered what was ruled a fumble at the Dallas 4-yard line.

In the press box, Tex Schramm, the Cowboys' general manager, erupted with rage over the call.

"One of the worst calls I've ever seen in my life," he bellowed.

Three plays later, after runs by Chuck Foreman and Tarkenton, Foreman scored from the 1.

The Cowboys weren't able to move against the Vikings' defense in the first half. The closest they came to points was a shanked field-goal try by Toni Fritsch in the second quarter.

In the third quarter, however, Staubach led Dallas on a 72-yard drive that tied the game. At the Vikings' 4, on third-and-goal, almost everyone in the stadium was expecting Staubach to pass. Instead, Landry sent in a running play. Reserve fullback Doug Dennison took the ball and burst into the end

Vikings quarterback Fran Tarkenton was as elusive as always, scrambling for 32 yards on three carries. He also passed for 135.

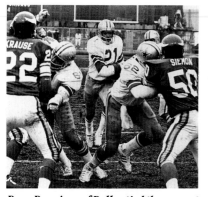

*Doug Dennison of Dallas tied the score at 7-7 **with a four-yard touchdown run.***

zone almost untouched.

Then on the first play of the fourth quarter, Fritsch made a short field goal to give the Cowboys a 10-7 edge.

"I really felt our defense was outplaying them," Landry said. "It wasn't a spectacular game to that point. But we were playing very well." But Tarkenton rallied the Vikings. Accounting for 57 of 70 yards with his scrambles and short passes, Tarkenton set the stage for another one-yard touchdown plunge, this one by Brent McClanahan, sending Minnesota ahead 14-10.

During the commercial, Reverend Tarkenton suddenly gasped and lurched forward in his chair. An ambulance was called. They were pretty sure it was a heart attack.

At about the same time, the Cowboys faced a desperate situation. After the Vikings' touchdown, Dallas had been unable to move and had to punt the ball back to Minnesota. Now, just seconds before the two-minute warning, Dallas braced for the third-and-three play. Landry called for a blitz. Tarkenton wanted to run a roll-out option.

Cowboys safety Charlie Waters was the blitzer. If Tarkenton had turned the opposite direction, he might have made the first down and Minnesota more than likely could have run down the clock and moved on in the playoffs.

But Tarkenton turned directly into Waters, who tackled him for a loss, and the Vikings had to punt.

At the Cowboys' 15, Staubach was looking around the lingering twilight. He felt guilty for what he was thinking: *We don't have much of a chance. All I can do is try hard. . .do it on instincts.*

Drew Pearson also was somber. He hadn't caught a pass all game. He hadn't had one thrown his way.

That was getting ready to change.

Staubach completed a seven-yard pass to Drew Pearson, then a nine-yard pass. But then the Cowboys sputtered. Staubach had two consecutive incompletions, then mishandled John Fitzgerald's poor snap and was dropped for a six-yard loss.

Schramm banged his fists together and muttered a soft curse. Metropolitan Stadium was rocking. Fourth-and-16.

Toni Fritsch gave Dallas a 10-7 lead with a 24-yard fourth-quarter field goal as Bruce Walton (78) blocked.

No plays were coming in from Landry. Under two minutes and it's up to the quarterback. A few years earlier, wide receivers had suggested plays to Staubach and they'd worked.

"Got any ideas?" Staubach asked Drew Pearson.

"I think I can beat my man on a corner pattern."

"Which side of the field do you want?"

"To the right."

"We'll try it."

A new center had checked into the game: Kyle Davis, a rookie.

"I need a good snap and some blocking," Staubach said.

Staubach's pass was a little wide. Pearson's feet were planted, then he had to reach. He caught the ball just as cornerback Nate Wright hit him.

The Vikings pointed fingers, criss-crossing their arms. Out of bounds, they claimed. No good. Pearson didn't get his feet in bounds.

But head linesman Jerry Bergman called it a catch. The defender had knocked the receiver out of bounds. The ball was at the 50-yard line. A first down.

Pearson suddenly was gasping for breath. He hadn't had it knocked out of him. But he was tired. He couldn't breathe well.

"Can you run the same pattern?" Staubach asked. "Only go deep?"

With five minutes left, the Vikings made a bid for victory when Brent McClanahan scored for a 14-10 lead.

Roger Staubach's bruised ribs hurt when he tried to throw deep, yet his 50-yard touchdown pass won the game.

Pearson said no. Not this play. Too tired. Call something else. There were 37 seconds left to play.

A pass flew incomplete between receiver Golden Richards and halfback Preston Pearson. Now there were 32 seconds.

"I'm ready now," Drew Pearson said to Staubach.

Staubach raised his arm. His ribs were sore. Pearson lined up to the right. From the Shotgun formation, Staubach took the snap and took two steps backward.

"I made a little fake to the middle at about fifteen yards," Pearson said. "It's the same route, the same move I'd made the year before, when Clint Longley hit me with a long pass to beat the Redskins on Thanksgiving Day. Only that time, the defender took the fake. This time, he didn't."

Wright knew he had help over the middle, where safety Paul Krause was stationed. But when Pearson put on a burst, Wright turned to run with him.

"When I saw Wright turn like that, I felt we had a chance," Staubach said. "When they take their eyes off the ball, strange things can happen."

The pass wasn't picture-perfect. "I wound up and threw and said a prayer," Staubach said. The ball wobbled high and then started to come down short.

That's what caused one of the famous controversies in pro football history. Both Pearson and Wright saw the pass would be short. Both slowed up, trying to adjust to the ball's flight.

Wright suddenly fell down.

"He seemed to slip," Landry said.

"He was pushed," Grant said.

"I really don't know," Pearson said.

"I really can't say for sure," Wright said.

At the 5-yard line the ball first appeared to strike Pearson in the crotch, then on his hands. Then it seemed to slither along his hip, where, with one hand and an elbow, he secured it, pulled it up to his chest, and stepped into the end zone.

Something flew by Pearson's line of sight.

"I thought it was a penalty flag," he said. "It could have been. There probably was interference, I'm not sure. It could have been called on either one of us."

It was an orange. Someone in the stands had hurled it onto the field.

Pearson looked around. The referee had his arms raised.

"I realized I'd scored. . .we'd won."

And he turned around to find the Marlboro Man. Pearson took a running start and tried to hit him in

Staubach and Tom Landry conferred on the sideline as Dallas tried to pull off a miracle.

the hat, the cowboy hat, but the ball bounced off the scoreboard instead.

The Vikings protested the touchdown bitterly. The stunned crowd booed. "It was like having to sit and watch your home get robbed," Vikings offensive lineman Ed White said.

Staubach never saw the catch.

"I didn't think I could throw it that far, to the end zone," he said. "Figure I'm ten yards behind the line, which was the fifty. One time I threw a ball sixty-five yards. But I just didn't think I could reach all the way to the end zone."

Someone interrupted and told Staubach that he hadn't reached the end zone. Pearson had caught the ball on the 5.

"You mean he caught the ball and ran in for the touchdown? It was just a Hail Mary pass. . .a very, very lucky play."

At 3:15 P.M. in Savannah's Memorial Medical Center, Dallas Tarkenton, Sr., was pronounced dead on arrival, the victim of a massive heart attack. His son Fran heard the news after the game and left immediately.

PERFECT SWANN DIVES

Pittsburgh Steelers 21,
Dallas Cowboys 17
January 18, 1976

Doctors aimed little flashlights at his eyes each day in search of dilated pupils and other signs of trouble. Lynn Swann had suffered a concussion one week earlier. A clothesline tackle in the AFC Championship Game against the Oakland Raiders had sent the Pittsburgh Steelers' wide receiver to the hospital.

A week before Super Bowl X, Swann's status was uncertain. The gifted young man was dropping every pass thrown to him in practice. He was frustrated. Doctors were worried.

A brain scan had been negative; equilibrium and reflex tests had come out okay, but the post-concussion syndrome concerned the Steelers' doctors anyway.

And playing a football game against the Dallas Cowboys was not exactly a recommended prescription for a speedy, uneventful recovery.

"I'm worried about my timing," Swann told teammate John Stallworth two days before the game. "And my concentration isn't real good either."

Swann had told reporters he would not risk his health for the sake of one football game, even something as monumental as the Super Bowl. "But then when Cliff Harris started talking so much, I knew I was going to play."

Harris, the Cowboys' safety, had been trying to plant seeds of intimidation all week, saying things such as, "Getting hit really hard again has to be in the back of his mind."

On Saturday, Swann snarled, "He can't scare me. I'm playing."

In 1976, the United States was 200 years old and the Super Bowl was 10. In a few months, the NFL would spread its arms and welcome expansion teams from Tampa Bay and Seattle. Pittsburgh, the defending Super Bowl champion, and Dallas,

Cowboys rookie linebacker Thomas (Hollywood) Henderson returned the opening kickoff 53 yards on a reverse from Preston Pearson. He was driven out of bounds by kicker Roy Gerela, and Dallas failed to score.

an NFC wild-card entrant that had won seven of its last eight games, headed for the Orange Bowl in Miami.

Dallas, with quarterback Roger Staubach operating from the resurrected Shotgun formation and throwing to a stable of fleet pass receivers, had been a big-play team all season. But now the Cowboys had to go up against one of the league's best defenses, the Steel Curtain, and a 4-3 stunt alignment defensive coordinator George Perles had installed. Conversely, the Steelers had a relentless running game, an Ozark Ike quarterback named Terry Bradshaw, and the steadily improving deep threats of Stallworth and Swann. The Cowboys also had a defense called the Flex, in which players line up in staggered formations.

"I think it's a game of our offense against their defense," Staubach said earlier in the week.

Bradshaw said, "It's gonna be a matter of whether we can run on the Flex."

Chuck Noll, the Steelers' head coach, said, "It

Leaping, floating, and then lunging for the ball, Pittsburgh's Lynn Swann made a fingertip 53-yard catch over Dallas cornerback Mark Washington in Super Bowl X. Swann caught four passes for 161 yards in the Steelers' 21-17 win.

Drew Pearson gave Dallas a quick 7-0 lead in the first quarter when he darted past linebacker Andy Russell and scored on a 29-yard pass play from Roger Staubach.

might come down to big plays."

Cowboys assistant coach Ermal Allen said, "If we want to win, we have to stop the bomb."

Both teams were edgy; practices had become more physical than usual. Steelers reserve quarterback Joe Gilliam, whose job it was to impersonate Staubach and run the Cowboys' offense in Pittsburgh practices, said he hoped to live long enough for the real game to begin. The Steelers privately felt there was no way they were going to lose. They considered Dallas a team that relied on deception more than superior talent to win.

"They were going to have to trick us to beat us," running back John (Frenchy) Fuqua said.

The Cowboys also groused behind closed doors that the Steelers were loud-mouthed, dirty players and all their complaining about how Oakland had played "cheap-shot football" in the AFC title game in which Swann had been knocked unconscious, was the peak of hypocrisy.

"It suddenly became very emotional," said Cowboys safety Charlie Waters. "By game time, we were feeling pretty ornery."

Steelers defensive end L.C. Greenwood smiled when someone asked him if the Steelers disliked the Cowboys. "When you have to play a football game," Greenwood said coolly, "you don't like anyone. Yeah, we hate the Cowboys. That's 'cause we gotta play them."

This was the environment that Lynn Swann was supposed to be using for R&R from a head injury. Swann went to the Orange Bowl two hours

Pittsburgh's Terry Bradshaw passed for 209 yards and two touchdowns.

before the rest of his team, set his leather tote bag on the floor, piled several towels atop it, and lay down to take a nap.

"When I woke up," Swann said, "I felt great, so ready to play, so ready to show the Cowboys and everyone else Lynn Swann can't be intimidated."

In the pregame warmups, Swann held onto the passes thrown to him. The SOS warnings that had caused nature to backpedal and the swan to turn back into an ugly duckling, had reversed once more. He was Same Old Swannie again.

Fuqua waved to one of the Cowboys. Cornerback Mark Washington had been Fuqua's college roommate; each had been the other's best man at their weddings.

"Luck to you," Fuqua said to Washington as the two brushed by.

"You, too, Frenchy," Washington said.

Fuqua would play only a couple of plays; injuries had cost him his starting job the year before, and Rocky Bleier had played too well for

Tight end Randy Grossman caught a seven-yard scoring pass from Bradshaw.

Fuqua to win it back. Washington would play the entire game. His main responsibility was defending against Swann.

Dallas won the coin toss and chose to receive. Roy Gerela's kickoff was taken by Preston Pearson, who had been claimed on waivers after being released by the Steelers.

"We were thinking the Steelers might be really pumped up and going after their former teammate," said Dallas head coach Tom Landry.

Pearson suddenly handed the ball off to linebacker Thomas Henderson on a reverse. The game was two seconds old and the Cowboys already had opened their bag of tricks. Henderson, a rookie who had incredible speed for a linebacker, had only one Steeler to beat. But Gerela, who would prove to be a more dependable tackler than kicker this day, drove Henderson out of bounds after a 53-yard return.

The tackle was costly. Gerela cracked a rib, had to be fitted for a corset at halftime, and missed two field goals and an extra point.

The Steelers' defense forced a punt. But Dallas did the same thing on Pittsburgh's first offensive series. And when punter Bobby Walden muffed the

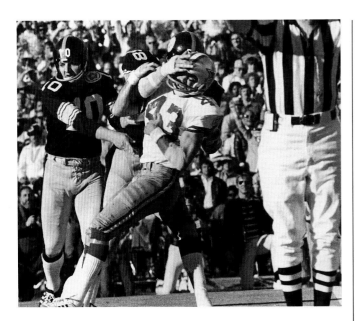

After Roy Gerela (left) missed a 36-yard field goal, Dallas safety Cliff Harris (43) mockingly patted him on the helmet, and Steelers linebacker Jack Lambert angrily threw Harris to the ground.

center snap and was smothered at the Steelers' 29-yard line, the Cowboys owned the first big break.

Moments later they had the first touchdown as Staubach hit Drew Pearson on a crossing pattern.

There was disgust on the Pittsburgh sideline.

"We're getting it taken to us," screamed all-pro middle linebacker Jack Lambert. "We're supposed to be the tough guys. We'd better damn well start playing like it."

The Steelers still were sputtering offensively. But Bradshaw threw a long pass on third down.

"At first it looked like a terrible play," Bradshaw said. "The Dallas guy's all over Swannie. He's got him covered perfect. No way we're gonna complete that ball."

Swann and Washington, striding along the sideline, looking for the ball, jumped in concert. In these moments it comes down to athleticism. Two men in the air, clawing for the ball. But Washington couldn't get his hands on it as Swann timed his leap perfectly. Both players lost their balance.

Only Swann still was under control. He got his right foot down just inside the out-of-bounds line, then his left, before he tumbled out of bounds with the ball secure in his grasp.

There would be no more worrying about Swann's ability to concentrate that day.

The 32-yard gain set up Bradshaw's short touchdown pass to tight end Randy Grossman that tied the game.

It also was the start of a 40-minute Steelers' famine on offense. The Flex seemed to confuse the Steelers. Its design is to take away the run and make trap-blocking, in which the Steelers specialized, ineffective. Pittsburgh's attack was sputtering, and

only some inspired defense was keeping the Steelers in the game. And the defense was without its star, tackle Joe Greene, who played very little because of a pinched nerve in his neck.

Toni Fritsch's second-quarter field goal gave Dallas a 10-7 halftime lead.

In that quarter, after Gerela missed a field goal, Dallas's Cliff Harris playfully patted the kicker on the helmet and mockingly applauded the effort.

An incensed Lambert ran over and flung Harris to the ground.

"That guy's gotta learn the Steelers don't get intimidated," Lambert said after the game. Lambert had ripped his teammates at halftime because of the Dallas "arrogance."

Still, Dallas held onto its three-point lead as the fourth quarter began.

As the Cowboys' offense huddled, a woman ran onto the field and into the huddle. She handed Dallas's Rayfield Wright a sterling silver horseshoe.

"It's good luck for y'all," the woman said.

"Maybe I should have accepted it," Wright said later.

On the next play, the Cowboys were called for clipping, forcing them to punt.

Reggie Harrison was a Steelers' reserve fullback who'd been claimed on waivers from St. Louis to help out on special teams. Harrison later admitted, "I was always afraid to try to block a kick. I thought I'd get hurt."

As Dallas lined up and Mitch Hoopes readied to punt the ball away, Harrison was one of two Steelers digging in over center. Pittsburgh had 10 players on the line of scrimmage.

"We knew the game had settled into one where field position was increasingly important," Noll explained later. "We felt Hoopes took a little longer getting rid of the ball when he was trying to really boom one. That's why the punt-block was on."

Harrison burst through, blew right by another Cowboy and blocked the punt.

"With my face," Har-

Under pressure from Steelers such as tackle Steve Furness (64), the Cowboys' Roger Staubach passed for 204 yards and two touchdowns and scrambled five times for 22 yards. But he also threw three costly interceptions.

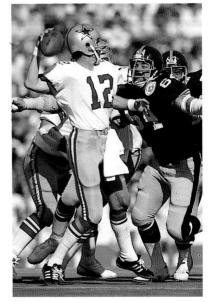

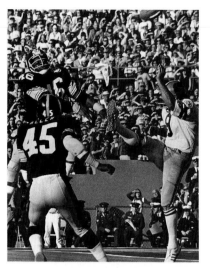

Pittsburgh's Reggie Harrison (46) blocked Mitch Hoopes's punt for a safety.

rison proudly said later, his speech hampered slightly by a gash on his tongue.

The ball bounded into and out of the end zone for a safety.

"That's when the game really changed," Landry said. "That blocked kick really amounted to a five-point play for them."

That's because the free kick by the Cowboys following the safety was taken by Pittsburgh and promptly cashed in for a field goal by Gerela that gave Pittsburgh a 12-10 lead.

The Cowboys tried to strike back quickly. On first down, Staubach looked over the middle for Drew Pearson. The Cowboys were running the same play on which they scored the game's first touchdown. Steelers films had indicated the Pittsburgh secondary was quick to close forward on first and second downs. The Cowboys were hoping Pearson could sneak behind coverage once more.

But safety Mike Wagner was ready. He intercepted, and the Steelers quickly tacked another field goal by Gerela to their lead. From the press box, Steelers president Dan Rooney and NFL Commissioner Pete Rozelle made their way toward the field.

With less than four minutes to play, the Steelers tried to use ball control to preserve the lead. But, on third down, five yards were needed for a first down.

"We gotta throw, guys," Bradshaw said in the huddle. "Okay, 69 Maximum Flanker Post."

Swann's eyes lit up.

"That's slick. . .we're going for it all," he thought to himself.

The Cowboys also knew the Steelers had to pass. So they planned a blitz. There actually were two blitzes. First, linebacker D.D. Lewis would come. Then, after a delay, Harris would roar in from his safety position.

That would leave Washington alone, with no backup help, on Swann.

Bradshaw ducked under the arms of Lewis, stepped forward, and was hammered in the jaw by Harris's helmet.

But he got the pass off first.

Explained Swann, "I just ran straight past

Washington. No moves, no fakes, just straight-ahead juice."

Washington retreated. His only hope at breaking up the play was to try to strip the ball.

"He missed," Swann said.

The 64-yard touchdown play brought the crowd to its feet, but not Bradshaw. He was knocked out, done for the game.

Gerela's extra-point try hit the upright. But Steelers fans figured a 21-10 lead was more than enough to win. For the first time all day, Dan Rooney smiled, relief on his face, as he shook hands with Rozelle on the sidelines.

The Cowboys struck back quickly, however, using just 67 seconds and five plays to go 80 yards, with Staubach flipping a 34-yard touchdown pass to rookie wide receiver Percy Howard.

The memory of Hail Mary still burned fresh. Dallas had beaten Minnesota earlier in the playoffs on a last-second miracle pass. Could the Cowboys do it again?

"We needed the ball first," Staubach said.

The onside kick was coming. Noll dispatched the usual wide receivers, running backs, and other good-hands people to the front. And one player wearing jersey number 72 was right in the middle.

"Moon had great hands," Noll said. "He used to be a tight end."

Gerry (Moon) Mullins was an obvious target for the onside kick. Sure enough, it dribbled toward him.

He just as surely recovered the ball. Now the Cowboys would be forced to use their time outs.

Terry Hanratty, taking over for the still-dazed Bradshaw, handed off on three consecutive plays.

The Steelers led 12-10 when safety Mike Wagner intercepted a Roger Staubach pass and returned it to the Dallas 7 to set up a field goal for a 15-10 lead.

Just after he released his 64-yard touchdown pass to Lynn Swann (celebrating below), Terry Bradshaw was tackled by safety Cliff Harris (43) and hit in the jaw by Harris's helmet and knocked out.

On fourth down and nine at the Cowboys' 41, everyone expected Walden and the punting unit to come on.

Instead, Noll directed Hanratty to go for it. Bleier, running laterally to run time off the clock, was stopped at the 39, and the Cowboys took over.

Noll defended his decision. "I was worried about the blocked kick," he said. "They'd already tackled my punter once. Two other times they came close to blocked kicks. Dallas needed a touchdown; if they'd needed a field goal, we would have punted. But they needed a touchdown. As it was they needed sixty yards and they were out of time outs. And we consider our defense one of our strengths."

Staubach promptly scrambled for one first down and passed for another and the Cowboys were at the Steelers' 38-yard line. There were 22 seconds left in the game.

In the press box, somebody realized that's how much time was left when the Steelers pulled off their Immaculate Reception against Oakland three years earlier. Somebody else was looking up how much time remained when the Cowboys' Hail Mary -defeated Minnesota.

Noll later insisted he wasn't worried.

"I know a man who always worried about getting hit by a car," he said. "But he never got hit by a car. He had a nervous breakdown."

Two Cowboys passes fell incomplete. There was time for one last play.

Wagner never joined the Steelers' defensive huddle. Instead he camped out on the goal line. Drew Pearson ran downfield, Staubach's pass hung in the sky . . .

"We had position," Wagner said, "but you never know. A Dallas guy could pop out of nowhere. I mean, how many times have you seen it before?"

Drew Pearson sighed and said, "Hail Mary II was just a little high."

Wagner tipped the ball, and it went to safety Glen Edwards, whose interception ended the game.

On the field, the Steelers' Dwight White and the Cowboys' Harvey Martin, teammates at East Texas State, embraced. Pittsburgh linebacker Jack Ham sought out Preston Pearson for the usual nice-game pleasantries. Fuqua looked for Washington, but never found him.

Dallas struck back as Percy Howard caught a 34-yard touchdown pass.

L.C. Greenwood, who had three of the seven sacks on Staubach, held up a badly swollen hand and said, "Damn, my new ring's not gonna go on for a while . . . not till the swelling goes down."

Harrison was enjoying his sudden celebrity. Bradshaw was in the trainer's room.

Franco Harris summed up the back-to-back Super Bowl victories.

"We have the blood of champions in us," he said.

Noll was asked if the Steelers were setting up a dynasty along the lines of Green Bay or Miami. He smiled and said, "I leave those judgments to the historians."

Lynn Swann, whose four catches for 161 yards had won him the game's most-valuable-player award, predicted he'd have "a terrible headache tomorrow morning because I'm going to party all night."

JINXED RIVALRY

Minnesota Vikings 24,
Los Angeles Rams 13
December 26, 1976

In the final minute, with all those people in the stands bundled up in purple celebrating and counting down the seconds, Tom Mack gasped at the terrible truth he suddenly was seeing.

"They've done it to us again," said the offensive guard of the Los Angeles Rams. "I don't know how I'm going to be able to live with this one."

The Minnesota Vikings were going to the Super

The Vikings became the first team to qualify for four Super Bowls when an opportunistic defense and quarterback Fran Tarkenton (eluding tackle Merlin Olsen) helped turn back the Rams. This frustrating defeat was the last game for Olsen after a 15-year career.

Bowl. The Rams were going home. For the third time since 1969, the Rams and Vikings had played the NFL or the NFC Championship Game at Metropolitan Stadium. The Rams had lost all three.

"Are we ever going to win at this place?" Mack said as the gun went off and he made the slow, pitiful trudge to the locker room.

"What is it about this place?"

The Vikings shocked the Rams in the first quarter when Nate Allen (25, above) blocked Tom Dempsey's short field-goal attempt, and Bobby Bryant (20, below) scooped up the ball and ran 90 yards to the game's first touchdown.

the Vikings. . .it's always so damn cold here, too."

The frustration was escaping like a gas leak, getting more toxic, more bitter.

"You look at that game and tell me they deserved to win," Jessie said. "It's ridiculous. You know where it all came down to, don't you? Their goal line. Man, we scored two touchdowns and the officials took them away from us. Then they blocked our kick and got a lucky bounce and they took it 90 yards. What kind of game is that?"

On their second possession, the Rams had driven into Vikings territory as Lawrence McCutcheon and John Cappelletti ran over and around the Minnesota defense. On second-and-goal at the Vikings' 4-yard line, quarterback Pat Haden called for a little trickery. A flanker reverse, with Jessie getting the ball. It fooled the Vikings, and Jessie was near the end zone when he was pushed out of bounds.

"I was in," Jessie said. "I couldn't believe the official spotted the ball three inches from the line."

On third down, Haden called for a quarterback sneak. As the Rams lined up, Vikings linebacker Wally Hilgenberg was playing a guessing game.

"My two guesses were halfback up the middle or quarterback sneak," Hilgenberg said. "I guessed sneak."

Haden took the snap and Hilgenberg crashed into him immediately. Haden was knocked back, then lunged forward and was buried by Vikings.

"I made it," Haden said. "I know I made it in the end zone on my second surge."

The Rams argued in vain. As the huddle formed, Mack was shaking his head. The Vikings' 1-yard line. What cruel irony.

Two years earlier, also with a trip to the Super

In the 13 games the two teams had played at Metropolitan Stadium since the Vikings came into the NFL, Minnesota had won 11. There had been two ties, including the 10-10 overtime game earlier in the season in which the Rams' potential game-winning field goal was blocked.

As Mack walked off the field after the 24-13 loss, he already was ripping tape off his hands and throwing the wads in front of him in disgust.

"I didn't think losing could hurt worse than the '74 game. But this one might," he said.

The Vikings, at first inspection, had won a game in which they were outplayed. They had led 10-0 at halftime and had less than 90 yards of total offense. They had made two big offensive plays all game. The Rams had a punt blocked that led to a field goal, a field goal blocked that was turned into a 90-yard touchdown return, four offensive thrusts inside the Vikings' 40 that yielded no points, and enough mistakes to force Minnesota to accept victory.

"There is more than one way to win in football," Vikings head coach Bud Grant said in his usual deadpan manner. "Kick it, catch it, block it. Whatever has to be done."

"It's got to be this stadium," said Rams wide receiver Ron Jessie. "It's hard when you're playing

Vikings linebacker Matt Blair blocked Rusty Jackson's second-quarter punt, setting up a field goal that put Minnesota ahead 10-0 at halftime.

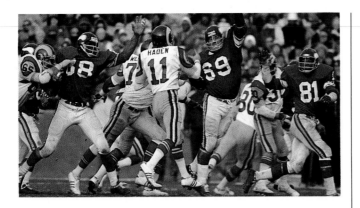

The Vikings, with pressure like this from Alan Page (88), Doug Sutherland (69), and Carl Eller (81), held Rams quarterback Pat Haden to just 9 completions in 22 attempts. Minnesota led 17-0 before the Rams scored.

Bowl at stake, the Rams had mounted a majestic 98-yard drive to the Vikings' 1-yard line. Same place, same stadium. Only when the Rams tried to get in the end zone, a yellow flag fell. Movement in the offensive line. The guilty party was Mack. The five-yard penalty had forced the Rams to pass, and there was an interception by Hilgenberg. The Vikings won that one 14-10.

The 1-yard line.

Rams head coach Chuck Knox remembered that scenario of two years ago, too. Get this close—get something out of it. He called for the field goal. This time, it was early, still the first period. The Rams had moved the ball well. Tom Dempsey lined up the kick. The ball would be spotted on the 7. It's automatic from here, closer than an extra point.

Vikings cornerback Nate Allen leaned forward.

"I thought I could block every kick there was," Allen said later. "The Vikings were the best in football at blocking kicks. We got fifteen of them that year. I got three myself."

On the snap there was a quiver of malfunction. Nothing noticeable, but the exchange from center to holder wasn't perfect.

Chuck Foreman's 62-yard third-quarter dash set up his own two-yard touchdown run that gave the Vikings their 17-0 lead.

"It gave them a tenth of a second to come at us," Dempsey said. "I guess that's all they needed."

Allen blocked the kick and the ball bounced toward the left sideline. Safety Bobby Bryant, whose broken arm in preseason had made it necessary for the Vikings to obtain Allen from San Francisco, picked up the ball and ran 90 yards to a touchdown.

"If we could come

right back at them," Knox explained afterward, "we wouldn't have started remembering back to 1974 and 1969."

After the kickoff, the Rams marched steadily upfield, reaching the Vikings' 21, where on first down, Cappelletti tried to sweep right end. But he was stripped of the ball and linebacker Matt Blair recovered.

"I couldn't believe it was happening," Haden said.

The Vikings were doing nothing offensively. Quarterback Fran Tarkenton seemed more bothered by the 12-degree weather and the whipping gusts of wind than anyone. Minnesota punted the ball back to Los Angeles.

At their 16, the Rams went right back to Cappelletti, who broke a tackle and held onto the ball and gained eight yards. But a holding penalty against

guard Dennis Harrah brought the play back. Three plays later, the ball still was at the 16 and punter Rusty Jackson was on the field.

"We knew Jackson was a little slow in his kick mechanics," Allen said. "He'd gotten two blocked the week before against Dallas. We went after him."

Jackson dropped the snap, retrieved it, and tried to kick. Blair blocked the kick, and the Vikings had the ball at the Rams' 8.

"We work on kick blocking every day," Grant said. "It just takes penetration on one side. It also doesn't hurt to have the punter fumble the snap."

Once again the Vikings were stopped, but Fred Cox kicked a 25-yard field goal for a 10-0 lead.

At halftime, the Rams looked around at each other, embarrassed. "No way we should be losing," Harrah said.

"Let's make this half our half," Knox said.

On the second play of the second half, Chuck Foreman, the Minnesota tailback, broke free up the middle and raced 62 yards. An ankle tackle by cornerback Rod Perry downed him at the Rams' 2-yard line. Two plays later, Foreman scored.

The Rams scored their second touchdown after defensive end Jack Youngblood, chased here by guard Charles Goodrum and tackle Ron Yary, returned a fumble to the Vikings' 8-yard line.

After Youngblood's fumble return, Haden threw a scoring pass to Harold Jackson.

It was 17-0 and the Vikings had managed, in all truthfulness, one good offensive play.

But then the Vikings came alive as Tarkenton hit on several short passes that carried Minnesota inside the Los Angeles 20-yard line.

"A touchdown then would probably have broken them for good," Tarkenton said.

But cornerback Monte Jackson intercepted for the Rams. And, just like that, they came alive. A pass to Harold Jackson for 40 yards was the big play. McCutcheon's 10-yard run scored the touchdown.

"We felt . . . better," Haden said. "At least we didn't feel like there was a curse on us. We were just beating ourselves. But we had enough time to still come back and win."

On the extra point, several Vikings got good penetration and Dempsey's rushed kick fluttered off to the left.

"I'll tell you the secret of rushing kicks after the Super Bowl," Grant told reporters later.

But the Rams were revived, both offensively and defensively. Tarkenton was swarmed under by defensive linemen Fred Dryer and Merlin Olsen. Tarkenton fumbled, and Rams defensive end Jack Youngblood picked up the ball and ran it to the Minnesota 8-yard line.

"It seemed like things were going just the reverse," Knox said. "Things were happening in our favor for a change."

Three plays later, Haden passed to Harold Jackson for a touchdown, and Minnesota's lead was only 17-13.

"I was sure we were going to win," Youngblood said. "We were making the big plays. We were making plays that get you to the Super Bowl."

Haden agreed. "I felt we'd come back and score right away," he said. "We'd score every time we had the ball."

The Rams reached the Vikings' 33 and 39 on their next two possessions. Hilgenberg blitzed and sacked Haden to kill the first threat. Then, with 2:31 to play, Bryant stepped in front of Jessie and intercepted at the Vikings' 7-yard line.

After Bryant's interception, Tarkenton threw a middle screen pass to Foreman, who broke a couple of tackles and ran 57 yards before he was knocked out of bounds at the Rams' 12-yard line.

Foreman was hurt on the play. His replacement, Sammy Johnson, scored with 33 seconds left.

In the Vikings' locker room, Grant said it was a credit to the Rams to come back the way they had. "They had so much adversity," he said. "But my team has a way of creating that adversity. We seem to find ways. It's a team game, and we can never forget that. This team plays with more emotion than any of my other Vikings teams. It's an added dimension that might, on our fourth try, help us win a Super Bowl."

Knox's press conference was filled with measured words. Like the rest of his team, he probably felt they were robbed, they should have won, and there really was a Metropolitan Stadium jinx.

But Knox talked in generalities, in polite coaching cliches. But then someone asked if Knox really felt the Vikings are "a great team."

Knox smiled and said with a resigned shrug, "A great team somehow finds a way to beat you. And one thing you have to say about the Vikings, they do know how to win. They do find those ways."

The Vikings were leading just 17-13 when Bobby Bryant's late fourth-quarter interception in front of Ron Jessie killed the last Rams' hope.

Sammy Johnson clinched the game for Minnesota with a 12-yard touchdown run.

GHOST TO THE POST

Oakland Raiders 37,
Baltimore Colts 31
December 24, 1977

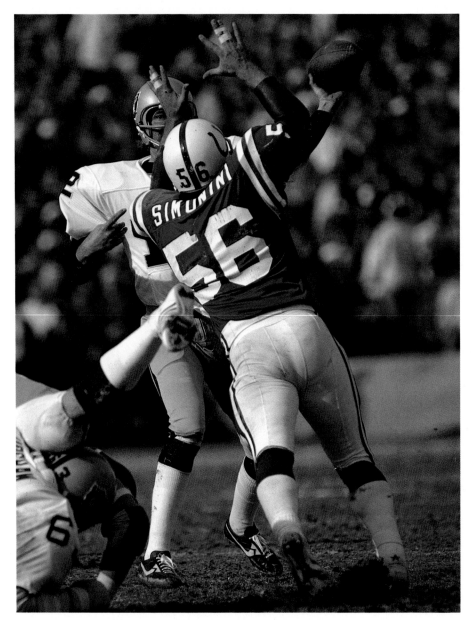

Despite pressure from Colts such as linebacker Ed Simonini, Oakland's Ken Stabler passed for 345 yards and three touchdowns—all to tight end Dave Casper. Stabler worked the ball around to five different receivers, however, as the lead changed hands eight times in the game.

'Twas the night before the night before Christmas and a man with a bag was passing out presents. There were motivational strings attached.

Gifts from the boss, Al Davis.

"Little trophies," head coach John Madden said. "Exact miniature replicas of the Lombardi Trophy we'd gotten for winning Super Bowl XI the year before."

The message was implicit: Let's do it again. Sometimes it's hard to hold onto a thought, difficult to remember the huge sense of pride winning creates. The little silver-chromed brass reminders only could help, Madden figured.

Especially since the Raiders' ticket into the playoffs had Wild Card stamped on it. Denver had come on strong in the second half of the season with its Orange Crush defense and edged the Raiders for the AFC West title. It meant Oakland's defense of the Super Bowl crown would be on the road. And the Raiders never had won a playoff game away from home.

The Raiders were in Baltimore, where the Colts had hoisted their third consecutive AFC East championship pennant.

"Bert Jones scares me. . .we have to contain Bert Jones," Madden told players, assistants, reporters, and anyone who got near him.

"That's our whole game plan. Three words: Contain Bert Jones."

Of course, Madden had worries other than the Colts' quarterback. For instance, he was concerned with the Baltimore pass rush and how it might affect his own offense, in particular, Raiders quarterback Ken Stabler.

"They have forty-seven sacks," Madden said. "That's a bunch. We could be in trouble."

Coaches are famous pessimists. They can conjure up the most horrible scenarios possible. Madden was one of the best/worst at such head games. It was all a part of preparation. In his mind's eye, Madden figured the Baltimore defensive front four of John Dutton, Fred Cook, Joe Ehrmann, and Mike Barnes could have a Christmas feast on Stabler.

With that unlikely happenstance planned for, Madden then could go about devising ways to keep this from happening. Pessimism has an antidote.

"This really isn't the way I like to celebrate the Christmas holidays," Madden said, excusing himself. "I'm going to bed."

When he woke up, his first thought was weather. What kind of blizzard was happening outside?

Instead, it was 47 degrees. Madden frowned. Then smiled. That's not so bad.

But that was only one less worry. On the bus ride to the stadium, visions of Bert Jones didn't dance in his head; they strafed and dive-bombed.

Madden admitted he didn't feel the least bit overconfident as the Raiders and Colts got ready to tee it up.

Memorial Stadium was jumping; almost 60,000 people had jammed into the old ball park. A three-game losing streak late in the season had people grumbling. Colts head coach Ted Marchibroda had fallen out of favor. There even were those who wanted a new quarterback ("Hey, I'd vote for that," Madden had bellowed) to replace Jones.

But, as Christmas Eve headed for high noon, all was forgiven. It was time to play football.

Marchibroda fretted as the Raiders warmed up. He also had his fears, although they were not as animated or demonstrative as Madden's.

"Stabler scares me to death," Marchibroda had said at a press conference earlier in the week. "And he's got all those receivers. And their pass rush is tremendous. And they're well-coached, too."

If Madden was worried about playing on the road, Marchibroda was wondering if his team was going to make another token appearance in the playoffs and lose in the first round, as it had each of the previous two years.

Mercifully, the game began. On the second play, Mark van Eeghen, the Oakland fullback who had run for a conference-leading 1,273 yards, fumbled and Baltimore recovered. Madden fumed.

It wasn't until the Raiders' defense had thrown back the Colts and the turnover had gone for naught that it appeared the burly coach was breathing again.

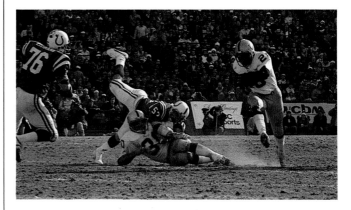

Both offenses seemed passive through most of the first quarter. Then Oakland came alive.

With less than two minutes left in the first period, halfback Clarence Davis broke loose and ran 30 yards into the end zone.

Oakland took a 7-0 lead when Clarence Davis raced 30 yards for a touchdown behind this block by running back Mark van Eeghen on linebacker Stan White. Van Eeghen was also the game's leading rusher with 76 yards.

"They are a left-handed team," Marchibroda explained later. "This is because they have two people who will probably be Hall of Fame offensive linemen playing the same side. Look at the films and see if [Art] Shell and [Gene] Upshaw didn't make big blocks on Davis's run."

They had. Then, too, the Colts' defense, despite all those quarterback sacks, had momentary lapses of poor tackling during the season.

A few minutes later, Oakland had another threat going. In the stands, there was a churning and growing disenchantment. Boos filtered down.

Stabler's eyes were slits as he looked at the Colts' defense. He had sent three receivers—Cliff Branch, Fred Biletnikoff, and van Eeghen—to the same side. It was third-and-six and the Raiders wanted to flood the Colts' coverage to see where the leak might be.

Stabler chose van Eeghen.

Baltimore safety Bruce Laird rotated in the Colts' zone.

in total yardage. Stabler hadn't been sacked yet. The Raiders were not playing poorly. They simply weren't scoring. Madden left the field ready to moan. But by the time he got to the locker room, he had talked himself out of it.

Taking the same thoughtful walk was Marchibroda, who had his own propaganda ready.

"They're staying close only because Bert got sacked three times to ruin our momentum and their punter [Ray Guy] is having a great day," Marchibroda said. "We've been backed up almost every series with no field position to work with. Otherwise we'd probably be way ahead."

Two coaches were making something out of very little. If you could believe what was said at halftime, each team had the other just where it wanted it.

"We need some consistency and we need some big plays," Madden told his team.

In the Colts' locker room, Marchibroda was clapping his hands and talking about special teams.

"Their kicker [Guy] is outkicking his coverage," the coach said. "We can break something on them with good blocks."

On the first play of the Raiders' first possession of the third quarter, Stabler sent van Eeghen over right guard for a yard. On second down, van Eeghen headed for the same hole again. Stabler turned and faked the handoff.

The Colts tied the score at 7-7 in the second quarter when safety Bruce Laird returned this interception of a Ken Stabler pass 61 yards for a touchdown.

"I had the flat," Laird said, "and I read the pattern and I just looked at Stabler, waiting for him to throw the ball."

The pass floated toward van Eeghen, but Laird stepped in front.

"I took it right off his hip," Laird said.

Over the next 61 yards, the Colts reclaimed a lot of fickle supporters. Laird's touchdown run tied the score.

With seven minutes left in the half, after five consecutive third-down failures by the Raiders, the Colts' running game started rolling. Lydell Mitchell, who had run for 1,159 yards and led the NFL with 71 pass receptions, and fullback Roosevelt Leaks forced the Raiders' secondary to respect Jones's play fakes. This opened up pass plays to Freddie Scott and Don McCauley for key first downs. When the Raiders toughened at their 19, Toni Linhart kicked a field goal for a 10-7 lead.

The Raiders stormed back behind Stabler, moving to the Colts' 23 in less than a minute. Madden turned to linebacker Ted Hendricks and said, "Wonder how we'll stop ourselves this time?"

Then Davis, running up the middle, was leveled and lost the ball. Dutton recovered for the Colts.

When the half ended 46 seconds later, Madden wondered if there was anything he could say to inspire his team. Then he started thinking.

Jones really had not been a damaging factor. The only Baltimore touchdown was the interception return. Oakland had almost doubled Baltimore

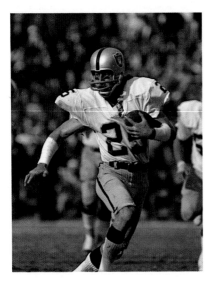

Oakland's Fred Biletnikoff caught seven passes for 88 yards.

Although Baltimore scored 31 points, quarterback Bert Jones did not throw a touchdown pass. He completed 12 of 26 attempts for 164 yards.

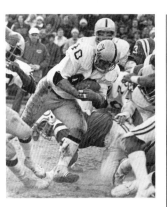

Ron Lee (left) gave Baltimore a 24-21 lead in the fourth quarter with this one-yard touchdown run. But Oakland matched that when Pete Banaszak (right) also ran a yard for a score, and the Raiders went back in front 28-24.

The Raiders' major personality trait always has been the long pass. They run a lot of timing routes, longer patterns that require an extra second or two of pass-blocking. Getting the defense to slow its charge because it thinks the ball is being handed off is crucial.

This time, the fake fooled everyone, and van Eeghen was buried by three Colts. Meanwhile, Stabler was lofting a 41-yard strike to Branch at the Baltimore 28. Shell and Upshaw escorted van Eeghen for runs of 16 and four yards, and on second down at the 8, Stabler threw a touchdown pass to tight end Dave Casper.

Madden pumped a fist into the air. That was more like it. His offense was alive at last.

Guy put the ball on the tee and prepared to kick off. Marshall Johnson stood on the goal line.

If Guy, the punter, overkicked his coverage, then Guy, the kickoff man, underkicked it.

Johnson ran up to catch the kick at the 13, made it through the wave of Oakland tacklers at the 25, then exploded down the sideline. Guy was the last Raider with a chance to make the tackle. But Johnson ran away from him. The Colts had regained the lead 17-14.

Madden stomped over to Stabler and said, "Gotta get it right back. Right now."

On second down, Stabler faded back, looking for Casper.

He didn't see Laird again.

"It got really weird," Laird said later. "Everything just started going crazy."

Laird's second interception gave the Colts the ball at the Raiders' 40. Jones tried to get another touchdown quickly.

Raiders defensive tackle Otis Sistrunk, however, had other ideas. Sistrunk deflected a pass, then sacked Jones, forcing David Lee to punt.

Ted Hendricks, however, got in the way and blocked the punt.

"Nobody in the history of football has ever been better than Ted Hendricks at punt blocking," Madden said. "He just has a real knack."

At the Baltimore 16, the Raiders tried two running plays before Stabler looked for Casper again.

"This time I also remembered to look for Laird, too," Stabler said.

The 10-yard touchdown pass gave Oakland back the lead, 21-17.

The fourth quarter began and it looked as if the winner would be the team that forced mistakes and cashed them in over the last 15 minutes.

Marchibroda continued to believe in Jones, even if the natives in the bleachers were getting restless.

Eight seconds into the fourth quarter, the Colts

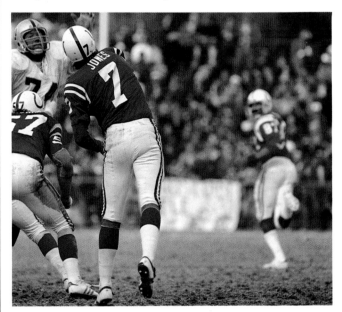

started an 80-yard, 13-play march to the go-ahead touchdown. Jones passed for first downs three times. Another important development was a pass interference penalty on Raiders rookie cornerback Lester Hayes, who was playing in place of injured veteran George Atkinson. Hayes, who excelled in aggressive, tight man-to-man coverage, bumped Glenn Doughty at the 1-yard line.

The Raiders held three consecutive times, forcing Marchibroda to make a tough decision: kick a field goal or go for it on fourth down?

"It wasn't so tough," the Colts' head coach said. "A field goal still kept us behind. We wanted the touchdown."

Fullback Ron Lee squeezed into the end zone, and Madden dropped to one knee in disappointment.

The Colts answered Banaszak's touchdown with a 73-yard touchdown drive of their own, highlighted by Jones's 30-yard pass to tight end Raymond Chester (87, downfield).

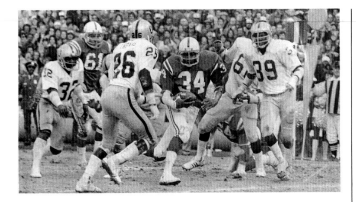

Baltimore culminated its 73-yard, fourth-quarter drive when Ron Lee broke off left tackle and raced 13 yards to the end zone. His second touchdown gave the Colts a 31-28 lead with 7:45 left in regulation.

Another long return by Carl Garrett—44 yards—set up Oakland, and the dizzying tempo continued. A 23-yard pass to van Eeghen and a pass interference penalty against the Colts' Nelson Munsey moved the ball to the Colts' 1. From there, Pete Banaszak, Madden's designated short-yardage man, dived over right guard and Oakland led again, 28-24.

"We really had it going," Madden said. "But so did they. Things were really back and forth."

It had taken the Raiders 63 seconds to get back into the lead. It took the Colts 68 seconds to reclaim it. Jones passed 30 yards to tight end Raymond Chester, a former Raider, then 16 yards to Lee. From the Raiders' 27, Lee swept around left end for 14 yards, then burst through left tackle for the final 13 yards and a touchdown and a 31-28 Baltimore lead.

Almost eight minutes still remained. At this rate, the final score was going to sound more like a basketball game had been played. But then came another downshift of action as the defenses stabilized. There was an exchange of punts, and, when the Raiders got the ball with almost three minutes left, everyone figured it was Last Chance time.

"We had time so it wasn't like we needed a miracle," Madden said. "Snake [Stabler] was so good at using the clock. So we weren't really worried.

"Well, put it this way, we weren't any more worried than usual."

After Stabler passed for one first down, the Raiders came up with the single most critical play of the game.

Ghost to the Post.

On a team of free spirits, with Snakes and Mad Storks and Lester the Molesters, tight end Dave Casper had a poltergeist nickname, albeit a friendly one. All afternoon the Ghost had been running short curls and crossing patterns underneath the Colts' zone defense. This time he took off on a deep post route.

"The pass was kinda like a wounded duck," Stabler later said.

"The pass was right over my head," Casper said. "Kenny throws such a soft ball that it really was a piece of cake to catch. If it looked tough, it really wasn't. I just ran under it and it stuck in my hands."

The 42-yard piece of cake brought the picnic to the Baltimore 14 and the crowd back to its feet. Three consecutive carries by Banaszak did little more than move Raiders kicker Errol Mann a little closer to the goal posts, where his 22-yard field goal tied the game 31-31 with 26 seconds left.

"When I heard the crowd groan," Hendricks said, "I knew the kick was good. I couldn't stand to watch it—I could hardly even bear to listen."

Chester felt the Colts had an advantage as the overtime period began. His former teammates were older and larger, each a factor when talking about stamina. But fatigue, obviously building up for everyone, never was a factor.

"It was automatic-pilot time," Chester said. "There was so much at stake. Everybody played so damn hard."

The Raiders had first chance at the victory, driving to the Colts' 33. But Mann's field-goal try was blocked by Barnes.

"I didn't feel good about things then," Madden said. "I was afraid that would be our only chance."

But the Colts were done offensively. Their two possessions of the overtime were three-and-out failures. With 4:16 left in overtime, by benefit of the

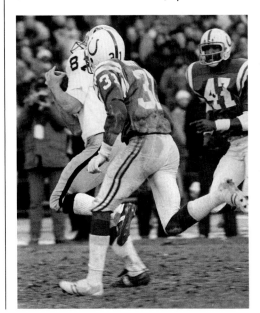

Trailing 31-28 with time running out, the Raiders streaked to the Colts' 14 on this 42-yard catch-and-run by Dave Casper. Nelson Munsey (31) and Tim Baylor gave chase.

With just 29 seconds remaining in regulation, Oakland's Errol Mann kicked a 22-yard field goal to tie the game at 31-31. Baltimore defensive end John Dutton (right) expressed his frustration at the Raiders' comeback.

inching war of field position, with Ray Guy either the ruler or the yardstick, Oakland took over at its 42-yard line.

As he came to the sideline, Raiders linebacker Monte Johnson, who was in on 20 tackles during the game, listened to something he'd been hearing for the last hour.

"I had this humming in my ear," he said. "The crowd had been yelling so loud and so long that I couldn't hear them anymore. I couldn't really hear anything."

Stabler completed three passes to Biletnikoff, the NFL's prototype possession receiver, and another to Branch, and the Raiders were back within Mann's kicking range. The overtime period ended with the Raiders at the Colts' 13.

"Things didn't look good," Laird said. "But we were hoping. It'd take a miracle but we were still hoping."

As it turned out, the Colts didn't have a ghost of a chance.

Madden noticed the Colts still were trying to cover Casper with one player.

He sent in a pass play.

Cornerback Munsey stood flat-footed as Casper ran past him, headed for the corner of the end zone. Munsey realized what was happening, but to no avail. Stabler's pass was caught by Casper in the seventy-fifth minute and forty-third second of the game.

The Raiders had won 37-31.

There was no real celebration in the Raiders' locker room. Only quiet relief. There was no crum-

bling agony by Baltimore, either. Only silent acceptance. Everyone agreed it had been a great game. Most, even on the Raiders, stopped short of calling it "fun."

Dave Casper said a better word for it might be "hell."

"I didn't like the game very much at all," he said. "When it goes back and forth like that, it's not a case of having fun. It's pressure and anxiety and fear you're going to lose. Playing checkers with your daughter is fun. Not this. This was the hardest football game I ever played."

John Madden in later years, after he left coaching, would describe the day as "the most exciting game I ever was involved with. That game had everything."

Almost two hours after the ordeal was over, Casper still wore his uniform.

"I'm suddenly so tired," he said as he sat at his locker. "I'm too tired to get undressed. I really don't think I can move."

In the Colts' locker room, Chester was moving just as slowly. The game had been exhausting, he said, "both mentally and physically. But we are not ashamed. We lost. We played hard.

"And tomorrow's still Christmas, no matter what."

In the second overtime, Casper finally ended the game when he clutched his third touchdown pass from Ken Stabler, this one a 10-yarder.

THE EARL OF HOUSTON

Houston Oilers 35,
Miami Dolphins 30
November 20, 1978

A week earlier, in the halftime highlights of "Monday Night Football," Howard Cosell had set the stage, as only he could:

"Next week, The Rose of Tyler, Texas. Earl Campbell, the Heisman Trophy winner, has taken the league by storm, along with the rest of the Houston Oilers, the hottest team in the National Football League. This kid is sensational and Bum Phillips knows just how to use him. But he'll get his sternest test because the Oilers must play the Miami Dolphins. Yes, the Dolphins, who are on their usual track to make the playoffs. Don Shula will come up with some way to try to stop young Mr. Campbell. And don't forget — he's got Delvin Williams, who happens to lead the NFL in rushing these days. And he's also got Bob Griese, apparently healthy again. Griese, who's led the Dolphins to so many big victories before. Earl Campbell and the Houston Oilers. Next Monday night, in the Houston Astrodome, you won't want to miss this one."

There were several minutes before the Houston Oilers would head down the runway to the field.

The night was already electric with anticipation. The Astrodome was bulging, packed to the rafters with fans. The syrupy fight song bounced back and forth and created a slight vibrating effect in the runway. There were blue pom-pons everywhere,

Earl Campbell scored four touchdowns in a classic Monday night shootout.

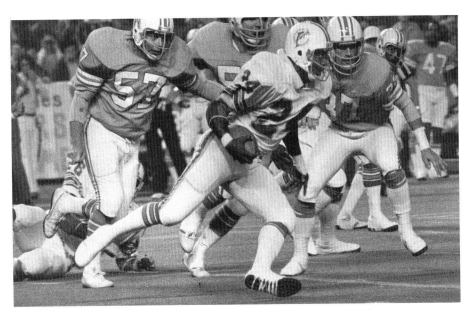

Miami's Delvin Williams, who came into the game as the NFL's leading rusher, gained 73 yards on 18 carries and scored on a one-yard run. But Campbell's 199-yard night shot him right past Williams for the rushing lead.

along with those corn-pone "Luv Ya Blue" placards.

Bum Phillips and his football team had seized the spotlight in Houston.

Soon it would touch a nation.

Soon the Oilers and Dolphins would play what arguably might be called the greatest Monday night game ever.

Soon prime-time America would get its first extended look at Earl Campbell.

"Hey, Rook—need about four from you tonight," said Carl Mauck, the Oilers' veteran center.

Campbell smiled, momentarily breaking his intensity.

"I'll try my hardest," he said.

Mauck, an 11-year veteran and one of the Oilers' captains, also smiled. He couldn't believe what he had just told the soft-spoken rookie running back. Four touchdowns? Against the Dolphins? In a Monday night game?

"Nothing like dumping a load on somebody, huh?" Mauck would say later.

In an opposite runway, where the Dolphins also were kicking in their stall with eagerness, the

talk was of containment, of defense.

Doug Betters, the defensive lineman with the red mountain-man beard and the hidden fire, was uncharacteristically demonstrative.

The Dolphins were walking slowly, cloaked in their usual Don Shula-inspired calm, heading for the light at the end of the runway. Betters suddenly beat a taped paw against his chest.

"Gotta kick ass tonight," he yelled.

Betters's declaration wafted through the Miami ranks. There were nods of agreement down the line.

"Earl Campbell... tonight we meet," linebacker Steve Towle said to nobody in particular.

The Astrodome noise was like a blast from a heat furnace. You could feel it. The Dolphins' head coach, Don Shula, frowned and immediately looked for his quarterback, Griese. Calling cadence would be a problem if the crowd chose a particular moment to get excited. Across the field, on the other sideline, Phillips, the Oilers' head coach, also was concerned with the runaway enthusiasm. His team wasn't used to a glaring spotlight. Youthful mistakes, generated by wanting to please the home crowd, might be a problem.

In the ABC booth, Frank Gifford sensed the communal energy that kept building in the bleachers

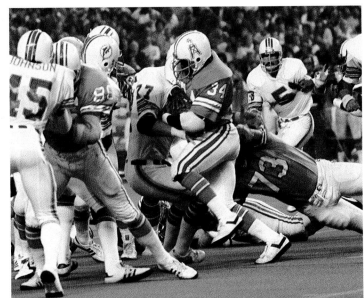

Campbell's four touchdowns came on runs of 1, 6, 12, and 81 yards, the last one clinching the Oilers' victory late in the fourth quarter.

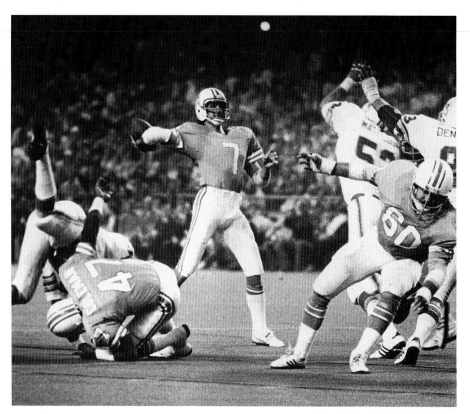

In the preseason, Griese had torn ligaments in his knee. He didn't return to the Miami lineup until the end of October. Throughout his career, the quiet Griese always had had Larry Csonka or Paul Warfield to deflect fame. Bob Griese was the guy who handed off or threw the occasional third-down pass.

Against the Oilers, however, Griese put his name on the top of the marquee. His right arm became a flamethrower. When the night finally was done, Griese had completed 23 of 33 passes for 349 yards and two touchdowns.

Although Houston stayed mainly on the ground, Dan Pastorini passed for 156 yards and a touchdown.

with each shake of the pom-pons, each twangy note of the Oilers' fight song. "Boy, this is fun," he said.

And the opening kickoff still was a minute away.

There seems to be a pattern to a football game that makes it classic even while it is still happening, a form in which emotion knocks the wind out of its witnesses, a level of intensity that somehow keeps strangling perception that the last play is the best one yet.

For three quarters, the Oilers and Dolphins traded touchdowns. Three apiece. One a quarter.

"We actually felt we were doing a good job on Campbell," Dolphins linebacker Rusty Chambers said. "But the thing we noticed was how he seemed to get stronger. Every time he got the ball, he seemed to run harder."

Campbell had scored the Oilers' first touchdown on a one-yard run, tying the score. The Dolphins had taken an early lead on Griese's 10-yard scoring pass to wide receiver Nat Moore.

The Oilers also were feeling comfortable with the way their defense was handling Williams and the Dolphins' veteran offensive line. Although the Miami running back did get into the end zone in the second quarter (on a one-yard run), the Oilers generally lassoed Williams and ultimately limited him to 73 yards on 18 carries.

"But we weren't ready for what Griese did to us," Phillips said.

"There were times," Phillips said, scratching his famous flattop, "that there wasn't a dadgum thing we could do to stop him."

The Oilers scored on a pass from quarterback Dan Pastorini to tight end Mike Barber in the second quarter to take a brief lead, before Griese drove Miami downfield to set up Williams's plunge.

A good football game became a great one in the second half, and the world got a good look at what Campbell was all about.

"I knew he was something special before the season ever started," said Oilers linebacker Robert Brazile, "when he showed up at all our minicamps, even the tryout camps. Imagine that—the Heisman Trophy winner at a tryout camp. Sometimes you worry about a guy who has a big reputation coming out of college. But Earl? Earl's Earl."

Phillips put it in more Bum-like terms.

"I don't know if Earl Campbell's in a class by himself," Phillips said. "But it sure don't take long to call the roll."

Campbell, who became an Oiler when Houston traded four draft choices and tight end Jimmie Giles to Tampa Bay for the number-one pick in the 1978 NFL college draft, had 44 yards at halftime.

In the third quarter, the Oilers took the lead on a six-yard run by Campbell. Miami tied it later in the period on a touchdown run by Leroy Harris.

"Just a terrific football game," Cosell said.

Houston's Bum Phillips consoled Miami's Don Shula after the Oilers delighted their fans with a 35-30 victory.

With 12:25 to play, blitzing Miami linebacker A.J. Duhe burst through and dumped Pastorini in the end zone for a safety. The Dolphins had a 23-21 lead, and Houston had to give the ball back.

"Aw, that safety wasn't gonna decide the game," Phillips said. "It wasn't major because there was so much time left. It wasn't something we wanted to give up. But it sure wasn't what was gonna decide the game. I knew that for sure.

"Earl was gonna decide it."

But after a punt to put the ball in play, the Dolphins took over at their 45-yard line.

"That was the key series in the game," Griese said afterward.

Miami couldn't capitalize. It had to punt the ball back to Houston.

"We just stalled," Shula said. "It was probably the point where the game turned."

With 4:46 to play, the Oilers took a 28-23 lead on a 12-yard run by "Souperman," "The Rose," or the other nicknames the many posters around the Astrodome had for Campbell. "No. 34—A Gusher of a Rusher" read one banner in the end zone.

Griese rallied the Dolphins once more, silencing the 50,290 fanatics with a drive down the field. But with 3:05 left, Griese's pass to tight end Andre Tillman was tipped by safety Mike Reinfeldt and floated into the hands of Oilers linebacker Steve Kiner at the Houston 7.

It had come down to this: The Oilers needed a first down, maybe two . . . enough to kill off the remaining time. The Dolphins needed the ball back. They needed one last chance for Griese.

"There ain't no secrets," Phillips said. "Everybody knows what we're gonna do and who's gonna do it."

Tim Wilson carried the ball on first down. Two runs by Campbell produced a first down. Then Campbell was up for a yard gain. It was second-and-9 at the Oilers' 19. There was 1:22 to play when Pastorini gave the ball to Campbell.

Speed and uncommon quickness for a man of 225 pounds got Campbell around the right corner. Miami linebacker Kim Bokamper had a shot, but

missed. So did defensive back Curtis Johnson. Suddenly there was only one man to beat.

Steve Towle seemed to have the angle. Then he didn't.

Campbell was headed for Lubbock, with Towle in his rearview mirror. Eighty-one yards. The cheer blocked out even Howard Cosell.

"Earl messed up our game plan there," Phillips deadpanned. "The plan was to run for a first down, then run out the clock. But I still wouldn't trade him for all the peppers in Mexico."

The celebrating pile in the end zone, not to mention the journey to get there, claimed Campbell's breath. His rib cage heaved. He headed for the oxygen. That seemed only fair because his late-blooming heroics had rendered the rest of the house breathless.

The Dolphins scored a meaningless touchdown on the game's final play. But the night belonged to the Oilers. Or was it the Earlers?

As the team left the field, the 35-30 final score still burning brightly over the numb, exhausted crowd, Earl Campbell waved a University of Texas Hook-'em-Horns gesture and flashed a wide grin.

He wound up with 199 yards on 28 carries. And, yes, four touchdowns.

After his four-touchdown, 199-yard night, Earl Campbell flashed the "Hook 'em Horns" sign from his alma mater, Texas. After winning the Heisman Trophy at Texas in 1977, he won the NFL rushing title (1,450 yards) in 1978.

SUPER SUPER BOWL

Pittsburgh Steelers 35,
Dallas Cowboys 31
January 21, 1979

"One roll of film and one pack of gum," said the cashier in the gift shop of the Fort Lauderdale hotel.

"Are you going to the game?"

"Yes ma'am, my dad's playing in it." Without being asked, the 14-year-old boy added, "Jackie Smith, number eighty-one for the Cowboys."

Darrell Smith carefully inserted the film into his Instamatic. He would try to remember to save a couple of shots for after the Super Bowl in the Cowboys' locker room. Hopefully, they would be victory pictures.

The kickoff for Super Bowl XIII still was five hours away. Darrell Smith looked outside at the hard rain, at the wind blowing in all directions, and he wondered what a hurricane must feel like.

Forty miles away, at the Fountainbleu Hotel, Terry Bradshaw was waking up. The Pittsburgh Steelers' quarterback had switched rooms around midnight, after his telephone kept ringing.

Wide open in the end zone, Dallas tight end Jackie Smith wound up on his back after dropping Roger Staubach's potential touchdown pass in the third quarter. The Cowboys settled for a field goal and lost Super Bowl XIII 35-31.

"Then I had the strangest dreams," Bradshaw remembered. ". . . about Billy Kilmer."

When his 8 A.M. wake-up call came, Bradshaw pulled himself to the side of the bed, and, still drowsy, got to his feet and pulled open the curtains.

"I saw all the rain and I just laughed," he said. "I always liked playing in rain and mud. Maybe it's the little boy in me. I saw that as a good sign."

An hour later, Bradshaw went downstairs to breakfast. "When I walked in the restaurant," he said, "who was sitting there in a booth? Billy Kilmer. That seemed like a pretty good sign, too."

Bradshaw decided that dreams do come true.

Jackie Smith was thinking the same way.

Years later, Bradshaw would remember Super Bowl XIII "as the most fun I ever had playing football. It was a great game but it was just so much fun, too."

Jackie and Darrell Smith don't remember the game quite like that. It was the last game Jackie Smith, a 16-year veteran who had been signed as a free agent by the Dallas Cowboys three months earlier, would play. In the crowded locker room after the game, he announced his retirement, a cruel punctuation point to a sterling all-pro career with the St. Louis Cardinals.

Darrell Smith never did take the last two pictures on his roll of film. He never even got it developed.

This was the Super Bowl in which people realized pregame buildup could become so monstrous it would be almost impossible for the actual game to live up to expectations. But this one did.

Pittsburgh 35, Dallas 31.

For a week, the buzzword among the two teams had been intimidation. There was taunting and chest-thumping. And there was Thomas (Hollywood) Henderson.

A linebacker with stunning speed and strength, Henderson splashed a week of audacity upon the international media.

"Terry Bradshaw couldn't spell 'cat' if you spotted him the 'c' and the 'a,'" Henderson said.

Each day produced further outrages.

Henderson called Steelers tight end Randy Grossman, who would re-

John Stallworth gave Pittsburgh a 7-0 first-quarter lead with this 28-yard touchdown catch over cornerback Aaron Kyle. Safety Cliff Harris (43) arrived too late. Stallworth caught three passes for 115 yards and two touchdowns.

place the injured Bennie Cunningham, "nothing but a sub. How much respect can you have for a backup tight end? He's the guy who comes in when everyone else is dead."

And then came the ultimate insult. Hollywood desecrated Jack Lambert, his all-pro counterpart on the Steelers.

"I don't care for the man," Henderson said. "He makes more money than I do, and he don't have no teeth. He's Dracula. Count Lambert, that's what I'm gonna call him."

Ten Super Bowls earlier, Joe Namath had sent similar shock waves through the pro football establishment, guaranteeing victory in Super Bowl III. Was Hollywood like Broadway?

Obviously, the two best teams in the NFL had made it to Super Sunday. But they also were teams with strong, colorful personalities.

Jackie Smith spent the week before the game in virtual anonymity. He'd expected it. Smith had become a Cowboy only because reserve tight end Jay Saldi had broken an arm. Smith, who would be 39 in a month, enjoyed almost uncontested privacy all through the blustery week.

That would change by Sunday night.

As the game time approached, there was a meteorological shift of momentum. The wind calmed, the rain stopped, and there were streaks of sunshine to greet early birds at the Orange Bowl.

Nobody was ready for the lightning that was coming.

On the first play from scrimmage, Dallas's Tony Dorsett ran for nine yards. He ran for 16 more on the second. Two plays later, he sped for 13 more. It was first down at the Steelers' 34, and the Steel Cur-

On the last play of the first quarter, Tony Hill of Dallas escaped on a 39-yard touchdown catch-and-run that tied the score at 7-7.

Thomas (Hollywood) Henderson wrapped up Pittsburgh quarterback Terry Bradshaw from behind, and fellow linebacker Mike Hegman stole the ball and ran 37 yards for a touchdown. It gave Dallas a 14-7 second-quarter lead.

tain seemed in shreds.

Landry then decided to try a gadget play, a double reverse. But Drew Pearson fumbled the second handoff. Defensive end John Banaszak recovered for Pittsburgh at the Steelers' 47-yard line.

Quickly, the Steelers faced a third down. Nine yards were needed for a first down. Third-and-long is a test of a quarterback, and Bradshaw had been criticized long before Henderson did it.

"They all called me a dumb blond for a lot of years," Bradshaw said. "Then I started losing my hair. Sure, it hurt to be called dumb. But the only way to get rid of a reputation is show everybody they're wrong. Third-and-long is a good way."

Bradshaw sensed a blitz. His quick pass to Stallworth, crossing over the middle, was on target. First down. Two plays later, on another third-and-long, Bradshaw came through again. This time it was to Grossman, who caught the ball and lunged for another first down.

At the Dallas 28, Bradshaw dropped back, saw Stallworth breaking free on the left, and "just put it up so he could go after it." The touchdown came with 9:47 left in the first quarter.

Dallas roared back. It was typical Roger Staubach, typical Cowboys. But with second down at the Steelers' 39, Staubach was trampled by tackle Steve Furness. Loss of 12. On the next play, defensive end Dwight White broke through to sack Staubach. Loss of 10. Typical Steelers.

After a punt, the Cowboys' defense teetered; the Flex was in a state of flux. Bradshaw connected with Franco Harris for 22 yards, Lynn Swann for 13.

Then Bradshaw made a mistake.

"Yeah, a *dumb* mistake," he said.

At the Cowboys' 30, Bradshaw tried to link up with Stallworth again.

"I looked at him all the way, never took my eyes off him," Bradshaw said.

Dallas linebacker D.D. Lewis never took his eyes off Bradshaw. Lewis simply got into the line of sight and waited for the interception that arrived momentarily.

Late in the first quarter, Bradshaw fumbled as he was hit by defensive end Harvey Martin. Dallas struck quickly. From the Shotgun, Staubach looked one way, then back to Tony Hill just as the wide receiver was putting a sideline move on Steelers safety Donnie Shell. It was perfect choreography, receiver and quarterback. Shell fell for it, bit, and Hill ran by him. Mel Blount was late arriving. Hill's touchdown ended the quarter. It was the only first-quarter score the Steelers had allowed all season.

After the kickoff, the Steelers soon faced their customary third-and-long dilemma. Landry sent both linebackers on a blitz. Henderson got there first. He locked his arms around Bradshaw and twirled him around. The ball was stripped free. Mike Hegman, the other Dallas blitzer, grabbed the ball before it hit the ground and ran 37 yards to the end zone.

Bradshaw, in obvious discomfort, wobbled to the

Pittsburgh's John Stallworth pulled away from Dallas cornerback Benny Barnes (31) on a 75-yard scoring pass from Terry Bradshaw in the second quarter. Stallworth's second touchdown tied the score at 14-14, and the Steelers went on to lead 21-14 at halftime.

The Steelers threatened to break away later in the second quarter. But Landry blitzed two linebackers once more, and Bradshaw was nailed. Roy Gerela's 51-yard field-goal attempt hit the crossbar.

Then the Cowboys erupted, five plays, from their 34 to the Steelers' 32. But Blount intercepted. In frustration, the Cowboys were called for piling on.

One play later, Ed (Too Tall) Jones was pointing at a Pittsburgh lineman, then to the yellow flag on the ground. Holding.

"But the thing about Bradshaw that day," Landry said, "was his accuracy downfield and his ability to make big plays all game."

Down the right sideline, Bradshaw to Swann for 29. Over the middle, Swann again, this time for 21 yards. First down, 47 seconds left in the half.

On third down at the 7, the Steelers needed a yard for a first down. The clock was running, and 30 seconds remained.

"I was hoping they'd be wondering if we'd just try to get the first," Bradshaw said. "I was hoping they'd play the run."

Bradshaw rolled right. Run or pass? Dallas was ready for a run. Bradshaw flipped a pass toward Rocky Bleier, who had brushed a block and curled into the end zone.

"I threw the dang thing too high," Bradshaw said. "Had to . . . . Someone with long arms was all over me."

The Cowboys had third down at the Steelers' 10 in the third quarter, when Roger Staubach passed to a wide-open Jackie Smith (81, top) in the end zone. But, as he fell down, Smith couldn't catch the ball.

bench, his shoulder shooting with pain. The appearance of the trainer and the team doctor huddled over the quarterback started a buzz that shot around the Orange Bowl. When Bradshaw handed the ball off to Harris twice in a row on the next possession, the whispers became rumors.

Something was wrong with Bradshaw, and it was third-and-five at the Steelers' 25.

"Aw, there was nothing wrong with my passing arm," Bradshaw said later. "I had a little pain in my left shoulder was all. Henderson twisted me pretty good. But I could still throw."

Swann ran a deep pattern, but he was smothered. Bradshaw looked for somebody else, and Stallworth was breaking open.

The pass was perfect and the next 65 yards were a foot race. The score was tied.

Bleier jumped as high as he could. The referee raised both hands. The touchdown gave Pittsburgh a 21-14 lead.

In the third quarter, the Steelers suddenly went stale. Or conservative. Two straight possessions—three downs and out.

"Stallworth had some leg cramps," Bradshaw insisted later. "That's why we weren't throwing."

After an exchange of punts, the Cowboys had

Leading 21-17, Pittsburgh got a big break in the fourth quarter when wide receiver Lynn Swann (88) and Dallas cornerback Benny Barnes collided at the Cowboys' 23. Interference was called on Barnes to set up a touchdown.

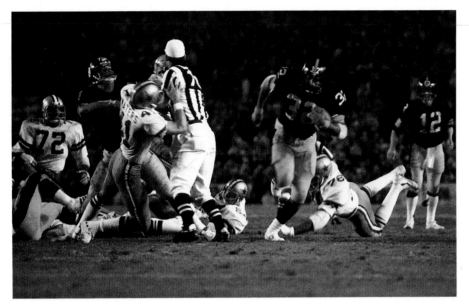

The Steelers grabbed a 28-17 lead on Franco Harris's 22-yard touchdown burst up the middle on a trap play. Dallas safety Charlie Waters (41, left) was screened off by umpire Art Demmas. Harris ran for 68 yards in the game.

good field position. Landry decided on another trick. Rookie cornerback Ron Johnson excelled in recognizing a running play, then closing in for the tackle. When Staubach handed the ball to Dorsett, Landry figured Johnson would charge to the line.

When Dorsett wheeled and lateraled the ball back to Staubach, Landry hoped Johnson would already have abandoned his coverage on Tony Hill. Staubach's pass was perfect. Hill reached for the ball. It never arrived.

It was batted away by Johnson, who never was fooled by the play fake.

"Man, what a play," Bradshaw said. "I know Roger thought he had six on that one. It was about ten inches away from perfection. Then Johnson made the play."

But the Cowboys would not surrender. They got the first down on a pass to Preston Pearson. From the Steelers' 30, the Cowboys set up in a double-tight end alignment. Jackie Smith ran onto the field.

Darrell Smith clicked off a picture from his seat in the stands.

Smith had not caught a pass in the regular season. He had planned to retire the year before, when a doctor told him he was risking permanent paralysis because of a nagging neck injury. But the lure of being a champion, of playing in a Super Bowl at last, had drawn him back. He was selling real estate and running a restaurant in October. Then Landry called him.

The Cowboys used three consecutive running plays and gained a first down at the 17. Two more plays gained seven yards. On third down, Dallas needed three for the first down, 10 for the score.

Staubach called a time out. Landry stood on the sidelines, arms folded.

"We wanted to be certain," Landry said. "We wanted the touchdown."

Now it was the Steelers' turn to wonder: run or pass?

Staubach barked signals, trying to make his cadence uneven and draw the Steelers offside. Lambert, the defensive captain, figured Staubach would be passing and called a blitz, charging up the middle himself.

"Staubach's cool," Lambert said. "You can't rattle him. You have to wrap him up. Just getting close to him won't do it."

Lambert got close. But Landry had called a perfect play. Staubach had already spotted Smith, who was ridiculously alone in the end zone.

"I took something off the pass," Staubach said afterward. "I saw him open. I didn't want to drill it through his hands. The ball was low. It could have been thrown better."

Jackie Smith said, "I just dropped it."

The soft pass was low, a little behind Smith.

"Not enough to miss it," Smith said. "I was so wide open. I tried to get down, tried to be over-cautious. On a ball like that, you want to get it in your hands and pull it close to your body. Then my left foot stuck and my hip went out from under me. The ball hit my hip pad and then my chest."

Lynn Swann gave the Steelers a 35-17 lead with this 18-yard touchdown catch midway through the fourth quarter. It was Terry Bradshaw's fourth scoring pass.

Smith flopped over backward on the painted grass. The ball rolled away. The field-goal unit came on and Smith walked off. The Cowboys settled for a field goal and still trailed by four points.

In the fourth quarter the Steelers began another drive. On a second-and-five from his 44, Bradshaw dropped back, looking once more for Swann.

"Post pattern," said Bradshaw.

But Cowboys' cornerback Benny Barnes was with Swann all the way. At the Cowboys' 23, the two bumped, and Barnes fell. Swann tried to make his cut. He went down as well. The pass fell, untouched.

But there was a flash of yellow, a penalty flag. Field Judge Fred Swearingen waved his arms. It was interference, but offensive or defensive? Call it either way: Lynn Swann or Benny Barnes?

Barnes was called for tripping.

Barnes exploded with anger and shock, rolling on the ground in disbelief.

Suddenly, it was third-and-nine at the Cowboys' 22. The Dallas Flex is supposed to be trap-proof. Steelers head coach Chuck Noll is one of those people who believe execution of his trap-blocking offense can overcome anything. Bradshaw knew the Cowboys were expecting a pass. And he out-thought them once again. The Steelers ran a textbook trap over left tackle. Franco Harris ran untouched into the end zone, giving the Steelers a 28-17 lead with 7:10 to play.

The kickoff flew on a line toward Randy White, the big defensive tackle. White's left hand was fractured in the regular season; it was in a cast. He couldn't control the ball. The Steelers recovered.

Bradshaw surveyed the field, then hit Swann on an 18-yard touchdown pass. Only 6:51 remained. The quarterback with the hot hand was spelling doom for Dallas.

But Dallas lashed back with a fury. Staubach, the consummate competitor, tried for a miracle. The Cowboys went 89 yards in eight plays, Staubach passing to Billy Joe DuPree for the touchdown.

Of course, there was an onside kick, and, of course, the Cowboys recovered. Dallas scored quickly, this time Staubach passing to Butch Johnson.

But there were only 22 seconds left. The drama was exquisite.

Everyone was on his feet for a possibly impossible finish to a thoroughly amazing game. Rafael Septien's onside kick dribbled forward.

There was a pile, a scramble. On the bottom, squeezing the ball, was Rocky Bleier. On top of him, clawing desperately and trying to recover one

last grasp at glory, was the Cowboys' Jackie Smith.

Moments later, the Steelers became the first team to win three Super Bowls.

Bradshaw was surrounded by reporters. He spat tobacco juice into a paper cup and said, "I told you this son-of-a-gun was gonna be fun."

Bradshaw had set three Super Bowl records. His team had won. He had been named most valuable player. And his paper cup runneth over with great expectorations.

In the other locker room, Smith emerged from the shower, naked except for a towel, and found almost as many reporters and broadcasters waiting for him as waited for Bradshaw.

Darrell Smith stood off to the side, waiting to go home. His father's team had lost.

The crowd of journalists asked the same embar-

Dallas uncorked a dramatic rally late in the game, scoring two quick touchdowns. Tight end Billy Joe DuPree got the first on a seven-yard pass from Roger Staubach.

rassing questions over and over. Some would leave and others would take their place. Smith tried to comb his hair, but microphones blocked his path. Once, the crowd lurched and a reporter lost his balance and his felt-tip pen brushed across Smith's back, leaving a black streak on his shoulder blade.

The ear-to-ear grin of Bradshaw and the solemn gaze of Jackie Smith were perfect contrasts as Super Bowl XIII ebbed into darkness.

Celebrity subsided for Smith one final time. He had dressed and looked to escape. But the embers smoldered and burst back into flame when somebody stuck a tape recorder in his face and wanted to hear the story once more. What happened? Why did you drop the pass? How do you feel? Did you cost your team the game?

The crow's feet around Smith's eyes were drawn tight. He said with a voice soft as a prayer, "I've had about all I can take. All these years, all the work, all the wait. Is this all everyone's going to remember?"

And he waved to his son. It was time to go home. On the way out the door, they saw Benny Barnes. He was in a hurry, too.

THE DOUBLE COMEBACK

Dallas Cowboys 35,
Washington Redskins 34
December 16, 1979

Linebacker D.D. Lewis (50) and defensive end Harvey Martin celebrated Dallas's remarkable come-from-behind 35-34 victory over Washington in 1979.

On the final day of the 1979 regular season, the Dallas Cowboys took their hardened, reinforced stereotype of being a cold, mechanical team made of football software and tele-circuitry—robots with stars on their helmets—and shattered it over the heads of the Washington Redskins.

In their long, sometimes unfriendly, always charismatic rivalry, the Cowboys and Redskins had played many games with dramatic finishes. But none ever topped this. No defeat ever was so cruel. No victory was so fine. No game had higher highs or lower lows than when the Cowboys beat the Redskins 35-34 at Texas Stadium.

"The greatest Cowboy comeback," said a beaming Tex Schramm, the Cowboys' president and general manager. "And that's saying a lot."

Washington head coach Jack Pardee wiped away a tear in the postgame locker room and said there never had been a defeat, not as a player nor a coach, that hurt as badly.

That was saying a lot, too.

"It hurts so deeply," Pardee said, his voice barely a whisper.

What the Cowboys did that December afternoon was come back twice, first from a 17-0 deficit, finally from a 34-21 disadvantage, scoring the winning touchdown with 39 seconds to play. The eight-yard pass from quarterback Roger Staubach to wide receiver Tony Hill not only wrested the NFC East divisional title away from the Redskins, it kicked Washington out of the playoffs (the Chicago Bears wound up with an NFC wild-card spot instead).

"They got what they deserved," said Cowboys defensive end Harvey Martin. "Nothing."

Cowboys blood had been boiling for more than a month. In November, the Cowboys had been humbled 34-20 by the Redskins. When Pardee sent kick-

Trailing 17-0, the Cowboys scored on a one-yard touchdown run by Ron Springs.

er Mark Moseley onto the field with nine seconds remaining to kick a field goal that seemed only to compound the insult, the Cowboys grumbled and flashed real fire, not the computerized kind. So often this team was perceived as some mechanical mirror of its head coach, the steely Tom Landry, whose next outburst of emotion would be his first. That was his reputation and his team's as well.

"But it was false," Landry said. "You can't play football without emotion. You can't coach it without emotion. You don't have to show it in public during a game. It is within our character to respond to situations like this. And we did."

"They rubbed our faces in it," Martin growled after the game in Washington.

Actually, the Redskins had genuine method to their apparent madness. Because of the NFL's system for determining the wild card with a complicated point-differential clause for tiebreakers, Washington had been correct in trying to score as many points as possible.

"As it turned out, we should have faked that field goal and gone for the touchdown," said Joe Theismann, the Redskins' quarterback.

The bitter aftertaste lingered on the Cowboys' charter flight home. For one, Martin didn't like what he was hearing. Some of his teammates actually were smiling and laughing and having a good time.

"I went crazy," Martin admitted.

Walking down the aisle, Martin said in a booming voice, "Used to be when Dallas lost to Washington you could hear a pin drop. It hurt to lose. It's supposed to hurt. Losing ain't worth a damn. This isn't a happy time. Fellows, some of the older players are upset. *Really* upset."

The plane was quiet except for the low rumble of the engines. Martin stood stoically for several seconds, letting his stinging words settle. Then he added, "If you don't hurt when you lose, you're gonna lose again."

In one of the seats, defensive tackle Larry Cole was making a list: Ten Things Wrong With Our Team.

Number one and underlined three times: Attitude.

The next day, a meeting was planned for the defensive team. No coaches were allowed. The meeting was postponed. That morning, Tom Landry handed linebacker Thomas (Hollywood) Henderson his walking papers.

"It was something that had to be done," Martin said. "Then other players started wondering who's next. We started our turnaround that day."

The next day, the defense did meet to stomp out the little prairie fires that were flaring all over the Cowboys' ranch. An attitude adjustment. Cole read his list of grievances. Martin and linebacker D.D. Lewis spoke. Even cornerback Benny Barnes got up to say something. "We were really surprised," Martin said. "Benny never speaks up."

The Cowboys' play did improve and the stretch run to the playoffs smoothed out. Then came the final Sunday, and the Washington Redskins.

Running back Preston Pearson made a falling, 26-yard touchdown catch to bring Dallas to within three, 17-14, at halftime.

The scoring differential system had thrown an interesting scenario into the day. Earlier, the Bears had run it up on the St. Louis Cardinals 42-6. That meant the 33-point advantage the Redskins carried into the final week was gone. That meant the Redskins had to beat the Cowboys; they had to win the division outright.

In the Cowboys' meeting room, someone had written something on a chalkboard: ATTITUDE. It was underlined three times.

The game began, and the Redskins, who had every right to be aroused themselves, leaped to a

The Cowboys scored 21 successive points for a 21-17 lead. But, after a Mark Moseley field goal pulled Washington to within a point, John Riggins sent the Redskins ahead again, 27-21, with this one-yard touchdown run.

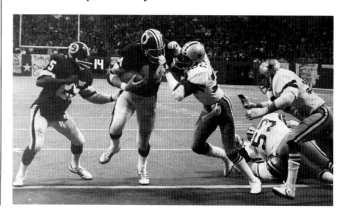

Wide receiver Tony Hill of Dallas was the game's leading receiver with eight catches for 113 yards, including the winning touchdown. Cowboys quarterback Roger Staubach completed 24 of 42 passes for 336 yards.

17-0 lead on a short touchdown run by Theismann, a long touchdown pass to running back Benny Malone, and a field goal by Moseley.

Then it was the Cowboys' turn.

"That was what made that game so thrilling," Dallas quarterback Roger Staubach said. "There were so many scoring shifts. They got seventeen straight, then we scored the next twenty-one, then they got the next seventeen. Then we got the last fourteen. It was so exciting—up and down, back and forth all game."

As the Cowboys, who played without injured running back Tony Dorsett, tried to get their act together, Staubach and Landry discussed offense the way someone might go over a grocery list.

"When you get down, you don't think about big comebacks or rallies," Staubach said. "You just talk about plays and how to execute them."

The Cowboys scored one touchdown early in the second quarter, and, with nine seconds left in the half, Staubach's 26-yard touchdown pass to Preston Pearson suddenly lifted the team and its fans out of their despondency.

Never in team history had the Cowboys come back to win a game from 17 points behind. But when Robert Newhouse scored on a two-yard run early in the third quarter, Dallas took the lead.

Theismann turned to John Riggins, his fullback, and said, "Riggo, this can't be happening."

Early in the fourth quarter, Moseley kicked a field goal to make it 21-20. Moments later, at midfield, Staubach threw a pass "that hit [Redskins safety] Mark Murphy right in the numbers, a really bad pass by me."

The Redskins regained the lead as Riggins bulled over from a yard out. Then with 6:54 to play, Riggins swept around end, burst down the sideline and rumbled 66 yards for what appeared to be a crushing, championship-clinching touchdown.

When the Cowboys failed to move the ball on the next possession, things were bleak on the Dallas sideline. Two minutes later, when the Redskins were pounding time off the clock, desperation had set in.

"We need a damned miracle," Schramm bellowed from his seat in the press box. "I don't know if we've used up our ration, but we need another miracle."

Fans were filing out of the stadium when Texas lightning struck. Washington's Clarence Harmon took a handoff and Cowboys safety Cliff Harris met him almost immediately.

Harris's helmet dug into Harmon's midsection and jarred the ball loose. The fumble bounced into the arms of tackle Randy White, who was lying on the ground and "couldn't have got out of the way of that ball if I'd tried. It was like we were supposed to have that ball."

The sudden bolt of fate was, according to Landry, "just one of about four key plays that allowed us to get back in the game."

And, according to Staubach, "It was opportunity that had 'Last One Available' stamped all over it."

From the Cowboys' 41, Staubach coolly gunned holes in the Redskins' secondary, completing passes of 14 yards to Butch Johnson, 19 yards to Tony Hill, and, finally, 26 yards to Ron Springs for the touchdown.

Two minutes and 20 seconds were left.

Was it enough for Dallas?

"The way Riggins was running—no," Randy White said. "They played ball control so well. They only needed one first down to force us to use all our time outs."

Moments later, it was third-and-two at the Redskins' 33-yard line. The classic football dilemma. And Washington had the classic player for just such a situation. Riggins already had carried the ball 21 times, already had gained a one-game career-best 153 yards. Everybody knew who would get the ball.

Including Cole.

"I took two gambles," he said. "One was that he would get the ball, which wasn't something you needed to be a brain surgeon to figure out. The other was that he would run right."

At the snap of the ball, Cole deliberately made his charge to the left. If the Redskins and Riggins had run the other way, Cole would be taking himself out of the play entirely.

Instead he ran directly into Riggins. The classic confrontation resulted in a two-yard loss. The Red-

Hill eluded cornerback Lemar Parrish for the winning eight-yard touchdown catch, which came with just 39 seconds left in the game. It was Staubach's third touchdown pass and finished off a 75-yard, seven-play drive.

skins were forced to punt.

"I had more speed than I thought and Riggins showed more indecision than I expected," Cole said later.

"Cole's play saved us two time outs," Landry said.

After a punt, the Cowboys had the ball at their 25, two time outs, and 1:46 to play with. In the huddle, Staubach could sense the booming confidence.

"We suddenly realized we didn't have to rush," he said. "We had time."

The Cowboys also had Staubach's hot hand. There had been so many of these last-minute marches to victory with Staubach at the helm. Completions of 20 yards to Hill and 22 and 25 to Preston Pearson moved the Cowboys to the Redskins' 8-yard line: first-and-goal.

"We called a play for [tight end] Billy Joe Du-Pree," Staubach said.

But Staubach had some special instructions for Hill: "If your man 'dogs' you, run a Fast Nine."

If Washington came with the blitz, that meant cornerback Lemar Parrish would move to the line of scrimmage, in Hill's face, to "dog" him man-to-man. Because of the blitz, the Cowboys wouldn't have time for any intricate pass patterns.

A "Fast Nine" is a simple fade to the corner of the end zone.

Landry told Staubach to line up over center instead of going into a Shotgun formation.

The Dallas quarterback saw the Redskins' linebackers inching closer. Two of them were coming, he figured. Hill watched Parrish slide into his path on the right flank, ready to "dog" him.

It's only a game, right? One game in a career, right? Tom Callahan, a columnist then for the *Washington Star*, wrote the next day, "When a house collapses, does the contractor say it was only a house?"

Staubach's pass feathered softly into Hill's hands. The impact was a piano falling out of a fifth-floor window.

The Redskins were crushed.

Parrish only could say, "It was perfect. Anything else I could have covered. It was a perfect play."

Tex Schramm banged his table with his fists, screaming, "Yeah, yeah, yeeeaaahh."

The remaining 39 seconds allowed one final twist in everyone's well-churned stomach. A pass interference call near midfield gave Washington one last gasp. Theismann's pass to tight end Don Warren at the Cowboys' 43 brought immediate pleas for the Redskins' final time out. Theismann claimed there was one second still showing on the clock. The Redskins claimed Moseley should have been allowed to come on to try a 60-yard field goal that would have won the game.

Referee Bob Frederic refused. There were nothing but zeroes left on the clock, he said, pointing to the scoreboard. The game was over.

"When you come back from the dead twice in the same game," Schramm said, "it's a miracle. No . . . . It's a double miracle."

The Cowboys had engineered so many of these implausible conclusions that one player decided to rank them. Wide receiver Drew Pearson, who had caught a last-minute pass to beat Minnesota in a 1975 playoff game, said amid the uncommon bedlam in the Dallas locker room, "This puts Hail Mary in second place."

Outside, the near-empty stadium was serenaded by country music blasting over the public address system—a Willie Nelson song: "Cowboys ain't easy to love and they're harder to hold. . . ."

The Redskins' locker room was like a morgue. Head coach Jack Pardee, whose team was eliminated from the playoffs by the loss, said, "I'm heartbroken."

THE CLASSIC SHOOTOUT

San Diego Chargers, 41
Miami Dolphins 38
January 2, 1982

Scrambling Dan Fouts passed for three touchdowns and a playoff-record 433 yards for the winning Chargers.

Sometimes, because physical fatigue and emotional exhaustion cause a sensory overload, you don't know what to feel. Sometimes, a football game is so good, so thrilling, so boggling, that when it finally is over, nobody's really sure. Sometimes, it's "A Day in the Life," and the final piano chord is so rich and resonant you think you're still hearing it and you're not really certain it ever ended.

"It's one game that will always be vivid for me," said Dan Fouts, who was quarterback for the San Diego Chargers that day. "The effort by both teams was just unbelievable...absolutely unforgettable."

Don Shula, the Miami Dolphins' head coach, agrees. But because his team lost, it has taken the catharsis of time to heal the hurt and help him to see the game for its everlasting quality.

"I can't remember a game where emotions ran away with you like they did that day," Shula said. "It was...a great game."

But immediately after the Chargers beat the

Dolphins 41-38 on a field goal 13:52 into overtime at the Orange Bowl, Shula, whose team had erased a 24-0 lead, actually led until the final minute, had its own potential winning field goal blocked on the final play of regulation, and flubbed another game-winner in overtime, could only snarl, "Great game? We lost."

A moment later, Shula cooled to the point he could concede, "It had to be a great game, maybe one of the greatest ever. But it's really tough for me to talk about something being great, realizing we didn't win."

Time has allowed the participating players and others involved to unravel the wads of action that flew in the air of a warm, humid early evening in Miami. Put enough distance between a blinding, dazzling moment, and perspective improves.

Two days before the game, on the San Diego charter flying to Miami, head coach Don Coryell's face was its usual clenched fist as he tried to

Chuck Muncie's one-yard dive in the first quarter built San Diego's early lead to 17-0 on the way to 24-0. The powerful Muncie gained 120 yards to lead all rushers in the game and also caught two passes for five yards.

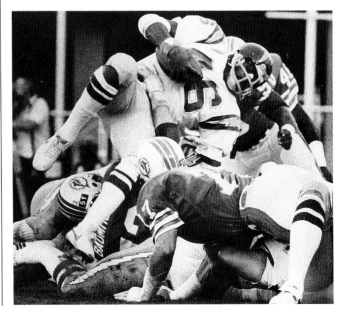

Exhausted by his effort in the muggy heat, San Diego's Kellen Winslow was helped off the field after the game by teammates Billy Shields (left) and Eric Sievers. Winslow caught 13 passes and blocked a Miami field goal.

James Brooks of the Chargers scored on an eight-yard pass for a 24-0 lead.

think of every angle. The game plan was set but the local weather report bothered him. By game time, rain squalls were due to stop and temperatures were supposed to be in the mid-80s, with a humidity level to match. The stifling heat was a trademark of the Dolphins' home-field advantage, and Coryell frowned with concern. The longer the game went, the more likely someone not used to that kind of weather would wilt. There was the threat of cramps, dehydration, and exhaustion.

Coryell told business manager Pat Curran to find bananas for the team. For the potassium, Coryell explained; that'll help fight off the cramps. What Coryell didn't explain was where, even in Miami, was someone to find eight dozen bananas at 8 o'clock at night on New Year's Eve?

"I wound up paying a dollar a banana and bribing people with game tickets," Curran said later.

The Chargers came into the playoffs preceded by a reputation. Their defense ranked twenty-seventh in the NFL, and successive blow-out losses to Cincinnati and Seattle in the last month had people wondering if even the San Diego offense—those lightning bolts on their helmets were perfect symbols—could outscore its defense.

Then there was the other reputation. There were whispers that the Chargers didn't have the psychological stuff to be champions. They lacked the heart it takes. That's what people were saying as the

Don Strock came off the bench in the second quarter and led the Dolphins' amazing rally, passing for 403 yards and four touchdowns.

opening kickoff neared.

Tight end Kellen Winslow was asked about it in a press conference. Winslow was the 6-foot 5-inch, 242-pound tight end who had redesigned the position, improving on the blueprints Mike Ditka and John Mackey had drawn years earlier. Winslow was a tight end who could go deep—the key ingredient in the flying circus known as Air Coryell.

"They call me the sissy, the San Diego chicken," Winslow said in his high-pitched voice. "I'm the tight end who won't block. They say I need a heart

transplant. In fact, that our whole team has no heart."

Winslow then paused and smiled at the nervous reaction that was obvious from the roomful of reporters.

Miami tight end Joe Rose eluded safety Pete Shaw to catch Strock's 15-yard touchdown pass in the third quarter. It finished a Dolphins' run of 24 successive points and tied the score for the first time at 24-24.

"But I'm very self-confident," Winslow added. "I know what I can do. I know what we can do."

The Dolphins were a team in transition. David Woodley, at 23 the youngest quarterback ever to start a playoff game, had his training wheels yanked off early and became the replacement for Bob Griese, who had retired. Shula also had veteran relief quarterback Don Strock, who had come off the bench five times in the regular season when Woodley was ineffective.

At the end of the first quarter, Miami wide receiver Duriel Harris looked at the scoreboard and dropped his head.

"Twenty-four-zip . . . embarrassing," he said.

Nose tackle Bob Baumhower said the mood was equal parts anxiety and frustration. "But somehow we managed to keep our poise while everything was going wrong," he said.

After marching to a field goal on the opening drive, the Chargers' defense forced the Dolphins to punt. On came Tom Orosz, whose specialty was a deliberately short kick that rolled and bounced and practically negated any kind of return.

But Coryell had a scheme. In addition to his regular return man, the flashy rookie James Brooks, Coryell also sent out wide receiver Wes Chandler. Chandler would be stationed 30 yards downfield; his job was to field those short kicks before they hit the ground.

"I was thinking I'd be fair-catching," Chandler said, "but the punt didn't have much height. My next thought was to get away from the first man down because I could see the wall [of blockers] forming."

Chandler's 56-yard return for a touchdown shocked the Orange Bowl crowd. But that was only an appetizer for San Diego. On the ensuing kickoff, Rolf Benirschke's kick caught in the wind and bounced in front of three Dolphins around the 30-yard line and headed backward, where San Diego's Hank Bauer recovered. A few plays later, running back Chuck Muncie scored and it was 17-0.

Another chunk of the Dolphins' sky fell a couple of plays later when Chargers defensive back Glen Edwards intercepted a pass by Woodley and returned it 35 yards. Fouts promptly threw a touchdown pass to Brooks and it was 24-0.

"They scored so quickly it was breathtaking," said Miami's Bob Kuechenberg, who had helped solidify the Dolphins' offensive line during their Super Bowl teams of the 1970s. "We were so far behind, we were really staggering."

Shula looked around the sideline, waved to Strock and told him to start warming up.

Chargers wide receiver Charlie Joiner said later, "A team like Miami is always going to make a run at you, no matter the score. We expected it and we got it."

"We weren't going to the desperation stuff," Strock said. "It was only the second quarter; the short stuff was open. We'd start airing it out if it was late. But even though we were down twenty-four, we still had enough time to do something about it."

Strock immediately led the Dolphins downfield. San Diego linebacker Linden King said, "You could sense the difference. Strock had real presence out there and you could tell the rest of the Dolphins were responding to him."

But things almost blew up in the Dolphins' face once more. Strock threw a pass, and Chargers safety Pete Shaw was in perfect position to intercept. But Shaw dropped it. The Dolphins settled for a field goal by Uwe von Schamann, "our most dependable player all year," according to Kuechenberg.

With less than three minutes left in the half, the Dolphins scored again, Strock throwing a touchdown pass to tight end Joe Rose.

Stung by the touchdown, the Chargers roared back. After stalling at the Miami 37, Benirschke's 55-yard field-goal try was short.

There were 30 seconds left in the half. Strock and Shula huddled. "We were thinking maybe we could get another field goal," Strock said.

Three passes and 23 yards later, six seconds were left on the clock and the ball was on the San Diego 40. The Dolphins had just taken their final time out

Dolphins tight end Bruce Hardy streaked away from San Diego linebacker Woodrow Lowe on a 50-yard, third-quarter touchdown pass that tied the score again, this time at 31-31.

and Strock asked Shula, "Should we try Herd?"

That was the Dolphins' formation designed for the Hail Mary play; three or four receivers line up on the same side, everyone heads downfield and the ball is thrown up for grabs.

Shula shook his head. He said, "Let's try 87 Circle Curl Lateral."

Strock said, "Which side do you want it?"

The play is from the flea-flicker family—a short pass to a wide receiver and a quick lateral to a running back trailing behind along the sideline. For the play to work, the defense had to be overly aggressive against the receiver. Shula looked at the Chargers on the field. Edwards and Willie Buchanon manned the left side of the secondary for Coryell. Both were big hitters.

"Right," Shula said.

Strock called the play and running back Tony Nathan asked, "Are you sure?"

"It's what the man wants," Strock said.

Harris didn't think it would work. He would be the primary receiver and he was supposed to lateral the ball to Nathan. The Dolphins had tried the play

Tony Nathan held the ball up after he put Miami ahead 38-31 with a 12-yard, fourth-quarter touchdown run.

twice before. Once, Nathan had run the wrong way. The other time Harris dropped the pass.

Shaw saw the play developing. "I was happy," he said. "They were throwing short. Harris ran a hook and I thought we'd make the tackle and that would be it."

Nathan had to be careful not to get knocked down coming through the line. Then he turned to the outside. "I saw the sideline was wide open," Nathan said. "They were all going after Duriel."

Buchanon was deep man in the zone. Linebacker Linden King was dropping back to help. Strock's pass to Harris was caught, the lateral was made.

"All of a sudden," King said, "Nathan's hauling ass to the end zone. All of a sudden they're back in the game."

Buchanon said he doubted if anybody on the Chargers' defense ever saw Nathan.

"It was just perfect execution," Buchanon said.

And it was just another coat of shellac on a game that would get glossier and glossier.

The Dolphins took the second-half kickoff and marched 74 yards to a game-tying touchdown on Strock's 15-yard pass to Rose.

Chargers linebacker Jim Laslavic explained, "We could have folded our tents at any time. The way things had gone late in the year, we were almost conditioned to things eventually going bad. And because we were used to that sudden disappointment, we didn't panic."

Especially Fouts, who revived the Chargers and helped them reclaim the lead at 31-24. He threw a 25-yard touchdown pass to Winslow. A block by reserve fullback John Cappelletti made everything possible. Cappelletti picked up a blitzing Dolphin, allowing Fouts the time to pump-fake, reload, and hit Winslow over the middle.

The crowd marveled at the aerial shootout. Fouts and Strock each would finish with more than 400 yards passing, 433 and 403, respectively, the first time in NFL history two quarterbacks both passed for more than 400 yards in the same game.

When Strock threw a 50-yard touchdown pass to reserve tight end Bruce Hardy, there was a feeling that whoever had the ball last would win. But the Dolphins finally grounded the Chargers. An interception by safety Lyle Blackwood led the way for Nathan's 12-yard sweep into the end zone on the first play of the fourth quarter. Then Miami, leading 38-31, stopped San Diego once more, and it appeared the game finally would calm down.

When the Dolphins used up the next seven minutes, grinding the ball down to the Chargers' 21, they seemed to have the game in control. But San Diego gang-tackled fullback Andra Franklin, with Gary Johnson wrapping up the rookie running back and King stripping the ball free. Shaw recovered at the San Diego 18. The Chargers still had a chance.

Fouts completed six of seven passes in a hurried drive downfield, the last a nine-yard touchdown pass to Brooks in the back of the end zone with 58 seconds left to play.

"Busted play," Fouts explained. "I was throwing to Kellen. But he was so beat up and tired that he had to jump to get it."

The ball flew over Winslow's head, and Brooks, who wasn't supposed to be in the area, made the catch. Benirschke's kick tied the game 38-38.

"When I caught the ball, Kellen gave me this 'Where'd you come from?' look," Brooks said. "I knew Fouts didn't see me. I was just glad to be where I was."

But given the nature of the game and its explosiveness, 58 seconds was a lifetime. Sure enough, Strock had the Dolphins back on the move. With four seconds to go, von Schamann was going to

Miami running back Andra Franklin (upper left) looked on in disgust as San Diego's Pete Shaw (44) recovered his late fumble on the Chargers' 18-yard line. San Diego then drove for the touchdown that sent the game to overtime.

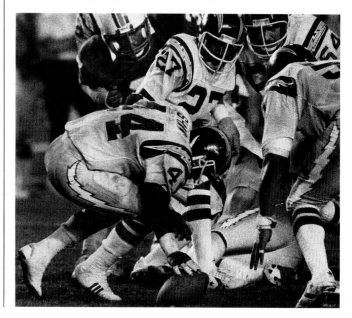

try a 43-yard field goal that could win the game.

Winslow, who had been carried off the field twice, once with a shoulder injury and another time with cramps in his neck and back, came in.

In the huddle, Winslow said to tackles Louie Kelcher and Gary Johnson, "Get me some penetration, guys, so I can have a chance at the block."

The Chargers had blocked just one kick in the 16 games of the regular season.

"If they had called a fake," said San Diego assistant coach Marv Braden, "they could have walked in. We had all eleven men going for the ball."

The snap was high. Strock got the ball down and in place and von Schamann swung his leg. The sound of the well-struck football was followed immediately by another unexpected sound, a second thump in the night. It was the right hand of Kellen Winslow swatting down the football.

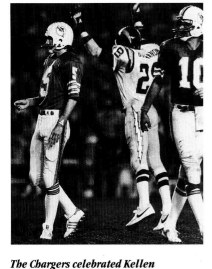

The Chargers celebrated Kellen Winslow's block of Uwe von Schamann's (5) field goal with four seconds left.

"My whole body cramped up after that, all the way up to my neck," Winslow said. "I couldn't stand up, but I figured if we lost, I had six months to heal."

In the overtime, Kuechenberg said, "Everyone was so beat up and tired that we were going on remote control. We kept waiting for the heat to get to San Diego and it got to us at the same time.

"It was a shame, the way both teams gave it everything they had, that the thing couldn't have just ended in a tie. Nobody deserved to lose."

A few minutes into the overtime, though, Benirschke was set to finish what Fouts and his frequent flyers had begun. San Diego had charged and the weary Dolphins were almost helpless.

"What was it—twenty-seven yards?" Shaw said afterward. "I was already pulling the tape off my wrists. Rolf just doesn't miss from there."

But the kick hooked left.

The Dolphins moved quickly, the big play coming on a 21-yard pass to Jimmy Cefalo. At the San Diego 25, von Schamann came on, intent to atone for his miss at the end of regulation. The Dolphins' placekicker had won four games for Miami during the season with field goals. For this one, he was concentrating on getting maximum height on the kick, getting it up quickly and before Winslow or anyone could put a hand on it.

"But I scuffed the ground," von Schamann explained later.

The off-balance kick went on a line into the arm of the Chargers' Leroy Jones.

Fouts led the Chargers downfield again, with passes of 20 yards to Chandler and 29 to Joiner setting up a first down at the Miami 10-yard line.

Benirschke came on once more.

Kellen Winslow crouched to block. How much more, he wondered. How much longer? Five seconds longer. Benirschke's kick was perfect. Winslow was flat on his back.

"I didn't hear anything, no noise," he said. "The silence was beautiful. I knew we'd won."

A Miami player offered him a hand to get up. Winslow said no. "I just wanted to lay there a moment," he said.

Finally he got up, walked a couple of yards, and started to reel. Two teammates had to help him.

"Thank God it's over," Winslow whispered as he walked off the field, holding onto his teammates. "It's the closest to death I've ever been."

Baumhower sat in the locker room, staring at a pile of discarded uniforms.

"It was all guts and emotion," he said. "Nobody has anything left. Someday I'll be proud to have been part of this game. But to play so hard and lose, it's tough. Real tough."

Four hours and three minutes, more than 1,000 yards of combined offense. Ninety grown men brought themselves to the verge of collapse, and when it was over it was hard to tell the winners from the losers. . . except for the tired smiles.

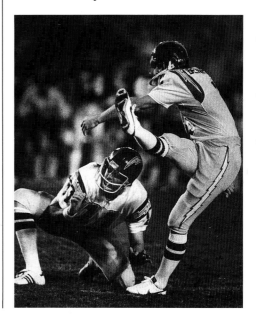

The long, long game ended with 13:52 elapsed in overtime when Rolf Benirschke kicked the winning 29-yard field goal.

THE CATCH

San Francisco 49ers 28,
Dallas Cowboys 27
January 10, 1982

It's about recognition, seeing what's happening and being where you're supposed to be.

Double coverage, thought 49ers wide receiver Dwight Clark, looking around, noticing the way Dallas Cowboys safety Michael Downs was easing toward him. A couple yards directly ahead, cornerback Everson Walls crouched, hands up like a karate fighter, ready. Walls already had made two interceptions, already had fallen on a fumble. Clark already had caught seven passes.

The San Francisco receiver bent into his three-point stance and decided it was a good thing he wasn't primary receiver on this play—probably the most important in the history of the 49ers' franchise. Third-and-three at the Cowboys' 6, a minute to play, six points behind, and the championship of the National Football Conference on the line.

Maybe the double coverage would help teammate Freddie Solomon get open, Clark was thinking as he turned to listen for quarterback Joe Montana's cadence.

The thing is to run the route anyway. Be disciplined, always be where you're supposed to be.

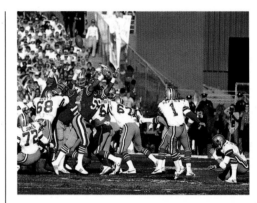

Rafael Septien kicked a 44-yard field goal for Dallas's first points. The Cowboys took a 10-7 lead later in the first quarter on a touchdown pass by Danny White.

When you come into the NFL hanging by your toenails, a tenth-round draft pick with slowpoke speed, you don't cut any corners. You can't.

How many hours had Montana and Clark spent practicing? How long had they worked on timing, drilling over and over, being so precise and so routine that pitcher and catcher could tell where the other was even if it were dark?

"Plenty," is what Dwight Clark would say later, shrugging. "If you want to play and you don't have all the gifts some players do, you just have to be stubborn and hang in there anyway. You have to out-work and out-prepare."

He was going to be a decoy and he was going to drag two Dallas Cowboys along with him. But even the decoy routes deserve attention to detail. Even they have to be run with the same discipline—a left-to-right drag, then a hairpin cut that winds up 15 yards deep, in this case, along the back line of the Cowboys' end zone—or else the synchronized nature of head coach Bill Walsh's space-age offense might break down.

In the huddle a few moments earlier, when Montana had called Sprint Right Option, Clark was wondering if the call would work. It had earlier, when Solomon caught an eight-

Freddie Solomon gave the 49ers a 7-0, first-quarter lead when he scored on an eight-yard pass from Joe Montana. Solomon caught six passes for 75 yards.

The 49ers' Dwight Clark—who says he can't jump very well—practically jumped out of the stadium to catch Montana's six-yard touchdown pass, which overcame Dallas 28-27 (after the conversion) in the 1981 NFC title game.

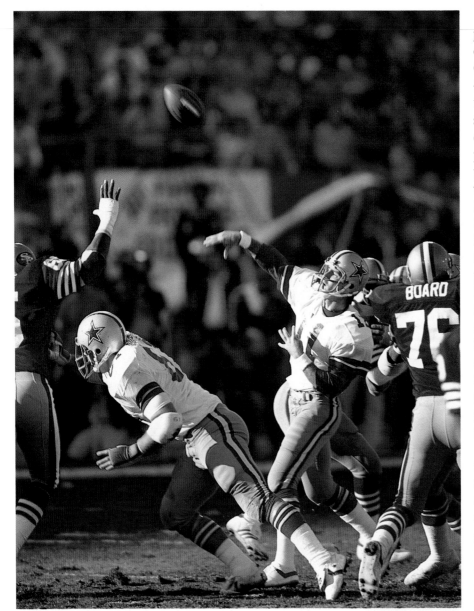

There were 60,061 people standing, the largest crowd in the history of Candlestick Park. The 49ers never had won anything bigger than a division title before. A lot of disappointments had piled up through the years; in the Bay Area where Oakland had flaunted its beloved Raiders for so long, 49ers fans were the poor cousins. As recently as two years before, the 49ers had lost 14 of 16 games. Maybe that's why everyone was standing as Montana hunched over center and called signals at the Cowboys' 6, a minute to play and a trip to the Super Bowl up in the air. Or about to be.

Montana looked over the Cowboys' defense. He spotted the double-team on Clark. He looked to the area where Solomon was going to be.

That's the charm about football in the modern era. You don't throw to certain players;

Tony Dorsett gave the Cowboys a 17-14 halftime lead with this five-yard touchdown run. Dorsett led all rushers with 91 yards.

Danny White, who brought Dallas from behind three times during the championship game, passed for 173 yards and two touchdowns, one to Tony Hill and one to Doug Cosbie. He completed 16 of his 24 attempts.

yard pass for a touchdown. But the Cowboys' pass rush had been pretty relentless lately, especially from the left side, where defensive end Ed (Too Tall) Jones lurked. Montana would be rolling directly into the Cowboys' best pass rusher.

Clark quickly put the fear out of his mind. He had learned a long time ago not to wonder about Walsh's offensive theory. It, as much as anything else, was the reason the 49ers were closer to the Super Bowl than ever before.

"If Bill thinks it will work, it will," Clark would say later.

So he'd just line up and run his pattern and see what happened. . . .

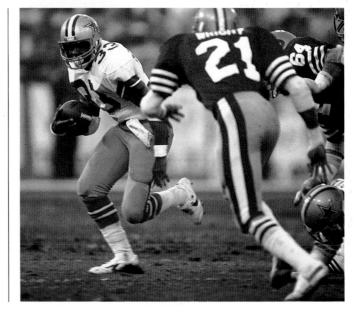

San Francisco's Johnny Davis wrapped the ball up tightly when he scored on a two-yard run in the third quarter. The 49ers went back in front 21-17.

you throw to certain areas. That's why that confidence is so important. You need to know someone's going to be someplace, even if you can't see them.

Montana took center Fred Quillan's snap and moved to his right. Immediately he realized the timing was shot. There was none. The Cowboys' defensive line had shredded the blocking and gotten penetration. Montana had hoped to throw a quick pass to Solomon but he instead was running for his and the 49ers' lives.

Too Tall was getting Too Near. Larry Bethea also was closing in. Montana was close to out of bounds; he almost could feel the white-chalked line underneath him. "I couldn't see anyone ex-

Early in the fourth quarter, San Francisco's Walt Easley ran for four yards, but fumbled, and cornerback Everson Walls of Dallas recovered at the 50. The turnover set up the touchdown drive that gave the Cowboys a 27-21 lead.

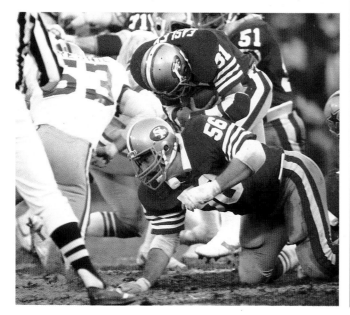

cept Too Tall Jones," Montana said.

It was only third down. Montana could step out of bounds, or throw the ball away and try again on fourth down. Guard Randy Cross was drifting over, unable to do much of anything but watch.

Cross said, "Joe's funny—he scrambles on purpose, trying to mess up coverages. And you'd better get to him because... well, you saw what happened."

Montana seemed indecisive as he backed up. He jumped off his back foot and threw the ball.

"I knew Dwight had to be back there," Montana explained later. "He always is. But I sure couldn't see him. I jumped up and threw the ball and went down and rolled over.

"And then I heard the crowd."

Clark can't jump. There seemingly is no way he could have reached Montana's pass, which was a high floater that might have been batted down had Too Tall not mistimed his leap at Montana.

Dallas tight end Doug Cosbie held the ball aloft when he raced into the end zone with a 21-yard touchdown pass on the fourth play after Walls recovered Easley's fumble. Drew Pearson escorted Cosbie into the end zone.

"I thought the pass was too high," Clark said. "I was tired, I'd had the flu for a week, I had trouble catching my breath all during the last drive. And I really don't jump too well."

But Clark caught the ball.

He landed at the back line of the end zone, his feet inches inside, just where they're supposed to be.

When Montana saw a replay of the play later, he gasped.

"I knew it was high but...Dwight must have jumped three feet to get that. I don't know how he got it. He can't jump that high."

Clark said, "You get it from somewhere. How does the mother pick up the car that has her baby trapped? You just get it from somewhere."

The 49ers' starving fans screeched and celebrated. There was hardly any thought to the fact the dramatic touchdown, gold-plated capper to a stirring 14-play, 89-yard drive, only tied the game.

Kicker Ray Wersching still had an extra point to

With Dallas leading 27-21, Joe Montana tried to throw deep for the 49ers, but Everson Walls (24) intercepted the ball and celebrated on the sideline.

kick before the 49ers could take over the lead.

And there were 51 seconds left to play.

And those were the Cowboys on the other sideline. The same Texas grinches who seemingly held a working patent on the ridiculous, last-second, Hail Mary, over-the-rainbow miracles that could supersede even the Montana-to-Clark miracle.

The 49ers' defensive unit was huddling on the sideline. They seemed vulnerable. What if their three rookies in the secondary suddenly acted their age? Jack Reynolds, their 36-year-old linebacker, might act his as well. What if Keena Turner, their linebacker who came down with chicken pox on the eve of the game, got woozier, more exhausted?

In the Dallas huddle, after Wersching's conversion, quarterback Danny White prodded his teammates. "All we need is a field goal," he said.

From the Shotgun, White set up and the Cowboys wheeled into motion. Wide receiver Drew Pearson glided downfield, made a quick cut to the middle, and there was the ball.

"I looked ahead and saw nothing but the goal posts," Pearson said, recalling the moment. "I

thought, oh my God, we're going to do it again."

Two hands belonging to Dwight Clark made the day for San Francisco. One arm saved it.

Pearson was a step or so away from a 75-yard dagger to the heart, and the body count at Candlestick would have set a record.

Cornerback Eric Wright's eyes bulged with fear.

"He's gone," Wright was thinking. He'd been beaten to the inside by Pearson. There was nobody else to help. Pearson was about to pull away. There was time only for one desperate final lunge.

The scoreboard showed 1:15 remaining and San Francisco behind by six points, when Montana huddled with coach Bill Walsh to talk strategy. The quarterback went back on the field and completed the winning 89-yard drive that sent the 49ers to Super Bowl XVI.

On second-and-10 at the Dallas 13, Lenvil Elliott swept left end for seven yards, and the 49ers called time out with 58 seconds left.

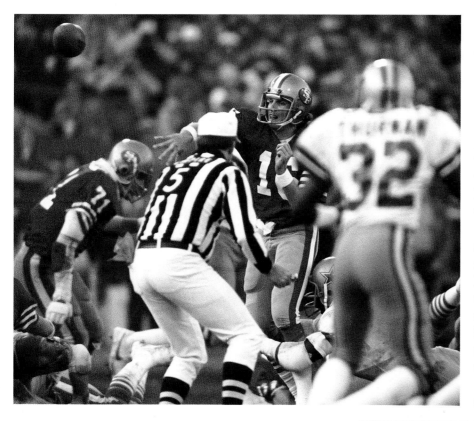

Then we're watching our lives pass before our eyes. You can't imagine our relief when we saw Pearson get pulled down."

In the Cowboys' huddle, White was thinking he needed only 15 more yards. Then Rafael Septien could come on and kick the field goal that would win the game.

San Francisco reserve defensive lineman Lawrence Pillers looked at Kurt Petersen's feet. He tried to figure how the Cowboys' guard would block him. He tried to think how he could get by the block.

"I don't really remember what I did," Pil-

Although the Cowboys intercepted three of his passes, Montana burned them for 286 yards and three touchdowns, including the six-yard lob that Dwight Clark pulled out of the sky for the winning score with 51 seconds left.

Around the neck, by the jersey, his number 88 suddenly twisted, then wadded, Pearson was collared and pulled down after a 31-yard gain on a one-arm tackle by Wright. But there would be no touchdown.

"It's just amazing how a game can change so quickly," Montana said. "Here we were, celebrating like we've never done just a few seconds earlier.

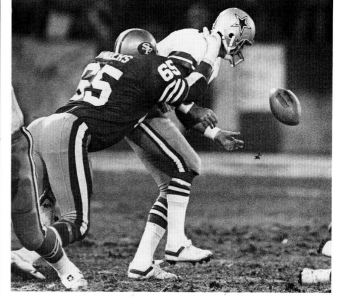

On the first play after the 49ers took the lead, Drew Pearson caught a 31-yard pass for Dallas, but cornerback Eric Wright's one-arm tackle saved a touchdown—and the game.

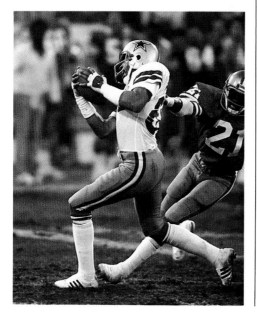

lers said afterward. "I just did something that got me a free shot at White."

White was hammered. He fumbled. And 49ers defensive end Jim Stuckey

With 38 seconds left in the game, Dallas was at the 49ers' 44, but defensive end Lawrence Pillers sacked quarterback Danny White and forced a fumble. End Jim Stuckey recovered for San Francisco to clinch the victory.

fell on the ball, smothering the Cowboys' last hope and setting off an earthquake of celebration.

The 49ers raised their helmets in triumph. Their coach rode on the shoulders of the moment. The 49ers were champions of the NFC.

IT'S A FUNNY GAME

Washington Redskins 37,
Los Angeles Raiders 35
October 2, 1983

In a game of rallies and comebacks, the most important is never the biggest or the best or the most impressive. Just the last.

At RFK Stadium, with Joe Washington back-pedaling and reaching for the pass from Joe Theismann, the game that had exhausted everyone's senses with so many big plays, suddenly stopped. A tapestry was unfolded, and some street-corner salesman was yelling "come look."

The tapestry shows this little running back, hands straining because the football is a little high for him to reach and still keep his balance. The final picture of Washington holding onto the ball and falling backwards into the end zone is a wonderful image of pro football.

You want to add a little more to the tapestry? Stitch a clock that shows 33 seconds left to play. And make it clear that the Redskins once led this game comfortably, then watched the Raiders score 28 points in a row with wild and passionate strokes of genius that included a 97-yard punt return. Then, because Washington really did wind up winning the game, scoring 17 consecutive points, somebody must draw some sort of conclusion about the unsinkable Redskins.

"We didn't quit . . . they didn't quit," said Redskins quarterback Joe Theismann. "At the end, nobody could stop anybody. It came down to who had the ball last."

Then Theismann,

Charlie Brown started Washington's winning 17-point rally when he caught an 11-yard touchdown pass from Joe Theismann midway through the fourth quarter. It cut the Raiders' lead to 35-27, and an exuberant Brown spiked the ball.

who wound up with more than 400 yards passing, added, "I think people are going to remember this game for a long time."

The Redskins had been expecting fireworks.

"But what we weren't expecting was all the offense," said Washington. "They were supposed to be hurting."

Marcus Allen, the Raiders' young running back, was injured; a bruised hip the week before had made him doubtful. Head coach Tom Flores said he wouldn't risk Allen compounding the injury.

Of the Raiders' first four possessions, three ended in interceptions as quarterback Jim Plunkett struggled. Washington built a 10-0 lead in the second quarter and had the Raiders backed up to their 1-yard line.

"I looked at Marcus real hard about then," Flores said. "We really needed some kind of boost."

Plunkett dropped back and hit wide receiver Cliff Branch with a pass, and, 99 yards after that, Flores

On a day of spectacular plays, the scoring began quietly when Washington's John Riggins gave his team a 7-0 lead with a two-yard touchdown run. The powerful Riggins was the game's leading rusher with 91 yards.

decided he didn't really want to ask Allen to play.

"I thought we were going to be right back in the game after that big play to Branch," Flores said.

Instead, the Redskins quickly marched to another touchdown, with Washington catching a five-yard scoring pass. Early in the third quarter, the Redskins led 20-7. Raiders defensive end Howie Long came to the bench and shouted, "We'd better get our asses in gear. This is embarrassing."

On the bench, Branch sat glumly. He had pulled a hamstring on his NFL record-tying touchdown. He was done for the day.

But Calvin Muhammad wasn't. The reserve wide receiver came on to score two touchdowns on passes of 35 and 22 yards, and the Raiders took a 21-20 lead. When tight end Todd Christensen pulled in another touchdown pass from Plunkett, Washington head coach Joe Gibbs felt the game was slipping out of his team's control.

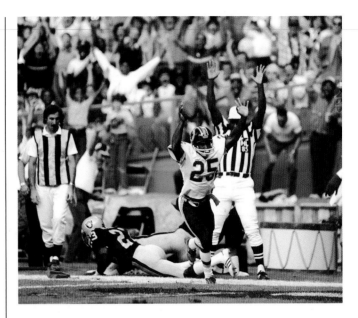

When Greg Pruitt inexplicably fielded a punt at his own 3—football logic suggests that punts landing inside the 10-yard line are best left alone—it appeared the Raiders had made a mental mistake that would help the Redskins reclaim the lead. But Pruitt broke a tackle, side-stepped another one, then raced to a 97-yard touchdown.

The Raiders led 35-20 with 7:31 left.

"Then I don't know what it was," Theismann said later, "but all of us just got so in tune with

The Raiders trailed 10-0 when Jim Plunkett (above) dropped back in his own end zone and threw a pass to Cliff Branch (below) that went for a 99-yard touchdown. Branch was the fifth player in NFL history to score on a 99-yard pass play.

the game. Charlie Brown and Little Joe [Washington] were simply fantastic. I started hitting my passes."

In those final minutes, Theismann passed for 190 of his 417 total yards. The Redskins stormed to a quick touchdown, with Brown scoring on an 11-yard pass. A big play during the drive was a short pass in the left flat to Washington, who turned it into a 63-yard gain.

On the sideline, Redskins running back John Riggins watched. His back was acting up. But that wasn't why he was out. The Raiders' big lead had made him and his ball-control style useless. Washington had taken his place.

But even after closing the gap to 35-27, things looked bleak. Riggins looked at the scoreboard. Marcus Allen also looked at the scoreboard.

We need to use up some clock, he thought.

The Redskins were going to try an onside kick. But special teams coach Wayne Sevier noticed all the running backs and receivers Flores had deployed to the front line. He counted them—nine.

Sevier told kicker Jeff Hayes to try a low, hard kick instead of the usual onside dribbler.

"If we could get the ball past that first line of players, then get down before the deep men came up, we had a fifty-fifty shot at the ball," Sevier said.

How perfect was Hayes's kick?

"Magnificent," Sevier said.

"Just about the worst thing that could have happened," Flores said.

The kick bounced off someone's foot, identity unknown except it belonged to a Raider. Most

Joe Washington gave the Redskins a 17-7 halftime lead when he caught a five-yard scoring pass from Joe Theismann. Washington had five catches for 99 yards and two touchdowns, including a 67-yard run with a screen pass.

agreed the foot was linebacker Jack Squirek's, but he swore mistaken identity. Dokie Williams, the Los Angeles wide receiver, retreated back and was first to reach the ball. It squirted from his grasp. The Redskins recovered at the 32-yard line.

Mark Moseley's 34-yard field goal inched the Redskins closer. Now they trailed by five points.

Allen snapped on his helmet. He ran onto the field. No more of this onside kick nonsense. When the Redskins tried it again, "I was all set to get it, no matter where it went."

But 4:28 was left to play, and Hayes's kick sailed deep. Allen turned to throw a block.

"When our defense came up with some really big plays and forced them to punt," Gibbs said, "I think all of us started believing we were going to win the game after all."

thing I see is him reaching up for the pass."

Because of Riggins and because of the Redskins' style—"If we have the ball, you can't score," Gibbs said—Joe Washington had scarcely played during the season.

"Then suddenly he's our star of the year," Theismann said. "It's a funny game."

Indeed. In January, the two teams played again. This time in Tampa, in Super Bowl XVIII. The Raiders won 38-9 as Marcus Allen set a Super Bowl record for rushing with 191 yards. The turning point in the game, both teams said, came shortly before halftime when Theismann tried to throw a short pass to Washington in the flat. Squirek, the Raiders linebacker, made no attempt to jam the Redskins' runner at the line of scrimmage. He simply stepped forward, intercepted the pass, and ran it into the end zone.

"It's the same play that worked so well against them back in October," Theismann said. "You know, it's a funny game."

Greg Pruitt completed the Raiders' 28-point rally with a 97-yard punt return for a touchdown. Punter Jeff Hayes (5) was one of the Redskins who missed him.

Trailing 20-7, the Raiders scored four consecutive touchdowns to take a 35-20 lead. In this 28-point assault, Calvin Muhammad (on ground) caught 35- and 22-yard touchdown passes. For the day, Muhammad caught five passes for 112 yards.

"The Raiders were in prevent but they also were without two of their starters [Vann McElroy and Ted Watts]," Theismann said. "The replacements weren't real familiar with what we were trying to do against the prevent."

Starting at the Redskins' 31, Brown caught passes for 9, 26, and 28 yards, and suddenly the ball was at the Raiders' 6.

Linebacker Rod Martin was assigned to cover Washington on the second-down play. Martin inched forward, set to jam the little running back.

"I got a piece of him but he's so hard to really get a good shot on," Martin said, reliving the touchdown. "He ducked under me or something. The next

The Redskins won the wild, wild game with 33 seconds left when Washington (Joe, that is) made a leaping, falling catch of a six-yard touchdown pass from Theismann. The Redskins scored 17 points in the last 6:15 for victory.

THE DRIVE

Denver Broncos 23,
Cleveland Browns 20
January 11, 1987

It finally had happened. As the erector set of a stadium rattled with anticipation and a huge blast of civic pride blew harder than the wind gusting off nearby Lake Erie, the quarterback of the Denver Broncos could sense something.

For probably the first time in his professional life, John Elway faced an apparently insurmountable obstacle. Yet, he felt a surge.

It was first down and 98. Five minutes left in the season. Unless. . . .

The botched kickoff return had been spotted between the 1- and 2-yard lines. So it was an optimist's first-and-98. The Cleveland Browns had the field mined with Nickel backs. The ancient turf was frozen and skinned and burned by ice, which is how it always is for football at Cleveland Municipal Stadium in January. The crowd was loud. And barking. A remark by Browns cornerback Frank Minnifield had become a flag around which a city could rally. In 1987, the Cleveland Browns were a bunch of Dawgs nobody loved, with only a few million exceptions. And now, as the Broncos huddled in their own end zone, a touchdown behind, there was no way to shut up the mongrel crowd, no way to uncook this goose. Unless. . . .

First-and-98. Browns outside linebacker Clay Matthews ran up beside nose tackle Bob Golic and slapped a gloved fist on his teammate's shoulder pad. "This is it," he bellowed. The Browns were going to win; they were going to go to the Super Bowl. There was no way they were going to lose

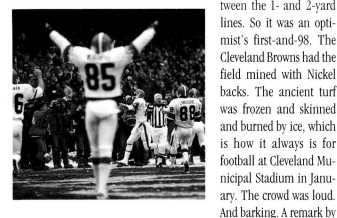

Herman Fontenot caught a six-yard first-quarter touchdown pass from Bernie Kosar to give the Browns an early lead.

Everybody always knew John Elway had the tools to be one of the NFL's best quarterbacks, but it took one memorable five-minute march down the Cleveland Stadium field to transform his potential into tangible greatness.

this game. Unless. . . .

Unless a large chunk of potential got cashed in. Unless greatness manifested itself in what would have to be one of the greatest touchdown drives ever. Unless John Elway and the Denver Broncos could maneuver the length of an unfriendly terrain against the most aroused of opposition in a matter of moments.

At last an underdog. All his life, Elway has been expected to excel; God's Gift to Quarterbacks is how he had been perceived since before he was old enough to grip a football. When he was in college at Stanford, the NFL scouting reports on him used to come back singing praises. He gave the greatest first impression in memory.

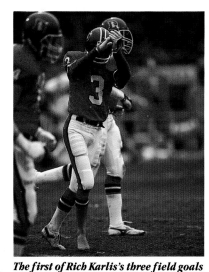

The first of Rich Karlis's three field goals put Denver on the board and heightened his mother's mixed emotions.

But now, with first-and-98 at Municipal Stadium, the designer quarterback sensed nobody could honestly expect this largest boulder yet to be pushed aside. And Elway smiled. Sometimes, it looks as if he's smiling when he isn't. This is because he has large teeth. Bright and white teeth, straight teeth. But as the Broncos formed their huddle, John Elway really was smiling.

Guard Keith Bishop was hunched over, waiting for the play to be called and Elway said, "Well, we got these guys right where we want them."

Not everyone laughed. Those who did really didn't think it was funny — it was more a nervous response to an overwhelming situation.

But Elway smiled. All the tons of expectation had been forklifted away. At last, an underdog. What a free feeling.

On the Browns' sideline, some players already

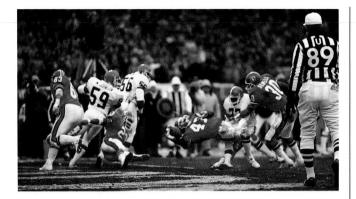

After linebacker Ken Woodard recovered Kevin Mack's fumble at the Browns' 37 and John Elway scrambled for 34 yards, Denver faced a fourth-and-goal situation at the 1. Gerald Willhite delivered a 10-7 lead with his touchdown plunge.

were celebrating. In the Broncos' end zone, only a few yards away from John Elway and the Denver huddle, dog biscuits were bouncing on the hard ground. There was a steady howl echoing around the majestic stadium.

"And then I suddenly flashed on something I was thinking about before the game," Elway said later. "Great quarterbacks make great plays in great games.

"That's what it's all about, isn't it?" he asked. "Until I can do that, I can't be considered a great quarterback."

The Broncos had waited for their leader to produce the pocketful of miracles he'd been saving for just this very occasion. Elway stepped forward, still smiling, and yelling to make himself heard, called for a short pass to running back Sammy Winder. The Drive began.

Bernie Kosar stared at Elway. The Browns' quarterback was trying to think along with his counterpart, guess which plays would be called, compare them with what he would call. He would pretend it was Bernie Kosar instead of John Elway who had first and 98, five minutes left in the season.

Kosar and Elway had a lot in common for two guys who looked like total opposites with the one exception they both did the same kind of work. If Elway was ultra-glide in cool, with style and technique and a throwing motion that came out of a textbook, Kosar was Big Bird, only a little more lumbering and gawky and with a variety of throwing motions that could give the old baseball pitcher, Luis Tiant, a run for his money. Yet Kosar arrived in the NFL from Miami with only slightly less fanfare. His quarterbacking skills, which were lacking only in cosmetic, eye-of-the-beholder beauty, likewise got him unfairly anointed as some resident savior once he hit the Cleveland city limits.

The perceptional difference was that while Bernie *could* do it, John *should* do it.

Kosar's 48-yard touchdown pass to Brian Brennan moments earlier had broken a 13-13 tie. It had convinced Cleveland fans that even when their curly-haired hero wasn't having a great game, like the week before when Kosar passed for almost 500 yards in the overtime victory against the Jets, he still knew how to make the big play that could win the big game.

Elway's first-down pass to Winder was one of those breathing-room flares. A five-yard gain helped.

In the huddle, Broncos' wide receiver Vance Johnson looked at Elway. Later, Johnson said, "The man was perfectly cool. I'm wondering how in hell are we going to get back in this game. And John was feeling no pressure at all. Just cool and calm."

The quick pitch to Winder on second down was read quickly by Browns defensive end Reggie Camp but Winder

Twenty seconds before halftime, 38-year-old Mark Moseley tied the score at 10-10 with a 29-yard field goal, his first of two.

gained three yards anyway. It was third-and-two, and the Browns were thinking pass. Broncos center Billy Bryan drove out against Golic. Bryan had no assignment as to which direction he was to block Golic. Whichever way Golic went, Bryan would also. It's called an influence block. Elway handed the ball to Winder, whose job was to read which way Golic and Bryan were headed, then go the opposite. And, oh yeah—make the first down.

Winder gained two yards and several inches. Only 88 to go.

"It doesn't look good, stuck way back like that," Broncos head coach Dan Reeves said afterward. "But when you've got John Elway on your team, you've always got a chance. Always."

In the stands, Helen Karlis pulled her winter coat tight. Her son Rich is the placekicker for the Broncos, but she's an Ohioan, from nearby Salem, where Rich went to high school. She's also a long-time Browns fan. Now she was playing a mental tug-of-war game with herself. Whom should she root for?

Maybe the Browns, she thought. Since the Broncos were trailing and stuck so far back. No need to open her coat and show off the nice orange and blue Broncos sweater her son had given her. Not yet, anyway.

For the fourth consecutive play, Winder got the ball, taking a handoff off right tackle for three yards. Fine with us, the Browns were saying. Grind it out, eat the clock.

"We knew Elway was the guy we had to stop," Golic said. "We had to get good pressure on Elway. But we also had to keep him contained."

On second down, Elway faded back, looking for flanker Steve Sewell, one of the fastest Broncos, who had lined up as a halfback. If Sewell could get isolated on a linebacker, maybe there was a miracle on the horizon.

But Sewell was knocked down and taken out of the play. Elway looked for a secondary receiver, then stepped up in the pocket to escape the clutch of defensive end Sam Clancy. Carl Hairston reached to put the clamps on Elway, but the quarterback dodged to the left, found himself outside the containment, and ran 11 yards, sliding down at the 26.

Mack rushed for 94 yards, including seven carries for 34 yards on a key drive to a field goal early in the fourth period.

Clancy later would complain the Browns' 3-4 defense couldn't get enough pressure on Elway, claiming, "During the game, we used a four-man line several times, and every time we did, we popped him pretty good. I think we made a mistake by not using more four-man during that drive."

Free safety Chris Rockins agreed, adding, "When you have someone who can scramble like Elway, three people rushing just won't do it. It seemed like every time we had good coverage, he was off and running. There's no doubt it hurt us."

On the sideline, Kosar was shaking his head. His thoughts rarely include scrambling for anything beside survival because quickness isn't part of his quarterback arsenal. The Broncos still were 74 yards away from a tie, but Kosar could feel it.

A play-fake to Gerald Willhite froze the Browns' underneath zone coverage, and Sewell easily romped to an open area, where the pass almost whistled to him. The 22-yard gain to the Denver 48 caused a change of attitude among the Broncos. Elway wasn't the only one who was smiling.

On the Denver sideline, veteran linebacker Tom Jackson was a cheerleader, as usual. Jackson had grown up in Cleveland. His father was sitting in the

stands. There were growing reports that this would be Jackson's final season; he would retire. But let it be in Pasadena, he was thinking. Let it be from the locker room of the Super Bowl.

Brian Brennan's 48-yard touchdown reception, now almost lost in the memory banks, gave Cleveland a 20-13 lead with 5:43 remaining, stunning the Broncos and sending the home crowd into a happy delirium.

Elway passed to Steve Watson for 12 yards and another first down. At last Denver was on the Cleveland side of the field. There was 1:59 to play. Elway and Reeves talked during the two-minute time out.

Browns head coach Marty Schottenheimer tried to cross up Elway. He called for zone coverage; Cleveland's cornerbacks, Hanford Dixon and Frank Minnifield, usually play man-to-man.

It was a terrific move. Reeves and Elway had decided on a play that would exploit the tight man-to-man coverage. Elway dropped back, saw the play wouldn't work, and tried to throw the ball away. Around the Browns' 5-yard line, safety Ray Ellis lunged. He was the closest to the ball. The pass was catchable; it could be the interception that would end any last-hurrah nonsense. But because he was so close to out of bounds and because it would have taken a circus catch to make the interception anyway, Ellis couldn't hold on.

Nose tackle Dave Puzzuoli came onto the field as Golic went off. Fresh legs, thought Schottenheimer. We have to keep pressure on Elway.

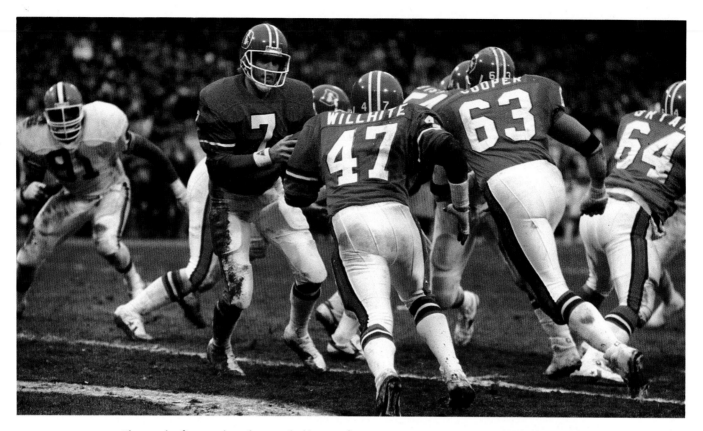

Elway took a five-step drop, then saw the blitzing Clay Matthews coming in wide. Elway stepped forward, and Puzzuoli blocked the way. Elway tried to move to his left, but Puzzuoli stormed after him and caught him for an eight-yard sack. In addition, Elway's tender left ankle, which had been sprained the previous week, got twisted. He called time out and the swagger was now a limp as he headed for another talk with Reeves.

Golic ran onto the field and tapped Puzzuoli, who was surprised he was going out.

"It turned out to be my only time on the field the whole drive," Puzzuoli said. "It was hard for me to believe."

In the stands, the dancing had resumed. Surely the sack finished the Broncos. Unless. . . .

Back at the Cleveland 48 and facing third down, 18 to go for the first down, and 1:47 to play, Elway looked at Reeves and smiled. Reeves smiled back.

"Just try to get half of it," said the coach. "We'll get the rest on fourth down."

From the Shotgun formation, Elway lifted his foot and slammed his heel into the ground, the signal for a silent cadence count to begin. Center Bryan then counted to himself and snapped the ball.

"But when I put my heel down," Elway explained later in the locker room excitement, "I also pointed to Watson to start him in motion. I'm supposed to point first, then give my heel signal.

The stage was set when Ken Bell bobbled a kickoff and was pounced upon at the Broncos' 2-yard line. With the 1986 season steadily ticking away, John Elway and the Denver offense had to face the growling Dawgs from their own end zone. Their dramatic 98-yard drive took 15 plays.

"So here comes Watson and I'm saying to myself, 'Please get out of the way, Steve, please get out of the way.'"

Elway raised his hands to try to stop Watson, who was by then between him and the center. At the same time, Bryan snapped the ball.

"It grazed his butt," Elway said.

The ball wobbled back to Elway and he fielded it off the ground. After back-pedaling several yards, Elway threw a pass to Mark Jackson that sizzled in the wintry air. The 20-yard strike was good for a

Flushed from the pocket on a second-and-7 pass play, Elway frustrated the Cleveland pass rushers, picking up a first down with an 11-yard scramble.

The Drive was completed when Mark Jackson made a sliding catch to tie the game with 37 seconds remaining.

first down to the Cleveland 28.

"If you want to pick one play," Schottenheimer said glumly in his postgame press conference, "that one sticks out."

"If Steve had been just a little more in the way of the snap, we probably would have lost the ball," Elway said. Then he added, "Game of inches, huh?"

Going without a huddle, Elway threw a timing pass to Watson, who ran a fade route to the end zone. Minnifield had it figured and stayed with Watson all the way. Elway threw the ball away on purpose.

Everybody was standing now. Nobody was barking and the mood was like the lake. Eerie.

In the coaches' box on the press level of the stadium, Broncos offensive coordinator Mike Shanahan telephoned down to Reeves that a screen pass might work. But only if the Browns stayed in their man coverage.

Sewell gained 14 yards on the soft lob. There was less than a minute left. In regulation, that is. . . .

"It was getting pretty dramatic out there," Elway said. "But we were relaxed. I just called plays and let things happen."

The officials ruled Watson was out of bounds when he caught Elway's next pass near the goal line. On second down at the 14, Reeves sent in the next play—a quarterback draw.

The Browns charged and Elway had to loop to the outside to escape. He was run out of bounds at the 5. It was third-and-1 and there were 39 seconds remaining.

"Release 66," Elway said in the huddle. He set up over center, and sensed Brown linebacker Chip Banks was coming on a blitz. He was.

There are games within the game—the race to get to somebody before the other guy gets to him. Elway still was backing up when he had to throw the ball. Only a great arm, only a great athlete, only a great quarterback, could make the play.

"It was low and hot," said Mark Jackson. "I had to go down to get it."

Jackson slanted from left to right, Banks had his arms up, Elway threw the pass and the ball stabbed Jackson in the chest. Touchdown, Broncos.

Helen Karlis stood up. What if Rich misses the extra point, she worried. That barefoot stuff always confused her. Former Browns kicker Lou Groza always wore shoes.

Her fear was heedless. The kick was good. Overtime was coming.

Kosar shook his head again. Things didn't look good.

"Last week when we went into overtime against the Jets," Kosar said later, "we knew there was no way we were going to lose. I had the feeling this time, things were exactly reversed."

The Browns won the toss. Elway slumped. The comeback would mean nothing if the Broncos lost.

But the Broncos held as linebacker Karl Mecklenburg stacked up Herman Fontenot two yards away from the first down. Cleveland punted the ball. And things became anticlimactic.

Elway completed two passes for 50 yards, and Winder ran into the middle three times so Karlis could wheel his size 8½ foot into a 33-yard winning field goal that had his mother jumping up and

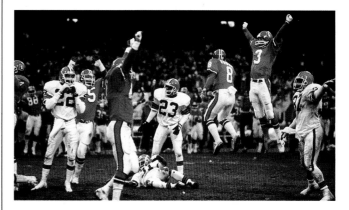

down with joy while most of the rest of the 79,973 in attendance groaned.

Afterward, everyone talked about The Drive. They still talk about it.

Given new life, the Broncos were the attackers in overtime. On their first possession, Elway took them 60 yards in nine plays before Rich Karlis came through with the game-winning field goal that gave Denver the AFC title.

Johnny E. played like Johnny U. John Elway had taken the Broncos 98 yards in 14 plays; he had completed six passes for 78 yards; he had run for 20 yards.

And when someone wants to know which play was great, which play was the one Elway can use to remind him of his pregame vision? Which play reaffirms the terrible swift sword of greatness, of potential realized, of potential that can transform into a force more vast than mere space, more sudden than simple time?

All of them.

APPENDIX

ALLEGHENY AA 4, PITTSBURGH AC 0
November 12, 1892, at Pittsburgh

PAC	0	0	—	**0**
AAA	4	0	—	**4**

AAA —Heffelfinger 35 fumble return (kick failed)

CHICAGO BEARS 19, NEW YORK GIANTS 7
December 6, 1925, at New York

Chicago Bears	12	0	0	7	—	**19**
NY Giants	0	7	0	0	—	**7**

ChiB —J. Sternaman 2 run (kick failed)
ChiB —J. Sternaman 6 run (kick failed)
NYG —White 12 run (McBride kick)
ChiB —Grange 35 interception return (J. Sternaman kick)

CHICAGO BEARS 9, PORTSMOUTH 0
December 18, 1932, at Chicago

Portsmouth	0	0	0	0	—	**0**
Chicago Bears	0	0	0	9	—	**9**

ChiB —Grange 2 pass from Nagurski (Engebretsen kick)
ChiB —Safety, Wilson tackled in end zone

CHICAGO BEARS 23, NEW YORK GIANTS 21
December 17, 1933, at Chicago

NY Giants	0	7	7	7	—	**21**
Chicago Bears	3	3	10	7	—	**23**

ChiB —FG Manders 16
ChiB —FG Manders 40
NYG —Badgro 29 pass from Newman (Strong kick)
ChiB —FG Manders 28
NYG —Krause 1 run (Strong kick)
ChiB —Karr 8 pass from Nagurski (Manders kick)
NYG —Strong 8 pass from Newman (Strong kick)
ChiB —Karr 19 lateral from Hewitt, who caught 14 pass from Nagurski (Brumbaugh kick)

CHICAGO BEARS 73, WASHINGTON 0
December 8, 1940, at Washington, D.C.

Chicago Bears	21	7	26	19	—	**73**
Washington	0	0	0	0	—	**0**

ChiB —Osmanski 68 run (Manders kick)
ChiB —Luckman 1 run (Snyder kick)
ChiB —Maniaci 42 run (Martinovich kick)
ChiB —Kavanaugh 30 pass from Luckman (Snyder kick)
ChiB —Pool 15 interception return (Plasman kick)
ChiB —Nolting 23 run (kick failed)
ChiB —McAfee 34 interception return (Stydahar kick)
ChiB —Turner 24 interception return (kick failed)
ChiB —Clark 44 run (kick failed)
ChiB —Famiglietti 2 run (Maniaci pass from Sherman)
ChiB —Clark 1 run (pass failed)

RUSHING — Washington — Seymour, 4 for 17; Johnson, 4 for 14; Filchock, 3 for 3; Justice, 1 for 2; Zimmerman, 2 for -15; Baugh, 1 for -16. **Chi. Bears** — Osmanski, 10 for 107, 1 TD: Clark, 7 for 75, 2 TDs; Nolting, 11 for 67, 1 TD; Maniaci, 5 for 62, 1 TD; McAfee, 7 for 32; Famiglietti, 4 for 19, 1 TD; McLean, 3 for 18; Nowaskey, 1 for 7; Manders, 2 for 1; Luckman, 1 for 1, 1 TD; Snyder, 2 for -8. **PASSING — Washington** — Filchock, 8 of 23 for 101, 4 int.; Baugh, 9 of 16 for 91, 2 int.; Zimmerman, 3 of 12 for 34, 2 int. **Chi. Bears** — Luckman, 4 of 6 for 102, 1 TD; Snyder, 3 of 3 for 36; McAfee, 0 of 1. **RECEIVING — Washington** — Millner, 6 for 94; Masterson, 3 for 34; Johnson, 3 for 9; Malone, 2 for 51; Hoffman, 2 for 8; Farkas, 1 for 19; Seymour, 1 for 7; Justice, 1 for 4; McChesney, 1 for 0. **Chi. Bears** — Maniaci, 2 for 44; Kavanaugh, 2 for 32, 1 TD: Swisher, 1 for 36; Mihal, 1 for 14; Nolting, 1 for 12.

CLEVELAND 15, WASHINGTON 14
December 16, 1945, at Cleveland

Washington	0	7	7	0	—	**14**
Cleveland	2	7	6	0	—	**15**

Cle —Safety, Baugh's pass hit goal post
Wash —Bagarus 38 pass from Filchock (Aguirre kick)
Cle —Benton 37 pass from Waterfield (Waterfield kick)
Cle —Gillette 44 pass from Waterfield (kick failed)
Wash —Seymour 8 pass from Filchock (Aguirre kick)

RUSHING — Washington — Condit, 9 for 18; Rosato, 6 for 17; Akins, 6 for 16; DeFruiter, 1 for 15; Hare, 2 for 6; Todd, 1 for 1; deCorrevont, 1 for -2; Bagarus, 5 for -4; Filchock, 3 for -32. **Cleveland** — Gillette, 17 for 101; Gehrke, 7 for 29; Greenwood, 9 for 19; West, 3 for 17; Reisz, 3 for 14; Koch 2 for 1; Waterfield, 3 for -1. **PASSING — Washington** — Filchock, 8 of 14 for 172, 2 TDs, 2 int.; Baugh, 1 of 6 for 7. **Cleveland** — Waterfield, 14 of 27 for 192, 2 TDs, 2 int. **RECEIVING — Washington** — Bagarus, 3 for 95, 1 TD; Hare, 2 for 20; Dye, 1 for 44; Turley, 1 for 11; Seymour, 1 for 8, 1 TD; Condit, 1 for 1. **Cleveland** — Benton, 9 for 125, 1 TD; Gillette, 2 for 45, 1 TD; Pritko, 2 for 17; West, 1 for 5.

CLEVELAND 35, PHILADELPHIA 10
September 16, 1950, at Philadelphia

Cleveland	7	7	7	14	—	**35**
Philadelphia	3	0	0	7	—	**10**

Phil —FG Patton 15
Cle —Jones 59 pass from Graham (Grigg kick)
Cle —Lavelli 26 pass from Graham (Grigg kick)
Cle —Speedie 12 pass from Graham (Grigg kick)
Phil —Pihos 17 pass from Mackrides (Patton kick)
Cle —Graham 1 run (Grigg kick)
Cle —Bumgardner 1 run (Grigg kick)

RUSHING — Cleveland — Jones, 6 for 72; Motley, 11 for 48; Bumgardner, 4 for 18, 1 TD; Graham, 3 for 3, 1 TD. **Philadelphia** — Ziegler, 17 for 57; Scott, 13 for 46; Craft, 4 for 28; Myers, 5 for 12; Mackrides, 2 for 2; Parmer, 2 for 2; Thompson, 1 for 1. **PASSING — Cleveland** — Graham, 21 of 38 for 346, 3 TDs, 2 int. **Philadelphia** — Thompson, 8 of 24 for 73, 2 int.; Mackrides, 3 of 8 for 45, 1 TD, 1 int. **RECEIVING — Cleveland** — Speedie, 7 for 109, 1 TD; Jones, 5 for 98, 1 TD; Lavelli, 4 for 76, 1 TD; Bumgardner, 3 for 37; Motley, 2 for 26. **Philadelphia** — Pihos, 4 for 51, 1 TD; Ferrante, 3 for 24; Myers, 2 for 29; Ziegler, 2 for 14.

CLEVELAND 30, LOS ANGELES RAMS 28
December 24, 1950, at Cleveland

Los Angeles Rams	14	0	14	0	—	**28**
Cleveland	7	6	7	10	—	**30**

LA —Davis 82 pass from Waterfield (Waterfield kick)
Cle —Jones 27 pass from Graham (Groza kick)
LA —Hoerner 3 run (Waterfield kick)
Cle —Lavelli 37 pass from Graham (kick failed)
Cle —Lavelli 39 pass from Graham (Groza kick)
LA —Hoerner 1 run (Waterfield kick)
LA —Brink 6 fumble return (Waterfield kick)
Cle —Bumgardner 14 pass from Graham (Groza kick)
Cle —FG Groza 16

RUSHING — Los Angeles — Hoerner, 24 for 86, 2 TDs; Smith, 4 for 11; Davis, 6 for 6; Waterfield, 1 for 2; Pasquariello, 1 for 1. **Cleveland** — Graham, 12 for 99; Motley, 6 for 9; Jones, 2 for 4; Bumgardner, 5 for 2; Lavelli, 0 for 2. **PASSING — Los Angeles** — Waterfield, 18 of 31 for 312, 1 TD, 4 int.; Van Brocklin, 0 of 1, 1 int. **Cleveland** –Graham, 22 of 32 for 298, 4 TDs, 1 int. **RECEIVING — Los Angeles** — Fears, 9 for 136; Hirsch, 4 for 42; Smith, 3 for 46; Davis, 2 for 88, 1 TD. **Cleveland** — Lavelli, 11 for 128, 2 TDs; Jones, 4 for 80, 1 TD; Bumgardner, 4 for 46, 1 TD; Gillom, 1 for 29; Speedie, 1 for 17; Motley, 1 for -2.

DETROIT 17, CLEVELAND 16
December 27, 1953, at Detroit

Cleveland	0	3	7	6	—	**16**
Detroit	7	3	0	7	—	**17**

Det —Walker 1 run (Walker kick)
Cle —FG Groza 13
Det —FG Walker 23
Cle —Jagade 9 run (Groza kick)
Cle —FG Groza 15
Cle —FG Groza 43
Det —Doran 33 pass from Layne (Walker kick)

RUSHING — Cleveland — Jagade, 15 for 104, 1 TD; Jones, 3 for 28; Reynolds, 6 for 16; Carpenter, 3 for 14; Renfro, 4 for 11; Graham, 5 for 9. **Detroit** — Hoernschemeyer, 17 for 47; Layne, 11 for 46; Gedman, 8 for 29; Walker, 3 for 7, 1 TD. **PASSING — Cleveland** — Graham, 2 of 15 for 20, 2 int.; Ratterman, 1 of 1 for 18. **Detroit** — Layne, 12 of 25 for 179, 1 TD, 2 int.; Walker, 0 of 1. **RECEIVING — Cleveland** — Jagade, 1 for 18; Lavelli, 1 for 13; Reynolds, 1 for 7. **Detroit** — Doran, 4 for 95, 1 TD; Box, 4 for 54; Hoernschemeyer, 2 for -2; Dibble, 1 for 22; Walker, 1 for 10.

DETROIT 31, SAN FRANCISCO 27
December 22, 1957, at San Francisco

Detroit	0	7	14	10	—	**31**
San Francisco	14	10	3	0	—	**27**

SF —Owens 34 pass from Tittle (Soltau kick)
SF —McElhenny 47 pass from Tittle (Soltau kick)
Det —Junker 4 pass from Rote (Martin kick)
SF —Wilson 12 pass from Tittle (Soltau kick)
SF —FG Soltau 25
SF —FG Soltau 10
Det —Tracy 1 run (Martin kick)
Det —Tracy 58 run (Martin kick)
Det —Gedman 2 run (Martin kick)
Det —FG Martin 13

RUSHING — Detroit — Tracy, 11 for 86, 2 TDs; Johnson, 5 for 20; Gedman, 6 for 13, 1 TD; Rote, 4 for 5; Cassady, 3 for 5. **San Francisco** — McElhenny, 14 for 82; Perry, 13 for 52; Babb, 2 for 3; Arenas, 1 for 2; Tittle, 3 for -12. **PASSING — Detroit** — Rote, 16 of 30 for 214, 1 TD, 1 int. **San Francisco** — Tittle, 18 of 31 for 248, 3 TDs, 3 int. **RECEIVING — Detroit** — Junker, 8 for 92, 1 TD; Cassady, 3 for 37; Doran, 2 for 51; Middleton, 2 for 27; Tracy, 1 for 7. **San Francisco** — Wilson, 9 for 107, 1 TD; McElhenny, 6 for 96, 1 TD; Owens, 1 for 34, 1 TD; Conner, 1 for 10; Babb, 1 for 1.

BALTIMORE 23, NEW YORK GIANTS 17
December 28, 1958, at New York

Baltimore	0	14	0	3	6	—	**23**
NY Giants	3	0	7	7	0	—	**17**

NYG —FG Summerall 36
Balt —Ameche 2 run (Myhra kick)
Balt —Berry 15 pass from Unitas (Myhra kick)
NYG —Triplett 1 run (Summerall kick)
NYG —Gifford 15 pass from Conerly (Summerall kick)
Balt —FG Myhra 20
Balt —Ameche 1 run (no extra point attempted)

RUSHING — NY Giants — Gifford, 12 for 60; Webster, 9 for 24; Triplett, 5 for 12, 1 TD; Conerly, 2 for 5; King, 3 for -13. **Baltimore** — Ameche, 14 for 59, 2 TDs; Dupre, 11 for 30; Unitas, 4 for 26; Moore, 9 for 24. **PASSING — NY Giants** — Conerly, 10 of 14 for 187, 1 TD; Heinrich, 2 of 4 for 13. **Baltimore** — Unitas, 26 of 40 of 361, 1 TD, 1 int. **RECEIVING — NY Giants** — Gifford, 3 for 14, 1 TD; Rote, 2 for 76; Schnelker, 2 for 63; Webster, 2 for 17; Triplett, 2 for 15; McAfee, 1 for 15. **Baltimore** — Berry, 12 for 178, 1 TD; Moore, 5 for 99; Mutscheller, 4 for 63; Ameche, 3 for 14; Dupre, 2 for 7.

PHILADELPHIA 17, GREEN BAY 13
December 26, 1960, at Philadelphia

Green Bay	3	3	0	7	—	**13**
Philadelphia	0	10	0	7	—	**17**

GB —FG Hornung 20
GB —FG Hornung 23
Phil —McDonald 35 pass from Van Brocklin (Walston kick)
Phil —FG Walston 15
GB —McGee 7 pass from Starr (Hornung kick)
Phil —Dean 5 run (Walston kick)

RUSHING — Philadelphia — Dean, 13 for 54, 1 TD; Barnes, 13 for 42; Van Brocklin, 2 for 3. **Green Bay** — Taylor, 24 for 105; Hornung, 11 for 61; McGee, 1 for 35; Moore, 5 for 22; Starr, 1 for 0. **PASSING — Philadelphia** — Van Brocklin, 9 of 20 for 204, 1 TD, 1 int. **Green Bay** — Starr, 21 of 34 for 178, 1 TD, 1 int.; Hornung, 0 of 1. **RECEIVING — Philadelphia** — McDonald, 3 for 90, 1 TD; Walston, 3 for 38; Retzlaff, 1 for 41; Dean, 1 for 22; Barnes, 1 for 13. **Green Bay** — Knafelc, 6 for 76; Taylor, 6 for 46; Hornung, 4 for 14; McGee, 2 for 19, 1 TD; Moore, 2 for 9; Dowler, 1 for 14.

DALLAS TEXANS 20, HOUSTON 17
December 23, 1962, at Houston

Dallas Texans	3	14	0	0	0	3	—	**20**
Houston	0	0	7	10	0	0	—	**17**

Dall —FG Brooker 16
Dall —Haynes 28 pass from Dawson (Brooker kick)
Dall —Haynes 2 run (Brooker kick)
Hou —Dewveall 15 pass from Blanda (Blanda kick)
Hou —FG Blanda 31
Hou —Tolar 1 run (Blanda kick)
Dall —FG Brooker 25

RUSHING — Dallas Texans — Spikes, 11 for 77; McClinton, 24 for 70; Haynes, 14 for 26, 1 TD; Dawson, 5 for 26. **Houston** — Tolar, 17 for 58, 1 TD; Cannon, 11 for 37; Smith, 2 for 3. **PASSING — Dallas Texans** — Dawson, 9 of 14 for 88, 1 TD. **Houston** — Blanda, 23 of 46 for 261, 1 TD, 5 int. **RECEIVING — Dallas Texans** — Haynes, 3 for 45, 1 TD; Spikes, 2 for 24; Arbanas, 2 for 21; McClinton, 1 for 4; Bishop, 1 for -6. **Houston** — Dewveall, 6 for 95, 1 TD; Cannon, 6 for 54; McLeod, 5 for 70; Hennigan, 3 for 37; Tolar, 1 for 8; Smith, 1 for 6; Jamison, 1 for -9.

CHICAGO BEARS 61, SAN FRANCISCO 20
December 12, 1965, at Chicago

San Francisco	0	13	0	7	—	**20**
Chicago Bears	13	14	13	21	—	**61**

ChiB —Sayers 80 pass from Bukich (kick failed)
ChiB —Ditka 29 pass from Bukich (LeClerc kick)
SF —Parks 9 pass from Brodie (Davis kick)
ChiB —Sayers 21 run (LeClerc kick)
SF —Crow 15 pass from Brodie (kick failed)
ChiB —Sayers 7 run (LeClerc kick)
ChiB —Sayers 50 run (LeClerc kick)
ChiB —Sayers 1 run (kick failed)
SF —Kopay 2 run (Davis kick)
ChiB —Jones 8 pass from Bukich (LeClerc kick)
ChiB —Sayers 85 punt return (LeClerc kick)
ChiB —Arnett 2 run (LeClerc kick)

RUSHING — San Francisco — Willard, 10 for 24; Crown, 6 for 23; Brodie, 1 for 13; Kopay, 2 for 0, 1 TD; Lewis, 1 for -2. **Chicago Bears** — Sayers, 9 for 113, 4 TDs; Arnett, 10 for 30, 1 TD; Bull, 6 for 25; Livingston, 3 for 14; Bukich, 1 for 1. **PASSING — San Francisco** — Brodie, 19 of 37 for 250, 2 TDs, 2 int.; Mira, 4 of 7 for 22, 1 int. **Chicago Bears** — Bukich, 16 of 32 for 347, 3 TDs; Bull, 1 of 1 for 54. **RECEIVING — San Francisco** — Parks, 9 for 129, 1 TD; Willard, 3 for 22; Casey, 3 for 12; Messer, 2 for 41; Kopay, 2 for 23; Crow, 1 for 15, 1 TD; McFarland, 1 for 14; Burke, 1 for 11; Stickles, 1 for 5. **Chicago Bears** — Morris, 5 for 95; Jones, 3 for 113, 1 TD; Sayers, 2 for 89, 1 TD; Ditka, 2 for 45, 1 TD; Livingston, 2 for 15; Bivins, 1 for 35; Arnett, 1 for 8; Bull, 1 for 1.

GREEN BAY 13, BALTIMORE 10
December 26, 1965, at Green Bay

Baltimore	7	3	0	0	0	—	**10**
Green Bay	0	0	7	3	3	—	**13**

Balt —Shinnick 25 fumble return (Michaels kick)
Balt —FG Michaels 15
GB —Hornung 1 run (Chandler kick)
GB —FG Chandler 22
GB —FG Chandler 25

RUSHING — Baltimore — Hill, 16 for 57; Matte, 17 for 57; Moore, 12 for 33; Lorick, 1 for 1; Gilburg, 1 for -5. **Green Bay** — Taylor, 23 for 60; Hornung, 10 for 33, 1 TD; Pitts, 3 for 14; Moore, 3 for 5. **PASSING — Baltimore** — Matte, 5 of 12 for 40. **Green Bay** — Bratkowski, 22 of 39 for 248, 2 int.; Starr, 1 of 1 for 10; Hornung, 0 of 1. **RECEIVING — Baltimore** — Mackey, 3 for 25; Moore, 2 for 15. **Green Bay** — Anderson, 8 for 78; Dowler, 5 for 50; Hornung, 4 for 42; Dale, 3 for 63; Taylor, 2 for 29; Moore, 1 for -4.

GREEN BAY 34, DALLAS 27
January 1, 1967, at Dallas

Green Bay	14	7	7	6	—	**34**
Dallas	14	3	3	7	—	**27**

GB —Pitts 17 pass from Starr (Chandler kick)
GB —Grabowski 18 fumble return (Chandler kick)
Dall —Reeves 3 run (Villanueva kick)
Dall —Perkins 23 run (Villanueva kick)
GB —Dale 51 pass from Starr (Chandler kick)
Dall —FG Villanueva 11
Dall —FG Villanueva 32

GB —Dowler 16 pass from Starr (Chandler kick)
GB —McGee 28 pass from Starr (Chandler kick)
Dall—Clarke 68 pass from Meredith (Villanueva kick)
RUSHING—Green Bay—Pitts, 12 for 66; Taylor, 10 for 37; Starr, 2 for -1. **Dallas—**Perkins, 17 for 108, 1 TD; Reeves, 17 for 47, 1 TD; Meredith, 4 for 22; Norman, 2 for 10. **PASSING—Green Bay—**Starr, 19 of 28 for 304, 4 TDs. **Dallas—**Meredith, 15 of 31 for 238, 1 TD, 1 int. **RECEIVING—Green Bay—**Dale, 5 for 128, 1 TD; Taylor, 5 for 23; Fleming, 3 for 50; Dowler, 3 for 49, 1 TD; McGee, 1 for 28, 1 TD; Pitts, 1 for 17, 1 TD; Long, 1 for 9. **Dallas—**Reeves, 4 for 77; Norman, 4 for 30; Clarke, 3 for 102, 1 TD; Gent, 3 for 28; Hayes, 1 for 1.

GREEN BAY 35, KANSAS CITY 10
January 15, 1967, at Los Angeles

Kansas City	0	10	0	0	—	**10**
Green Bay	7	7	14	7	—	**35**

GB —McGee 37 pass from Starr (Chandler kick)
KC —McClinton 7 pass from Dawson (Mercer kick)
GB —Taylor 14 run (Chandler kick)
KC —FG Mercer 31
GB —Pitts 5 run (Chandler kick)
GB —McGee 13 pass from Starr (Chandler kick)
GB —Pitts 1 run (Chandler kick)
RUSHING—Kansas City—Dawson, 3 for 24; Garrett, 6 for 17; McClinton, 6 for 16; Beathard, 1 for 14; Coan, 3 for 1. **Green Bay—**J. Taylor, 16 for 53, 1 TD; Pitts, 11 for 45, 2 TDs; D. Anderson, 4 for 30; Grabowski, 2 for 2. **PASSING—Kansas City—**Dawson, 16 of 27 for 211, 1 TD, 1 int.; Beathard, 1 of 5 for 17. **Green Bay—**Starr, 16 of 23 for 250, 2 TDs, 1 int.; Bratkowski, 0 of 1. **RECEIVING—Kansas City—**Burford, 4 for 67; O. Taylor, 4 for 57; Garrett, 3 for 28; McClinton, 2 for 34, 1 TD; Arbanas, 2 for 30; Carolan, 1 for 7; Coan, 1 for 5. **Green Bay—**McGee, 7 for 138, 2 TDs; Dale, 4 for 59; Pitts, 2 for 32; Fleming, 2 for 22; J. Taylor, 1 for -1.

LOS ANGELES RAMS 27, GREEN BAY 24
December 9, 1967, at Los Angeles

Green Bay	7	3	7	7	—	**24**
Los Angeles Rams	0	7	10	10	—	**27**

GB —Dale 30 pass from Starr (Chandler kick)
LA —Snow 16 pass from Gabriel (Gossett kick)
GB —FG Chandler 32
LA —Snow 11 pass from Gabriel (Gossett kick)
LA —FG Gossett 23
GB —Williams 104 kickoff return (Chandler kick)
LA —FG Gossett 16
GB —Mercein 4 run (Chandler kick)
LA —Casey 5 pass from Gabriel (Gossett kick)
RUSHING—Green Bay—Williams, 12 for 26; Starr, 2 for 23; Anderson, 7 for 20; Wilson, 7 for 17; Mercein, 4 for 12, 1 TD. **Los Angeles—**Josephson, 19 for 73; Bass, 11 for 18; Gabriel, 4 for 11. **PASSING—Green Bay—**Starr, 10 of 20 for 138, 1 TD, 2 int. **Los Angeles—**Gabriel, 20 of 36 for 227, 3 TDs, 2 int. **RECEIVING—Green Bay—**Dowler, 4 for 71; Dale, 2 for 43, 1 TD; Wilson, 2 for 4; Williams, 1 for 14; Mercein, 1 for 6. **Los Angeles—**Casey, 5 for 97, 1 TD; Josephson, 5 for 51; Snow, 4 for 48, 2 TDs; Truax, 2 for 14; Bass, 2 for 5; Pope, 1 for 12.

GREEN BAY 21, DALLAS 17
December 31, 1967, at Green Bay

Dallas	0	10	0	7	—	**17**
Green Bay	7	7	0	7	—	**21**

GB —Dowler 8 pass from Starr (Chandler kick)
GB —Dowler 46 pass from Starr (Chandler kick)
Dall—Andrie 7 fumble return (Villanueva kick)
Dall—FG Villanueva 21
Dall—Rentzel 50 pass from Reeves (Villanueva kick)
GB —Starr 1 run (Chandler kick)
RUSHING—Dallas—Perkins, 17 for 51; Reeves, 13 for 42; Meredith, 1 for 9; Baynham, 1 for -2; Clarke, 1 for -8. **Green Bay—**Anderson, 18 for 35; Mercein, 6 for 20; Williams, 4 for 13; Wilson, 3 for 11; Starr, 1 for 1, 1 TD. **PASSING—Dallas—**Meredith, 10 of 25 for 59, 1 int.; Reeves, 1 of 1 for 50, 1 TD. **Green Bay—**Starr, 14 of 24 for 191, 2 TDs. **RECEIVING—Dallas—**Hayes, 3 for 16; Reeves, 3 for 11; Rentzel, 2 for 61, 1 TD; Clarke, 2 for 24; Baynham, 1 for -3. **Green Bay—**Dowler, 4 for 77, 2 TDs; Anderson, 4 for 44; Dale, 3 for 44; Mercein, 2 for 22; Williams, 1 for 4.

OAKLAND 43, NEW YORK JETS 32
November 17, 1968, at Oakland

New York Jets	6	6	7	13	—	**32**
Oakland	7	7	8	21	—	**43**

NYJ —FG J. Turner 44
NYJ —FG J. Turner 18
Oak—Wells 9 pass from Lamonica (Blanda kick)
Oak—Cannon 48 pass from Lamonica (Blanda kick)
NYJ —Namath 1 run (pass failed)
NYJ —Mathis 4 run (J. Turner kick)
Oak—Smith 3 run (Lamonica pass to Dixon)
NYJ —Maynard 50 pass from Namath (J. Turner kick)
NYJ —FG J. Turner 12
Oak—Biletnikoff 22 pass from Lamonica (Blanda kick)
NYJ —FG. J. Turner 26
Oak—Smith 43 pass from Lamonica (Blanda kick)
Oak—Ridlehuber 2 fumble return (Blanda kick)
RUSHING—NY Jets—Snell, 21 for 46; Mathis, 4 for 23, 1 TD; Joe, 2 for 9; Namath, 1 for 1, 1 TD; Boozer, 4 for -13. **Oakland—**Dixon, 14 for 75; Smith, 10 for 53, 1 TD; Banaszak, 7 for 18. **PASSING—NY Jets—**Namath, 19 of 37 for 381, 1 TD. **Oakland—**Lamonica, 21 of 34 for 311, 4 TDs, 2 int. **RECEIVING—NY Jets—**Maynard, 10 for 228, 1 TD; Lammons, 6 for 95; Sauer, 2 for 37; Mathis, 1 for 21. **Oakland—**Biletnikoff, 7 for 120, 1 TD; Smith, 4 for 76, 1 TD; Cannon, 3 for 87, 1 TD; Dixon, 3 for 6; Wells, 2 for 22, 1 TD; Banaszak, 2 for 0.

NEW YORK JETS 27, OAKLAND 23
December 29, 1968, at New York

Oakland	0	10	3	10	—	**23**
New York Jets	10	3	7	7	—	**27**

NYJ —Maynard 14 pass from Namath (J. Turner kick)
NYJ —FG J. Turner 33
Oak—Biletnikoff 29 pass from Lamonica (Blanda kick)
NYJ —FG J. Turner 36
Oak—FG Blanda 26
Oak—FG Blanda 9
NYJ —Lammons 20 pass from Namath (J. Turner kick)
Oak—FG Blanda 20
Oak—Banaszak 5 run (Blanda kick)
NYJ —Maynard 6 pass from Namath (J. Turner kick)
RUSHING—Oakland—Dixon, 8 for 42; Banaszak, 3 for 6, 1 TD; Smith, 5 for 1; Lamonica, 3 for 1. **NY Jets—**Snell, 19 for 71; Boozer, 11 for 51; Namath, 1 for 14; Mathis, 3 for 8. **PASSING—Oakland—**Lamonica, 20 of 47 for 401, 1 TD. **NY Jets—**Namath, 19 of 49 for 266, 3 TDs, 1 int. **RECEIVING—Oakland—**Biletnikoff, 7 for 190, 1 TD; Dixon, 5 for 48; Cannon, 4 for 69; Wells, 3 for 83; Banaszak, 1 for 11. **NY Jets—**Sauer, 7 for 70; Maynard, 6 for 118, 2 TDs; Lammons, 4 for 52, 1 TD; Snell, 1 for 15; Boozer, 1 for 11.

NEW YORK JETS 16, BALTIMORE 7.
January 12, 1969, at Miami

New York Jets	0	7	6	3	—	**16**
Baltimore	0	0	0	7	—	**7**

NYJ —Snell 4 run (J. Turner kick)
NYJ —FG J. Turner 32
NYJ —FG J. Turner 30
NYJ —FG J. Turner 9
Balt—Hill 1 run (Michaels kick)
RUSHING—NY Jets—Snell, 30 for 121, 1 TD; Boozer, 10 for 19; Mathis, 3 for 2. **Baltimore—**Matte, 11 for 116; Hill, 9 for 29, 1 TD; Unitas, 1 for 0; Morrall, 2 for -2. **PASSING—NY Jets—**Namath, 17 of 28 for 206; Parilli, 0 of 1. **Baltimore—**Unitas, 11 of 24 for 110, 1 int.; Morrall, 6 of 17 for 71, 3 int. **RECEIVING—NY Jets—**Sauer, 8 for 133; Snell, 4 for 40; Mathis, 3 for 20; Lammons, 2 for 13. **Baltimore—**Richardson, 6 for 58; Orr, 3 for 42; Mackey, 3 for 35; Matte, 2 for 30; Hill, 2 for 1; Mitchell, 1 for 15.

KANSAS CITY 23, MINNESOTA 7
January 11, 1970, at New Orleans

Minnesota	0	0	7	0	—	**7**
Kansas City	3	13	7	0	—	**23**

KC —FG Stenerud 48
KC —FG Stenerud 32
KC —FG Stenerud 25
KC —Garrett 5 run (Stenerud kick)
Minn—Osborn 4 run (Cox kick)
KC —Taylor 46 pass from Dawson (Stenerud kick)
RUSHING—Minnesota—Brown, 6 for 26; Reed, 4 for 17; Osborn, 7 for 15, 1 TD; Kapp, 2 for 9. **Kansas City—**Garrett, 11 for 39, 1 TD; Pitts, 3 for 37; Hayes, 8 for 31; McVea, 12 for 26; Dawson, 3 for 11; Holmes, 5 for 7. **PASSING—Minnesota—**Kapp, 16 of 25 for 183, 2 int.; Cuozzo, 1 of 3 for 16, 1 int. **Kansas City—**Dawson, 12 of 17 for 142, 1 TD, 1 int. **RECEIVING—Minnesota—**Henderson, 7 for 111; Brown, 3 for 11; Beasley, 2 for 41; Reed, 2 for 16; Osborn, 2 for 11; Washington, 1 for 9. **Kansas City—**Taylor, 6 for 81, 1 TD; Pitts, 3 for 33; Garrett, 2 for 25; Hayes, 1 for 3.

OAKLAND 23, CLEVELAND 20
November 8, 1970, at Oakland

Cleveland	0	10	7	3	—	**20**
Oakland	3	10	0	10	—	**23**

Oak—FG Blanda 9
Oak—Smith 27 pass from Lamonica (Blanda kick)
Oak—FG Blanda 42
Cle —Kelly 10 pass from Nelsen (Cockroft kick)
Cle —FG Cockroft 42
Cle —Scott 63 run (Cockroft kick)
Cle —FG Cockroft 32
Oak—Wells 14 pass from Blanda (Blanda kick)
Oak—FG Blanda 52
RUSHING—Cleveland—Scott, 14 for 101, 1 TD; Kelly, 18 for 31; Nelsen, 1 for -2. **Oakland—**Smith, 16 for 73; Dixon, 14 for 47; Hubbard, 6 for 21; Todd, 4 for 15; Blanda, 1 for 4. **PASSING—Cleveland—**Nelsen, 9 of 28 for 110, 1 TD, 3 int. **Oakland—**Blanda, 7 of 12 for 102, 1 TD, 1 int.; Lamonica, 7 of 20 for 68, 1 TD. **RECEIVING—Cleveland—**Kelly, 5 for 65, 1 TD; Morin, 2 for 25; Scott, 2 for 20. **Oakland—**Smith, 4 for 43, 1 TD; Sherman, 4 for 35; Wells, 2 for 45, 1 TD; Biletnikoff, 1 for 17; Chester, 1 for 13; Dixon, 1 for 9; Todd, 1 for 8.

MIAMI 27, KANSAS CITY 24
December 25, 1971, at Kansas City

Miami	0	10	7	7	0	3	—	**27**
Kansas City	10	0	7	7	0	0	—	**24**

KC —FG Stenerud 24
KC —Podolak 7 pass from Dawson (Stenerud kick)
Mia—Csonka 1 run (Yepremian kick)
Mia—FG Yepremian 14
KC —Otis 1 run (Stenerud kick)
Mia—Kiick 1 run (Yepremian kick)
KC —Podolak 3 run (Stenerud kick)
Mia—Fleming 5 pass from Griese (Yepremian kick)
Mia—FG Yepremian 37
RUSHING—Miami—Csonka, 24 for 86, 1 TD; Kiick, 15 for 56, 1 TD; Griese, 2 for 9; Warfield, 2 for -7. **Kansas City—**Hayes, 22 for 100; Podolak, 17 for 85, 1 TD; Wright, 2 for 15; Otis, 3 for 13, 1 TD. **PASSING—Miami—**Griese, 20 of 35 for 263, 1 TD, 2 int. **Kansas City—**Dawson, 18 of 26 for 246, 1 TD, 2 int. **RECEIVING—Miami—**Warfield, 7 for 140; Twilley, 5 for 58; Fleming, 4 for 37, 1 TD; Kiick, 3 for 24; Mandich, 1 for 4. **Kansas City—**Podolak, 8 for 110, 1 TD; Wright, 3 for 104; Taylor, 3 for 12; Hayes, 3 for 6; Frazier, 1 for 14.

PITTSBURGH 13, OAKLAND 7
December 23, 1972, at Pittsburgh

Oakland	0	0	0	7	—	**7**
Pittsburgh	0	0	3	10	—	**13**

Pitt —FG Gerela 18
Pitt —FG Gerela 29
Oak—Stabler 30 run (Blanda kick)
Pitt —Harris 60 pass from Bradshaw (Gerela kick)
RUSHING—Oakland—Smith, 14 for 57; Hubbard, 14 for 44; Stabler, 1 for 30, 1 TD; Davis, 2 for 7. **Pittsburgh—**Harris, 18 for 64; Fuqua, 16 for 25; Bradshaw, 2 for 19. **PASSING—Oakland—**Stabler, 6 of 12 for 57; Lamonica, 6 of 18 for 45, 2 int. **Pittsburgh—**Bradshaw, 11 of 25 for 175, 1 TD, 1 int. **RECEIVING—Oakland—**Chester, 3 for 40; Biletnikoff, 3 for 28; Smith, 2 for 8; Banaszak, 1 for 12; Siani, 1 for 7; J. Otto, 1 for 5; Hubbard, 1 for 2. **Pittsburgh—**Harris, 5 for 96, 1 TD; Shanklin, 3 for 55; Fuqua, 1 for 11; McMakin, 1 for 9; Young, 1 for 4.

DALLAS 30, SAN FRANCISCO 28
December 23, 1972, at San Francisco

Dallas	3	10	0	17	—	**30**
San Francisco	7	14	7	0	—	**28**

SF —V. Washington 97 kickoff return (Gossett kick)
Dall—FG Fritsch 37
SF —Schreiber 1 run (Gossett kick)
SF —Schreiber 1 run (Gossett kick)
Dall—FG Fritsch 45
Dall—Alworth 28 pass from Morton (Fritsch kick)
SF —Schreiber 1 run (Gossett kick)
Dall—FG Fritsch 27
Dall—Parks 20 pass from Staubach (Fritsch kick)
Dall—Sellers 10 pass from Staubach (Fritsch kick)
RUSHING—Dallas—Hill, 18 for 125; Staubach, 3 for 23; Garrison, 9 for 15; Morton, 1 for 2. **San Francisco—**V. Washington, 10 for 56; Schreiber, 26 for 52, 3 TDs; Thomas, 1 for -3. **PASSING—Dallas—**Staubach, 12 of 20 for 174, 2 TDs; Morton, 8 of 21 for 96, 1 TD. **San Francisco—**Brodie, 12 of 22 for 150, 2 int. **RECEIVING—Dallas—**Parks, 7 for 136, 1 TD; Garrison, 3 for 24; Alworth, 2 for 40, 1 TD; Sellers, 2 for 21, 1 TD; Montgomery, 2 for 19; Hayes, 1 for 13; Ditka, 1 for 9; Hill, 1 for 6; Truax, 1 for 2. **San Francisco—**Riley, 4 for 41; G. Washington, 3 for 76; Schreiber, 3 for 20; V. Washington, 1 for 8; Kwalick, 1 for 5.

MIAMI 14, WASHINGTON 7
January 14, 1973, at Los Angeles

Miami	7	7	0	0	—	**14**
Washington	0	0	0	7	—	**7**

Mia —Twilley 28 pass from Griese (Yepremian kick)
Mia —Kiick 1 run (Yepremian kick)
Wash —Bass 49 fumble return (Knight kick)
RUSHING—Miami—Csonka, 15 for 112; Kiick, 12 for 38, 1 TD; Morris, 10 for 34. **Washington—**Brown, 22 for 72; Harraway, 10 for 37; Kilmer, 2 for 18; C. Taylor, 1 for 8; Smith, 1 for 6. **PASSING—Miami—**Griese, 8 of 11 for 88, 1 TD, 1 int. **Washington—**Kilmer, 14 of 28 for 104, 3 int. **RECEIVING—Miami—**Warfield, 3 for 36; Kiick, 2 for 6; Twilley, 1 for 28, 1 TD; Mandich, 1 for 19; Csonka, 1 for -1. **Washington—**Jefferson, 5 for 50; Brown, 5 for 26; C. Taylor, 2 for 20; Smith, 1 for 11; Harraway, 1 for -3.

OAKLAND 28, MIAMI 26
December 21, 1974, at Oakland

Miami	7	3	6	10	—	**26**
Oakland	0	7	7	14	—	**28**

Mia—N. Moore 89 kickoff return (Yepremian kick)
Oak—C. Smith 31 pass from Stabler (Blanda kick)
Mia—FG Yepremian 33
Oak—Biletnikoff 13 pass from Stabler (Blanda kick)
Mia—Warfield 16 pass from Griese (kick failed)
Mia—FG Yepremian 46
Oak—Branch 72 pass from Stabler (Blanda kick)
Mia—Malone 23 run (Yepremian kick)
Oak—Davis 8 pass from Stabler (Blanda kick)
RUSHING—Miami—Csonka, 24 for 114; Malone, 14 for 83, 1 TD; Griese, 2 for 14; Kiick, 1 for 2. **Oakland—**C. Davis, 12 for 59; Hubbard, 14 for 55; Banaszak, 3 for 14; Stabler, 3 for 7. **PASSING—Miami—**Griese, 7 of 14 for 101, 1 TD, 1 int. **Oakland—**Stabler, 20 of 30 for 293, 4 TDs, 1 int. **RECEIVING—Miami—**Warfield, 3 for 47, 1 TD; N. Moore, 2 for 40; Nottingham, 1 for 9; Kiick, 1 for 5. **Oakland—**Biletnikoff, 8 for 122, 1 TD; Branch, 3 for 84, 1 TD; B. Moore, 3 for 22; C. Smith, 2 for 35, 1 TD; C. Davis, 2 for 16, 1 TD; Hubbard, 1 for 9; Pitts, 1 for 5.

DALLAS 17, MINNESOTA 14
December 28, 1975, at Bloomington, Minnesota

Dallas	0	0	7	10	—	**17**
Minnesota	0	7	0	7	—	**14**

Minn —Foreman 1 run (Cox kick)
Dall —Dennison 4 run (Fritsch kick)
Dall —FG Fritsch 24
Minn —McClanahan 1 run (Cox kick)
Dall —D. Pearson 50 pass from Staubach (Fritsch kick)
RUSHING—Dallas—Dennison, 11 for 36, 1 TD; P. Pearson, 11 for 34; Newhouse, 12 for 33; Staubach, 7 for 24; Fugett, 1 for 4. **Minnesota—**Foreman, 18 for 56, 1 TD; Tarkenton, 3 for 32; McClanahan, 4 for 22, 1 TD; Marinaro, 2 for 5. **PASSING—Dallas—**Staubach, 17 of 29 for 246, 1 TD. **Minnesota—**Tarkenton, 12 of 26 for 135, 1 int. **RECEIVING—Dallas—**P. Pearson 5 for 77; D. Pearson, 4 for 91, 1 TD; Newhouse, 2 for 25; Richards, 2 for 20; Fugett, 2 for 13; DuPree, 1 for 17; Dennison, 1 for 3. **Minnesota—**Marinaro, 5 for 64; Foreman, 4 for 42; Gilliam, 1 for 15; Lash, 1 for 15; Voigt, 1 for -1.

PITTSBURGH 21, DALLAS 17
January 18, 1976, at Miami

Dallas	7	3	0	7	—	**17**
Pittsburgh	7	0	0	14	—	**21**

Dall—D. Pearson 29 pass from Staubach (Fritsch kick)
Pitt —Grossman 7 pass from Bradshaw (Gerela kick)
Dall—FG Fritsch 36
Pitt —Safety, Harrison blocked Hoopes's punt through end zone
Pitt —FG Gerela 36
Pitt —FG Gerela 18
Pitt —Swann 64 pass from Bradshaw (kick failed)
Dall—P. Howard 34 pass from Staubach (Fritsch kick)
RUSHING—Dallas—Newhouse, 16 for 56; Staubach, 5 for 22; Dennison, 5 for 16; P. Pearson, 5 for 14. **Pittsburgh—**Harris, 27 for 82; Bleier, 15 for 51; Bradshaw, 4 for 16. **PASSING—Dallas—**Staubach, 15 of 24 for 204, 2 TDs, 3 int. **Pittsburgh—**Bradshaw, 9 of 19 for 209, 2 TDs. **RECEIVING—Dallas—**P. Pearson, 5 for 53; Young, 3 for 31; D. Pearson, 2 for 49, 1 TD; Newhouse, 2 for 12; P. Howard, 1 for 34, 1 TD; Fugett, 1 for 9; Dennison, 1 for 6. **Pittsburgh—**Swann, 4 for 161, 1 TD; Stallworth, 2 for 8; Harris, 1 for 26; Grossman, 1 for 7, 1 TD; L. Brown, 1 for 7.

MINNESOTA 24, LOS ANGELES RAMS 13
December 26, 1976, at Bloomington, Minnesota

Los Angeles Rams	0	0	13	0	—	13
Minnesota	7	3	7	7	—	24

Minn — Bryant 90 blocked field goal return (Cox kick)
Minn — FG Cox 25
Minn — Foreman 2 run (Cox kick)
LA — McCutcheon 10 run (kick failed)
LA — H. Jackson 5 pass from Haden (Dempsey kick)
Minn — Johnson 12 run (Cox kick)
RUSHING — Los Angeles — McCutcheon, 26 for 128, 1 TD; Cappelletti, 16 for 59; Jessie, 1 for 3; Haden, 3 for 3. **Minnesota —** Foreman, 15 for 118, 1 TD; Miller, 10 for 28; Johnson, 2 for 12, 1 TD; McClanahan, 1 for 2; Tarkenton, 1 for -2. **PASSING — Los Angeles —** Haden, 9 of 22 for 161, 1 TD, 2 int. **Minnesota —** Tarkenton, 12 of 27 for 143, 1 int. **RECEIVING — Los Angeles —** H. Jackson, 4 for 70, 1 TD; Jessie, 2 for 60; McCutcheon, 2 for 18; Cappelletti, 1 for 13. **Minnesota —** Foreman, 5 for 81; Rashad, 3 for 28; Miller, 3 for 24; Grim, 1 for 10.

OAKLAND 37, BALTIMORE 31
December 24, 1977, at Baltimore

Oakland	7	0	14	10	0	6	—	37
Baltimore	0	10	7	14	0	0	—	31

Oak — Davis 30 run (Mann kick)
Balt — Laird 61 interception return (Linhart kick)
Balt — FG Linhart 36
Oak — Casper 8 pass from Stabler (Mann kick)
Balt — Johnson 87 kickoff return (Linhart kick)
Oak — Casper 10 pass from Stabler (Mann kick)
Balt — R. Lee 1 run (Linhart kick)
Oak — Banaszak 1 run (Mann kick)
Balt — R. Lee 13 run (Linhart kick)
Oak — FG Mann 22
Oak — Casper 10 pass from Stabler (no kick)
RUSHING — Oakland — van Eeghen, 19 for 76; Davis, 16 for 48, 1 TD; Banaszak, 11 for 37, 1 TD; Garrett, 1 for 6. **Baltimore —** Mitchell, 23 for 67; R. Lee, 11 for 46, 2 TDs; Leaks, 8 for 35; Jones, 6 for 30; McCauley, 2 for 9. **PASSING — Oakland —** Stabler, 21 of 40 for 345, 3 TDs, 2 int. **Baltimore —** Jones, 12 of 26 for 164. **RECEIVING — Oakland —** Biletnikoff, 7 for 88; Branch, 6 for 113; Casper, 4 for 70, 3 TDs; van Eeghen, 2 for 39; Davis, 2 for 35. **Baltimore —** Mitchell, 3 for 39; Scott, 2 for 45; R. Lee, 2 for 22; McCauley, 2 for 11; Chester, 1 for 30; Doughty, 1 for 20; Pratt, 1 for -3.

HOUSTON 35, MIAMI 30
November 20, 1978, at Houston

Miami	7	7	7	9	—	30
Houston	7	7	7	14	—	35

Mia — Moore 10 pass from Griese (Yepremian kick)
Hou — Campbell 1 run (Fritsch kick)
Hou — Barber 15 pass from Pastorini (Fritsch kick)
Mia — Williams 1 run (Yepremian kick)
Hou — Campbell 6 run (Fritsch kick)
Mia — L. Harris 1 run (Yepremian kick)
Mia — Safety, Pastorini tackled in end zone by Duhe
Hou — Campbell 12 run (Fritsch kick)
Hou — Campbell 81 run (Fritsch kick)
Mia — Cefalo 11 pass from Griese (Yepremian kick)
RUSHING — Miami — Williams, 18 for 73, 1 TD; L. Harris, 12 for 51, 1 TD; Moore, 1 for 3; Griese, 1 for 0. **Houston —** Campbell, 28 for 199, 4 TDs; T. Wilson, 10 for 35; Barber, 1 for 13; Renfro, 1 for 9; Coleman, 2 for 9. **PASSING — Miami —** Griese, 23 of 33 for 349, 2 TDs, 1 int. **Houston —** Pastorini, 10 of 16 for 156, 1 TD, 1 int. **RECEIVING — Miami —** L. Harris, 5 for 25; D. Harris, 4 for 79; Bulaich, 4 for 46; Moore, 3 for 84, 1 TD; Tillman, 3 for 45; Williams, 2 for 20; Rather, 1 for 39; Cefalo, 1 for 11, 1 TD. **Houston —** Barber, 3 for 56, 1 TD; Burrough, 2 for 37; Caster, 2 for 31; Renfro, 2 for 24; Coleman, 1 for 8.

PITTSBURGH 35, DALLAS 31
January 21, 1979, at Miami

Pittsburgh	7	14	0	14	—	35
Dallas	7	7	3	14	—	31

Pitt — Stallworth 28 pass from Bradshaw (Gerela kick)
Dall — Hill 39 pass from Staubach (Septien kick)
Dall — Hegman 37 fumble return (Septien kick)
Pitt — Stallworth 75 pass from Bradshaw (Gerela kick)
Pitt — Bleier 7 pass from Bradshaw (Gerela kick)
Dall — FG Septien 27
Pitt — Harris 22 run (Gerela kick)
Pitt — Swann 18 pass from Bradshaw (Gerela kick)
Dall — DuPree 7 pass from Staubach (Septien kick)
Dall — B. Johnson 4 pass from Staubach (Septien kick)
RUSHING — Pittsburgh — Harris, 20 for 68, 1 TD; Bleier, 2 for 3; Bradshaw, 2 for -5. **Dallas —** Dorsett, 16 for 96; Staubach, 4 for 37; Laidlaw, 3 for 12; P. Pearson, 1 for 6; Newhouse, 8 for 3. **PASSING — Pittsburgh —** Bradshaw, 17 of 30 for 318, 4 TDs, 1 int. **Dallas —** Staubach, 17 of 30 for 228, 3 TDs, 1 int. **RECEIVING — Pittsburgh —** Swann, 7 for 124, 1 TD; Stallworth, 3 for 115, 2 TDs; Grossman, 3 for 29; Bell, 2 for 21; Harris, 1 for 22; Bleier, 1 for 7, 1 TD. **Dallas —** Dorsett, 5 for 44; D. Pearson, 4 for 73; Hill, 2 for 49, 1 TD; B. Johnson, 2 for 30, 1 TD; DuPree, 2 for 17, 1 TD; P. Pearson, 2 for 15.

DALLAS 35, WASHINGTON 34
December 16, 1979, at Irving, Texas

Washington	10	7	0	17	—	34
Dallas	0	14	7	14	—	35

Wash — FG Moseley 24
Wash — Theismann 1 run (Moseley kick)
Wash — Malone 55 pass from Theismann (Moseley kick)
Dall — Springs 1 run (Septien kick)
Dall — P. Pearson 26 pass from Staubach (Septien kick)
Dall — Newhouse 1 run (Septien kick)
Wash — FG Moseley 24
Wash — Riggins 1 run (Moseley kick)
Wash — Riggins 66 run (Moseley kick)
Dall — Springs 26 pass from Staubach (Septien kick)
Dall — Hill 8 pass from Staubach (Septien kick)
RUSHING — Washington — Riggins, 22 for 151, 2 TDs; Malone, 7 for 20; Theismann, 5 for 16, 1 TD; Harmon, 3 for 10; Forte, 2 for 9. **Dallas —** Springs, 21 for 75, 1 TD; Newhouse, 9 for 22, 1 TD; Johnson, 1 for 13; Staubach, 1 for 0. **PASSING — Washington —** Theismann, 12 of 23 for 200, 1 TD. **Dallas —** Staubach, 24 of 42 for 336, 3 TDs, 1 int. **RECEIVING — Washington —** Buggs, 2 for 49; Harmon, 2 for 31; McDaniel, 2 for 19; Thompson, 2 for 19; Malone, 1 for 55, 1 TD; Forte, 1 for 14; Warren, 1 for 9; Hammond, 1 for 4. **Dallas —** Hill, 8 for 113, 1 TD; Springs, 6 for 58, 1 TD; P. Pearson, 5 for 108, 1 TD; D. Pearson, 1 for 20; Johnson, 1 for 14; DuPree, 1 for 5; Laidlaw, 1 for 4.

SAN DIEGO 41, MIAMI 38
January 2, 1982, at Miami

San Diego	24	0	7	7	3	—	41
Miami	0	17	14	7	0	—	38

SD — FG Benirschke 32
SD — Chandler 56 punt return (Benirschke kick)
SD — Muncie 1 run (Benirschke kick)
SD — Brooks 8 pass from Fouts (Benirschke kick)
Mia — FG von Schamann 34
Mia — Rose 1 pass from Strock (von Schamann kick)
Mia — Nathan 25 lateral from Harris after pass from Strock (von Schamann kick)
Mia — Rose 15 pass from Strock (von Schamann kick)
SD — Winslow 25 pass from Fouts (Benirschke kick)
Mia — Hardy 50 pass from Strock (von Schamann kick)
Mia — Nathan 12 run (von Schamann kick)
SD — Brooks 9 pass from Fouts (Benirschke kick)
SD — FG Benirschke 29
RUSHING — San Diego — Muncie, 24 for 120, 1 TD; Brooks, 3 for 19; Fouts, 2 for 10. **Miami —** Nathan, 14 for 48, 1 TD; Woodley, 1 for 10; Hill, 3 for 8; Franklin, 9 for 6; Vigorito, 1 for 6. **PASSING — San Diego —** Fouts, 33 of 53 for 433, 3 TDs, 1 int.; Muncie, 0 of 1 int. **Miami —** Strock, 29 of 43 for 403, 4 TDs, 1 int.; Woodley, 2 of 5 for 20, 1 int. **RECEIVING — San Diego —** Winslow, 13 for 166, 1 TD; Joiner, 7 for 108; Chandler, 6 for 106; Brooks, 4 for 31, 2 TDs; Muncie, 2 for 5; Scales, 1 for 17. **Miami —** Nathan, 9 for 114, 1 TD; Harris, 6 for 106; Hardy, 5 for 89, 1 TD; Rose, 4 for 37, 2 TDs; Cefalo, 3 for 62; Vigorito, 2 for 12; Hill, 2 for 3.

SAN FRANCISCO 28, DALLAS 27
January 10, 1982, at San Francisco

Dallas	10	7	0	10	—	27
San Francisco	7	7	7	7	—	28

SF — Solomon 8 pass from Montana (Wersching kick)
Dall — FG Septien 44
Dall — Hill 26 pass from D. White (Septien kick)
SF — Clark 20 pass from Montana (Wersching kick)
Dall — Dorsett 5 run (Septien kick)
SF — Davis 2 run (Wersching kick)
Dall — FG Septien 22
Dall — Cosbie 21 pass from D. White (Septien kick)
SF — Clark 6 pass from Montana (Wersching kick)
RUSHING — Dallas — Dorsett, 22 for 91, 1 TD; J. Jones, 4 for 14; Springs, 5 for 10; D. White, 1 for 0. **San Francisco —** Elliott, 10 for 48; Cooper, 8 for 35; Ring, 6 for 27; Solomon, 1 for 14; Easley, 2 for 6; Davis, 1 for 2, 1 TD; Montana, 3 for -5. **PASSING — Dallas —** D. White, 16 of 24 for 173, 2 TDs, 1 int. **San Francisco —** Montana, 22 of 35 for 286, 3 TDs, 3 int. **RECEIVING — Dallas —** J. Jones, 3 for 17; DuPree, 3 for 15; Springs, 3 for 13; Hill, 2 for 43, 1 TD; Pearson, 1 for 31; Cosbie, 1 for 21, 1 TD; Johnson, 1 for 20; Saldi, 1 for 9; Donley, 1 for 4. **San Francisco —** Clark, 8 for 120, 2 TDs; Solomon, 6 for 75, 1 TD; Young, 4 for 45; Cooper, 2 for 11; Elliott, 1 for 24; Shuman, 1 for 11.

WASHINGTON 37, LOS ANGELES RAIDERS 35
October 2, 1983, at Washington

Los Angeles Raiders	0	7	14	14	—	35
Washington	7	10	3	17	—	37

Wash — Riggins 2 run (Moseley kick)
Wash — FG Moseley 28
LA — Branch 99 pass from Plunkett (Bahr kick)
Wash — J. Washington 5 pass from Theismann (Moseley kick)
Wash — FG Moseley 29
LA — Muhammad 35 pass from Plunkett (Bahr kick)
LA — Muhammad 22 pass from Plunkett (Bahr kick)
LA — Christensen 2 pass from Plunkett (Bahr kick)
LA — Pruitt 97 punt return (Bahr kick)
Wash — Brown 11 pass from Theismann (Moseley kick)
Wash — FG Moseley 34
Wash — J. Washington 6 pass from Theismann (Moseley kick)
RUSHING — Los Angeles — Hawkins, 15 for 64; Plunkett, 2 for 21; King, 7 for 20. **Washington —** Riggins, 26 for 91, 1 TD; J. Washington, 4 for 10; Theismann, 2 for -3. **PASSING — Los Angeles —** Plunkett, 16 of 29 for 372, 4 TDs, 4 int.; Pruitt, 0 of 1. **Washington —** Theismann, 23 of 39 for 417, 3 TDs; J. Washington, 0 of 1. **RECEIVING — Los Angeles —** Muhammad, 5 for 112, 2 TDs; Christensen, 5 for 70, 1 TD; Barnwell, 3 for 75; Branch, 1 for 99, 1 TD; King, 1 for 9; Hawkins, 1 for 7. **Washington —** Brown, 11 for 180, 1 TD; J. Washington, 5 for 99, 2 TDs; Warren, 3 for 62; Monk, 3 for 59; Walker, 1 for 17.

DENVER 23, CLEVELAND 20
January 11, 1987, at Cleveland

Denver	0	10	3	7	3	—	23
Cleveland	7	3	0	10	0	—	20

Cle — Fontenot 6 pass from Kosar (Moseley kick)
Den — FG Karlis 19
Den — Willhite 1 run (Karlis kick)
Cle' — FG Moseley 29
Den — FG Karlis 26
Cle — FG Moseley 24
Cle — Brennan 48 pass from Kosar (Moseley kick)
Den — M. Jackson 5 pass from Elway (Karlis kick)
Den — FG Karlis 33
RUSHING — Denver — Winder, 26 for 83; Elway, 4 for 56; Lang, 3 for 9; Sewell, 1 for 1; Willhite, 3 for 0, 1 TD. **Cleveland —** Mack, 26 for 94; Fontenot, 3 for 3; Kosar, 4 for 3. **PASSING — Denver —** Elway, 22 of 38 for 244, 1 TD, 1 int. **Cleveland —** Kosar, 18 of 32 for 259, 2 TDs, 2 int. **RECEIVING — Denver —** Watson, 5 for 55; Sewell, 3 for 47; Mobley, 3 for 36; V. Johnson, 3 for 25; M. Jackson, 2 for 25, 1 TD; Kay, 2 for 23; Willhite, 2 for 20; Winder, 2 for 2; Sampson, 1 for 10; Lang, 1 for 1. **Cleveland —** Fontenot, 7 for 66, 1 TD; Brennan, 4 for 72, 1 TD; Langhorne, 2 for 35; Mack, 2 for 20; Weathers, 1 for 42; Slaughter, 1 for 20; Byner, 1 for 4.